SHARDS
OF
EARTH

BY ADRIAN TCHAIKOVSKY

SHADOWS OF THE APT

Empire in Black and Gold
Dragonfly Falling
Blood of the Mantis
Salute the Dark
The Scarab Path
The Sea Watch
Heirs of the Blade
The Air War
War Master's Gate
Seal of the Worm

ECHOES OF THE FALL

The Tiger and the Wolf
The Bear and the Serpent
The Hyena and the Hawk

THE FINAL ARCHITECTURE

Shards of Earth

Guns of the Dawn

Children of Time
Children of Ruin

The Doors of Eden

SHARDS OF EARTH

The Final Architecture: Book One

ADRIAN
TCHAIKOVSKY

orbitbooks.net

Orbit
Hachette Book Group
1290 Avenue of the Americas
New York, NY 10104
orbitbooks.net

First U.S. Edition: August 2021
Originally published in Great Britain by Tor, an imprint of Pan Macmillan, in May 2021

Orbit is an imprint of Hachette Book Group.
The Orbit name and logo are trademarks of Little, Brown Book Group Limited.

The publisher is not responsible for websites (or their content) that are not owned by the publisher.

The Hachette Speakers Bureau provides a wide range of authors for speaking events. To find out more, go to www.hachettespeakersbureau.com or call (866) 376-6591.

Library of Congress Control Number: 2021936739

ISBNs: 978-0-316-70585-1 (hardcover), 978-0-316-70582-0 (ebook)

Printed in the United States of America

LSC-C

Printing 1, 2021

*We've come a long way since 2007. This one is for Simon,
who made a great many things happen.*

CONTENTS

SHARDS
OF
EARTH

PROLOGUE

In the seventy-eighth year of the war, an Architect came to Berlenhof.

The lights of human civilization across the galaxy had been going out, one by one, since its start. All those little mining worlds, the far-flung settlements, the homes people had made. The Colonies, as they were known: the great hollow Polyaspora of human expansion, exploding out from a vacant centre. Because the Architects had come for Earth first.

Berlenhof had become humanity's second heart. Even before Earth fell, it had been a prosperous, powerful world. In the war, it was the seat of military command and civilian governance, coordinating a civilization-scale refugee effort, as more and more humans were forced to flee their doomed worlds.

And because of that, when the Architect came, the Colonies turned and fought, and so did all the allies they had gathered there. It was to be the great stand against a galactic-level threat, every weapon deployed, every secret advantage exploited.

Solace remembered. She had been there. Basilisk Division, Heaven's Sword Sorority. Her first battle.

*

The Colonies had a secret weapon, that was the word. A human weapon. Solace had seen them at the war council. A cluster of awkward, damaged-looking men and women, nothing more. As the main fleet readied itself to defend Berlenhof, a handful of small ships were already carrying these "weapons" towards the Architect in the hope that this new trick would somehow postpone the inevitable.

Useless, surely. Might as well rely on thoughts and prayers.

On the *Heaven's Sword*, everyone off-shift was avidly watching the displays, wanting to believe this really *was* something. Even though all previous secret weapons had been nothing but hot air and hope. Solace stared as intently as the rest. The Architect was impossible to miss on screen, a vast polished mass the size of Earth's lost moon, throwing back every scan and probe sent its way. The defending fleet at Berlenhof was a swarm of pinpricks, so shrunk by the scale they were barely visible until she called for magnification. The heart of the Colonies had already been gathering its forces for dispatch elsewhere when the Architect had emerged from unspace at the edge of the system. Humanity was never going to get better odds than this.

There were Castigar and Hanni vessels out there, alien trading partners who were lending their strength to their human allies because the Architects were everybody's problem. There was a vast and ragged fleet of human ships, and some of them were dedicated war vessels and others were just whatever could be thrown into space that wasn't any use for the evacuation. Orbiting Hiver factories were weaponizing their workers. There was even the brooding hulk of a Naeromathi Locust Ark out there, the largest craft in-system—save that it was still dwarfed by the Architect itself. And nobody knew what the Locusts wanted or thought about anything, save that even they would fight this enemy.

And there was the pride of the fleet, Solace's sisters: the Parthenon. Humans, for a given value of human. The engineered warrior women who had been the Colonies' shield ever since the fall of Earth. *Heaven's Sword*, *Ascending Mother* and *Cataphracta*, the most advanced warships humanity had ever designed, equipped with weapons that the pre-war days couldn't even have imagined.

As Solace craned to see, she spotted a tiny speckle of dots between the fleet and the Architect: the advance force. The tip of humanity's spear was composed of the Partheni's swiftest ships. Normally, their role would have been to buy time. But on this occasion, the *Pythoness*, the *Ocasio*, the *Ching Shi* and others were carrying their secret weapon to the enemy.

Solace didn't believe a word of it. The mass looms and the Zero Point fighters the *Heaven's Sword* was equipped with would turn the battle, or nothing would. Even as she told herself that, she heard the murmur of the other off-shift women around her. "Intermediaries," one said, a whisper as if talking about something taboo; and someone else, a girl barely old enough to be in service: "They say they cut their *brains*. That's how they make them."

"Telemetry incoming," said one of the officers, and the display focused in on those few dots. They were arrowing towards the Architect, as though planning to dash themselves against its mountainous sides. Solace felt her eyes strain, trying to wring more information from what she was seeing, to peer all the way in until she had an eye inside the ships themselves.

One of those dots winked out. The Architect had registered

their presence and was patiently swatting at them. Solace had seen the aftermath of even a brush with an Architect's power: twisted, crumpled metal, curved and corkscrewed by intense gravitational pressures. A large and well-shielded ship might weather a glancing blow. With these little craft there would be no survivors.

"It's *useless*," she said. "*We* need to be out there. Us." Her fingers itched for the keys of the mass looms.

"Myrmidon Solace, do you think you know better than the Fleet Exemplars?" Her immediate superior, right at her shoulder of course.

"No, Mother."

"Then just watch and be ready." And a muttered afterthought: "Not that I don't agree with you." And even as her superior spoke, another of the tiny ships had been snuffed into darkness.

"Was that—?" someone cried, before being cut off. Then the officer was demanding, "Telemetry, update and confirm!"

"A marked deviation," someone agreed. The display was bringing up a review, a fan of lines showing the Architect's projected course and its current trajectory.

"So it altered its course. That changes nothing," someone spat, but the officer spoke over them. "They *turned* an Architect! Whatever they did, they *turned* it!"

Then they lost all data. After a tense second's silence, the displays blinked back, the handful of surviving ships fleeing the Architect's renewed approach towards Berlenhof. Whatever the secret weapon was, it seemed to have failed.

"*High alert*. All off-shift crews make ready to reinforce as needed. The fight's coming to us!" came the voice of the officer. Solace was still staring at the display, though. *Had* they accomplished nothing? Somehow, this secret Intermediary weapon had shifted the course of an Architect. Nobody had made them so much as flinch before.

Orders came through right on the heels of the thought. "Prepare to receive the *Pythoness*. Damage control, medical, escort." And she was the third of those, called up out of the off-shift pool along with her team.

The *Pythoness* had been a long, streamlined ship: its foresection bulked out by its gravitic drives and then tapering down its length to a segmented tail. That tail was gone, and the surviving two-thirds of the ship looked as though a hand had clenched about it, twisting every sleek line into a tortured curve. That the ship had made it back at all was a wonder. The moment the hatch was levered open, the surviving crew started carrying out the wounded. Solace knew from the ship's readouts that half its complement wouldn't be coming out at all.

"Myrmidon Solace!"

"Mother!" She saluted, waiting for her duties.

"Get this to the bridge!"

She blinked. *This* was a man. A Colonial human man. He was skinny and jug-eared and looked as though he'd already snapped under the trauma of the fight. His eyes were wide and his lips moved soundlessly. Twitches ran up and down his body like rats. She'd seen him before, at the council of war. One of the vaunted Intermediaries.

"Mother?"

"Take him to the bridge. Now, Myrmidon!" the officer snapped, and then she leant in and grabbed Solace's shoulder. "This is *it*, sister. This is the weapon. And if it's a weapon, we need to use it."

5

There were billions on Berlenhof: the local population as well as countless refugees from the other lost worlds. Nobody was going to get even a thousandth of those people off-world before the Architect destroyed it. But the more time they could buy for the evacuation effort, the more lives would be saved. This was what the Parthenon was spending its ships and lives for. That was what the Hivers would expend their artificial bodies for, and the alien mercenaries and partisans and ideologues would die for. Every lost ship was another freighter off Berlenhof packed out with civilians.

She got the man into a lift tube, aware of the wide-eyed looks he'd been receiving as she hauled him from the dock. He must be getting a far worse case of culture-shock; regular Colonials didn't mix with the Parthenon and before the war there'd been no love lost. Here he was on a ship full of women who all had close on the same face, the same compact frame. Human enough to be uncanny but, for most Colonials, not quite human *enough*.

He was saying something. For a moment she heard nonsense, but she'd learned enough Colvul to piece together the words. It was just a demand to wait. Except they were already in the lift, so he could wait all he wanted and they'd still get where they were needed. "Wait, I can't..."

"You're here...Menheer." It took a moment for her to remember the correct Colvul honorific. "My name is Myrmidon Solace. I am taking you to the bridge of the *Heaven's Sword*. You are going to fight with us."

He stared at her, shell-shocked. "They're *hurt*. My ship. We jumped..."

"This is your ship now, Menheer." And, because he was shaking again, she snapped at him. "*Name*, Menheer?"

He twitched. "Telemmier. Idris Telemmier. Intermediary. First class."

"They say you're a weapon. So now you have to fight."

He was shaking his head, but then she had him out of the lift and the officers were calling for him.

The battle displays formed a multicoloured array in the centre of the bridge, showing the vast fleet as it moved to confront the Architect. Solace saw that they were finally about to fire on it: to do what little damage they could with lasers and projectiles, suicide drones, explosives and gravitic torsion. But their goal was only to slow it. A victory against an Architect was when you made yourself enough of a nuisance that they had to swat you before they could murder the planet.

They got Idris in front of the display, though Solace had to hold him upright.

"What am I—?" he got out. Solace saw he didn't have the first clue what was going on.

"Whatever you can do, *do*," an officer snapped at him. Solace could see and feel that the *Heaven's Sword* was already on its attack run. She wanted desperately to be on-shift at the mass loom consoles, bringing that ersatz hammer against the shell of the Architect. She didn't believe in this Intermediary any more than she believed in wizards.

Still, when he turned his wan gaze her way, she mustered a smile and he seemed to take something from that. Something lit behind his eyes: madness or divine revelation.

Then their sister ship's mass loom fired and Solace followed the *Cataphracta's* strike through the bridge readouts. It was a weapon developed through studying the Architects themselves, a hammerblow of pure gravitic torsion, aiming to tear a rift in their enemy's crystalline exterior. Operators read off the subsequent damage reports: fissuring minimal but present; target areas flagged up for a more concentrated assault. The *Heaven's Sword*'s Zero Point fighters were flocking out of its bays now and dispersing, a hundred gnats to divert the enemy's time and attention from the big guns.

The whole bridge sang like a choir for just a moment as their own mass loom spoke, resonating through the entire length of the ship. Solace felt like shouting out with it, as she always did. And kept her mouth shut, because here on the bridge that sort of thing would be frowned on.

Idris gasped then, arching backwards in her arms, and she saw blood on his face as he bit his tongue. His eyes were wider than seemed humanly possible, all the whites visible and a ring of red around each as well. He screamed, prompting concerned shouts from across the bridge, eclipsed when the Fleet Exultant in command called out that the Architect had faltered. Impossible that so much inexorable momentum could be diverted by anything short of an asteroid impact. But it had jolted in the very moment that Idris had yelled.

The mass loom sang again, and she saw the *Cataphracta* and the *Ascending Mother* firing too, all targeting the same fractures in the Architect's structure. Smaller ships were wheeling in swarms past the behemoth's jagged face, loosing every weapon they had, frantic to claim an iota of the thing's monstrous attention. She saw them being doused like candles, whole handfuls at a time. And then the Architect's invisible hands reached out and wrung the whole length of the *Cataphracta* and opened it out like a flower. A ship and all its souls turned into a tumbling metal sculpture and cast adrift into the void. And it would do exactly the same to Berlenhof when it reached the planet.

The Locust Ark was annihilated next, fraying into nothing as it tried to throw its disintegrating mass into the Architect's path. Then the *Sword*'s loom spoke, but the choir was in discord now, the very seams of the warship strained by the power of her own weaponry. Idris was clutching Solace's hands painfully, leaning into her and weeping. The Architect had halted, for the first time since it entered the system, no longer advancing on the planet. She felt Idris vibrate at that point, rigid as he did *something*; as he wrestled the universe for control over the apocalyptic engine that was the Architect. Her ears were full of the rapid, efficient patter of the bridge reports: stress fractures, targeting, the elegant physics of gravity as a bludgeoning weapon. Damage reports. So many damage reports. The Architect had already brushed them once and Solace had barely realized. Half the decks of the *Heaven's Sword* were evacuating.

"It's cracking!" someone was shouting. "It's cracking open!"

"Brace!" And Solace had to brace for herself and Idris too. Because his mind was somewhere else, doing battle on a field she couldn't even imagine.

*

There was a terrible impact and the screens briefly malfunctioned. Then in the chaos, as the *Heaven's Sword* died, the Fleet Exultant gave Solace her last orders. In response, she grabbed the Intermediary—the little Colonial man who might be their greatest weapon—and hustled him through the wreckage. She bundled him through the surviving sections of the ship to the life pods. She prioritized him even over her sisters because he'd been made her responsibility, but also because he was hope: the universe now had one destroyed Architect; before the Battle of Berlenhof that number had been zero.

*

Later, in the vast medical camp planetside, Solace had been there holding Idris's hand when he awoke. They'd been surrounded by other casualties from the *Heaven's Sword*, all the other lucky ones who'd managed to escape with injuries rather than obliteration. Between the fight and its explosive end, half the fleet and a dozen orbitals had been crippled.

Idris had squeezed her hand, and she'd hugged him impulsively, just as she would have hugged a sister. There was more fighting to come, but right then they were just two comrades in arms. A pair who'd stood before the inevitable and still turned it aside, and the war owed them time to heal.

Six years later, the Intermediaries would finally end the war, though not by destroying or even defeating the enemy. The Architects, after almost a century of hounding humanity from world to world, would simply not be seen any more, vanished off into the endless space of the galaxy. Nobody could say where they had gone. And nobody knew when or if they might return.

Thirty-nine years after that, they woke Solace from cold storage one more time and said her warrior skills were needed. Not because the Architects were back, but because the Parthenon and the Colonies were on the brink of war.

PART 1
ROSHU

1.

Solace

Solace had thought her squad would assemble in the shuttle bay, all military precision and gleaming armour as befitted a Monitor Superior's formal escort. But instead, the Monitor called them to the Grand Carrier's main viewport first.

"What you are about to see is an object lesson," she told them. "I am aware that Myrmidon Executor Solace has seen this already, but for the rest of you, this is where you came from. We all came from Earth originally, and don't let anyone tell you any different."

It had been a long time. Over a decade of Solace's personal history, in and out of suspension; forty years of objective time, whatever that meant. Nothing had changed. Earth would always be the same now.

Earth was like a flower, forever turned towards the sun. An alien flower whose exemplar might grow in some fecund jungle on a distant world. A thing of creepers and reaching shoots, something more than vegetable, less than animal.

Earth's mantle and crust had been peeled back, like petals whose tips formed spiralling tendrils a thousand kilometres long. The planet's core had gouted forth into yearning, reaching shapes, formed into rings and whorls, arches, curved arms... A hundred separate processes shaped from the living core of the planet as it writhed and twisted, then was left to cool. A flower twenty thousand kilometres across, splayed forever in full bloom; a memorial to ten billion people who hadn't made it to the ships in time.

That had been all Solace had been able to think about, the first time she saw the lost home of her species. She remembered there had been parties, speeches and celebrations that the war was finally over, that they'd, what, won? Perhaps it was *survival* rather than victory, but sometimes just surviving was your definition of a win. And she'd gone to another big room then, the place where the real diplomats would be talking it out soon enough. She'd stood with a handful of other veterans, looked down on Earth and thought about how many lives had been snuffed out.

It was beautiful, in a horrible way. You couldn't look at that intricately crafted floriform sculpture and not appreciate just how magnificent, how perfect it was. Not mindless chaos unleashed upon the planet. In the sculpture's exacting workmanship, its eye-leading symmetries, there was a plan. Even to human eyes, the glorious, lethal artwork that Earth had become was intentional and organized, all the way down to the atomic level. That was why the things that had come to Earth—and to so many other planets—were not known as Destroyers or Unmakers. The traumatized survivors of humanity had named them *Architects*. This was what they did— they rebuilt. Nobody knew why, but very plainly there was a reason, because they were exacting and careful in their work. They had stringent criteria. Most particularly, the worlds they made into their art or machines or messages had all been inhabited. As though the final artistic flourish involved something on the surface looking into the stars and knowing its own doom.

Coming back to the present, Solace saw the wide eyes, the taut faces of her squad. These young myrmidons had never faced their history before. She went among them, gently reminding them they were all soldiers together. Or had been, while there was a war. Now it was time to practise diplomacy on Lune Station.

*

They had come to the ruins of their ancestral home in the Grand Carrier *Wu Zhao*. Not a dedicated warship, but big enough for the Parthenon to remind every other human-descendant who had the big guns. The sight of the *Wu Zhao* approaching Lune Station like a vast segmented silverfish would chill more than a few spines.

Solace and her squad of half a dozen sisters wore light engagement armour—probably sufficient to take the station, if someone decided to declare war while they were aboard. Even light armour noticeably bulked out their short, compact frames. It made them look as though they'd evolved for higher gravities and crushing atmospheres.

Monitor Superior Tact had her head tilted back, angled slightly to the left—a polite shorthand indicating she was conducting a conversation over her implant. She at least had dressed for diplomacy, wearing a long grey gown of sheer, shimmering material. There was a ring of leaden discs at her neck and a circlet of similar material at her brow, guaranteed to be packed with electronic countermeasures and some kind of emergency armament. Similarly, just because Tact was a thin, stately old woman didn't mean she wasn't fully up for hand-to-hand combat.

"And we have clearance for docking," she announced to them all. "Executor Solace, prêt à combattre?"

"Pret, Mother." Ready for combat, ready for anything. An exchange that had so infused Partheni culture that it now covered any confirmation between superior and inferior. Child Solace had responded to her teachers the same way every morning, long before anyone put a gun in her hand.

The *Wu Zhao*'s gravitic fields carried their shuttle smoothly out of the carrier's docking bay and towards the station, where Lune's own field generator would pick them up. "It's been a while," Tact said philosophically. "Last time I was on Lune Station, it was for our secession."

"That was on Berlenhof, wasn't it?" Solace said before she could stop herself; correcting superiors wasn't a good habit.

"The diplomatic song and dance was, later. But we formally cut ties with the Council of Human Interests right here, before an audience of about a dozen of their grandees. No surprise to anybody by then, but you could cut the fear in that room with a knife, daughter." Seeing her soldiers' expressions, Tact added, "Yes. On both sides. *Everyone* thought it might mean war. And neither the Partheni nor Hugh wanted more war—especially human against human."

"We should empty the *refugia*," one of the escort put in bluntly. "Saving your authority, Mother."

Tact's lips pressed thinly together. "Ah yes, the *refugia*." Meaning a dumping ground for excess genetic variability. Meaning all of non-Parthenon humanity. "Nobody is to use that term while on-station, or start calling them 'refugeniks' or anything of the sort. Because you can be absolutely sure that Hugh knows exactly how insulting it's intended to be. Est-ce compris?"

When the Architect had begun its cataclysmic work, Earth's moon had been flung off into space. Nobody had even tracked where it had gone, what with all attention on humanity's desperate attempts to evacuate. One more piece of the past lost beyond recall.

Lune Station was named in memory of that lost satellite. As they moved closer, Solace could see the hollow bowl of its central hub, its exterior transparent so all occupants could see what the Earth had become. Around the outside of the bowl spread great fans of solar collectors, communications equipment and the arms of the station's brachator drive.

Tact interrupted her thoughts as the *Wu* took them in for their final approach. "Daughter," she said, "I trust you are fully aware of what your current role entails. You're not just a squad-sister now, est-ce compris?"

"Compris," Solace confirmed, as their craft drifted to a stop. In her heart of hearts, she would always be a squad-sister. But she'd been around for long enough to know that putting an accelerated projectile into someone wasn't always the best way to defend the interests of the Parthenon. And unlike her younger sisters, who'd never seen the war, she'd mixed with Hivers, regular humans and aliens. They'd all been in it together against the Architects. That was why it had been hard to wake up now to find everyone so estranged.

The lurch as the Lune Station docking control took hold of them was entirely avoidable. Some Colonial controller waving his genitals in their direction as far as Solace was concerned. She felt the shift and sag as Lune's induced gravity engaged, the same Earth-standard 1G she recognized from the *Wu*.

"Remember," Tact informed them all, "put on a good show. Efficiency, discipline, restraint, est-ce compris? We are the pride of the galaxy, the shield of humanity, the armoured fist, the banner unfurled." Her voice was abruptly hard, ringing from the metal walls like a hammer. "We start no fights here, but make them believe that we will damn well finish them."

"Compris, Mother," the escort chorused, standing and forming up.

The Council of Human Interests—"Hugh"—hadn't sent out a similarly pugnacious party to meet them. There were a handful of clerks in knee-length belted smocks, what passed for well-to-do white-collar garb here. The man at their centre was wearing much the same—save that the extravagant cloth of his over-robe fell all the way to his shiny shoes. To Solace it looked absurdly impractical, but that was the point, she supposed. Here was a man who didn't need to throw his own punches.

He kissed Tact on either cheek, the way the Partheni did. She clasped his hand—elbow to elbow—in the "Colony handshake." All deeply symbolic of the divided fragments of humanity clinging together, or some such nonsense.

"Monitor Superior Tact," he greeted her with a bland smile, speaking Parsef smoothly enough. "I was expecting some battlefield officer, bloody to the elbows."

"Commissioner Poulos. And I trust you've had the chance to table the additional motion I sent."

Solace caught the momentary evasion in his eyes before the man turned from Tact to look over her escort.

"It's been too long since I saw the infamous Partheni myrmidons," he declared, though Solace reckoned he could happily have gone to his grave without ever seeing them again. He made a show of examining their company badges, stopping at hers because she alone displayed the winged blade and the serpent, rather than the *Wu Zhao*'s sunburst icon. *Myrmidon Executor Solace, Heaven's Sword Sorority, Basilisk Division.* That she was a long way from her assigned ship obviously didn't escape him.

"You've brought an apprentice, Tact?" he asked mildly, while Solace squirmed within her armour at his scrutiny. "The sword is for the ship, and the snake, that's artillery division... Angels of Infinite Fortitude, they used to call you?" Old nicknames from when the Partheni were humanity's shield against the Architects, not the enemy.

"No, menheer," and then, because she couldn't keep it in, "Angels of Punching You in the Face, menheer," watching at least an eighth of the poetry in him wither.

"Ah," he said. "Well. I suppose we'd better..." And they set off, leaving both entourages to jostle for primacy, a contest that the armoured Partheni won. Solace sensed Tact's eyes on her, and felt she wasn't living up to the role of apprentice diplomat as well as she might.

"We have a full slate of trade agreements to rubber-stamp," the Commissioner was saying. "As for your other motion..."

"Yes, as for the other?" Mother Tact enquired. Because she hadn't come all this way just to talk about shipping tariffs.

"It's been tabled," was all the man would say.

*

The Partheni escort received hard looks on the way to their temporary quarters. Many Lune staff clearly saw them as a threat, but Parthenon armour was proof against hard looks. It wasn't proof against boredom, though, while they waited for Tact to wade through trade permits and shipping concessions with a roomful of Hugh diplomats in impractical clothes, forging towards the one issue that was actually important right now.

Tact's message to Solace, when it finally arrived, came in as a series of brief encoded packets designed to avoid Colonial surveillance.

Their Liaison Board has no interest in sharing Intermediary Program data, Tact confirmed to her. *Their Ints remain "weapons technology," not to be shared with foreign powers.*

But Intermediaries aren't designed to be weapons against us... and the Architects are gone anyway, Solace shot back.

While our technology exceeds theirs, they'll do us no favours. The Ints are the one thing they have that we don't. And those they're turning out these days are under government control. There's no way we could get hold of one for study without starting a war. This might just be the Parthenon's next step, Solace knew. The problem was that not only were the Intermediaries the best weapon against any return incursion of the Architects: as navigators they gave their ships the freedom of the galaxy. A warship with an Int pilot could turn up anywhere, strike and vanish, uncatchable. And the Parthenon had the best warships, but the Colonies had *all* the Ints.

What are my orders, Mother? Solace pictured breaking into Hugh data stores, kidnapping officials and punching information out of them. All for the good of the Parthenon, which was the prime good of the universe, but still...*I do not want to be the name children learn when they're taught how the next war started.*

I'm sending you coordinates in-station. Go there. Someone wants to meet you. Bon chance. Tact was being uncharacteristically cryptic.

This someone. They want to meet me *in particular?* Solace was puzzled as she was neither spy nor diplomat. Not yet anyway. After waking her, they'd rushed her through basic training. But up to this point, her whole adult life had been spent working behind some sort of gun, whether on a personal or starship scale.

That is correct. Maximum diplomacy, est-ce compris? Meaning no weapons or armour.

Compris, Mother. And she was shrugging into a belted tunic in the Colonial style, the sleeves to mid-bicep and the hem down past her hips. All in Partheni blue-grey with her company badges left of her heart. She reckoned turning up in nothing but her under-armour body sleeve would be more provocation than the staid Colonials could take.

Her destination was in the station's underside, the part turned away from the sun where the work was done. Here were docking bays, machine rooms, the cramped quarters of the staff. She ended up on a gantry overlooking a dry-dock where a lander was being outfitted. The domed, six-footed ship was mostly complete, with waldo-wearing engineers and the scarecrow shape of a Hive frame moving the final pieces into place. They'd be taking it down to Earth's tortured surface, maintaining a token presence so that some politician somewhere could claim the homeworld wasn't completely abandoned.

"Myrmidon Executor Solace," said a voice close by on the

gantry, and she started out of her reverie, cursing herself. The newcomer had arrived without warning. He—it—was just there.

Seeing it, recognizing it, she stood very still and waited to see what it would do. They called it Ash, and "the Harbinger." It had come to Earth on a trading ship, immediately before the war and told everyone that a colossal alien entity was about to reshape the planet. The Castigar crew that had brought it were as ignorant of its meaning as the humans of Earth.

What would happen later would be as much a harsh revelation to the Castigar as to humans. Ash told people that the end was nigh, and although almost nobody believed it, that *"almost"* gave just enough leeway so that, when the Architect did arrive and begin its terrible magnum opus, some vessels were ready. They took on passengers and headed out for Earth's colonies. The Harbinger's warning saved millions, even if billions more were lost.

After that, Ash had turned up here and there across the breadth of the human Polyaspora—respected, revered, feared. And now it was standing next to her on a gantry at Lune Station.

Ash wore a human-type robe, draped oddly across its peculiar physiology. There was a writhing nest of pseudopod feet at its base and two tree-like branches at its apex. One of these supported Ash's head, or at least its sense organs: a handful of reddish orbs that guttered dimly with their own light. Beneath them, set into Ash's leathery grey-black skin, were a series of vertical slits—function unknown. Ash was the only one of its kind anyone had ever met and nobody had been given the opportunity to study its physiology. The other branch was contorted into one sleeve of the robe, a rubbery knot of tendrils projecting from the opening in a creditable mockery of a hand. The other sleeve was empty, pinned across the robe's chest. All in all, not a very good impersonation of a human being, and that head was a good half-metre taller than most humans. Yet it was just humanoid enough that one could stand there and talk to it and pretend there was something similar to you talking back.

Some worshipped it, God's messenger who had saved so many. Others called it a devil, part of the Architects' schemes. Not that anybody knew what *those* were.

"You again," said Solace, because it wasn't her first encounter with this damned alien. Last time had been at Berlenhof, just before the battle. Popping up like the spectre of death.

"Me," it said, "again." Ash's rich, deep voice came from its body, nothing to do with its pseudo-head. It had always conversed in whatever language it chose, and now it spoke perfect Colvul, the stitched-together tongue of the Colonies.

"At least speak something civilized," she grumbled in Parsef—a blend of three Earth languages, with added French for formalities.

"You'll need your Colvul where you're going," Ash said conversationally. She'd heard the damn thing give rousing speeches, pronouncements, mystic warnings. It had even stolen the punchline of someone's joke.

"Where's that, exactly?"

"The Parthenon seeks Intermediaries." Ash pronounced the words carefully.

"And you care about that why?"

"You know why," it rumbled, cocking its false head at an unnatural angle. "The Partheni navy is humanity's preeminent military force. Lacking Intermediary navigators impacts your ability to travel between stars. Their lack also strips you of a key weapon against the enemy."

"The Architects?"

"Even so."

"And if the Architects are never coming back? It's been forty years, right?"

"They are always coming back," Ash said.

For a moment Solace felt a chill, presumably as intended. *What does it know?* Then she thought of a smaller, sadder truth. Ash claimed it was the last of its kind, sole survivor of a species destroyed by the Architects long ago. For Ash, the Architects were always coming. That was why it had devoted its life to warning others.

"There aren't many Intermediaries," it observed. "Fewer than you'd think. Most human brains can't take the conditioning. The old ones don't last and the new ones are fragile. The transformation is hard for them."

Solace stared at it, meeting those glowing pits with a shock of contact, just like eyes.

"You recall Idris Telemmier?"

Solace blinked. "Dead, surely." *He must be ancient. He was always so frail.*

"Alive. Alive and free. Not bound to Hugh or its Liaison Board. Free to make his own choices regarding his allies. If you can win his trust. Again."

Somehow the damnable alien injected something salacious into its phrasing. Solace felt herself colouring. And yes, after Berlenhof, the two of them had been together—for a while. Many of her sisters had experimented. And he'd been so vulnerable and alone. To someone brought up within a culture of self-sufficiency and unity, this had exerted a strange fascination.

I wonder if he remembers me. Because if Ash could be believed, this was what her superiors needed. An Int who could be bought or talked into coming over to the Partheni. A way of combating the Architects should they return. *Or a way of cancelling out the Colonies' one advantage…*

Her implant offered up data as it spoke, somehow routed to avoid Lune Station's own channels. A ship's name, a location—out on the fringes of human space, where the rule of law ran thin.

"Thank you." She wanted to ask questions, but didn't want to hear the answers. A creature like Ash…maybe it would pronounce her own death, the death of her ship, her fleet, everything. It had been the voice in the night foretelling the fall of Earth. There was no kind of doom that might not follow in its shuffling footsteps.

On the way back to the docking bay, she reported to Tact, who showed no surprise. By the time she rejoined her squad, Tact had already made arrangements. Solace was leaving her own kind to take on yet another new role. She was to play spy amongst the *refugia*—the human stock her people had left behind. *And all I ever wanted was to be a soldier.*

2.

Idris

In the year "51 After" as Colonial reckoning went, in the thick of the war, an Architect had exited unspace above the colony world of Amraji.

The colonists had begun to evacuate immediately, having seen what happened to Earth fifty-one years before. By this point, practically every human community across the galaxy was living with flight plans under its collective pillow, a bag packed and everyone ready to go.

On the ground, everyone who'd been able to had boarded every ship there was. Then those ships got the hell off the planet as quickly as possible, fleeing even as the Architect's bulk eclipsed half the sky. Some arrived at the nearest colonies, half their passengers traumatized, deranged, even catatonic, because there hadn't been enough suspension beds to put everyone under before entering unspace. Some arrived with parts of their hull twisted into elaborate streamers and fili-gree, because they'd come too close to the Architect at work. Some never arrived. Every evacuation had its tally of lost vessels. Hurry, panic, untrained navigators, badly repaired gravitic drives, there were so many reasons why.

The *Gamin* had been a mid-sized freighter, fitted out to

ship live bodies for the evacuation. Not well enough, as it turned out. It had left Amraji with a crew of four and over seven hundred passengers, headed for the colony of Roshu. It never arrived.

A year ago—over seventy years since the *Gamin* was lost— a Cartography Corps expedition discovered the vessel. Some error in its course had taken it off the known Throughways of unspace, and it had come out into the real so far from home its weak distress beacon had gone unheard for decades. The Cartography expedition that discovered it reported the find, then continued to reach out into unmapped unspace, seeking new Throughways that less adventurous ships might be able to use to reach unknown stars. An antiquated freighter wasn't much use in itself, but it was an important historical artefact. Eventually the Colonial Heritage Foundation commissioned one of the few independent salvagers with the means to navigate out to where the *Gamin* could be found. And while the benevolent mission was talked about on all the fashionable mediotypes, the Foundation somehow never got around to mentioning that the name of the salvage craft was the *Vulture God*, because that might be seen as bad taste.

You had to screw your eyes up really hard to make the *Vulture God* look like any kind of bird. Perhaps a very fat bird with enormous claws and stubby little wings. The central bulk of its barrel body contained its oversized gravitic drive, which could displace enough mass into unspace to bring back the *Gamin*. Projecting out at cross-angles were the blunt little "wings" of its brachator drive that would give it purchase on real space and let it manoeuvre. The actual mass drives for fine manoeuvring were almost inconsequential, a handful of vents about the bloat of its hull. Slung notionally "underneath"—

a direction determined by onboard gravity—was the great clenched tangle of its docking arms. The *Vulture* could latch on to just about anything and haul it around, and now it had reached the *Gamin* it was ready for action.

Idris was already awake, as always, though having stared unspace in the eye for the last day he was feeling washed-out and tired. Ready to nap for about a hundred years, not that it was going to happen.

He alone had been awake in the deep void, guiding the *Vulture God* across unspace. He'd covered vast empty light years in moments to emerge, a ridiculous distance from anywhere, near where the *Gamin* had somehow ended up. There was the promised distress beacon, sounding loud and clear. There was the lost freighter, tumbling slowly through space, the beacon its only live system. There had been some suggestion that people might still be in suspension, aboard, but Idris knew cobbled-together ships like the *Gamin* and they didn't lend themselves to miracles.

He made some scratch calculations for an approach and burned some fuel in the mass drives for cheap and dirty momentum. Then he had the brachator drives reaching out to that liminal layer where unspace and real space met, that quantum foam of transient gravity nodes which their "grabby drives" could latch on to. The *Vulture God* sheared sideways through space as its inertia was shifted through thirty degrees, scudding closer towards the distant winking signal that was the *Gamin*. Idris tutted at his own inelegant piloting and made a few adjustments, spinning the vessel on its axis, stabilizing its drift, grabbing at another handful of the universe to pull them along a slightly different angle of approach.

After that, he had the ship's mind reconstitute itself enough to make him a cup of much-needed kaffe. Then he set about waking the others.

*

The *Vulture God* boasted a crew of seven, five of whom were human. They made for an odd mix by the standards of ships that stuck to the regular Throughways—the readily navigable pathways within unspace that dictated where most vessels could and could not travel. There were no standards for deep void ships, though. There just weren't enough of them. Most species didn't even have a means of navigating off the beaten track and, even where such means existed, they were hard to engineer and needed delicate treatment. Idris certainly felt like *he* needed treating delicately.

He hadn't ever been meant for *this*. He'd only ever been intended as a living weapon. Long past his use-by date now, Idris was still lurching on like a lot of Colonial civilization—most certainly like the *Vulture God*. He'd been on board for four years now, so it was hard not to be sentimental about the ship. It had always come through for them and never quite broken down beyond repair. And if there was one thing the war had taught Colonial humanity to become very, very good at, it was patch repairs on failing starships.

Unspace had made him sweat unpleasantly, so by the time the rest of the crew were stirring he'd blasted his body clean in the dry shower and printed out fresh clothes. This was one of the delights of long-range spaceflight on a shoestring budget. They were basically the same clothes he'd taken off, chewed up and reconstituted as nominally "clean." White undershirt, black short-sleeved tunic, grey breeches and sandals made up his outfit. When he cinched his toolbelt about his waist, he felt almost ready to deal with the universe at large.

His quarters were down near the drone bay, which doubled as engineering control. He could hear Barney complaining loudly within about the list of systems that had developed faults since they set out. Olli would be prepping the *Vulture*'s claws, ready to clasp to the *Gamin*, and Medvig would be... doing whatever the hell Medvig did when they didn't have anything constructive to contribute. Idris sloped forwards towards the command compartment, where Rollo was going over the initial scans.

Rollo Rostand was a stocky, square-faced man, brown-bronzed by decades of low-level radiation exposure, his hair and moustache wispy and dark grey. He had a rare weight-retaining physiology and the *Vulture* had been doing well enough to keep his paunch over his belt. He supplemented the standard printed crew clothes with a military-surplus jacket he claimed had been his father's, the war hero. The details of these heroics tended to change with the telling, but everyone of that generation had done *something*. Idris, the actual veteran, was more than happy with Rollo's embellishments because it meant nobody would ask about his truths.

"Well hola now, my children," the man was saying as Idris ducked into the compartment. "How's it looking across the board?"

"Everything's broken to shit," came Barney's sour voice through their comms. "I am sending you a shopping list for when we're back on Roshu."

"Are you also sending Largesse to pay for it?" And, interpreting the pregnant silence as a negative, "In which case I recommend you make do and mend like a good son of Earth. Olli?"

"One of the drones is a lost cause," the remote specialist's slightly distorted tones came in. She'd slept the unspace flight in her control pod, Idris knew, which was not best operating procedure.

"Make do—"

"And mend, I know, I know. Only it's more making do than mending right now."

Rollo beamed around at Idris as though this was the best news he could have expected. "We've just matched tumble with our prey, my children. I'm flagging up our access point. Should bring us into the *Gamin*'s crew spaces. Maybe."

"Maybe?" Idris asked.

"When they refitted that bucket for passengers nobody filed their new plans with the proper authorities, see right? So we do the best we can." Rollo settled back in his chair and put his bare feet up on the console. "Since you're here, my son, you do the honours," he invited, and Idris dropped into the pilot's seat. The *Vulture God* was now moving in-sync with the *Gamin*, so precisely that they might as well have been stationary. Idris engaged the brachator drive, nudging the salvage ship ever closer—while maintaining all the other vectors of their travel so that they drifted into the shadow of the freighter like a parasite tentatively approaching its host.

This close, he opened up the mass drives as well, trimming their motion carefully as they ghosted across the ugly, weld-scarred hotch-potch of the *Gamin*'s hull. The freighter's crew compartment was set midway into one side. Most of the space above it would be for cargo—in this case the passengers—while the gravitic drive formed a lopsided torus around the freighter's circumference. Lopsided because part of it was missing, a section of the ring torn open and warped into strange spiralling fingers that clawed at the void.

Rollo shook his head. "Looks like they cut it too fine getting out." There was no mistaking Architect-inflicted damage.

Idris couldn't imagine what it had been like for the *Gamin's* crew: enter unspace with a damaged drive or stay and risk the Architect's attention. Likely he'd have made the same decision.

"Olli," he transmitted. "Ready for you."

"On it." His board lit up to show she had control of the *Vulture's* claws and was deploying them to bridge the final gap between vessels.

"What are we getting besides the beacon?" Rollo asked. "Kittering, send it over."

Kittering's real name sounded like nails on a chalkboard, made with a rapid stridulation of some of his mouthparts. The crab-like alien would be hunkered down in his own compartment, a space entirely adapted for his physiology and comfort. His chief role was managing accounts and logistics. Still, he was a good second engineer and when a job was afoot, everybody worked.

Even Kris. The last member of the crew—Idris's business partner—hadn't shown yet. She made a habit of taking her sweet time over actually reporting for duty. And if it hadn't been for Idris's value to the venture, Rollo would likely have dumped her somewhere along the way. Idris needed her, though, and the *Vulture* needed Idris to get out into the deep void. Otherwise it was just one more salvager among many, scrabbling for work along the Throughways.

Kittering sent over what the *Vulture's* ailing sensor suite had gleaned from the *Gamin*. Aside from the beacon, just some low power readings: a few failing systems still labouring within the otherwise dead ship.

"You don't think we'll actually..." The thought of finding working suspension pods bobbed for a moment in Idris's mind.

"Find people? Alive...Be the fucking heroes of the universe, hey?" Rollo shook his head. "Go on though, bet me a thousand Halma we'll find them, bet me five-kay Largesse. Bet me anything?"

"I won't," Idris said quietly, and Rollo nodded.

"No more would I."

The frantic board showed that they had drifted close enough to set off all their collision alarms, but Olli had full control of the great convoluted mess of the claw. It was unfolding like a mechanical tarantula from the *Vulture*'s underside, to grope for the freighter's hull. Olli was a top-notch remote operator with a rare gift—able to run non-humanoid rigs as though they were her own body. Right now she would be *"in"* the docking claw, its seven articulated limbs stretching and flexing until she had them clamped to the *Gamin*, magnetically locked.

"Nice work, Olli, my sweet child," Rollo told her. "Smooth as a baby's ass. Now get the cutters ready."

"You're not going to hail them?" The new voice came from the control compartment's hatch. Idris glanced up and nodded as Kris came in. Here on board ship she was dressed in a variant of the same printed clothes, though she had one of her signature scarves about her neck, same as always. She was a dark woman a shade taller than him, her hair a carefully shaped mass of fine curls. She was also running from her own trouble, but getting out of trouble was her speciality skill.

"Nobody to hail," Rollo insisted, but a moment later he grudgingly went through the motions. If they cut through the hull and someone fell out and died in space, at least they could hide behind a trail of proper procedure. This was the sort of trouble that Kris specialized in.

*

They could just have hauled the whole ship off like an unopened present to give to the Heritage Foundation. That was all the contract required. Rollo was always on the lookout for a bonus, though. What if the *Gamin* held some unexpected treasure? What if there really were living refugees? Why give the kudos to the Heritage people when the *Vulture*'s crew could cash in?

They could have gone in through a hatch, like civilized people. However, four years ago a fellow salvager had been destroyed by actual honest-to-goodness booby traps left by the long-dead occupants of the ship it had opened up. Trapped in stranded ships, the mind went to strange places, especially if it had been exposed to unspace for long. The crew of the *Vulture God* were taking no chances, and going in through the wall instead, Olli cut smoothly along some of the pre-existing repair seams until the side of the freighter had been peeled back. There was no rush of stale atmosphere, only vacuum meeting vacuum. *Could have been worse*, Idris allowed.

"Right then, let's get this business underway," Rollo announced. "Olli, move your remotes in, and have Medvig follow up with his little fellows. And you, shyster," he said to

34

Kris, "may as well get a camera drone in there. The medio-types will be worth something. Double-time, everybody! And that does not mean double pay, before anyone asks."

The crew spaces of the *Gamin* were adrift with small objects. Back in the earliest days of space travel nobody would have dared fit out a ship with so much loose junk, but people had been taking artificial gravity for granted for generations before the Architect came to Amraji. It was a small side-use of the same engines that moved the ships through space. The *Gamin*'s gravitic drives were lifeless though. The viewfeed from Olli's drones showed her remotes jetting carefully through a swirl of odd items: data clips, slates, gloves, a gleaming silver locket, a stiffly frozen plush toy. Of the crew themselves there was no sign, and Idris wondered if they had taken a shuttle and tried to get...where? Emerging unplanned from unspace in the middle of nowhere, drive burnt-out and the nearest star system light years away, where would you go?

"Atmosphere loss by slow leak, my guess," Olli's glitching voice came to them. "Or this junk'd be flushed out already. Moving towards the cargo."

"Check if there's pressure before each door," came Kris's input, following up with her cameras.

"My hands are in the carcass," announced Medvig, with that tinny edge of jollity that always tinged their artificial voice, no matter what the topic. Like many Hivers, they had accumulated a lopsided personality the longer they were separate from the wider hive mind of the Assembly.

Idris slouched down to the bay, feeling that even if he wasn't doing anything, he should at least be where the doing was done. Towards the ceiling, Olli hung in her pod, eyes closed as her three remotes cleared the way for Medvig inside the wreck. She was a pale doughy woman, grown bulky through inactivity even on a spacefarer's diet. Half obscured in her pod, the most obvious thing about her silhouette was her stunted, near-useless limbs. Her arms ended at the elbows with a tuft of half-formed fingers, one leg stopped at the smooth stump of her knee, the other absent altogether. Olian Timo—Olli—had been born so, and without any sense of proprioception—a stranger in her truncated body. But she'd been born to a colony where every single human being was a precious resource and they'd found where she excelled. Olli had trained with remotes of all kinds since she was three. Her mind could mould itself to any body shape, regardless of how its limbs and senses were configured. Three remotes at once was just another day at work for her.

The crew had set up an umbilical leading the three metres or so between hulls. It led "down" to the *Vulture's* crew— though its direction was meaningless to the dead spaces of the *Gamin*. Medvig's armless tripod frame was already squatting at the *Vulture* end, a metal assemblage of dull bronze and copper, their cylindrical body dominated by four square openings. Their long head was featureless save for a couple of mismatched yellow lights—humans liked to have something to focus on. Medvig's "hands" could act as his own personal remotes and he had already sent these small spider-like assemblages down the pipe and into the freighter to help Olli with the fine work.

Kris gave Idris a wave from where she sat on the floor, Kittering crouching beside her. The alien wasn't much more than a metre high but was half again as wide, lending him a crab-like gait when he moved through their human-designed corridors. High-status Hannilambra back home might lavishly ornament their armoured backs and the shield-like surfaces of their protective arms, to show their wealth and status. Kittering's were set with cheap screens that he used to communicate or rented out as advertising space.

"Suspension pods…" said Olli. Idris glanced up to the bay's main screen, flicking from one drone feed to another. Here was the main cargo space of the *Gamin*, lined with suspension beds. Their irregular layout and lack of uniformity spoke of the haste of their installation. None of the drones were picking up any power signatures.

"Could be worse," Kris said, and he could only nod.

"It will, of course, become worse." Medvig's cheery tones issued from their metal torso.

"Next cargo bay. I'm opening her up," Olli reported. And then, "It's worse."

Idris stared dully at the screen, noting that the conversion of the *Gamin* from cargo to passenger craft hadn't been complete by the time of its evacuation. That hadn't stopped its crew from nobly taking on as many people as they could.

There were no suspension pods in the next chamber, just bodies. They were vacuum-withered, dried-up like sticks, many with ruptured eyes and self-inflicted wounds. A few desiccated hands clutched makeshift weapons. Idris watched a gun drift past, an old-model accelerator that could certainly have put a pellet through the hull; perhaps that had lost them their atmosphere.

The *Vulture*'s drones pushed in through the open hatch, sending rigid bodies spinning away. It looked as though there had been a couple of hundred people packed into this hold, and they had not gone peacefully. Idris could almost hear an echo, across time, of the dreadful all-consuming panic that had swept through the hold like a flash fire; the madness gifted to each one of them alone.

It wouldn't have just been the knowledge that they were going to die. People could be remarkably sanguine when all hope was gone. It was that they had gone through unspace, awake. It was something he himself was intimately familiar with, but then he was an Intermediary. It was what he had not only been trained for but extensively engineered for. One of the lucky ones who'd survived the process.

Unspace travel while awake wasn't a death sentence; it wasn't *guaranteed* to drive a person into a stage of permanent madness either. But both outcomes were entirely possible. Unspace was *different*. Things from real space—such as humans—had a tenuous existence there. It was a terrible, lonely place, until you sensed something...*other*. Then being alone became preferable to the alternative. Regular navigators retired to their suspension beds after setting a course along the Throughways, and their ships woke them when they were ready to exit unspace at their destination. It was only when you went off the beaten track that someone had to keep the lamps burning, gazing into the abyss and having it gaze right back. That was what Intermediaries did. That was the invaluable service people like Idris provided to the post-war world, for as long as their minds held together.

Things went further downhill after Olli found the *Gamin*'s lone power signature, the one system still working in the whole ship. She tracked it down to one corner of the hold, finding an antique mediotype projector bolted lopsidedly to the wall. It was looping through an array of entertainment, brightly coloured figures that were partway between human and extinct Earth animals. They were still capering about, having adventures, teaching vacuum-silent lessons about space safety and friendship and making do. Because someone had wanted the children to have something to take their minds off the journey when they left their homes and went into space. Because of course there had been children here. Because of course.

After enough time had passed, Rollo's rough voice came through to them. "All right, my sons and daughters. Olli, Medvig, bring in anything loose that'll fetch a price. Then let's get this tomb back to Roshu. Soonest started, soonest finished. And Barney?"

"What now?" the engineer demanded from wherever he was in the ship.

"Run some component comparisons. I know she's old, but there's probably something on that ship that we could reuse on this one."

3.

Idris

Back Before, nobody came to Roshu for their health. It was a poisonous planet, the atmosphere full of sulphur, chlorine and arsenical compounds, the ground heavy with selenium and cinnabar. The external temperature could cook eggs even near the poles, which was where all the habitats were. The initial Roshu colony had been a small mining concern. After Earth, a lot of refugees ended up there. They lived out of their failing ships for a generation, while people built makeshift shelters on the ground or in orbit. Some ships failed, some shelters did too, yet people kept arriving. Roshu had been one of the few colonies that hadn't needed to encourage refugees to leave, but it was never going back to being a little mining colony. Enough people stuck from the Polyaspora, and the same Throughways that brought the refugees also made Roshu a stopover for merchants and haulers.

The *Vulture God* erupted out of unspace, close enough to set Roshu's traffic control systems complaining, and Idris began bootstrapping the ship's systems and waking the others. Roshu wasn't his favourite place in the galaxy, frankly.

Just about all human colonies had an AI kybernet to standardize legalities and trade within human space. At Idris's request, Roshu's version confirmed docking privileges at the planet's single groundbound spaceport, Roshu Primator, and he began their approach.

Rollo strolled in, wearing nothing but white long johns and munching on a stick of something purple-flavoured. He scratched idly at his paunch. "You fucked up the approach again. Careless, boy, careless."

Heritage had hailed them by then, wanting to take the *Gamin* out of the *Vulture God*'s claws. Money changed hands in the ghostly ether where the computer systems meshed. Job done, and Idris was happy to be rid of the wrecked freighter and all its grisly contents, even happier to count the Largesse added to the *Vulture*'s account.

Some of the older colonies still ran their own currencies but the Polyaspora had wrecked any wider human economy. The entire fugitive culture had been living from day to day for decades on a barter-economy. Largesse had started when people began swapping skills and services for whatever necessities could be gleaned. Colony kybernets had formalized it into a credit system, at least nominally backed by Hugh. It remained rough around the edges, intentionally shadowy, a cobbled-together system for a cobbled-together civilization.

"Well now, my happy little family," Rollo announced to the crew, as they levered themselves groggily from the suspension pods. "I would love to tell you all we just got rich, but take docking fees, repair costs and the usual bribes out of it and we're all just very slightly better off. Kit, Kris, Barney, Medvig: shore leave, one day. Idris and Uncle Rollo are going to see a man about putting bread on the table. Mesdam Olian, dearest of all my surrogate daughters, has drawn the short straw. She will be minding ship for the first day, during which she will doubtless attend to various niggling matters of maintenance. Those that do not require Menheer Barnier's technical acumen."

"Fuck off, Unca Rollo," from Olli, not best pleased at sitting out the first round of shore leave.

"Oho, yes indeed," Rollo twinkled, cranking the avuncular up to eleven. "For the rest of you reprobates, we will be on the ground two days maximum. Whoever fucks up the worst on day one gets to mind the ship on day two."

Rollo took oversight of their landing approach into the docks at Roshu Primator—"The Primate House" as the city had somehow become known. The docking ring was set around the very apex of the covered city's outer bubble as if the place was wearing some kind of hat. Under this encircling platform was a gravitic drive, whose ministrations maintained atmosphere over the landing pads, supported ships during the last few hundred metres of their descent and, not least, held up the whole unlikely city's structure. Idris could only imagine the maintenance schedule this demanded, and what might happen if someone cut corners.

With the surly exception of Olli, the crew assembled at the hatch, dressed for shore leave. For Idris and Barney this didn't require any changes to their printed ship gear. Idris liked not standing out, and Musoku Barnier had probably accepted he wasn't going to win any beauty contests. He'd been caught in some engineering-related mischance long before he joined the *Vulture God*'s crew. Wherever he'd been, the medical facilities had been efficient but utilitarian. Half his face was craggy bronze-brown and deeply lined. The other half was greying pink, smooth as youth, the eye a milky marble. Kris said the true root of Barney's ill temper was that the grafted side looked better than the original.

Kris had donned her fancy clothes: the long tunic with wide sleeves, the artfully draped poncho. On her slim frame, all that unnecessary cloth served to at least mimic the impression of wealth and good living. The red scarf around her neck was vivid as a murder scene. Anyone seeing them stepping off the ship would take her for a passenger, slumming her way across the galaxy before taking up a position in her parents' company.

Medvig didn't dress up. They were a three-legged armless frame, with a head purely for the convenience of dealing with humans. However, the crew's other non-human member had made his own planet-appropriate arrangements.

Hannilambra weren't really like crabs, because crabs came from Earth. Yet to any human who'd seen a shellfish farm, the comparison was unavoidable. Evolution had designed the Hanni to present their armoured backs to predators, protecting a broad body set on three pairs of legs that let them skitter in just about any direction. Kittering's focal point was a fork-shaped prong jutting from under the butterfly-wing curve of his shell. Five round amber eyes stared unwinkingly from this, with the bellows of his two breathing membranes rising and falling on either side. The sagging sack of his belly was mostly hidden by his shield arms, evolved for defence but co-opted for display. Above the arms, a cluster of mouthparts was in constant fidgety motion. Kittering's eye-crown didn't come much past Idris's waist, but the little accountant pushed through his human crewmates with perfect assurance. The screens set into his back and shields displayed a lurid advertisement for some no-holds fight match. Kittering was always on the lookout for a little extra Largesse.

Rollo himself had slung a reinforced jacket over his ship clothes. Old miners' gear, his one concession to a night on the town. None of them were carrying obvious weapons, because Roshu had strict regulations about anything that could punch a hole in the dome.

As the hatch opened, revealing a quicksilver-coloured sky dotted with toxic clouds, Kris rapped Idris on the shoulder.

"Eyes open."

"Like they cut off the lids," he agreed, and then the crew were going their separate ways.

"Got a call from a Cheeseman," Rollo explained to Idris. "Deep void work. Wants to see if we've got what it takes." Cheesemen were fixers who matched jobs to skills. They claimed the name came from "chessmen," after their legendary logistical skills. Everyone else said it came from "cheese-paring" after their legendary tight-fistedness.

Idris nodded glumly. Intermediaries were rare, so being exhibited like some human curio was part of the deal.

They were pushing down a narrow corridor, cluttered with spacers, miners and colony staff. Here tawdry establishments sought to bilk the impatient of their currency before they reached the main dens of vice on the lower levels. And Idris had an itch between his shoulder blades. His paranoia told him someone was following them, but then paranoia was one of the things you ended up with if you kept your eyes open through unspace. He shook off the feeling irritably.

The crowds had blinded Idris and Rollo to trouble, so they practically bounced off the two large men who stepped in front of them. Idris was just making apologies when one of them said, "Idris Telemmier. You come with us now."

He froze. Strangers knowing his name was never auspicious, especially when it preceded an order and not an invitation. The voice wasn't the nasal Roshu twang either, but something heavier with rolled consonants, from a planet less cosmopolitan than this.

"He's going nowhere with you, friend," Rollo started and got slammed against the corridor wall for his trouble, with a whoof of lost breath. The other man seized Idris's arm in a vice hold. The two heavies were just that. Most people who'd come out of the lean war generations were small, clawing to their majorities out of half-starved childhoods. This pair's ancestors hadn't had any worries on that score. They were each a good two metres tall and broad across the shoulders. They wore bottle-green uniform jackets, busy with gold trimming about the shoulders and cuffs. Their long faces had bristly moustaches, and hair worn in wire-bound braids that reached to their chins. Everything about them screamed money and casual violence, and there was only one place that really did the two together so well: Magda.

"We don't need any trouble!" Idris proclaimed loudly. But everyone was just rushing past, in a hurry not to see any trouble either, in case it was contagious.

"Detaining you under 'Liaison Board Order Three, Rogue Intermediaries,'" one of the Magdan heavies grunted, like someone reading the words with difficulty from a book.

"Kris." Idris tried the radio, but they'd hit a complete dead zone. *Worse and worse.*

"Whose authority?" Rollo choked out, more for the form of it.

"Our lord desires justice," one of them said. "A fugitive Intermediary. Very dangerous. To be repatriated to Colonial service. And you talk too much, fat man. Accessory, we think."

His friend flashed a slate that might or might not display some manner of permit.

Idris got as far as "I'm not—" before his arm was wrenched behind his back, hard. Then he and Rollo were being frog-marched away.

Solace

Partheni weren't renowned for travelling incognito. When she stepped off the passenger-hauler at Roshu, Solace was followed by a fair-sized a-grav trunk that held her armour and weapons. The sight of her Parthenon greatcoat put a good metre of clear space around her, which had its pluses and minuses. The long military coat, marked with her company badges and rank, attracted a lot of foul looks these days. The last few decades had seen the rise of an ugly subculture of "Nativists" in the Colonies, who were dead against anything except "natural-born humans" on their worlds. At the same time, the uniform was notorious enough that nobody dared to give her any trouble. Worst came to worst, the intimidation factor might just start opening doors for her purely so that their owners could get rid of her more quickly.

It struck her that the phrase *Parthenon diplomacy* might become Colvul parlance to describe exactly the way she was behaving, and she wasn't sure if that was funny or not.

There weren't many places on Roshu for high-profile guests, but the Aspirat—the Parthenon's covert ops division— had an account with the Orrery of Man. It was part hotel, part monument to poor taste and gold paint, but at least it was in a "good" part of the moneyed upper dome. More scowls were evident as she entered the lobby, and that concerned her a little more. The Partheni were always going to be anathema to the grass-roots "real humans for real humans" movement within Hugh. By Nativist lights they were vat-grown genetic freaks, and they'd become a military threat when they left Hugh's control thirteen years ago. Hostile stares from snooty staff and the cosseted rich, even in this hellhole, didn't bode well for the future. *Fear not the gun but the finger on the trigger*, as the saying went.

Soon after, a very different Solace slipped out of a staff exit, dressed in olive-coloured ship clothes and sandals. She retained the bleeding wing tattoo under her left eye, but Roshu's underside was rough, diverse and full of transients of all descriptions.

The Parthenon's Aspirat section maintained a sympathizer in the city administration—a grey-haired woman with the stern demeanour of a vengeful librarian. Solace only needed to say, "Show me the *Vulture God*," and she received a packet of information, delivered hand to hand—the old way, so nobody could pluck it from the kybernet in transit.

The *Vulture*'s file held only its most recent flight plan and a crew manifest with images and biometrics, mostly so local authorities could identify any bodies after bar fights. Solace flicked across the pictures: hostile-looking moustache, good-looking woman with a double chin, half-face guy, better-looking woman with a scarf and an intriguing grin, cheap-ass Hanni, battered-looking Hive frame...and there was her mark.

Idris Telemmier. She stared at the picture below the sparse details. It wasn't even listed that he was an Int. Another agent might have queried her superiors. *Are you sure?*

Except she knew. As Ash said, this was an old friend. A fellow veteran.

Of course she remembered him. She remembered Berlenhof, default HQ of the Council of Human Interests—wealthy and beautiful even before Earth fell. And she'd never forget the conflict that followed. She'd been with the first *Heaven's Sword*, a shining new ship with the latest mass loom technology. And after the battle, her surviving sisters had become the core of a new sorority for the next ship to bear the name.

Before the battle, with the Architect making its graceful approach past the outer planets, the Partheni had met Berlenhof's fellow defenders on one of its orbitals. While her superiors had discussed hard tactics with their opposite numbers, she'd sat with her fellow soldiers and just talked. This was back in the day when the Parthenon was humanity's great hope. The angels with their martial resolve and top-of-the-range technology. Their mission: to hold back the inevitable.

She felt a wave of nebulous emotion. A clutch of loss mixed with the soaring nostalgia of *When We Were Heroes*. She'd been twenty-five and had never seen anything more than a skirmish before. There had been Castigar warrior-caste members spoiling for a fight; Hannilambra merchant venturers, humans from every corner of the Colonies. And there had been a special weapon too. Four men, three women, one nonbinary. *Intermediaries*, the first class of them, right out of the labs; the weapon that a little corner of human science had been working on ever since the Miracle at Forthbridge.

Idris Telemmier had been among the group. Later, he'd

become the first man she'd ever met. A little younger than she was, dark bronzy skin like most Colonials, black unruly hair hacked short by someone whose barber status was defiantly amateur. Mostly she remembered how nervous he'd looked, flinching from every loud noise. And he had big ears, really quite outsize for his face. Odd what stayed with you.

Now she looked at his image and saw the same man, when she should have been looking at a face that might have belonged to his grandfather. Solace herself had been born over seventy years before, Earth standard, but she'd spent a lot of that time in suspension, a weapon waiting for an appropriate war. Colonials didn't do that; they only put themselves under when they travelled and, for Ints, not even then. She could only assume the image was seriously out of date.

Three of the eight Ints had died, at Berlenhof, and another two had been driven irretrievably insane in the course of duty. Idris could easily have been next. Yet when she met him on-planet after the battle, in the infirmary camp converted from a luxury hotel, he'd been lucid. Shaken, but that was to be expected after you'd touched the vast alien consciousness of an Architect with your mind.

Six years later, the war would end, thanks to Berlenhof's hard-won insights. In the Far Lux system, the Intermediary Program would finally establish contact with an Architect. No formal détente, no treaties, no demands. According to the surviving Ints, there had just been a...*noticing*. The Architects had discovered that humans existed. The war, which had raged for eighty years and cost billions of lives, had been fought without the knowledge of one of its parties. And on becoming aware of humanity, the Architects had simply vanished. Nobody knew where they went. Nobody knew where they had come from or why they'd done what they did. They had never been seen again.

*

When the *Vulture God* came into port, Solace put herself into a position to greet it. That was her initial plan: just step forward and raise a hand. She watched the same faces from the manifest appear, or most of them. Then it was Telemmier's turn, and Solace simply stared. If he'd had the slightest awareness about him, he'd have seen her immediately, all her training fled.

He really hadn't changed. The image she'd seen *was* up to date. Here was the man she'd known in the war. The man with the big ears and the worried expression from fifty years ago, not aged a day.

For a moment she was back in the war, when things had been simultaneously better and so much worse. Back fighting the Architects, which couldn't be fought in any meaningful way. Until they'd wheeled out Idris and his fellows, their secret weapon, the hope of humanity.

She stared, missed her moment, and the crew walked right by her.

The majority were very plainly out for a night on the town, or whatever passed for it on Roshu. Idris and Moustache peeled off from them, and Solace wanted to just shout his name, go and grab his shoulder. She was a soldier, after all, and he'd been her comrade-in-arms once. Easy to forget she was a spy now.

So she forced down all those easy, blunt ways of doing

things and just skulked after them, awaiting her moment, fending off people who tried to sell her things or interest her in their dubious services. Food, games, mediotypes, even...

"Forbidden delights of the warrior angels, Menheer?"

The words actually stopped her and she turned incredulously. For a moment—a very brief moment—she thought she saw a Partheni soldier soliciting a lurching freighter pilot. Then the garish lights opposite switched orientation, revealing a very risqué "uniform." The spacer obviously found the look authentic enough, because he changed tack and stumbled through the open door of the institution. The young woman posted outside looked speculatively at Solace.

"Mesdam, you?" She stretched a smile across her tired face. "Who knows the pleasures of our sex better than the wicked angels of the Parthenon?" Behind her, the frontage of the establishment lit up with decals of wings and phallic spaceships.

I should tell her, Solace thought, amused. She was curious as to what counted as "forbidden" on decadent Roshu. But she just shook her head and hurried to make up lost ground.

But she was too late. Through being circumspect, she'd lost her quarry to someone who *had* just done the soldierly thing and accosted them. Idris and Moustache were now in the company of a pair of decorated military clowns. Given the way the crowd was parting, they were recognized by the locals as having some manner of authority. Or perhaps it was merely that they were big men, plainly kitted out by someone with Largesse to spare.

For a moment she was going to just wade in, pit her Partheni skills against the brute squad and show them who bred better soldiers. However, she was in Colonial space, these two could be Hugh security services and that was how wars were started.

She brought out a slate and recorded the whole mess, tailing them until they reached what she identified as a bastion of the local administration. This validated her decision not to kick anyone's head in. Yet.

So what now? It wasn't as though the Parthenon had any diplomatic sway here on Roshu. She needed allies if she wasn't going to simply storm in like a one-woman army. And the *Vulture's* remaining crew were the only possible candidates... Wherever they were, they would be spending credit—her accomplice could pinpoint which dive was fleecing them. Then she could use them to break up whatever the hell was going on with Telemmier and friend. Solace flicked through the profiles of Idris's crewmates until she found the one she wanted—the woman with the scarf and the grin—and put her plan into action.

Her contact located the crew at a gaming den, where their Hannilambra factor was hustling two miners and a freighter pilot at Landstep. Solace was just in time to see the engineer, Barnier, heading off with a man and a woman. The trio looked very friendly, bound for one of the upstairs rooms. The woman Solace wanted was at the bar, looking far too elegant for Roshu, knocking back a beaker of the notoriously potent Colonial moonshine. She glanced at the approaching Solace briefly, then fixed on her. After all, Solace did have the distinctive Partheni face. It was inevitable when you grew your people out of vats from a carefully curated gene-line.

Solace saw her eyes widen, and knew the Colonial woman could denounce her to the entire establishment. It was time for her soldier routine, whether Solace wanted to go there or not.

"Your friends are in trouble," she said, to forestall a scene. "Your captain and navigator. They need you." Of all the crew, this woman's particular civilian talents were required right now. But because Roshu was that kind of place, and the uniforms had seemed that kind of people, she added, "and you need me."

4.

Idris

Magda was an Earth-like planet, cold but with a relatable biochemistry. Back Before, the colony had already been expanding, the original founders becoming an overclass above a mass of new colonists—introduced to run the expanding agricultural industry. Magda was the largest exporter of foodstuffs to overburdened Earth.

After, refugees had fled to Magda in their millions, knowing only that *here* was a planet with room for them. And the planet's landowners, the Boyarin, had taken in everyone, turned not one ship away. Which sounded grand until you understood that to set foot on Magda was to accept the life they gave you, one of service in the factories or fields. It was never quite slavery under Hugh definitions, but then Magda was one of the big dogs of Hugh. Remarkable how the authorities there could end up "not quite" any number of bad things. The word most enlightened outsiders applied to Magdan society was "serfdom." The Boyarin themselves called the system the "robot," which seemed to adequately sum up how they regarded the mass of their people.

It was one of the Boyarin themselves who came to look

in on Rollo and Idris, shortly after they were consigned to one of Roshu Admin's holding cells.

He looked young, although the Boyarin were certainly amongst those few with the wherewithal for a long life. His clothes were flamboyant: a loose-sleeved shirt of shimmering orange, hand-embroidered at the throat and cuffs; tight trousers and tight boots; a black half-cloak ornamented with gold. His body was lean and fit, his coldly handsome features graced with a small upwards-tilted moustache and a neat scar that curved from the corner of his mouth to his ear. The Magdan elite liked their duels, Idris had heard. His heavies—presumably Voyenni, house guards—stood impassively after announcing him as "The Boyarin Piter Tchever Uskaro."

Piter Uskaro was all skin-deep smiles, and he had eyes for Idris alone. "What fortune attends our meeting," he announced. It was as if his "guests" weren't stuck in a cramped, oven-hot metal box with one clear plastic wall. His tones, heavy with the Magdan accent, came to them through a speaker in the ceiling.

"Your Grandness, there's been some mistake," Rollo tried. "We're just salvagers. We're no criminals. I can provide references, work history."

Uskaro waved the virtual paperwork aside, still grotesquely pleasant, as though just waiting for a servant to turn up with wine. "Deep void work, yes. Which means you have in your possession a rare gem, a commercial Intermediary. Yet imagine my surprise when I asked after the details of your leash contract with the Liaison Board. And, alas, none is filed!" He rolled his eyes as though they were all just victims of Hugh bureaucracy. "Which can only mean that your man here is a *fugitive* from his contract, and you have been abetting him. I'm sure it's witless, Captain Rostand. Do I mean witless? Innocent, maybe, is the word. I'm sure you had no idea your man here was a dangerous renegade fleeing the service he owes to his people. Bad trouble, Captain. Very bad. You will of course be grateful when I take him off your hands. It is not the first time such a one has been apprehended by the Boyarin's tireless efforts in our drive for justice. We spearhead the advancement of our species, Captain. Our tireless navigators seek out Throughways as yet undiscovered, that we may open up a wealth of planets hitherto hidden from us. The future of humanity, Captain! Fresh colonies, perhaps even new Originator sites. Treasures beyond imagining!" His teeth were blinding white and perfectly even when he smiled.

Idris squinted into the sun of that expression and wasn't fooled. His fight-or-flight response was screwing his body into overdrive. Awkward, given he could do neither.

"What," he managed, "did your last Int die of?"

That perfect smile didn't falter. "It so happened that my family's best navigator suffered a mishap. How lucky for me that we were able to locate a replacement so swiftly. I am just concluding the legalities with Roshu kybernet, after which we shall be off. And then I shall decide whether charges should be filed against your captain here, as your accomplice. Perhaps a residual concern for his wellbeing will encourage you to accept your rightful lot. It's time you served the species that made you what you are."

"Your Grandness," Rollo started. "He is not under leash. He is a free man. You have no right—"

Uskaro gave him the look of a man who can purchase any right he wishes. "The kybernet is processing the matter now,

Captain Rostand. I shall return shortly to take possession of my new property. What happens to *you* depends on your decorum between now and then."

When he was gone, Rollo sat on the floor and stared at his sandalled feet. "Fuck all paymasters," he said, less a specific jibe at Uskaro so much as a familiar spacer oath.

Idris was still standing. He couldn't sit. His skinny body was vibrating with adrenaline which had nowhere to go. *I will fight*, he decided. *I will not go.* And he knew they couldn't force him, not really. They couldn't *make* him navigate for them. But they could beat and brutalize him, condition him, drug him. Drive implants into his brain, until his ability to resist their demands had been pared down to nothing. Mostly with the Liaison Board Ints, the Commercial Ints, it wasn't necessary. They came pre-compliant, resigned to drudgery until the horrors of unspace unhinged them. But when one of them went renegade and fled, well, you heard all sorts...

And he wasn't renegade. He'd never been on a leash. But it wasn't the first time someone had made the convenient assumption, and this time Kris wasn't here to sort it out.

"I won't go," he said, because the thought had bounced back and forth in his head so much it had to escape.

"We'll jump them," Rollo suggested. "On the way to their ship..." As though Rollo would even be getting out of the cell, Idris thought. "Or we'll come after you." As though they could, without Idris in the pilot's chair. "We'll...something." As though there was anything.

*

Around fifty-five years back, in the heart of the war, the freighter *Samark* exited unspace to find every wartime pilot's worst nightmare: an Architect bearing down on them. They were bound for Forthbridge Port, packed to the gills with displaced refugees. Faced with their imminent demise, the crew started packing people into shuttles and escape pods, of which there was an entirely inadequate supply. Meanwhile, the Architect reached out for them, intent on peeling the ship and arranging the hull into a configuration more pleasing to its alien aesthetics.

Yet, even as it began to warp the hull, it stopped. For a long moment the passenger freighter and the colossal alien entity hung there in space, both speeding towards Forthbridge Port. Then it withdrew. For the first time ever, an Architect just went away. What happened on board the *Samark* became legend. The most popular mediotype showed one of the passengers, a girl of fifteen, running onto the bridge. She was clutching her head, speaking in tongues, blood running from her nose. What was clear to everyone was that Xavienne Torino had somehow made the Architect leave. Her own testimony confirmed she'd forged a link between them, mind to mind.

She had been the first Intermediary, a natural. Over the next decade, humanity's best scientists would work with Saint Xavienne—as she became known—to try and replicate her abilities. The new corps would get its first outing at the Battle of Berlenhof in 78 After, and would go on to end the war.

But before *that*, everyone had realized Ints were good for more than just driving away Architects. That same uncanny sense let them tap into the fabric of unspace, to navigate beyond the established Throughways in a way no instrument or device could. Some species could manage something similar: the Castigar and the Hegemony for example. But even with them it was rare, and humanity had abruptly joined that select club. Ints went from being a secret weapon to a trading advantage. So the Liaison Board was born. They took in humanity's unwanted and they turned out a handful of commercial Intermediaries, through harsh conditioning and unrelenting surgery. All who survived the Program left under leash contracts, making them nothing but property until they'd paid back the colossal cost of their "treatment." Which meant, to all intents and purposes, never.

Idris was a free man, created before the Board existed, but who would believe him? And almost all the other free wartime Ints were dead. These cheery thoughts occupied him until the Boyarin Piter Tchever Uskaro returned, with his retinue, to "take possession."

"All is achieved," he said cheerfully to the two station guards. One opened the cell so a Voyenni trooper could pull Idris out; the other ensured Rollo stayed inside. Then they hauled him out to the clerks' office, where the staff did their best not to notice what was going on.

"Look at your face like thunder," Uskaro remarked drily to Idris. "You'd think you didn't want to serve humanity. You don't want people to take you for a *betrayer*, do you?" Idris noted that the word was given a particular spin and he suppressed a shudder. The "pro-humanity" Nativists had a strong foothold on Magda and they talked a great deal about *betrayal*. By the Parthenon, by aliens, by Intermediaries somehow in league with Architects. Anything to explain why humans didn't run the universe.

Idris faced up to the man, as much as he could given their

difference in heights. "Your Elegance, let it be known that—should you make me your navigator—I vow to guide that ship into the deep void where monsters dwell. I will wake everyone aboard, so your people may experience the nightmares of unspace. Once they've gone mad, torn out each other's throats and driven their own thumbs into their eyes, I will paint on the walls with their blood. Salvagers will find these words: 'the Boyarin Piter Tchever Uskaro did this, who is no respecter of human freedoms.'"

He felt a wash of catharsis, then immediately knew he'd gone too far. Uskaro's face had closed like a trap, the fake smile vanishing. A tightening grip on his arms told him that the two Voyenni were going to give him a beating as a matter of honour, and their master would plainly enjoy watching Idris learn his place. But perhaps not before these witnesses. So Uskaro merely nodded tightly and marched towards the exit, the Voyenni pulling Idris along in his wake.

Yet the doors didn't open, and one of the clerks called from behind them.

"Kybernet says to hold the Int," she explained when faced with Uskaro's disbelieving stare. "Administrative matter." When he demanded an explanation, she shrugged. "Don't know, Your Elegance. Doesn't say. Just routine."

A movement at floor level caught Idris's attention as he hung between the Voyenni. Like a rodent, a spider, a *hand*: a scuttling shape of metal and plastic. He knew it, of course. It was one of Medvig's remotes, detached from the Hiver's frame, come over to say hello.

Seeing that it had his attention it carefully balanced on three of its fingers and curled the rest in until it had made a creditable "thumbs up."

Bless you, Medvig. Somehow they'd found him. Now he just had to worry about Rollo...

When the outer door opened, it was Kris they all saw, and she already had Rollo free and clear beside her. She must have extracted him from the cells via some other route.

"What *is* this?" Uskaro stared at her. "Why is this man free and who is this woman?" He was briefly too baffled to be angry.

"Your Elegance, I am Keristina Soolin Almier. Acting as certified advocate to the Hugh Civil Court for my client Idris Telemmier."

Uskaro made a little spitting noise of utter incredulity. "It is not permitted a lawyer. *It* is under a leash contract."

"I am now calling upon the Roshu kybernet to act as arbiter," Kris announced grandly. "Respond, if you please."

The voice emanating from the clerk's console was flat and affectless. "Presence confirmed for the stated purpose."

"I request the release of my client, imprisoned under false pretences. I have filed a request for damages, plus compensation for emotional trauma and loss of liberty, against the Family Uskaro. This will be dealt with under separate hearing once my client is freed."

"He cannot be your client," Uskaro hissed at her. Then he protested to the air, as the kybernet had no physical presence, "It is *property*, under a leash contract."

The clerk, who looked as though she was enjoying herself, threw data up on a wallscreen. Idris's birth records, from seventy years ago. Idris's war record. Idris's work history. Idris, old beyond his face.

Uskaro's own features went slack, realizing simultaneously the sheer *value* of what he had seized, and that he wasn't legally able to keep "it." One of the original wartime Ints, with all those decades of skill and experience. But, for that self-same reason, out of his reach.

"But he's—"

"Old enough to be your revered grandpa, Boyarin. Real, real old." A grin from Kris, and Idris thought, sourly, *Thanks for that.*

"I look forward to your depositions regarding compensation, Your Elegance," she finished up brightly. "Doubtless your lawyers will be in touch."

She reached forward to take Idris's wrist and, as simply as that, he was out of the Voyenni's grasp. Medvig's artificial spider-hand scurried up to sit on Kris's shoulder, and Idris guessed the Hiver would have circumvented the office's privacy screens to transmit events to the rest of the crew.

"Now let's walk proudly out of Roshu Admin like free citizens of the Colonies," Kris said quietly. "Then let's get the fuck to the ship as quick as we can." She glanced back, and Idris did too—meeting Uskaro's bleak, hungry gaze. "I don't think the Boyarin will restrict himself to legal measures."

5.

Idris

Roshu Admin's holding cells were in one of the more civilized neighbourhoods of Roshu Primator. Reaching the docking ring—and the *Vulture God*—was going to involve some legwork through districts where a little violence could be overlooked. Idris was painfully aware just how big and healthy those two thugs of Uskaro's had been. Rollo could throw a punch and Kris was more than capable of looking after herself, but neither of them were professional heavies.

"Listen up, my children." Rollo was speaking low, sending to all crew. "Extricate yourselves from whatever foul vices you're engaged in and hightail it back to the *God* right now. We are no longer welcome here. Keep an eye out for Voyenni in green too."

"Are we fighting now?" came Barney's incredulous reply. "I mean, already?"

"No, my son, we are flying ahead of the shitstorm, like always," Rollo told him. "Olli?"

"Does this mean no shore leave for me?" the drone specialist's voice broke in.

"My poor luckless daughter, it does," Rollo confirmed. "And

I need the *God* ready for a speedy exit. Especially if bad neighbours turn up before we do."

Olli's response to that was anatomically challenging but probably indicated agreement.

"Kittering." Rollo was striding down the dignified street at an undignified hustle, heedless of the stares they were getting: two dirty spacers plus Kris, whose ersatz finery looked like the imitation it was in this district.

There was a rattle over the comms, then the translation chirped, "Scurrying in progress!" Converting Hanni to human Colvul was more of an art than a science.

"Tell me we have somewhere to go, Kit."

"Further employment has been secured through my own excellent offices, Captain! Good work, low risk!" Kittering's translator yapped.

"Anywhere but here," Rollo confirmed, as they hit the seedier side of town and prepared for trouble. "This way, children." He bundled Idris and Kris onto a cargo elevator. "Next time, my daughter, bring backup for a caper like this, see right?"

"I . . . did take out some fight insurance. What with you being incommunicado," Kris confessed. She had authority in emergencies, but ceding control made Rollo twitchy. "Seeing how the Boyarin get violent when they don't get what they want, I hired us some extra security." At his glower she added, "A concerned party who alerted me to your predicament, Captain, and offered their services."

"We are going to have a talk about what your executive authority actually covers," Rollo muttered, but then the elevator shuddered to a halt at a loading bay. They bulled their way out through a crowd of spacers and staff, all apparently trying to manoeuvre bulky a-grav crates and trolleys towards it at the same time.

Idris caught a flash of bottle-green uniform. "Trouble," he hissed. A couple of Voyenni were shoving through the throng towards them.

Rollo nodded and vaulted the next cargo flatbed, heading away. But before Idris could follow, a third Voyenni loomed abruptly beside him—a big man in shirtsleeves, no doubt dragged from some dive by his master's demands. For a moment he had Idris's collar, hoisting the smaller man off the ground. Then Kris's knife flashed out, its ceramic blade slashing the man's wrist so he let go with a howl.

Now we run. Their undignified hustle abruptly became a flat-out pelt over cargo crates and around startled haulers and loaders. Rollo jinked towards another elevator, but the car was already departing—and Idris saw another Voyenni elbowing towards them from that quarter, a head taller than most of the crowd.

There was only a railing in the opposite direction, surrounding a deep shaft. It had been built to transport containers into the bowels of the city from the docking ring above, and also housed the cargo elevator in which they'd arrived. Idris remembered seeing shafts like that as a child. It had seemed that you could step out into empty air and float down—just like those monolithic cargo pods. Except that each pod was controlled by the city's gravitic engines. Jump out into that abyss and you'd plummet to your death.

Kris swore and whirled towards the approaching Voyenni, knife at the ready. But her scarf seemed to strike up a life of its own, tugging her towards the railing and the drop. She swore and swatted at the hand-like remote plucking at her.

"Get with the program! On on on!" Medvig signalled. Their remote sprang from Kris to land on an automated pallet stacked high with containers as it glided slowly alongside the shaft, a tonne of stately metal in motion.

Rollo didn't hesitate, hauling Idris onto the pallet. A line of nacelles jutted from its upper surface, handles for gravitic steering, and Idris grimly wrapped his arms about one. Rollo boosted Kris up, then scrambled aboard himself. The Voyenni were already running, not seeing the plan but scenting there was one, and they now wielded short, studded bludgeons. Matters had gone past mere fisticuffs.

The pallet reversed dramatically, shunting pedestrians out of the way until it hit the buckling metal of the rail. "Grab on, organics!" Medvig chattered in their ears. "Rough transit alert!"

Without warning they broke through the rail, dropping into five storeys of empty space. Idris heard panicked screams as they began to plummet. A stomach-wrenching second later and they were climbing back up the shaft, the pallet clawing for purchase against the city's gravitic field.

"Medvig—my children—you'd better all know what you're doing!" Rollo yelled.

"In times of stress, have you considered singing happy songs?" Medvig, as an intelligence distributed across a knot of cyborg roaches, loved highlighting human frailties.

They passed the platform they'd just abandoned and the Voyenni were there, waiting for them. *Surely they're not going to—* but they were angry and their boss probably took failure out of their hides. One of them, the boldest or maddest, vaulted the crumpled rail. He hit the floating truck hard, one hand closed tight around a gravitic pontoon. Kris slashed the shoulder seam of his coat, drawing a little blood, but he hauled himself up, the truck lurching madly as his weight skewed its lift calculations. In moments, the second Voyenni had gone for the leap. He'd left it almost too late, hands grabbling for purchase and boots kicking as he tried to pull himself up.

Rollo feinted at the first thug, who blocked the punch contemptuously, receiving a blow to his gut as payment. Then he was on Rollo, lifting his opponent with the clear intention of just throwing him into the chasm.

Medvig's remote jabbed metal finger-legs at his eyes and the Voyenni reeled back. One huge fist caught the spidery machine and dashed it against a container's metal lid, smashing it into fragments. The Voyenni's other hand still gripped Rollo, and the man looked strong enough to lob the captain into the void one-handed.

Kris stabbed him. She looked ice cold for the three heartbeats it took to drive her duelling knife into his ribs four times, then horrified as the man toppled away. Rollo went with him.

Idris twitched to grab him and almost toppled from the wildly skewing container himself. It was Kris who snagged Rollo's wrist, bracing herself with a leg over the corner of the container. All of this had their conveyance skewed almost forty-five degrees from level, with everyone clinging to its uppermost edge to keep them from the chasm below. At that point the other Voyenni hauled himself up.

Idris kicked him in the face, resulting only in a snarl from his victim as he reached inside his jacket. Idris saw the stubby barrel of a gun—not a high-velocity accelerator, but a laser or chemical firearm would be quite sufficient to kill any or all of them.

Something swung overhead and he had the sense of an armoured figure with stubby wings—gravity handles just like the pallet's pontoons. The Voyenni jerked his arm up, appreciating the greater threat was above. But the flying figure dipped in the air, grabbed the thug's collar and jerked sideways, tearing the man off the container and into open air.

Idris winced, waiting for the drop, but the flyer swung its victim over a railing into a knot of gawking officials and space crew. Its work done, it ascended to hover above them, keeping perfect pace.

"Is that...?" Rollo stammered. "Kris, child, what did you *do?*"

You couldn't mistake that armour. Grey-blue metal and armour-plastic plate, a uniform that had been refined since the war but never really changed. Everyone knew the elite soldiers of the Parthenon, but you didn't expect to just run into one inside the Primate House.

"Meet your new crewmate!" Kris shouted.

Then they were up top, outside the dome and next to the docking ring. Past the lumpy, repair-scarred hull of an ore transporter and another couple of haphazardly parked ships was the reassuringly ugly hull of the *Vulture God*.

"Yes!" Rollo whooped, then their container lurched and tipped them all off. They just about hit the dock, rather than plummeting down the shaft, before Medvig abandoned the pallet to its fate. For a moment it was beginning the long, slow tumble towards the shaft's distant reaches, clanging thunderously off nearby traffic. Then the city's system caught up with it, cushioning its fall with invisible hands.

"More bad guys! *Move!*" came Olli's voice in their ears, and they pelted past the ore freighter towards the *Vulture*.

"Everyone aboard?" Rollo demanded.

"Full complement, aye," she confirmed. "Or will be when you get your behinds through the hatch."

"Ahead!" Kris shouted.

Idris, already feeling at least three decades too old for any of this, saw that the ordeal was nowhere near over. Another four Voyenni were charging towards them, emerging from the far side of the *Vulture God*. It hadn't exactly been a mystery where they'd been docked.

They had guns, and they had strength and training on their side even without those. What Idris had was...

A friend, apparently. Even as they ran for the *Vulture*, the armoured flyer dropped down, blocking the oncoming Voyennis' path.

One of the thugs had a gun levelled now, and in response the Partheni unslung her own weapon from its holding arms. An accelerator, about as absurdly illegal in this system as anything could be. If she'd turned it downwards she could have sent a hail of gravitically accelerated pellets through the city's dome and a score of its separate floors.

Still, there was only one of her and four Voyenni, who might also consider themselves the galaxy's elite. Not to mention they were all twice the bulk of the woman inside the armour. They began spreading out, grim looks on their long faces, determined to do right by their chief.

Then the *Vulture*'s hatch opened and Olli joined the fight.

Olli couldn't wear prosthetics or take grafts, born without any awareness of how those absent limbs might work. Instead she had embraced the unnatural. She called the workframe she wore her "Scorpion"—designed by the Castigar and never intended for human use. It stomped out on four legs, half a dozen tool-arms flanking her central pod. A couple of big pincer limbs arched down from the top and a long, segmented tail lashed from side to side behind her. She'd fitted *that* with a grabber and cutting saw—which struck sparks from the docking platform. In her Scorpion, Olli was three metres tall.

The Voyenni looked from her to the Partheni warrior and obviously decided they were outclassed. Mulishly, they backed off as the rest of the crew hustled to board their ship.

"Get us up!" Rollo bellowed. "And fuck docking control if they try to complain."

"Oh, I think they're very glad to be rid of us," Kris said. Idris could only nod weakly, dropping into the pilot's seat. He set the *Vulture*'s drive against the gravity of the planet below, sending them leaping into the sky—if not like an eagle, then at least like an old bird that would live to see another day.

*

"Right," Rollo said, when the *Vulture God* had broken atmosphere and was navigating the orbital debris that cluttered Roshu's night sky. "My children, let us not do that again. I, for one, am too old for shit even vaguely related to that."

Idris hunched awkwardly in the pilot's seat. He was swinging the *Vulture* hand over hand, using its brachator drives, until it was in an orbit high enough for them to escape at the slightest provocation. The *Vulture* was nobody's idea of a racer, but their foes no longer had an Intermediary. Idris would back himself against any pursuit. As part of what they'd made him into, he had an unmatched feel for the contours of space. He just had to open his mind to feel the texture of the gravitic foam that formed the barrier between the real and unspace, that the greedy little hands of the brachator could latch on to, to drag the ship about.

More than three hundred volunteers had been accepted onto the old wartime Intermediary Program, so he'd been told. Idris was one of just thirty who'd not only survived but left sane enough to do the job. The Liaison Board's post-war hit rate, using convicts and debtors, was only a tenth even of that. The process was also ruinously expensive, even for successes. Doubtless the Boyarin Uskaro had paid well for a "fugitive's" whereabouts. And now he knew Idris's provenance, he'd be even keener to take possession—legally or otherwise.

"How do we stand with ground control?" Rollo demanded.

"A crapton of complaints but no demands so far. Though they've forfeited our docking deposit," Kris told him.

"I want eyes all around: Olli, my children. A certain Boyarin bastard most definitely did not walk here from Magda. I don't want his ship on top of us before we know it. Barney, how're our feathers?"

"Fucking bedraggled," came the engineer's sour voice. "We can fly though."

"Where to?" Idris wanted to know.

"Kit?"

The Hanni hadn't decamped to his chambers yet and his screens were still flickering with Roshu-local adverts. A moment later he was displaying navigation data, ship specs, their new job's contractual details. The financial incentive was circled. Commercial transactions formed the chief common ground for human and Hannilambra dealings. Personal enrichment for them was a matter of life and death.

"Heading to Huei-Cavor," Rollo noted. "Pick a path, Idris. Why does Huei-Cavor ring bells with me, anyway?"

"Hegemony takeover in progress," Kris told him promptly. "It's going to be a bit turbulent."

"Frying pans and fires, and never a break from them." The captain shook his head. "And while I'm talking trouble, which of my unruly children suborned the city gravitic system to lug us about on that travelling trunk?"

Medvig's frame had been standing in the corner like a three-legged avant-garde sculpture. Now, in acknowledgement, they wriggled one of their remotes, currently plugged back into their chest.

Rollo scowled at the Hiver, but then his expression softened. "I am very grateful, but you can't go about hacking kybernet systems. It's outside your remit. They'll unlicense you." Medvig operated under a leash contract of their own, necessary in order to trade with humanity. The Colonies, having created the Hivers during the war, remained leery of the distributed intelligence now it had declared independence.

Medvig's three surviving remotes managed, between them, a very creditable spread-handed shrug. "Always a pleasure saving your pounds of flesh," came the artificial voice from their chest.

The smile that graced Rollo's face was not one of his jovial beams but something smaller and more genuine. "Just be careful, see right?" And then he looked up and his expression hardened. Following his gaze, Idris saw that their newest crewmate had entered the compartment.

She still wore most of her armour, though the wings were folded and the gun nowhere to be seen. She was short, compact-framed, her skin weirdly pale. And she was beautiful. Or perhaps she was just a well-finished product of the Partheni vats. Their warriors weren't identical, but followed an identical aesthetic. She was looking at him. And he knew her.

Idris felt a sudden sinking in his belly, knowing that the universe wasn't done messing with him, still ladling out his own personal ration of trouble.

"You," Rollo addressed her, moustache bristling as he made a big show of being unafraid, "pulled out your goddamn Mr. Punch inside Roshu Primator. That is death penalty stuff. I should poop you out the airlock right now."

For a moment the Partheni's face was blank, then she translated "Mr. Punch" as spacer slang for an accelerator, so named because of the inconvenient holes it made in ship and habitat walls alike. "I am of course extremely sorry," she said. "Also, you're welcome." Both statements delivered in exactly the same neutral tone of voice, as though giving Rollo the option of which he wanted to hear.

In the end, he decided on neither. "Kris, explain this nonsense to your Uncle Rollo because he can't make head or tail of it."

"She came and told me you and Idris had got scrobbled." The lawyer was cleaning her knife, not quite meeting Rollo's gaze. "She offered herself as security, wanted to sign on. I took an executive decision. And we did need her."

"She's a *Partheni!*" Rollo gesticulated wildly at the woman, then tried to face up to her again. "My newfound surrogate daughter, you do realize we are a crummy little salvage operation here? We are not going to be fighting any star battles while I'm captain."

"Sometimes you get tired of fighting," the woman said. Remembering her, Idris didn't believe it for a moment.

He should say something, he knew. He should unmask her as the Mysterious Woman From His Past, here for some underhand purpose that could only relate to him. Except something flipped inside him when he looked at her, and in the end he took the coward's way out and said nothing at all.

"Well." Rollo ran a hand through his thinning hair. "What do we even call you? Or do you just have a number?"

Solace, Idris recalled, just before she spoke. There had been rank and company after the name, back then, and she was plainly biting off something similar now. It must be hard to be just "Solace" without all that military armour to protect it. And there was something about that moment when she just said her name, bare and alone. She looked suddenly uncertain, a crack in that Partheni facade. Idris, who sometimes felt he was built entirely out of competing vulnerabilities, valued them in other people.

"Hoi, Captain," came Barney's voice. "Horizon trouble."

One of the command screens flashed up with the image of a ship just getting underway. It was a conspicuous piece of kit with a forked hull like two forward-curving claws, the ring of its gravitic drive spread like a peacock's tail. Barney identified it as the *Raptorid*, Boyarin Uskaro's craft.

"Flash bastard," Rollo decided. "Do we have a road to Huei?"

"We do," Idris confirmed, eyes still on Solace.

"Then everyone get to your couches for suspension for we're going under, my family. We have a working spare for our new friend?"

"Captain, I keep *all* the spares in working order," Barney's voice said bleakly. "Because all the regular couches are on the point of falling over."

"Then further discussion will wait," Rollo decided. "Kris, show the angel where she's to go. Idris?"

"Ready." He saw a twitch of frustration cross Solace's face. *Had her recruitment spiel lined up for me.* It seemed depressingly likely that she was just the friendly face of a deal similar to the Boyarin's. *Everyone wants a piece of me. Well she can at least wait until Huei-Cavor before trying it on.*

As he pulled the ship a politic distance from the planet before the unspace jump, he called up a quick lowdown of precisely what was happening on Huei-Cavor that had Rollo so gloomy, just in case that meant more personal trouble for him too.

Ah, yes. It's being taken over by the clams.

*

Human colonists, in the hopeful days Before, had finally met what they most feared. The Essiel Hegemony was a genuine space empire, complete with conquered species, all dominated by a race of alien overlords. When humanity appreciated what they'd found, they retreated in fear and disarray. Back then, nobody could imagine anything worse than an alien polity with designs on adding humans to their menagerie. Which was exactly what the Hegemony seemed to represent.

Except, as time went on, no warfleet appeared in the skies over Earth or any of its colonies. The Hegemony certainly wanted to talk to humanity, and human xenolinguists' best guess was that they wanted to discuss humans bowing to their almighty alien power, or else... something would happen, some species-wide calamity. But if the Hegemony was threatening humanity, they seemed very laid-back about it. Refusal caused no offence, just a repeat of the offer, demand or ultimatum at a later date.

It didn't help that the Essiel were very alien aliens, and their conquered under-species weren't much better. So, although the Essiel met with human diplomats and sent messages, with great pomp and ceremony, nobody was quite sure what they were saying—what threats were being made, what promises offered.

Then the Architects came and suddenly many things about the Hegemony became clear. The doom that the Essiel had been waving at humanity was not a threat, but a warning. The Hegemony was more than familiar with the Architects' predatory designs and could shield planets from their attentions. All they wanted in return was a world to swear itself to them, heart and soul.

A dozen human colonies joined the Hegemony for this reason, accepting the Essiel as their unquestioned overlords. That rate of defection had slackened since the war ended, of course, but now the Essiel had human underlings to translate for them. Hegemonic diplomats had appeared all over the Colonial Sphere, pushing their inscrutable masters' agenda. Their rule was peace and love, order and harmony, they said. The Essiel were the benevolent autocrats our ancestors had sought but never found—human nature being too flawed. They were a cult, basically. Nobody was even sure if what they spouted really represented what the Essiel and their Hegemony intended, filtered as it was through layers of mistranslation. The Essiel were, in a very religious sense, ineffable.

Huei-Cavor, the Essiel's latest "conquest," was busy with ships. So much so that Idris had a momentary flashback to evacuations during the war. Many were getting the hell off-planet with whatever they could carry. Other ships were turning up with diplomats, spies and information-hounds keen to mediotype every development for dispatch on the next packet ship. After a planet-wide vote and years of argument, the population of Huei-Cavor had decided to leave Hugh for the Essiel Hegemony. Huei-Cavor was a big win for the Essiel, a prosperous colony. The Hegemonic cult had been pushing hard for years. Preaching and pros-elytizing in the open—and likely worse things behind closed doors—to swing public opinion. And Nativists and Hugh loyalists had been fighting every step of the way, only to fall at the last fence. Even now, Idris gathered from the newsfeeds, the ceremonial barge of some Essiel overlord was due. Come to oversee the ritual obeisance of the col-ony's government and accept their fealty. And that would be that. Everyone would have to adjust the notional borders of their maps; Huei-Cavor would no longer be a human-governed world.

"Just promise me," Barney said, actually there in person, as all the *Vulture God*'s systems were good for the next twenty-four hours. "Whatever this job is, we're not getting involved in that mess."

Rollo glanced at Kittering, who fiddled a little ditty with a few of his mouthparts. His screens lit up with happy human faces. The captain just shrugged. "Our mark is the *Oumaru*. She's out from some Hegemony planet I can't even say prop-erly, freighter, human-built, human-operated. It's in the curio trade, decent value stuff. She's thirty-nine standard days late, and off the Throughways. We get her nav data and go hunting the deep void, same as we've done a hundred times. Only

77

this time we might get to be proper heroes and bring back a live crew."

Barney nodded, grudgingly satisfied. "We got shore leave on-planet?"

"On-station only, and when we're back. Too much shit going down right now. Uncle Rollo doesn't risk his family when there's a whole planet changing hands."

Barney accepted that glumly and sloped off. Idris got up and stretched.

"Go get some sleep," Rollo advised.

"Right. Of course." He'd been on the *Vulture* long enough for them to know that never happened.

When he reached his cabin, though, it was already occupied. Looking oddly nervous, Solace was sitting on his bed, waiting for him.

PART 2
HUEI-CAVOR

6.

Solace

The Parthenon arose, a fully formed fighting force, only a dozen years after Earth was destroyed. A phoenix from the ruins when the rest of humanity was running and grieving; humanity's miraculous angels in its darkest hour.

Truth was, of course, that its founder, Doctor Sang Sian Parsefer, had been preparing for a war brought by Earth. She'd been breeding a better version of humanity, after all. The old model would probably want to file a few objections. An outlaw scientist operating beyond the reach of Earth, her team of like-minded renegades included warship designers, weaponsmiths and geneticists. Solace always wondered whether Parsefer's martial intentions had been as defensive as the Partheni taught. When you've built the latest in superior military hammers, surely all your problems start looking like inferior Colonial nails.

All Parsefer's plans had been predicated on the political situation as it had existed Before, orbiting about the gravitational centre of Earth. Then the Architects changed everything; imminent civil war was converted to a story of heroism. Parsefer could spot a greater threat when she saw one, and her warrior angels became saviours. The only human force that could even slow an Architect to give a planet a chance at evacuation.

Yet their military might didn't end the war. That happened by way of the Colonials and their Intermediary Program. Saint Xavienne's chance mutation could never have emerged unaided from the curtailed genetic range of a Parthenon vat. Then the Colonies had refused to share their Int research, even in victory, and relations had only deteriorated since.

Which brought Solace here, to Idris Telemmier. Of all her sisters, she might be the only one to call an Int an old acquaintance. Idris was not just an individual navigator or weapon. He represented a trove of data on how an Intermediary was created. With his cooperation, the Parthenon could potentially engineer their own. They could take the fight to the Architects if the monsters returned. They could protect themselves against Colonial assault too if it came to *that*. On her shoulders rested, quite conceivably, the fate of her entire people.

Idris was frozen in the doorway, staring at her. That eternal flinch that made up so much of his facial expression was on full display. He looked as though he expected a slap from her, or perhaps from the universe at large.

He seemed no more than twenty-two but had to be more than seventy. She couldn't process it.

"It is you, isn't it?" he got out, voice little more than a croak. "Berlenhof."

"Yes, and I broke into your room. Can we get past that?" Solace found herself asking. "Except you don't lock your door, anyway."

"We trust each other here," Idris said, waving away the rest as he stepped in and slid the door shut.

A Partheni myrmidon, straight out of training, had more possessions than Idris. There was a shelf of mediotypes, the lack of formal labelling suggesting illicit copies. A cheap hologram cycled slowly through alien-looking plants, or Solace assumed they were plants. A printer-recycler was set into one wall, and the bed, she could attest from sitting on it, was hard as a board. Nothing to wash or crap in, so it was the ship's communal facilities for that. *At least that'll feel like home.* Except some of her messmates here were men and some were not human.

"We can skip the bit where I announce my ambitions don't include deep void scavenging, and you are completely surprised..." she prompted. When he still stood there dumbly, she went on, "They put you under, afterwards? Suspension via the Int Program? Or...they used relativistic travel...?"

"Kind of the opposite," he told her hollowly and finally sat on the bed, keeping as much space between them as possible. "I...Look, none of us first class out of the Program came out...right. *I'm* not right. So it's that. I haven't been on ice, like I guess you have. It's just that..." He was talking to his hands as they lay palm-up in his lap. "I haven't *slept*, Solace. I haven't slept properly since they did what they did to me."

Whatever her next line should have been, it fell out of her head at that. "You haven't slept in...?"

"Fifty years, and some. Not slept, not aged. Like they stuck a pin in me back then."

"Is this *all* Ints—?"

"Me. Just me. They fucked us all up, and no two of us the same. I hear the later classes got it even worse, the leashed ones. I don't know why I'm even telling you this. I'm sorry. You were about to threaten me or kidnap me or something. Don't let me stop you." His voice had sunk so low she had to rub shoulders with him to hear his words.

And yes, she should be pushing their deal—not threats but a proposal, a heartfelt plea. Except right then she just felt cold, as though the deep void was radiating out through him. She wondered if she should put an arm around him or take his hand, as if one of her sisters was having a hard time. The way things had started between them on Berlenhof; two wounded soldiers healing together.

"I'm not here to kidnap anyone," she said, honestly enough, though her next orders might turn that right around. "They sent me with an offer."

"And they sent you because we'd met."

"We're short on options." *And if we just liberated some poor bastard under a leash contract, even covertly, that would mean war.*

"The answer's no, by the way. To your offer." He was still talking to his hands but now he was very tense, in case kidnapping was on the menu after all.

"I haven't made it yet." Solace felt as though the pair of them were having two different discussions, side by side.

"I'm not joining you. Do you think I'd be here, on this ship, if I was interested in signing on with any side? I did my time in the last war. I want nothing to do with the next one."

"This isn't to fight…" Solace started but at last he looked up at her, not angry so much as accusatory.

"I won't be *owned*. Not by the Magdans, not by Hugh, not by the Parthenon. Or anyone else who wants to buy me."

Solace stared. "Is *that* what you think we want?"

"Doubtless you've dressed it up very nicely, but I reckon joining the Parthenon's a door that opens one way only. Not to mention that I've already had my footnote in the historio-types. I don't want to go down as the man who betrayed the Colonies as well." He blinked, as though seeing her as herself for the first time. "Hello, by the way."

Solace opened her mouth, found it empty of words, closed it again.

"I'm sorry. It would have been good to just...run into you again. By chance. Catch up on whatever interesting dreams you had in suspension." Idris obviously became aware he was talking too fast and made an effort to slow himself. "Because I remember...I don't sleep, I don't age and I don't forget—not the big things. I owe you my life. And I owe you double because you kept me sane after Berlenhof, after...first contact. But it's *you* I owe, not the Parthenon."

"I..."

"So you can get off at Huei-Cavor. Or go to plan B and we'll see how that works out, I suppose."

"I signed on for your next mission," she said. "So I guess I'm sticking around for that. Look, Idris...Can we start this again?"

"Not particularly."

"Not now. I'll go find my cabin, but next time I'd like to at least start with 'Hello.'"

"So you can work your way towards your offer again?"

"Yes, because that's my mission. I want to report that I got that far, when I go back empty-handed. But also...just, hello. It's actually good to see you. You're the only person outside my sisters that I ever met and liked."

She wasn't sure whether she was manipulating him or not. When she saw his face soften, even more vulnerable when unguarded, she wondered if she should feel guilty.

*

"Look at that bedamned fancyman," Rollo crowed. Everyone except Kittering and Barney was up in the control compartment, watching their approach to Huei-Cavor's orbitals. It was a long time since they'd been to any world with so much traffic. Its equator was ringed with a jewelled necklace of stations, shipyards, elevator hubs and the skeletal frames of superdocks for big freight vessels. Past that, they could see the blue-yellow swell of the planet itself. It was azure-white at its visible pole, showing copper-saturated ice deposits wisped with sulphur-tinged clouds. Despite the aggressive chemistry, a lot of people lived on Huei-Cavor's surface. Pills or body-mods enabled people to metabolize whatever the planet threw at them. Once they'd adjusted to local conditions, the regime was as good for health and longevity as a mineral spa. A number of well-heeled oldsters had set up down there over the years, funding much of the planet's burgeoning infrastructure.

And now all that wealth was being ceremonially handed over to alien overlords. *Why, if the Architects were gone?* Solace wondered. Maybe it was because Huei had an older population that remembered the war. Their childhoods had been characterized by the terror that, any day, something could just appear over the planet and obliterate it. They wanted the Essiel's much-vaunted protection.

Rollo's "fancyman" was the Hegemonic ambassador's enormous barge. Looking down on it, as it descended for landing, was like looking into the half-folded petals of a rose made from coral. The barge had no visible windows, engines, weapons, or any recognizable components at all. It fell towards the planet like a slow motion asteroid.

It would have a similar impact upon the planet's political sphere, given a sizeable slice of Huei-Cavor's population wasn't happy about the change in management. The newscasts were showing riots, bombings and thousands-strong protests. There would be bloodshed, now and for years to come. Perhaps not the best time to visit, Solace thought.

Now the newstypes were interviewing that bald white-bearded man who seemed so popular locally. He was wearing a remarkably elaborate robe, red with eye-catching geometric gold embroidery. Its remarkably high curved collar fanned out behind him, visible over the top of his head. He was standing with a few others in lesser finery, all looking serenely pleased with themselves. This was the Hegemonic cult, Solace understood: the human faction that had been pushing for the planet to leave Hugh for years. Baldy-beardy called himself Sathiel, because high-ranking cultists tended to adopt names that made them sound religious. Sathiel was apparently a big man from the Hegemony, here to assist in a smooth handover. The Essiel liked peaceful, well-run planets. The view changed to show the enormous crowd that had gathered at the landing site. This was mostly excited neo-cultists, keen for a glimpse of their new rulers.

"Response from Lung-Crow Orbital," Olli reported. She was reclining in the six-legged frame she used to get about the ship, after Idris had persuaded her to take a break from her control pod. She'd been trying to get hold of their contracting party aboard the nearby station. Unfortunately their new employer was the local administration, who had their plates full right now.

"Let's hear it." Rollo pulled comms over to his station. "This is *Vulture God*, reporting for duty. Do we have Lung-Crow Admin? Word is there's deep void work going begging."

On his screen, the Lung-Crow hung over the planet like a huge spindle. Within its windowed upper facets, people lived, worked and did business. From the slot-riddled lower half, ships passed in and out like bees from a hive. Then its image was shunted out of the way to reveal a lean woman, her eyes obscured by a battery of lenses.

"Factor Kittering?" she said doubtfully to Rollo.

The Hannilambra sent her a feed from his own console, appearing as an inset on the main screen. His mouthparts fiddled some sort of introduction.

"Ah, Captain Rostand, then. Admirably prompt."

"And looking to be just as prompt out the door," Rollo told her easily. "I get the impression you have plenty of bigger holes to patch than ours. You are..." A brief glance sideways. "Factor Luciel Leng, is it?"

"Your own factor there assures me you have a deep void-capable ship and navigator. I've seen your certification, but I want assurances that you're not puffing your profile. Because that's what I'm paying for."

"If you've seen the papers you've seen how it is," Rollo confirmed. "We're good for it."

Solace looked between them, wondering how many of these deals ended in fraud and acrimony. Rollo and Luciel seemed to be happy with just a word and a handshake.

"This is delicate and needs swift action. We're after the *Oumaru* out of Rrrt'k." She attacked the alien name gamely. "Mechanical failure, probably. It's not shipping anything particularly valuable, just Hegemonic set dressing for people keen to show our new chiefs just how on-side we are; tat, basically, not worth stealing."

"But worth blowing up for a political point," Solace suggested.

Luciel's faceted gaze shifted to catch a glimpse of Solace, probably wondering if the *Vulture* really had a Partheni on board and why. "I hope not," she replied. "But if you find anything... controversial, come back out-system, I'll have a Coffin on hand to bring both the *Oumaru* and your ship in covertly. We don't want to offend the Hegemony or help the Nativists score points, right?"

"I see you," Rollo confirmed. "We're good for it."

Luciel Leng seemed as reassured as she was going to be, relaxing back into her seat and nodding at Solace. "She real?"

"So I'm told," Rollo told her.

"I didn't think they were for hire?"

"The universe is wonderful and full of never-ending variety." The captain nodded to Leng. "My factor confirms the money and escrow arrangements. Let's go get your missing ship." He closed the channel and declared, "Suspension pods, my childer! And everyone run your own checks too this time. Bad dreams to the minimum, see right?"

"New girl, you okay? Need help with your pod?" the engineer, Barnier, grunted at her. She gave his mismatched features a tight smile.

"I'm good." She'd checked it over already and fixed a couple of minor glitches with the help of a built-in troubleshooter the crew hadn't ever accessed. The suspension pod and the ship were of very different vintages, and the pod was decidedly older.

One by one the crew shuffled off to their pods, leaving Idris at the pilot's station with Solace behind him.

He half glanced around, then looked back to his controls. "Better get yourself under. We're going into unspace the moment we're clear of traffic."

"Into the deep void."

"The abyss that gazes also," he agreed. "You've done that before, have you—stayed awake on a Throughway journey?"

"Part of the training," she agreed. "Didn't like it."

"Deep void's worse," he said, with some relish.

"I'll bed down when we're in. I wanted to say..." She saw him tense, and of course she'd wanted to repeat the Parthenon's offer. But she was a soldier, not a diplomat, and a few months' teachings didn't change that. So she said instead, "I didn't forget what happened, after Berlenhof."

"Me neither." His voice was very small. She wanted to put a hand on his shoulder, but he was slumped in the seat, hunched in on himself. He seemed as though he'd break if she touched him. "I guess they train you not to feel things, the scars left behind. In the Parthenon. Rock-hard warrior angels, all that." He sounded wistful.

"They train us to talk about it. They train us to heal, and not to deny we're in pain. Rock-hard is brittle."

"You going to be doing that around here?"

"Among Colonials? No." The thought made her feel ill. "You people never admit when you're hurting. Sign of weakness in your culture. Or that's what I was taught."

He made a nondescript noise. "It must be nice, to talk." Voice no more than a whisper.

And then he was gone, the pilot's seat apparently empty, the ship resoundingly vacant around her. She knew they'd entered unspace and she was the only person left on board, perhaps in the universe. The only person here, but not the only *thing*—and that way madness lay. It was the same for everyone on board too. Or would have been, if they'd been foolish enough to stay awake. Hurriedly she skipped over to her pod and climbed in, setting it to put her on ice the moment the clamshell lid closed.

Idris

Then Solace was gone, and Idris felt the familiar infinite echo of unspace. He glanced back, looking for even a fading ghost of her. Already, the control compartment was devoid of all life. Just him and the void now. More than once Idris had wondered if the secret of his own longevity could be found in these shadowy spaces; certainly nobody else had an explanation.

Everyone was alone in unspace, even on the Throughways. But, if you stepped away from them into the deep void, you were as alone as any sentient creature had ever been. Except not quite, not entirely alone.

Every species that entered unspace reported the same feeling. Even the hardiest found the transit traumatizing; some manner of suspension or sleep was everyone's preferred solution. It had been a prime piece of evidence in the case over whether Hivers were truly intelligent: that their composite minds reacted similarly to unspace. Unspace responded to intellect. A dumb computer couldn't pilot you there. Before Intermediaries, humanity could only navigate the Throughways—paths through space that the vanished Originators had left behind long ago, along with their enigmatic ruins. The Throughways connected populated star systems, which were populated precisely because the Throughways led there. Easy enough for a regular pilot to set their ship to travel a Throughway. It was like positioning a paper boat in a stream, knowing that soon enough it would beach at a particular turn. Not so the deep void.

Idris felt the shift as they left it all behind: not like breaching a membrane but as though he and the ship were falling into a chasm, away from everything there ever was. Lights receded to infinity and the only thing ahead was the abyss that gazed also. This was the truth of the void, the thing that had driven the passengers of the *Gamin* mad. After you'd finished wishing you weren't alone, you realized you *weren't*, and then you really wished you were.

Idris had as much experience of this as any human being alive. There was a comforting body of literature about how it was just a reaction of the mind to the absence of some key sensory feedback. Idris—and every other Int he'd talked to about it—didn't believe that for a moment.

He guided the *Vulture God* into the untracked spaces as if steering a ship on a horizonless ocean, past any hope of ever making land. And he knew, with absolute conviction, that far below in the depths something stirred. It slept, perhaps, but the wake that Idris's mind made on the surface troubled its dreams. One day it would truly wake and rise, maw wide to engulf whatever unfortunate had caught its notice. Perhaps that had already happened, because ships vanished into the deep void sometimes, even those with trained Int navigators.

Idris settled deeper in his chair, letting his unique senses unfold. His mind's eye began to draw unhelpful images of benthic abysses, slimy tresses of seaweed, chasms within chasms where lurked...something. Amidst all this distraction he was listening, reaching out. Mind's ear attuned, mind's fingers deft, testing the tautness of unspace as a spider plucks its web. He felt the texture of the cosmos against the tissues of his brain, each pucker and whorl a suggestion of mass and its attendant gravitic train. If he'd stayed with the Cartography Corps, or been conscripted by the Boyarin, this would have been his whole life. He'd have hunted down those traces, until at last he found something more than a mere will-o'-the-wisp: an unknown star, profitable new planets. Hopefully, even a Throughway to connect his discoveries to the rest of creation. Yet nobody stayed in the Cartography Corps for long. You got out after a tour or two, wild-eyed and trembling. Or you stayed and something went wrong in your head. Then one day you took your ship somewhere and never returned. Perhaps you finally understood what was behind that brooding sense of presence, and you went to the court of the abyss, to dance with its god-king forever and ever.

Idris kicked himself mentally.

Is it closer now? He always asked himself this. And it always seemed that the sense of *something*—down there, out there— was rising to meet him. He tried to write off that feeling as one more illusion and never convinced himself.

Idris Telemmier had been doing this for fifty years, wartime and after. He had endured when his peers had gone mad or killed themselves from the horror of it all. He'd outlasted the generation of Ints that came after him, and most of the next. He could have written a book, save that the final chapters would have degenerated into mystic ranting. *It has a purpose for me!* he could have screamed into the void.

He'd once heard another Int being bundled onto a ship during the war. *Don't make me go!* the woman had been shouting. *It knows me!* Over and over. He hadn't been into the deep void himself then. He hadn't understood.

Idris Telemmier reached out into the solitary infinite, like a man feeling for some precious dropped object in a dark room. And somewhere in that sightless expanse, he felt something was reaching back to seize his hand and pull.

But not today. He'd taken the telemetry and course data of the *Oumaru* and let it sit at the back of his mind; let his consciousness expand into unspace and found something that felt like a ship.

As he closed the trap of his mind, he could even tell that it felt like a ship of the *Oumaru*'s approximate size. It was drifting out beyond the Throughways that converged on Huei-Cavor. Not so very far off course but, without an Int navigator, even going slightly off the beaten track meant you never found your way back.

He felt a spark of hope, because the *Oumaru* hadn't even been lost for that long. Most likely the crew were still in suspension. Or they might be calling out for aid. How glad they'd be when the *Vulture God* surfaced beside them, an unlikely Samaritan.

With profound relief, he loosened the gravitic drive's hold on the fabric of unspace, sending them bobbing up—he couldn't not think of *up* and *down* despite himself—into real space. He was abruptly aware, somehow, of all the sleepers in their suspension pods around him. Then once more, unspace's great impassive Presence receded into the realm of the imaginary.

Next time, he felt it was saying, but it was always that way. He tracked the blip of mass he'd identified, which might be the *Oumaru*. Then the *Vulture*'s sensors showed him an image of what he'd found.

He choked.

Jolted back in his chair.

Heart almost stopped one moment, racing the next. When he tried to send the wake-up signal to the pods, his fingers stuttered over the keys and he couldn't. There was blood in his mouth. He'd bitten his tongue. For a moment he just wanted to send the ship back into unspace instead, to face the Presence.

The *Oumaru* was there, but there would be no tearfully grateful crew. The ship had been peeled, flayed and reshaped into an elegant sculpture of trailing metal, like a flower. It was a sight from the war, but the *Oumaru* had left dock only a few days before.

7.

Idris

"Tell me one thing only," Rollo said hoarsely. "Is...it gone?"

The entire crew had assembled in the control compartment. They could have examined the images from anywhere, but this seemed a good time to be in the company of others.

Idris had already engaged his senses, examining real space and its distortions, the same he would use to get the drop on another ship. *I'd know if it was here,* he told himself. If there was an Architect lurking in unspace, its malign presence must have cried out to him. More lessons learned from the war.

"There's nothing," he managed. "It's gone."

"It's gone," echoed Kris, "but *they're* back."

"We don't know that," Rollo said hurriedly. Everyone goggled at him, mutely indicating the evidence on the screens. "Look, my children," he told them, voice shaking, "we don't know. I mean, the Arch...the Architects..." His voice went hoarse and whispery as he tried to say the word, as though it might summon them anew. "They went *somewhere.* Maybe the *Oumaru* stumbled on them there. Maybe they were intruders, they were punished and left here. A warning for us, perhaps. 'Steer clear.' But it doesn't mean they're *back.* It doesn't mean..."

Kris sat down heavily next to Idris, who clasped her arm briefly, all the solidarity he could manage. Kittering was preening his minor legs obsessively, his screens showing nothing but a dimly lambent darkness. Barney reached out to Olli, who took his hand with the stumpy finger-buds at her elbow.

"Do you think they knew, at Lung-Crow?" Solace broke in. She was standing a little off from the others, outside their shared solidarity.

"No," Rollo said at once. "Not a hope. They'd have sent people with us, if they had. Or used a Hegemony navigator to get it themselves. This was routine retrieval business—right up to now." He mopped his brow, staring at the *Oumaru*'s delicately disembowelled hulk. "I want volunteers to suit up and go over there."

"Fuck off," Barney said immediately. "Why?"

"Because I have a bad feeling about how this job will go— and I want something we can sell, some hard data. Also, we don't know that there are no survivors. Some of the aft compartments look intact."

"I'm not seeing anything powered," Idris murmured.

"Suspension pods on emergency might not give out enough for us to smell it," Olli said. She grimaced. "I'll go in the Scorpion. Who's with me?"

"Me," Solace offered. Olli didn't like that, instantly bristling, but the Partheni said, "Your frame, my armour. We're best able to get back to the *Vulture* quick, if something does turn up."

*

After that, the crew waited. Idris had guided the *Vulture God* in as delicately as he could, clasping the most intact part of the *Oumaru*'s hull, of which there was little enough. To an onlooker, the two vessels would have looked as if a winged crab was trying to tackle some vastly strung-out jellyfish.

He had the gravitic drives running low, but enough to extend a field across *Oumaru*'s near end. Solace's armour and Olli's Scorpion both had gravitic handles that could claw a purchase in that field, allowing them to manoeuvre in vacuum. Idris watched them jockey out of the *Vulture*'s airlock and jink in zigzag lines across the tortured curve of the freighter's violated hull. They were heading for the ragged edge where the Architect had exposed the vessel's innards.

What if this is it? That's what everyone must be thinking. *What if this is the war?*

Forty years ago, Idris and two of his peers had gone before an Architect at Far Lux and made contact. For a mind-splitting moment, human thought and the ponderous cognition of a moon-sized entity had existed in the same frame of reference. The Intermediaries had done what they were created for.

They hadn't brokered an understanding. There hadn't even been a détente. But the Architect had become *aware* of them. And it had gone away, leaving the colony at Far Lux— mid-evacuation—untouched. And no Architect had been seen since. Humanity had been saved.

A generation had grown up since, without that terrible annihilating shadow. Except Idris was of the war generation, and could never forget.

"There's no sign of any crew," came Olli's voice. "I can see clear through to the far end of the ship. Everything in here's been...Architected. The inside's as fucked as the outside.

Crew and most of the cargo must have just...been blown out. It wouldn't have taken long to do this, right?"

"A ship of this size? Seconds," Idris confirmed hollowly, trying not to remember all the times he'd seen it happen. Planets took longer. Earth's reconfiguration had taken a whole hour, they said.

"What a mess," Olli said, and Idris suspected she wasn't referring to the ship's internal structure. Then, "Hey, what are you doing?"

"Taking samples," from Solace.

"Souvenirs, Patho?" Olli sounded disgusted.

"Samples," Solace repeated. "Architects have a signature, like fingerprints, when they affect matter. If nothing else, we can see if this is one we know—or some new one, fresh out of whatever hell they come from."

*

Barney suggested leaving the ship behind, but Rollo vetoed that. "My child, we have a job to do. There has been an unexpected *complication*. That is all." He sounded very much like a man trying to reassure himself. "We bring it back. We get paid. We go away and try to forget this ever happened."

"*Seriously?*" Olli demanded, slouched back in her walker frame now.

"This may just be...an aberration," Rollo said mildly, a wave of his hand dismissing the Architects and all they had done. "One incident. It's not..."

"The end of the world," Olli finished sourly.

"Ready to haul her back, my son?" Rollo asked Idris.

There was a fretting little fear at the back of Idris's mind that, when he moved the hulk into unspace, there would be something else attached to it. Something invisible in real space, but manifest in all its ghastly glory in the imaginary spaces beyond.

He would have plenty of time to dwell on happy thoughts like that on the journey through the deep void back to port.

"I suppose you'd better get to your pods then," he told the crew.

Factor Leng had asked them to plot an exit point far from any traffic, if they found anything problematic. She'd been thinking of sabotage and anti-Hegemony slogans, but he reckoned this counted. Idris brought them out well away from anyone who might catch sight of their grotesque cargo, and sent a single encrypted image to Lung-Crow Admin.

"I don't envy whoever gets to make a statement about this," Kris mused, once the crew had woken. "I mean, not our problem. But..."

"It's going to be a pain in the ass to do business anywhere for at least half a year," was Barney's massively understated contribution.

Due to suspension and unspace travel, a spacer's life usually involved surprisingly little waiting aboard ship, but with their covert approach, it would be a few hours before the Leng's Coffin could reach their position. They played Landstep and Brag, and Kris pulled out a curated handful of mediotypes from her collection. Throughout, Idris was aware of Solace's eyes boring into his back. Her unspoken offer hung in the air, visible only to the two of them.

In the end, though, when the Coffin was closing in, she just said, "You jumped straight into salvage, after the war?"

"Cartography Corps, for a few years, discovering planets."

He blinked up at her, still not convinced she wouldn't ambush him. "You ever been to Damasite? No, I suppose not. Well that was one of mine. Found it in the void, traced a Throughway back. There's a colony on it now, onto their second generation." He found her hard to look at, mostly because she was—if he was frank with himself—very easy to look at. The woman who'd engineered the Partheni genomes had had exacting standards when it came to appearance.

"And then?" she pressed.

"Then someone from the Liaison Board turned up and made me an offer," he told her shortly. "It was a very nice offer, on the surface. I'd have lived well on that offer. But I'd heard, by then, how they were treating the next class of Ints—and the hit rate they were getting with conscripts and criminals. I didn't want to be part of it anymore. I'd done my bit. I ended the war, Solace. Not alone, but I was one of the few."

"I'm amazed they let you just walk out." And this wasn't a Partheni criticizing the Colonial authorities. It was an old friend, glad for him. He felt broken edges grinding inside him and stilled those feelings brutally. *No, not doing this. She's just after me for one more goddamn government.*

"So after the Cartography Corps, you've been bumming about on ships like this, for all those years?" Solace asked, and he winced at the implicit criticism.

"I had a stint in prison. And I was a slave once."

"*What?*"

"Well, they slapped a leash on me. I fought it, and thankfully it wasn't anywhere like Magda, where the small print of the law's tattooed onto some gorilla's knuckles. But that's the why of Kris."

"You lawyered up?"

"She has saved me from that kind of shit on eleven separate occasions now."

"She sounds good," Solace noted. "Why's she slumming it with you?"

"Ask her." Idris shrugged. "Not my sunny personality, that's for sure. And now you're looking at me funny."

"Harbinger Ash," Solace said. "Idris, he sent for me. He told me where to find you." A moment later, she looked as if she wished she hadn't. It was just her making her offer by another route.

Idris shrugged. "Changes nothing." Yet he was keeping a lid on so much that *something* had to give. "But I'm glad he did. I always wondered. If I'd see you. I should. I should be grateful that he. I should...something. I'm sorry. I am a failed experiment most days, and a bad human being."

The Coffin pilot's voice had been buzzing away quietly and now it stopped, because the man had finally caught sight of the *Oumaru*. Rollo snorted, "You assholes get it now—why I've dragged you out to this hinterland? I'm not here for *my* health, see right?"

There was a ragged noise over the comms, someone's choked breathing, then, "Yeah," in awed tones. "No shit. We're opening the doors. Just get on inside."

There wasn't much call for the vast Coffin transporters: only really used to get large and delicate cargo down planet-side. Out in space, you could shunt fragile goods around without a worry, due to the inertial dampening effect a gravitic drive could muster. But the buffeting of atmospheric entry meant it was best to fully enclose anything you wanted to take down to the surface. Of course, cargo wasn't usually another ship. But the Coffin's size meant they could transport the *Oumaru* to the Lung-Crow Orbital without sparking a system-wide panic. Just putting off the inevitable, Idris knew. But that was life, wasn't it?

He guided the *Vulture God*, with the *Oumaru* in tow, into the great open maw of the Coffin. Then the bigger vessel's internal gravitics locked them in place. After that, there'd be more waiting as the Coffin lugged them in-system to the bustle of Huei-Cavor. Barney stomped off, claiming maintenance duties, and Kittering ended up playing a three-hander with Medvig and Olli instead. Rollo sloped away to get some sleep.

Idris looked up at Solace almost challengingly. "So, what about you?" he asked. "Would you like a drink? We can synthesize ... actually very little that tastes authentic. But you can at least tell me what you've been up to, if we're doing the old friends bit."

"I saw a little action, after the war." She shrugged. "I was on ice, off ice. You hear about the hostage standoff, on Britta Station? That was one of mine."

He had, and it was only a few years back. The Parthenon had saved three Colonial scientists from paranoid Nativists with a gripe. They ended up keeping the scientists and it had nearly started a war.

"As long as you're keeping busy," he managed weakly.

*

It seemed weirdly unreal that every news mediotype wasn't screaming about the return of the Architects. Instead, Huei-Cavor was entirely fixated on the Hegemonic ambassador's arrival to consecrate the planet. Idris watched the ritual unfold on one of the small screens, grimly aware that the absurdly elaborate process was suddenly a matter of life or death, if only anyone down there knew it. Huei-Cavor was about to move beyond the Architects' grasp.

The huge barge they'd seen earlier had landed, and a crowd of hundreds of thousands was kneeling for the ceremony. A hatch in the side of the barge had folded into a ramp and the newsfeeds were showing the Always Revered Emnir, the Bastion and the Gilded, process onto the soil of Huei-Cavor. Not that the alien luminary would actually *touch* the soil. That wasn't an Essiel thing. First came ranks of human cultists, in bright and impractical robes. Then came a scurrying host of things like segmented metal weasels, with six legs and a mouthful of weapon barrels—some Hegemonic subject race. Finally, the actual Essiel appeared before its new congregation.

"The Always Revered Emnir, the Bastion and the Gilded" was the human cultists' interpretation of its title of course. And the ceremony that followed—all three hours of it—was the cult's doing too. The Essiel just sat there for it, and occasionally waved some stick-thin limbs from its a-grav platform. This was five metres wide and made of real diamond, worked into intricate, symmetrical arabesques.

Human researchers' best guess was that the Essiel had evolved from some kind of sedentary exoparasite that attached itself to more mobile animals, and eventually began to manipulate their rides. Physically, they were two-valved shells, some three metres tall when stood upright. Where the shell halves diverged at the top end, a clutch of stalked eyes and articulated limbs projected. The alien overlords of the greatest known polity in the galaxy looked more like barnacles than anything else.

Idris tuned out most of the ceremony, although Barney and Kittering followed every move. Kowtowing to a shellfish seemed a small price for lasting security, given recent circumstances.

At last, the Coffin arrived at Lung-Crow. Factor Luciel Leng met them at the gangplank, looking strained and with a handful of security at her back.

"Captain Rostand, I commend you on your good work," she said, with a smile that looked tissue thin. "Obviously not quite what anyone was expecting, but good, very good. You're after some leave here?"

"I understand it is the done thing," Rollo said, deadpan.

"Then I will require certain assurances," Leng said. She was a short woman, now they saw her in the flesh. Her lenses clicked round, as though hunting out Rollo's weaknesses. "None of your crew are to divulge what you've found."

"Standard rates for non-disclosure. A contract shall be prepared," came the snappy tones of Kittering's translator.

"You think you can keep this to yourself?" Kris asked.

"For now. While the celebrations continue. For a little while," Leng told her. "And I don't want a crew of spacers shooting their mouths off about what they've found."

"You're Hegemony now, right?" Kris pressed. "I'd have thought you'd be shouting this from the rooftops. Your new overlords will love the boost it'll give their recruitment drive."

"We are considering how best to...broach this matter with the Divine Essiel. How best to..." *Exploit it* hung in the air, unspoken. A lot of people might be made or ruined in this transition of power, especially mid-level station administrators.

"So I am holding your ship until I've worked out how to manage this news," she told them flatly. "Go drink and game all you want, but if there's a riot and people start screaming the Architects are coming, I will not release your payment. You understand me?"

"Crystally," Rollo told her sourly. "You just hurry up and decide. More than a day in port, my crew get itchy feet."

More than a day and most ports are desperate to be rid of us, Idris reflected.

8.

Solace

Solace's new loyalties only went so far. She might be crew and an honorary Colonial, just like Kittering the Hannilambra. But that didn't mean she'd forgotten whose vat they'd decanted her from. As soon as she could, she broke from the others and sent a coded missive to Monitor Superior Tact. The Lung-Crow Orbital could play its games, but if the Architects *were* back, the Parthenon needed to know. In fact, the rest of the galaxy needed the Parthenon to know. *Keep it secret*, she requested and reckoned that would be in the Parthenon's interests too, for long enough that she hoped she wasn't screwing over the *Vulture God*.

Her duty done, she went to play Colonial, which meant shore leave and drinking. Ostensibly, she thought it might help her mission to get to know Idris's crewmates, although Kris Almier was distractingly eye-catching. The dark woman had peeled away to sit at the bar with a decidedly fancier drink than anyone else, and had been doing something technical with a slate. Solace saw it was some kind of game—bright, visually simple and yet deceptively difficult, like a lot of Colonial culture.

"So what's your story, precisely?"

Kris started as Solace sat down. "What's it to you, soldier?"

"Crewmate," Solace corrected without acrimony.

"Not really sure what you are." Kris tucked the slate away, as though the game contained the secrets of creation. "Except Idris is weird around you."

"We're old friends," Solace said easily, signalling for a drink.

"What are the odds, huh?" Solace could tell that Kris was wary of her, yet the woman still squared her shoulders pugnaciously and added, "If you cause trouble for my *client*—just be aware I'm up on Hegemonic law as well as Colonial. I can protect him from you wherever the hell we go outside your space. And Rollo and Kit know better than to take a job within reach of the Parthenon."

Solace's instinct was to hint darkly that the Parthenon's reach extended everywhere, including right here, right now. A moment later, the words unsaid, she felt deeply unhappy with herself.

"We're old friends," Solace repeated, less glibly now. "We were at Berlenhof. And yes, no coincidence running into him. I was sent. But... I'm not going to just stuff him in a sack and run off. I have an offer for him, when he's ready to hear it."

"And if he says no?"

"Then it's no, of course." *Until I get an order that it has to be "yes."* "Who are you, Kris? Never heard of a shipboard lawyer before."

"Keristina Soolin Almier, certified advocate out of Scintilla." The words were smart enough, but one of her hands twisted her bright scarf. Shimmering gold, this one; Solace hadn't seen her wear the same one on two consecutive days yet.

"Iceball," she noted, trying to remember anything else about the planet. They were crazy there, she recalled. Rich, educated, rigid society, weird customs. It was on a list of Colonial planets where any Partheni insertion was flagged as dangerous. "Would have thought you could do better than this," she noted. "And I'm not trying to cast shade, just saying."

"Outside the Parthenon, we don't always end up where we expect," was Kris's answer to that.

"You could come too, if Idris accepts my offer," Solace said frankly. *In the unlikely event he lets me even make it.* "Add Partheni regulations to your legal portfolio. You'd be in great demand. Precious few Colonials know their way around them." She lifted her eyebrows enquiringly.

"You think winning me over's the way to get him to play along?" Kris asked her. "Or..." She frowned abruptly. "Are you *coming on* to me, Myrmidon?"

Solace had a moment of being taken equally by surprise at the thought, then shrugged. "Well, you Colonials can be funny about that kind of thing but, if you were up for it..."

Kris goggled at her, and Solace waited to see if she had retained her settled-world prejudices, or if she'd picked up a spacer's more liberal mores. It was page one of the Partheni playbook that Colonials were weird about sex, in a hundred conflicting ways, and you shouldn't *ever* get into this sort of conversation. But Kris had brought it up...

In the end the woman coloured and looked away, fiddling with her scarf again. "Well, I...it's not my normal thing but...I guess I'm flattered."

Solace grinned despite herself. "Offer's there."

"I guess it is just women, for you people?" Kris went on slowly, in what Solace felt was an encouragingly intrigued manner.

"At home. When you get sent out, you experiment…" And without meaning to, she glanced across the bar at Idris. When she looked back, Kris was staring at her, wide-eyed.

"Idris? *Seriously?*" she said.

For a moment Solace thought she was jealous or horrified, but the woman's expression had resolved into something like mischievous glee. Solace found herself entirely wrong-footed, because she'd meant to keep that firmly under wraps. Apparently one drink was all it took to unshell her. She was saved from having to give further details when a large man pushed his way to the bar. He sat so close to Kris that he almost shoved her off her stool.

The lawyer opened her mouth to reproach him, but he looked bleakly at the pair of them and said, "The *Oumaru*."

Solace's fighting reflexes kicked in instantly. *Angels of Punching You in the Face*, and she was ready to make good on the name. The man was beefier than Colonials normally got, even broader than Magdan's Voyenni soldiers. His hair and beard were cropped to a stubble and his knuckly face was blotched with blue and purple discolorations. There was something very wrong with him too. His clothing was slit from the neck to the small of his back, because some creature was implanted there. It was a thing between a lobster and a bee, armoured in parts, bristly with jagged hairs. Several limbs were dug deep into the man's body, the flesh around them warped and lumpy. Its handful of stalked eyes flicked about, scanning the crowd. Solace had no idea what it was, except nasty. Very nasty.

Kris very carefully set down her plastic beaker, "*Oumaru*. Should that mean something?" she said.

The newcomer regarded them without humour. "You

brought her back from deep void." His Colvul was accented strangely. "My employer has an interest in her. Tell me where she is, please."

"Nope," Kris said.

"Not our fleas, not our circus," Solace added. Which, from their expressions, wasn't a saying that had travelled outside the Parthenon.

The man—the *symbiont*, Solace decided—smiled thinly. She wondered whether the joining of flesh also meant a joining of minds. "Do not make a game of this," he continued. "My employer is desirous that his staff have access to the ship. This can be a pleasant matter of contractual recompense or it can lead to matters less pleasant."

"Take this up with our factor. I'm just crew," Kris said carelessly.

"The Hanni says you are already under contract. I did explain that this was problematic to my employer, but the little crab would not be moved. To avoid the unpleasantness I come to the crew. Show me the ship now, please." He put his big hands on the bar and Kris instantly moved several steps away. Danger hung about him like he sweated it.

"You don't want to kick off any unpleasantness with me," Solace told him evenly.

He merely grinned. "You're the Patho they told me about. Good for you. You're not the only ones who fight. To the ship now, please."

Solace stood, calm and battle-ready now actual face-punching was imminent. When violence erupted from two tables away, it caught all three of them entirely by surprise.

She aimed a fist at the symbiont out of sheer reflex, and he'd gone for her in the same moment. She twisted aside as her blow glanced off a cheekbone hard as steel. A moment later, someone in red robes was thrown into the pair of them. Symbiont hit the bar with his elbow, cracking the counter and yelping in surprisingly high-pitched pain. Solace herself went with the momentum and put the bar between them. She ended up half covered by robes, shouldering aside the dazed cultist-turned-missile. When she put her head above the parapet, the whole room had erupted into fighting and Symbiont was gone. For a moment she thought Kris had been carried off as well, but the lawyer was also crouched behind the dubious cover of the cracked bar.

"What *is* this?" Solace demanded, feeling as though their own fight should have taken precedence over this random farrago. Even as she spoke, Kris shouted, "Idris!" and was off into the melee, drawing a narrow-bladed knife from her sleeve. Solace vaulted the bar and was right behind her.

At a booth across the room were Idris, Rollo and Olli. Solace's heart sank to see that someone had driven a dagger into their plastic tabletop, because she knew precisely what *that* bit of theatre meant. *The Betrayed. With their "humans for humans" sentiments.* Between her and them was a room full of brawling people either trying to get into or out of a fight, all representing a serious obstacle. A core of young Colonial men were going for anyone wearing cult robes or Hegemony regalia.

A cultist stumbled into her, robes flapping, and tried to punch her in the face. She blocked and elbowed him in the jaw with brutal efficiency. He spat blood from his savagely bitten tongue and reeled away. She felt absurdly indignant, because frankly none of this was their fight. However, a man had Idris by the collar, and she remembered that Intermediaries were on the Betrayed's long list of race traitors. How they'd identified Idris for what he was, she didn't know, but presumably that was why someone was trying to choke him to death. Rollo slugged the man, who let the Int go and lurched sideways. He hit an electrified prong that Olli had jabbed out from her walker frame and fell, shuddering. Then a bulkier opponent appeared, popped Rollo in the nose and kicked Olli back into the wall.

Solace powered through the fist-happy crowd. Halfway across the room she had a sudden crisis of conscience and looked for Kris, surely at the mercy of the mob. Except Kris was tight at her back, knife held along the line of her arm. Even as Solace glanced in her direction, the lawyer took a cultist's arm, twisting it viciously to bend the man backwards. She then kicked her victim's legs out from him, her blade remaining unbloodied. *No need to escalate just yet.*

A bundle of bodies cannoned into Solace even as they moved forwards: two spacers laying into a cultist. One of them saw her, processed her as an ally, then realized his mistake. He was a particularly ugly customer, his own Nativist sympathies on show with the cross-hilted knife inked onto his forehead. The Parthenon was right at the top of the Betrayed's hate-list.

She swayed back from his right fist's wild swing, and then his left came at her with a knuckleduster studded with nails. His friend was right behind with a knife.

Escalation it is, then. Knuckles came for Solace with both fists this time. She caught one, rammed it back into its owner's face, and then deflected the other so the knuckleduster raked across Blade's abdomen. Then Blade rammed into her, knocking her over. She rolled out from underneath him, ramming an elbow into his head, but Knuckles got a grip on her knee and drew back his fist full of nails for a pounding.

Kris cut his ear off.

For the briefest moment, mid-brawl, Solace and Knuckles both stared at the ear as it flopped to the floor. Kris had stepped back, knife poised, and the back of her other arm presented to block.

Knuckles rose, roaring, to his full height, Solace forgotten on the ground. He grabbed for Kris and received the myrmidon's booted foot right in the groin. She reckoned she'd fractured the man's pelvis. She kicked Blade in the head for good measure as Kris hauled her to her feet.

Over at the table, Barney had appeared and was wrestling fiercely with the man who'd hit Rollo. Solace punched their antagonist in the back of the head and floored him.

"Where's Idris?" Kris yelled.

"There!" Olli had righted herself and was pointing a truncated arm across the room. Solace spotted a knot of red and purple figures, with Idris's slender form in the middle.

"Oh for..." It seemed particularly unjust—in the middle of this fight-that-was-not-their-fight—that they'd have to go toe-to-toe with both sides. A moment later Idris was gesturing, apparently unharmed, and they shouldered their way over. Medvig was sheltering amongst the cultists too, Solace saw, and Kittering had been under the table all along. They had sensibly decided against getting trampled by a roomful of mad humans.

The cultists were armed with shock batons and coshes, more than ready to give any marauding Nativist a run for their money. Around that time station security finally arrived and started cuffing rioters, or at least any rioters without

Hegemony colours. Rollo made the call that perhaps they *were* with the cultists after all.

Soon the bar was quiet again and security were considerately removing the unconscious bodies. Solace stared at the dagger stuck into the crew's erstwhile tabletop.

"So that's a thing," Kris agreed, following her gaze. "The Betrayed. They'll all get rooted out of here sharpish by the cult, now the Hegemony's taken over."

Solace nodded. The Betrayed were a relatively new faction within internal Colonial politics. They were officially decried by Hugh and yet, mysteriously, they'd never been outlawed. The Parthenon didn't care for the legitimate Nativist movement either, which was all about returning to one unified human identity. They celebrated old Earth and embraced the rhetoric of humanity's past glories. The Betrayed went a step further, preaching that humanity would have been the galaxy's dominant species, if allowed to fight the Architects "properly." But Intermediaries had made some sort of sham peace, they claimed, part of a grand conspiracy to keep humans down. Needless to say, the Hegemonic cult was right up there in their sights as well, which brought them round to...

"Who are your new friends, my wayward son?" Rollo asked.

Before Idris could speak, a thin greying woman amongst the cultists said, "Captain Rostand, of the *Vulture God*?"

"A responsibility that seems to bring only trouble these days," he agreed warily.

She managed a creditable smile. "My hierograve has asked me to invite you to dinner, sir."

Rollo looked over the ruin of the bar, then back to her. "That so?" he asked, his usual loquaciousness deserting him in the fact of this unexpected development.

"He has a business proposition for you. Perhaps you and he—"

"Oh no, my friend, it's all of us or nothing at this point. This orbital has a case of the frothing fits on it. So make sure your table has something fit for a Hanni."

*

"Help me out." Rollo bent towards Kris as they followed the cultists through the orbital's quieter passageways. "Why wine and dine us when they run the place now? We've got nothing they need, surely?"

"The cult isn't unified. Right now various cells will be jockeying to see who gets to be the mouthpiece for their masters," she speculated. "The clams—" She bit off the slur. "The *Essiel* are very hands-off when it comes to how they rule, so long as they get what they want. Winning divine favour can get underhand and sneaky fast."

Solace had shuffled closer to Idris. "You all right?"

He looked at her warily. "For now. Except Barney was shooting his mouth off about deep void work to what turned out to be a knot of Betrayed."

And deep void work meant Ints. "You get that reaction a lot?"

"You're going to tell me it'd never happen in the Parthenon, right?"

She opened her mouth to say: *Well, it wouldn't.* Closed it again. *Still not the right time, but what would it take?* "Just give me a chance, Idris. Let me spiel and then I'll be out of your hair."

"'Give your spiel,'" he corrected, smiling a little. "Your Colvul's slipping."

"Also, you're changing the subject," she pointed out.

He shrugged. "Probably. I do that." And then they had arrived, apparently. They'd gone some way into the domestic areas of the orbital, amongst nests of rooms occupied by station staff and permanent residents. These cabins were stacked three or four high and separated every now and then by high atria and claustrophobic light wells. The latter had probably been intended as public squares, so long as your public was happy to gather in groups of no more than a dozen. Here, though, three units had been converted into some kind of eatery, decked out in Hegemonic colours. Plainly this neighbourhood was well ahead of the curve in adapting to the system's new masters.

There was a large table ready for them, half a dozen richly robed cultists already standing by their chairs. Staff bustled past, setting places. They'd even left spaces for Olli's walker and Medvig's frame and put in a high, narrow stool for Kittering. All in all, not a bad show.

"Please," the lead cultist invited them, and the crew sat cautiously. Solace saw Kris adjust the sit of her knife within her sleeve and Rollo squared his shoulders. Nobody really trusted this development not to go sour at the first opportunity.

Then their benefactor arrived—the hierograve from the way the other cultists reacted—and Solace burst out, "I know you!"

For a moment she couldn't quite place him. He was balding with a fringe of white hair about the ears and a well-groomed beard. She found herself wanting to stroke it: it was a novelty to Partheni eyes and looked soft and woolly as a blanket. Colonial men tended to misinterpret that kind of thing, though, so she kept her hands to herself. His high-collared robe was eloquent evidence of his cult standing but his eyes had a good-natured twinkle to them—suggesting he was as harmless as everyone's favourite grandfather. Solace, who had no male relatives of any kind, didn't trust him an inch, and she reckoned the rest of the *Vulture*'s crew were just as leery.

"His Wisdom the Bearer Sathiel," the cultist woman announced, and Solace abruptly recalled seeing the man in the news mediotypes. He'd been talking about Huei-Cavor entering a bold new age, and how his sect had been instrumental in converting the populace to Hegemonism.

"Well this is a grand honour and no mistake," Rollo said without enthusiasm. The restaurant staff began bringing out food, a mix of bland-but-nutritious Colonial staples and weird-looking dishes from Hegemonic worlds. Kittering received a bowl of something that looked like coarse-grained coloured sand that his mandibles picked at with gusto. Nobody seemed to know what to do with Medvig, but in the end the Hiver just co-opted whatever was going. When they had a pile of assorted foodstuffs in front of them, their insect-form selves swarmed out of their frame and attacked everything omnivorously, breaking it all down into proteins and energy.

Sathiel twinkled at Rollo, who smiled right back. For a moment Solace thought the pair were going to have an avuncle-off right there at the table. Then one of the hierograve's people bustled forward to remove his high collar and peel back his robe, revealing a thin mauve tunic underneath.

"They look hot, those things," Rollo said, around a spoon of algae.

"And heavy, but that's responsibility, isn't it?" Sathiel smiled, as though faintly embarrassed by all of it. "Captain, we have a mutual problem, you and I, and it's sitting in Bay 98 right now."

"You have a problem with my ship, friend?" Rollo asked him mildly.

"*You* have the problem," Sathiel said. "Right at this moment, a certain station administrator of our acquaintance is looking into impounding it for her own purposes. She wishes to retain control of a...sensitive cargo you brought back from the deep void."

"This is perhaps the worst-kept secret I've ever encountered in my long career," Rollo remarked.

"Some of the administrative staff know how our masters may be best-served," Sathiel said piously. "We therefore heard you have evidence of an Architect attack, a recent one too. You can appreciate this is of prime importance to the galaxy as a whole, and the Hegemony in particular."

"You mean if you parade our 'cargo' about in public, everyone will suddenly want to wear a fancy robe like yours," Olli said sharply.

The cultists bristled, but Sathiel took no overt offence. "Do you not think, Mesdam Timo, that people *deserve* the chance to save their worlds from destruction? Or should we wait until an Architect appears over Ossa or Faedrich perhaps?"

"Why not just swash your robes at station admin then?" Medvig's comment was even blunter than customary, perhaps because half of their processing power was devoted to eating.

"I think you've already discovered that we're experiencing some...unrest here," Sathiel told them. "And our local admins, who were vociferously anti-Hegemony, are now trying to grab power by any means possible. There are also

Nativist sympathizers in positions of authority. I would rather be in possession of the *Oumaru* and *then* ask permission, to stop anything happening to it."

"Wait," Solace broke in. "Do you have someone on your payroll who has a sort of...insect thing plugged into his back?" She exchanged glances with Kris.

"A Tothiat, you mean?" Sathiel asked. "Not in my retinue. It's a rare adaptation..."

So who was that "Tothiat," exactly? One more complicating factor.

"What are you proposing, Your Wisdom?" Rollo asked.

"I am suggesting that your people and my people go down to the bay, in defiance of the impounding order. I will ensure that all staff on duty are keen to earn favour with our masters, and thereby clear your way. You can then take your ship out and leave the *Oumaru* in full view outside the orbital. Everyone will see it and know just what happened," Sathiel said. "And then we can put all this ridiculous cloak-and-dagger business out of the way and proceed into the future like grown-ups. What do you say?"

Rollo glanced at Kittering, whose arm-screens were running with a screed of Colvul text: contractual terms and rates. Apparently the only variable the factor was concerned about was not doing it for free. Then the captain looked to Kris.

"Factor Leng won't be happy," the lawyer opined.

"A matter of less than no consequence to me," Rollo decided. "Nobody who wants to tie down my ship is a friend. And what about *your* lot?" A frank stare at Solace.

"Me?"

"Tell me you didn't skip straight off and tell your people

what we had here?" Not angry, but not smiling right now either. "Parthenon's already taking action to keep this for themselves, maybe? You tell me."

But Solace found she didn't know. Probably, if she contacted Tact right now, she'd be told the secret must be kept for a few more days to give the Parthenon room to manoeuvre. Except the Parthenon seemed very far away and the *Vulture* and its crew were right here. And their ship was their entire livelihood, their home and everything they had.

"Do it. Let's go," she heard herself say. She was keenly aware of Idris staring at her. "If there's Partheni trouble, I'll field it, Captain."

Rollo's gaze bored into her and he nodded curtly. "Welcome to the crew, my daughter," he said. She felt a spike of utterly misplaced pride, that she hated herself for only a moment later.

*

They finished the meal, because it was good eating. If you were Colonial, dinner invites didn't happen very often. Nobody could get very drunk under the circumstances, but the mood certainly lightened. Rollo and Sathiel ended up swapping anecdotes at the head of the table.

Then, after the last platter had been sent back to the recycler, the hierograve stood. "Let's go get your ship back," he told them, "and spread truth to the universe."

"Let's do just that thing, my children," Rollo agreed, pushing back his bench and nearly unseating Barney, who'd been sharing it.

Sathiel was obviously leery of his grandfatherly face being

seen subverting station authority. Instead he sent his deputy to appease station security, heading up a little red-clad delegation. Rollo was at her heels, talking with Kit about the next job the factor had lined up. "Anywhere but here," he was saying, and Solace wondered how much of the galaxy was out of bounds to the man.

"Hey." It was Idris, unexpectedly at her elbow. "Going native on us?"

A sharp answer died on her lips. "I don't know what I'm doing right now," she admitted. "Let's just get everyone out of here first, then we can reset to where we were."

"I appreciate it, though," he said implacably. "Helping us. Ship-family matters out here. More than cults, governments and what planet you come from. It's only when you spend your life planetside that people lose their minds over that sort of thing."

"And you don't want to be part of anything that big," she finished for him.

"I do not, no. No more of that for me, sorry."

The cultists were at the bay access hatch now and signalling to be let in, but their friendly collaborators inside were apparently playing it coy. Olli just trundled her walker forwards and found a diagnostic socket she could plug into. An eyeblink later she had the door open, with a derisive sound that said absolutely everything about Lung-Crow electronic security.

There were three lifeless bodies on the other side. They wore station security uniforms and they'd been burned by beam weapons. The lead cultist let out a yelp and shrank back, but Rollo just bulled forwards, shouting, "Goddamn it, my *ship*!"

The door on the far side of the security check was open and they piled through. There hung the hideous-beautiful flower of the *Oumaru*, still clutched in the *Vulture God*'s grasp. There were more dead security on the catwalk, plus a couple of ragged-looking spacers—whose co-conspirators were even now at the *Vulture*'s open hatch.

"Bastards!" Rollo hissed and snatched up one of the security men's guns, running for the cover of the railing. Solace was already moving, grabbing a weapon for herself, bitterly regretting that her armour and accelerator were inside the ship.

There were four men at the *Vulture*'s hatch, which probably meant some were already inside. Most were human, and their leader was mostly human too. The non-human part was that lobster-bee thing that had merged with his back. A *Tothiat*, Sathiel had called it, and now Solace was kicking herself because she hadn't asked what that meant. She shot him anyway. The security guns were hardly Mr. Punch, so wouldn't knock holes in the wrong walls. They punched a hole into the Tothiat easily enough though, right into the left side of his gut. He fell back against the *Vulture God*'s hull. Rollo tried a shot, too, striking sparks from his own ship. Barney had a third gun but was fiddling with it, and Solace had to yell how to disable the safety.

She risked a glance around. Kris and Idris were just taking cover, which was probably for the best. Olli was bustling forwards on her walker frame, her eyes fixed determinedly on the ship. Medvig's tripod body stalked after her, their remotes corkscrewing through the air towards the hijackers.

The men at the hatch were scattering for cover and Solace drilled another through the leg so that he landed hard on the gantry, howling in pain and distracting his friends. Barney and Olli pushed forward at that, clattering up shaky metal steps to a higher railing where they'd have a vantage point. The engineer was grimacing furiously but hadn't fired a shot yet. What the unarmed Olli felt she could contribute, Solace couldn't guess.

A figure appeared within the *Vulture*, not a human but a crablike Hanni—and it was tracking Barney with some kind of weapon mounted atop its shell. Solace shot it over the rim of its half-raised shield arms, hitting the clutch of limbs and mouthparts below its eyes. The creature's many legs jerked and it toppled limply out onto the gantry.

"Go!" said Rollo, taking his own advice and making a run for his ship. Solace registered a growing shudder throughout the bay and realized that someone on board had engaged the *Vulture*'s mass drives, ready to rip the vessel—and its salvage— free of the station's hold.

The hijackers in the hangar opened fire upon Rollo, then Medvig's remotes were on them, slapping, gouging and generally making a nuisance of themselves. The Hiver's body-frame was motionless, worryingly out in the open, as they devoted all their concentration to the task. Solace ran to back up Rollo, then shooting erupted behind her.

She whirled and saw that the hijackers had friends who'd been elsewhere, probably dealing with the docking controls. They'd just unloaded their weapons into the knot of cultists and cut them down. Worse, they had Idris. Kris was facing the human newcomers, her knife out against their guns. What had Idris was a Castigar, though. They came in all shapes, both natural and engineered, but this one looked the standard model: a four-metre black leech whose body terminated in a host of squirming eye-tipped limbs. It also sported a metal hood, equipped with pincers and weapon barrels. The pincers had closed about Idris's body, lifting the Int partway off the floor.

"Bring him! Get in the ship!" someone yelled, and Solace saw numbly that the Tothiat was back on his feet, despite the lethal hole she'd put in him. He wasn't even favouring his unhurt side, as he grabbed his comrade with the shot leg and practically threw him on board the *Vulture*. "Stand down or your man gets torn up" he yelled at Rollo, facing down the captain's levelled gun with equanimity.

"*You get off my ship,*" Rollo roared back furiously, gun shaking but not lowering an inch.

The Castigar surged forward. Rippling muscular waves swept down its body, sending it eeling along the gantry at the speed of a running man. Idris went jolting along in its vice-like grip. Solace had her weapon levelled at it, but it was deliberately keeping its victim between it and her. She didn't know enough about Castigar physiology to be certain of taking it down. Medvig's remotes hovered about it like flies, not daring a landing.

"My employer regrets this," the Tothiat boomed, "but we need your ship to move that piece of junk. Maybe we'll sell it back to you." His confederates had left cover to scurry over to the *Vulture*. Rollo took another frustrated step forward, right out into the open, his face purple with rage. The Tothiat levelled his gun as the Castigar and its fellows raced up a parallel gantry with Idris still jerking about like a doll.

"*Fuck you,*" Barney suddenly shouted from on high, finally getting his gun to work. His shot clipped the Tothiat's temple, almost spreading the symbiont's brains across the *Vulture*'s paintwork. Solace's gun took out one of the men at the hatch as the others returned fire. She heard Olli's cry of grief and froze, then Barney toppled over their walkway's railing, buckling the gantry below with his dead weight.

All hell broke loose.

The Castigar and friends were entering the ship now, the Tothiat gesturing frantically for them to hurry. Then something burst out of the hatch, a thing of legs and arms with a whipping, saw-edged tail. The sight was sudden and monstrous enough to even startle a yell from Solace. It was Olli's Scorpion frame and it moved like monkeys and spiders, claws and saw tearing into the nearest hijacker and ripping him apart. Up on the high gantry, Olli was slumped back in her walker, eyes closed as she remotely wrangled the Scorpion into a frenzy of destruction. Then the Castigar's headmount jolted as it unleashed a searing beam of energy against the Scorpion, followed by a rattle of accelerator pellets. They punched a dozen holes in the frame without slowing it but the distraction allowed Idris to twist out of its grip and run for his life, heading back down the walkway towards the crew. One of the other hijackers tried to retrieve him, and Solace put a bullet in the man's head on her second attempt.

The Tothiat rolled his shoulders then laid hands on the Scorpion's far greater bulk. Before Solace's incredulous gaze, he crouched and just tipped the half-tonne of machinery over a broken rail, leaving it flailing and clinging to the twisted metal with half its limbs. Then he leapt inside the *Vulture*, perhaps about to abandon his comrades and make off with the prize.

Medvig's remotes grabbed him, all three of them, latching on like hands. As they jetted away, they dragged him halfway out of the ship. The Tothiat shouted and tried to bring up his gun, but they wouldn't let him, yanking him left and right and spoiling his aim. Then the Castigar had lumped its long body up to the hatch, despite Solace putting a bullet into some part of it. Its weaponized hood swung round until it found the Hiver, and its beam lashed out again. Medvig's chest unit glowed red as their outer layers ablated away. Something inside them blew, showering molten metal and sparks. In the aftermath, Solace saw blazing insectoid bodies crawling frantically out from the hole, dropping to the ground and spinning on their backs as they crisped and died.

The Tothiat and a handful of his followers were aboard the *Vulture* now, and the Castigar snaked aboard after, turning to spray the bay with a salvo of accelerator shots. They drilled through walls and stanchions without significantly slowing. Solace felt the familiar shudder of an atmosphere bubble contending with unplanned apertures.

Then the *Vulture*'s hatch closed and the ship was on the move. It slid sideways out of the bay with a roar of thrusters, pulling its terrible cargo, forcing Rollo and the rest back. Solace instinctively tracked it with her purloined gun, but it wasn't designed to puncture a ship's hull.

A moment later and they were left in the ravaged bay, staring at Barney's corpse and Medvig's burnt-out shell.

9.

Havaer

Havaer Mundy, of Hugh's much-feared Intervention Board, wore clothes badly. It was as though they weren't quite right for his size or shape. It was a common Colonial problem born of too many generations of malnourishment and unreliable manufacturing. *Make do and mend.* Even with an orbital office over Berlenhof, Havaer's tunics still seemed as ill-fitting as an itinerant spacer's.

That he had a face designed by evolution for suspicious and mistrustful expressions had perhaps exercised some form of determinism, because he had ended up in a suspicious and mistrustful job. His features were gaunt and hollow, hung off big slanting cheekbones. Above them, his narrow eyes seemed to question everything. In his career at the Intervention Board— familiarly known as "Mordant House" because of the planet-side district their office had once inhabited, and because it sounded just sinister enough—he had driven three subordinates to confess misdeeds he hadn't even guessed at, just by sharing a room with them.

Today, Havaer wasn't feeling too sinister. He was looking forward to getting to grips with some unchallenging intel reports on a smuggling operation. A cartel had been bringing the Hegemonic drug Esh into a handful of colony worlds, and he suspected preventing it was a lost cause. Still, his job was to do, not to set policy, and current policy was to draw a hard border and try to control access to the stuff.

Midway through his morning, though, he was called in by Chief Laery. She was hunched like a spider in an a-grav chair behind her desk. Her brittle-boned limbs were like narrow pipes, slightly thicker at the elbows and knees. Her neural link threw images and holograms across her desk as she addressed him.

"Might have a problem. At Huei-Cavor."

Havaer gave his chief a look. "The Hegemony takeover isn't news, surely. And we can't do anything about it. Unless we really do want to butt heads with the Essiel?" Some of the more Nativist in the department had been pushing for just that: Hugh should take a stand against these damn aliens poaching their colonies.

"It's not the Hegemony, believe it or not." Laery's head shifted on her fragile neck and more information began to appear over the desk. "A ship just brought in a packet from a Huei-Cavor informer. Supposedly something special docked at an orbital there. Under cover, but someone reckoned they could make a little Largesse by selling us the news."

Havaer was scanning through the report. "More Architect gossip. This is nonsense."

"Almost certainly. And not the first time someone's tried to spread this particular rumour," Laery agreed, then paused expectantly.

"I thought they were going to repeal Standing Order Four," Havaer complained eventually, when he saw which way this was going.

"Still in committee," Laery agreed with a thin smile. "Likely it'll be done by the time you return from Huei-Cavor. Then they'll use it as a reason not to pay you overtime."

Standing Order Four came out of the period when any rumour of the Architects' return had caused immediate panic. Whole teams of Mordant House agents had been dispatched by the swiftest routes at vast expense. But those days were past, and Hugh was seeking to cut back on costs. Crack squads of veterans, led by hard-faced people like Havaer, cost money. Especially when they kicked in doors, kidnapped and interrogated witnesses, boarded ships and almost set off whole chains of subsidiary wars in their fervour.

Apparently someone had seen a salvage crew drag in a wreck that looked like it had been Architected. Havaer shrugged inwardly. A ship could explode in a variety of ways. You could get some pretty spectacular effects if a gravitic drive went wrong in the instant of transit. And these days, who'd even seen an Architect's handiwork first-hand? He already had his final report half composed in his head before he stood up. On Laery's desk, the details of his berth to Huei-Cavor flashed up. He frowned.

"This...looks a bit roughshod," he said uncertainly. "Roughshod" was an old operational term combining the word's actual meaning with "rough" and "slipshod." It was the way the service used to operate back in the old days: you got things done however, and lived with the discomfort. They were shipping him out on a Castigar vessel which made scant concessions to human passengers. It was definitely the quickest way to Huei-Cavor, using one of their near-mindless Savant-caste navigators to speed them through the deep void. "Chief, is there...something I'm not seeing here, about this job?"

Laery held his gaze, expressionless. "On paper, of course not. Just another nonsense fire we need to stamp out. Just come back and tell us we don't need to worry about it, Havaer."

"And off paper?"

She shut off the holographic display, and he knew that she'd also killed the recording of their meeting. "The Harbinger Ash is involved," she said.

Havaer wasn't important enough to have met Ash, but he knew it was still around, ageless and pointless in equal measure. Yet it kept turning up, and sometimes it said something. When it did, you listened.

"I didn't need to hear that," he muttered.

"You haven't. Not officially. Just a routine mission."

His heart was speeding and he had his internal dispenser give him a shot for it. "I'll go pack then, Chief."

*

The Castigar woke him at Huei-Cavor, just in time for him to discover everything had already gone mad. Even being shipped roughshod through the deep void hadn't been quick enough for him to get ahead of this.

The Castigar ship's bridge was a tube, inclined at forty-five degrees and half submerged in milky liquid. The worm-shaped aliens lounged in fat loops on the slope, their many-limbed heads buried in their instrumentation. A human-style display was set towards the high end of the space for his benefit—because Industry-caste Castigar tended to be helpful to a fault.

The Huei-Cavor system was in uproar, the Hegemony

takeover almost forgotten. Havaer's target had arrived unnoticed, the ship hidden within a Coffin transport. However, when the *Vulture God* left Lung-Crow station at speed, it had apparently been towing an Architect's leavings, there for all to see. Further investigation revealed that the ship had used force to escape the station, leaving a wake of deaths behind it—including station staff and the ship's own crew. Nobody was sure who controlled the vessel now. Speculation abounded.

He looked at the recorded *Vulture God* and its twisted cargo, cross-referenced the images on his slate to wartime wrecks.

He gave himself another shot to slow his heart.

All around him the Castigar were flashing warning colours across their slick, segmented bodies, twining their tail-tips together in agitation. The air stank with the acrid scent of their worry. He was entirely in agreement with them. He contacted the handful of Hugh and Mordant informers on Lung-Crow and sent them his credentials, requesting full cooperation and an introduction to station admin. He'd have to hope that Hugh writ still carried some weight, despite the recent regime change.

Then the Castigar craft was spiralling in towards the station, its speaker-delegate requesting docking permission.

Havaer Mundy retrieved his dossiers and reviewed his knowledge of the *Vulture God* and its crew.

Kris

After their arrest, Kris had expected them to be framed for the security staff's deaths. She'd already prepared legal arguments by the time His Wisdom the Bearer Sathiel pitched up at their cell. Part of her was numb after seeing Barney and Medvig die. However, she was still the crew's lawyer and she had to protect them.

Sathiel changed all of that—and it didn't hurt that he was pushing his own interests as well. He had a serious throw-down with station admin, accusing Leng of trying to hide the truth about the Architects. He also took responsibility for the *Vulture*'s crew being in the cargo bay, and Leng was plainly unwilling to arrest him or his people. Everyone ended up being turfed out of her offices onto the street.

Sathiel rushed off to capitalize on what he had, given that the actual evidence had been whisked away from him. The *Vulture* crew—if that was even what they were anymore— were left abandoned as the station resounded with the agitation of people still getting to grips with a possible return of everyone's worst nightmare.

"Right," said Rollo, and led them off to do their duty: to drink, brood and toast their lost companions.

"Musoku Barnier," Rollo said sombrely. They'd muscled everyone else out of an alcove in the nearest bar and now he stood while they sat. Even Solace, who'd never been at a spacer's wake before. "Born 92 After," he declared to them, "on Tsiolkovsky Orbital over Lumbali."

"Complaining son of a bitch," Olli put in promptly.

"Bad sore loser," Kittering's translator declared.

"Drank too much," Kris added.

"Couldn't keep money," Idris rounded up.

Rollo nodded, satisfied conventions were being followed. "My son, he was, my brother. Loyal to his ship and safe hands. Died in orbit—who should have died in space where he belonged. One of ours, he was."

And they chorused, "One of ours," with Solace a beat behind, caught out.

"Asset Medvig 99622," the captain went on. "Instanced 116 After and provided to us under a medium-duration leash contract out of Peace Hive Three."

"Bad sense of humour," Kris said.

"Finicky stand-offish type," Idris followed.

"Never put my stuff back where it belonged," growled Olli.

"Very expensive to maintain," Kit contributed.

"My children, they were, and comrades," Rollo said. "Good company and safe hands. Died amongst us, who should have gone back to their own, but they were ours."

"They were ours," the chorus came back to Rollo, and Kris saw tears making their tortuous way down the creases on his face.

Safe hands. For Colonial spacers, whose lives were strung from one mechanical failure to the next, for whom there would never be enough replacement parts and every little thing might be made to serve as something else just to get them into port, it was the greatest valediction.

"Now," Rollo said quietly, hands on the table. "In this time of grief, I have a favour to ask of you, my daughter." And he looked Kris in the eye.

"Oh, I know," she agreed. "I'm on it, Captain. I will find out who the hell those waste-makers were."

Rollo's smile was bleak. What, after all, could they do with the information? A handful of spacers who didn't even have a ship...But if all they could do was spread word to their peers, they'd do that.

Kris stood to go, shaking her sleeve slightly to make sure her duelling knife was hanging right. For a moment she thought to ask Solace to accompany her. You couldn't get better backup than a Partheni soldier. The woman looked distracted, though, and Kris wondered if she was planning to leave them soon. Instead she glanced at Olli.

"Oh yes," the remote specialist said. "Wouldn't miss it."

"Bring the Scorpion," Kris told her. "Stay back, don't loom, but bring it." And if they actually met any of the symbiont's confederates, Olli would ensure they properly rued the day.

Kris had done this sort of thing before. It was a development of the work she'd carried out as a student lawyer back on Scintilla, when the thought of a spacer's life would have set her laughing hysterically. Students did the beat work on senior advocates' cases, investigating witnesses, digging up dirt...which meant getting their hands dirty. She hit the Lung-Crow's kybernet with her credentials until she found a way in, then set automated seekers into the station's records. Next, she and Olli went around the docks, talking to spacers and the orbital's ground crew. Where people recognized her ship name, she took their sympathy and used it ruthlessly. The rest of the time she played whatever role seemed most apt: creditor, debtor, abandoned lover, old friend. Always her queries circled the identity of the Tothiat, perhaps a Tothiat who palled around with a vermiform Castigar with a beweaponed headmount.

The station records gave her some detail on Tothiats as a class, none of it good. They were from the Hegemony; the actual Tothir, the insect-thing, was technically a subject race of the Essiel. You didn't see them much outside a fishtank off-world, because they were very dependent on their planet's chemistry. However, the Essiel had many ingenious subordinates, and someone had felt it worth putting a great deal of effort into giving the nasty little critters the freedom of the universe. The solution had been to graft Tothir to other creatures—modified to produce the toxic chemicals the things needed. The results, so she read, had gone some way beyond the Hegemonic scientists' intentions. What came off the surgeon's table was neither host nor implant, but a conglomerate personality—seamlessly mixing both. Unsurprisingly, there were few volunteers for the process. On the other hand, Kris discovered grimly, the resulting hybrid had considerable conscious control over the host body's metabolism. The merged creature could push itself far past its usual limits, and repair damage very swiftly. They could even survive hard vacuum for an uncomfortably long period of time.

A super-symbiont. Great.

Kris had never expected to end up here, not the young Keristina Soolin Almier who'd won a scholarship to the law schools of Scintilla. She'd been brought up within the Harmaster asteroid belt, home to colossal resource-stripping factories. Her parents had been members in good standing with the Iron Co-ops, whose collective bargaining and strict union lines had turned poverty and hard graft into relative comfort and affluence by the time Kris was born. Harmaster ex-pats were turning up all over the Colonies by then, bringing their work ethics and Iron Coin bursaries with them. That had been enough to get her onto Scintilla. A lucrative white-collar future had beckoned.

Scintilla was ... difficult, though. The planet was old-money rich, like Magda. It had the old families to go with it, those left to their own devices since before Earth fell. It was a cold world, with cities carved into the sides of snow-swept mountains. The older students stalked the sparse, high halls of its best law college in black furs. Their junior assistants wore monkish robes and were forbidden to talk in the corridors. And then there was the duelling. It was constrained by all manner of legal restrictions, but students were expected to argue their way out of any repercussions if caught carrying the knife—that was part of the training. And if you didn't carry the knife, you weren't anyone. You could buy the knives legally, train openly, and everyone obsessed over the careers of the top fighters. Even the tutors. They harangued their classes on the evils of the atavistic and reprehensible practice, yet their eyes twinkled in encouragement even as they lectured. And it was hardly ever fatal these days.

Kris had picked up the knife because it was plain she'd never walk in the right circles unless she did. She held on to it because she found she loved it. Not the spilled blood— especially if it was hers—but everything else. It was a stupid aristocratic piece of bravado yet she turned out to be very good at it. Up to and including the point where she found her knife painted with the life's blood of a very promising young boy of very good family.

It hadn't been the legalities that got her, of course. She'd argued her way out of those in a way that would have made her tutors proud. But the family, they wouldn't forget. Vendetta was a serious business amongst the legal dynasties of Scintilla. Life gave her two choices then. Get off-planet or spend her days fending off challenges and assassins. She often wondered if she'd made the right choice. Especially now, shipless and penniless.

"We know this individual." Her benefactor, after a morning's enquiries, was a Hiver. This one resembled a metre-tall bird cage with six evenly spaced legs and not even the pretence of a head. They were an asset leased to the station dock crew and Kris suspected they didn't socialize with their human peers much. "We hear he killed your companions."

"Two crew down and our ship gone," she confirmed. "And we've no idea who they were."

"The absence of knowledge is a wound that will not heal." This Hiver's designation was Yuri, just another random label plucked from a list somewhere. "Of course I am not permitted to provide you with confidential station records, under the terms of my contract." Their voice vibrated reedily from the cage of their body. She could see a host of little insects within, whose constant communion produced the conscious entity that called itself Yuri.

"Well, look," Kris told them. They were in an abandoned cargo bay, next to a tangle of wiring that the Hiver was desultorily repairing. "I can probably work up a good legal argument for why we're entitled to this information, then spend all day getting it past the kybernet and station admin," she said. "Or I could find the shady outfit I damn well know exists somewhere on board, and have them hack the system. But I'd rather take the Largesse my factor has made available and transfer it to you. You can't tell me you don't have your own account separate from your leash."

Yuri managed a creditable chuckle. "We won't do it for the money," they said. "Although we *will* take the money, just to clarify. However, we will do it for your loss. We have looked you up on the Tally. Your Asset spoke highly of you."

Kris went still, parsing that. Yes, Hivers kept a record of who did right by them and who did not. She hadn't ever thought of Medvig doing that. But that was because, to her, Medvig had been people.

"Your Tothiat goes by the name of Mesmon. He shipped in aboard the *Sark*. The *Sark* itself departed peaceably after your ship was taken. Not connected by security with the theft. Mesmon seems a spacer freelancer. But, to one who has worked here under leash for many years, patterns become clear. He is a sworn man with the Broken Harvest Society."

"Ah," said Kris heavily, taking that in. *The mob.*

She had been expecting Nativists maybe, opposing Sathiel's cult. Perhaps even Hugh spooks. Yet the *Vulture God* had been stolen from them by actual thieves.

It was nothing personal, was her guess. Nobody on the crew had tangled with the Broken Harvest as far as she was aware. She set her covert search agents in motion once more and precious little they brought back was good. It looked as though Broken Harvest operated in the Hegemony as much as in the Colonies. If they'd taken their prize across the border— or rather, deeper into Hegemonic space, now—the *Vulture's* crew would be powerless to intervene.

She took a meagre lunch with Olli in a nearby canteen and went over what she'd found. The remotes specialist nodded, her capsule opened up so she could feed herself with the Scorpion's smaller arms.

"Where's the *Sark* out of?"

"Registered in a place called G'murc or something, in the Hegemony. Not that it means anything," Kris told her.

Olli frowned, chewing mechanically. "And if we knew where they'd gone? What then?"

"Depends where that was. Maybe we could…go after them. Book passage there? I don't know. If we wanted to butt heads with Broken Harvest, anyway."

"Rollo would," Olli decided. "Rollo is pissed. Don't know

if it's the ship or Barney and Med, but he's in a mood to cut the throat of God if he has to. What about you?"

Kris blinked at her. "The throat of God?"

"Or this Mesmon triggerman, anyway. Are you ready to do the same?"

Kris felt within and found the same urge that had led to her carrying the knife on Scintilla—now tempered and hardened by two dead friends. "Maybe," she allowed.

"Then let me link to the station and I'll show you a trick." Olli gave her a fierce smile.

It was simple, really. Kris almost laughed when she found out. It was the packet trade. Everyone carried news, after all. That was how word travelled from one planet to another through unspace. Everyone made a little money on the side by downloading encrypted communications to deliver at their destination. But to do so, you had to say where you were going.

The *Vulture God* had obviously not taken on packets in its violent exit from Lung-Crow. On the other hand the *Sark*, given its innocent departure, had. It was just what you did when you travelled, natural as breathing, second nature to any crew.

The *Sark* crew had taken on the packet for Tarekuma. Maybe it had been an elegant piece of misdirection. Maybe they weren't even heading for the same destination as the stolen *Vulture*, but it was all they had to go on.

10.

Havaer

New screens lined the corridors leading from the passenger bays. Kicking his heels at Lung-Crow customs, Havaer had plenty of time to see twenty different pundits making hay over the flight of the *Vulture God*. Some of the talking heads claimed the ship's captain was responsible, but the prevailing opinion was that parties unknown had hijacked the *Vulture God* and vanished it away.

There were several recordings that certainly seemed to show an Architected wreck clutched in the *Vulture*'s claws. And there was some panic, but there was also denial. Nobody wanted to admit what everyone was thinking. So: a fragile calm prevailed at Lung-Crow. No screaming exodus yet. In fact, now the planet was under Hegemony rule, maybe prices for a berth *to* Huei-Cavor would be climbing...Public opinion might sway towards the Essiel—here and elsewhere—when this news spread.

All the more reason to find the truth about the wreck.

At last Havaer was let through and he dusted off his credentials as mediotype opinionator, under which guise the office supplied a handful of articles a month below his byline.

Later that same day, having pulled some local strings, he

met with His Wisdom the Bearer Sathiel. The man was urbane, grandfatherly and opulently dressed, surrounded by worshipful followers. He clasped Havaer's bony arm warmly, in the Colonial fashion, as they ordered a cup of the Caffenado that humans drank in the Hegemony. It tasted like the best parts of coffee, lemon and almonds.

Havaer gave the man his attentive smile and decided he didn't trust Sathiel an inch, but then the whole cult business gave him the creeps. To his mind, inventing a religion venerating extraterrestrial barnacles was a ludicrous response to meeting an alien species. Except, he admitted, it did seem to provide a framework for human–Essiel interactions.

"You've been very vocal about the *Oumaru* rumours, Your Wisdom," he commented diplomatically, channelling his persona of highbrow mediotype reporter. They were in a small eatery, and most patrons were wearing cult heraldry— from a simple badge to full-on robes like Sathiel. Havaer's long-sleeved charcoal tunic, trousers and slip-ons were standard kit for someone out of the richer settled colonies, but in this mish-mash place, he stood out amongst both the spacers and Hegemonic types.

Sathiel lifted his beaker. "Caffenado," he breathed, as though the drink was rare and precious. "Serendipitous child of humans trying to adapt coffee to the soil of an alien world. Now one of the most widely partaken-of beverages known. A major import into the Colonies, as doubtless you're aware. And war-caste and breeder-caste Castigar can't get enough of it—which is an unlooked-for benefit. Goes to show what can arise, when humanity travels to the stars and welcomes the alien with open hands."

Havaer tried his smile again and made notes on his slate.

"Well, Your Wisdom, you'll understand that I'm not really here as a potential convert."

The cultist nodded understandingly. "My point, Menheer Mundy, is that there are those, even here, who don't drink Caffenado because of what it represents. Especially here. There are those who would do everything in their power to throw up hard barriers between humanity and its neighbours. Even if they have to murder their own to do it."

Havaer blinked, nodded, noted, the whole act. "*Alleged* proof that the Architects have returned has been taken from us—by unknown persons for unknown reasons. But are you... making specific accusations here, Your Wisdom?"

Sathiel's pleasant smile broadened and he looked down into the dark liquid before sipping. "I'd risk giving you, a mediotypist from the inner Colonies, something you cannot use... Your audience being less *pro-alien* than some?"

"My audience is cosmopolitan," Havaer assured him. "I mean, I'm no fool, I can see this could be controversial. If we hinted that humans tried to hide evidence of Architects, for selfish reasons. No doubt we'd get lots of angry responses, but that won't be the majority. I cater to an open-minded base."

"Well then, let me be frank. There would be nothing more fatal to the Nativist, pro-human bloc than proof that the Architects have returned. Not only because the Divine Essiel have within their power the ability to protect entire worlds from their depredations, but simply because when the Architects were a present threat, that was when humanity existed hand in hand with our neighbours. Right now there are those in power who would rather push them all away. How would that be perceived, if there was a new Architect war on the horizon?" Sathiel fixed Havaer with a gaze that abruptly had all the grandfather sucked out of it, nothing but steel remaining. "My point, Menheer Mundy, is just that, and if you *do* pass this shocking news on to your audience, you'd be acting in their interests. I appreciate that people within the Colonies find all this…" he picked at his richly embroidered sleeve, "unsettling. Our ritual relationship to the Divine Essiel looks like idolatry, perhaps even brainwashing. But I'll let you into a secret, Menheer. I'm not religious, not in the way you probably believe. However, the Essiel have the power to accomplish things that, try as we might, humanity cannot replicate. Humanity cannot proof our worlds against the Architects, using Originator regalia. We might happen upon a planet with Originator ruins, allowing us to keep the monsters away from only that world. But the Hegemony can ward their worlds at will. And if the Architects come back, as I believe they *have*; if the Architects *keep* coming back, what is best for humanity? To ignore the rest of the galaxy and sing stories of our greatness, until our last world is just some monstrous sculpture commemorating our end? Or should we accept that we are not self-sufficient, and take the help offered—at what is a very reasonable price?"

Havaer recorded it all, thanked Sathiel profusely, and made his retreat. The Caffenado had been very good, he agreed. Hard not to develop a taste for it. Out of the cultist's presence, even he found himself a little shaken. Not a madman, Sathiel, but a persuasive one. It would be profoundly unfortunate should he turn out to be right. Like most Colonials, Havaer had no wish to be ruled by alien overlords. But better than dying.

After that, it was time to find the *Vulture God*'s disinherited crew. When he set out, he'd assumed the whole Architect business was a hoax and the *Vulture* crew was at the heart of it. Now, with two of them dead and their ship taken, he wasn't sure what to think.

Havaer's contacts eventually tracked them to a maintenance bay by the freight docks. It was a cavernous space with the stripped shells of two shuttles hanging overhead like whale carcasses. A Hannilambra Envoy-class craft sat below these on uneven legs, as half a dozen crablike aliens and eight station engineers tried to scavenge sufficient parts to fix her gravitic drive. At the back of the bay, sitting on dented crates, were three of the *Vulture God*'s survivors.

The broad man was their captain, Rostand. The Hannilambra was the factor. And the skinny youngster was their pilot, Telemmier, the Int. It set Havaer's teeth on edge to think of such a valuable asset rusting at the fringes of Colonial space, rather than serving Hugh.

Rostand glowered up at him as he arrived. "Are you Pilchern?"

From the man's expression, this Pilchern was going to have a bad day when he did turn up. For a moment Havaer considered saying yes and just winging it, but there were too many unknowns. "Captain Rostand, I'd like a moment of your time."

"You and every other fucker," Rostand growled. He was well on the way to drunkenness, Havaer decided: red eyes and a reddening face. Though there was likely grief involved, for his lost crew.

"I'm not rag," Havaer replied, which he hoped was still spacer slang for newsmongers. He'd decided to ditch his mediotype persona, as the crew hadn't given any interviews so far. He pulled out his Hugh Intervention Board ID, the real one, and triggered its authenticator with his thumb. The little square of plastic confirmed his biometrics and bona fides.

Rostand stared belligerently at it, then shrugged. "You're out of your jurisdiction. Or haven't you been keeping up with current affairs around here?" Spacers were notoriously prickly about Hugh interference, mostly because they were usually doing something illegal.

Havaer hooked over an empty box and sat down, smiling. "Captain, I've no official power here, no backup, just a man investigating. You can imagine what."

"Word gets to Mordant House quickly these days," said Telemmier, not looking at Havaer. He'd pulled into himself when the ID came out, and Havaer could understand that. Under other circumstances, the man would be the focus of any Mordant operation here.

"We heard you brought something in," Havaer said frankly. "Then I arrive to find it's been taken from you."

"Along with a lot else," Rostand spat. "What do you want from us, Menheer Spook? Confirmation that we found what they say we found? Yes. Verification that any proof disappeared with my damn ship? Yes again. So there we have it. That's all there is, see right?"

"You're Colonial citizens, you two." Havaer looked to Rostand and the Int, ignoring the Hanni for now.

"Doesn't mean we do what you say," rejoined the truculent Rostand. "'Specially not here."

"I'm just hoping you have some loyalty to the Council of Human Interests, being human," Havaer went on patiently. "I'm not trying to be Nativist, just concerned. If what you found really..."

Telemmier broke in. "It did happen. And it was recent. I expect you've seen the *Oumaru*'s departure logs. *Something* pulled her off course into the deep void and did...*that* to her."

Havaer tried to meet the man's gaze, but the Int's eyes just kept sliding away as though fixed on a distant horizon. Standard for Intermediaries, though. You couldn't see what they saw without developing the "abyssal gaze." "Menheer Telemmier, would you be willing to—"

"No."

"I haven't—"

"No, I will not come and answer your questions about what I might have sensed or not sensed, felt or not felt... in unspace or real space or in the reaches of my imagination," Telemmier told him flatly. "I don't do government work anymore. I've served. I've earned the right to be left alone."

Havaer hadn't quite believed the file on Idris Telemmier. Crossed wires, surely; couldn't be the same man. Not enough years on the face for a start. Must be some escapee from a leash contract, so technically still the property of the state... Except Havaer could look into those too-young features and see the extra decades lurking beneath the surface like a rot.

"I can promise you—"

"I'm not going back," Telemmier said and Havaer prepared to push the matter. He only caught the iron behind the words in retrospect, as Telemmier burst out again, "I'm *not going back!*" He stood so suddenly that he kicked over his crate, fists balled abruptly. The Int was the least imposing physical specimen Havaer had ever seen, a true child of the Polyaspora, but the air about him seemed to flex, and one of the gutted

147

shuttles above creaked warningly. A coincidence, it had to be just coincidence. But Telemmier was one of the oldest Ints out there, junior only to Saint Xavienne herself. Who knew what they might become, in time?

Havaer smiled at him, which was hard but he was practised. "Understood," he said easily. "I'll leave you with my details, in case you recall something and want to pass it on. Anything will help. This isn't about you, it's about saving lives. Anything..." He trailed off. A woman had joined them. Havaer put a great deal of effort into maintaining his mild, friendly expression.

She was Partheni. He noted the badges on her regulation grey overcoat, the service-and-loss tattoo beneath her eye. But he'd have known her without those signs. Soldiers of the Parthenon all had a certain look to them, literally: beautiful and deadly like highly polished knives.

He nodded cordially to her and stood. "Thank you for your time, Captain."

The Partheni was standing protectively by Telemmier, regarding Havaer with narrow-eyed belligerence. She didn't return the nod.

On his way out Havaer was already composing his report in his head. *Parthenon involvement, request further instructions.*

Idris

Colonial tradition was for grieving to be brief; the living needed to move on. It came from when the dead had outnumbered the living, and there just wasn't time for protracted mourning. And it wasn't as though the end of the war had cured death. Spacers died; they died hard and they still died often. They were the lifeblood of the human sphere, from the crews of the huge, dilapidated freighters whose timely arrival with holds of food was the difference between plenty and starvation, all the way down to the packet runners who carried nothing but information and barely stayed out of suspension for longer than it took to download. They died when life support failed; they died crazy in the deep void. They died when decades of careful maintenance ceased to be enough to hold their ageing ships together. They died on both sides of pirate actions, of hereditary conditions, in impromptu brawls in sordid brothels or orbital bars. And their friends moved on, but you couldn't move on without a ship to move you. Losing a ship was a disaster that you literally could only walk away from.

Kittering had been searching for opportunities for the crew all morning, without success. No vessel would take them on as a group. Rollo was fiercely adamant that he'd take nothing less than a share-holding second, and Idris privately thought that he wouldn't want to be the captain who took Rollo on as a subordinate.

At some point, Idris knew, the crew would simply part under the stress of the situation, so that they would all drift outwards and probably never meet again. He certainly wasn't going anywhere without Kris to fight for him. He felt a cold shiver at the thought that she might turn to safe work on-planet as an advocate. She'd been running a long time, after all.

Around that point the spook turned up, which didn't improve anybody's mood much. And Idris had over-reacted, of course. Too much stress and grief over too short a time.

He'd let himself off his own personal leash, and that always left him feeling tired and sick. Probably the man really wasn't here with ulterior motives but then Solace had arrived. He would worry, later, what conclusions the Mordant House man would draw about Partheni involvement; Hugh attention was never welcome. Yet right then he'd never been so glad to see anyone as he was to have Solace beside him, and the spook had cleared out almost immediately. Solace's proprietary air should have got on his nerves but, with Kris absent, he clung to the thought that *someone* was looking out for him. *That's wretched, Idris; just wretched.* But he felt rubbed raw, as though every new development was salt on open wounds.

"I thought you'd left, gone back to..." Rollo made a vague gesture, presumably intended to indicate the whole institution of the Parthenon.

"I've been seeing what I can do," Solace told him. "As a member of your crew."

"And are you? Still?"

She met his bleary-eyed belligerence head on. "Do you still *have* a crew?"

Rollo dropped his gaze first. "I don't know, my daughter."

"If you do, then I'm still on it. Until the next job, when we can negotiate all over again. And...I have something to say, but where are Kris and Olli?"

Rollo glanced at Kittering, whose screens informed them that they were inbound, with word.

Solace nodded. "Then let's hear what they have for us."

*

"My ship's headed for Tarekuma?" Rollo echoed, after Kris had rattled out their news. "That figures, my children." He sighed, and said again, "Tarekuma. It's a goddamn armpit."

"Explain?" Solace asked and Rollo rolled his eyes at her.

"Not having to know about or go to Tarekuma is a profound incentive to back the Parthenon." He rubbed at his face as though trying to scrub the alcohol out of his skin. "It's... a shit-hole, is what it is."

"Back Before," Kris filled in, "there were plans for a *big* colony there. It was going to be a grand terraforming venture. Rocky planet, bad chemistry, but they had all the time and money in the world, didn't they. And what the place did have was *location*. Seven Throughways meet at Tarekuma. Then the Architects happened, and then the war. Whole lot of refugees ended up in Tarekuma, because it was so easy to reach. What didn't end up there was money or terraforming kit. People came there from everywhere. Aliens too. Gangs, warlords, cults... They got the vertical cities running, bought atmosphere modifiers, kept out *most* of the bad wildlife. Even now, Hugh's got only the loosest grasp over what goes on down there."

"Way I hear it, that's how they like it," Olli put in sourly. "Gives Hugh a place to bend their own laws, gives their spies a place to meet other spies—all sort of shadowy ballsack stuff."

Kittering chittered, his screens responding to a query Kris had raised. She read off the information:

"There are maybe a hundred major players on Tarekuma and any number of off-world cartels and syndicates who've got fingers in the pie. The Broken Harvest are some kind of criminal enterprise from out of the Hegemony," Kris reported.

"Wouldn't have thought their perfect paradise-empire would have gangsters," Idris said mildly.

"I don't pretend to understand it myself," Kris replied, "but the Essiel have a strange attitude towards outlaws and crime. They hate it and openly fight lawbreakers, and yet it's also a recognized part of their system somehow. So, yes, the Broken Harvest are some mob out of the Hegemony. But if they're on Tarekuma, they obviously stray beyond its borders."

"So why," Rollo demanded ponderously, "do they want *my* ship?"

"Maybe we were just unlucky," said Olli. "Surely they want the *Oumaru*, not the *Vulture*? Plenty of people would pay to control that evidence, either hide it or shove it up a flagpole." Olli eyed Solace. "You fuckers, for instance?"

The Partheni met the accusation without a frown. "Honestly, not our style."

"Harvest'll have a sale lined up for the *Oumaru*, or maybe they'll auction it. But the *Vulture*... I mean, it's a decent ship, but it's not the prize. Maybe we could even buy it back off them, cut a deal—work for the mob to secure it?"

Idris looked from one to the other, seeing how Olli's suggestion sat. Not well, but not beyond anyone's personal morality, was his conclusion. During his years with the *Vulture* they'd never worked for criminals directly. But you might have only had to go one step down the chain to find dirty money. On the other hand, working for the Broken Harvest meant clasping wrists with Barney and Medvig's killers—not something to be done lightly.

The same dilemma had probably played out in Rollo's head, for he said, "We *could* go there... See if they haven't already sold or scrapped her. Work passage over to Tarekuma and see how things lie. And if there's a chance for revenge…" His face went hard at that thought. He could be a vengeful man. Dangerous waters, Idris knew. *Am I getting cold feet?* Icy cold. But he couldn't abandon his crewmates.

"Kit," said Rollo at last. "Hunt down berths Tarekuma-ways, as passengers or crew, whatever it takes." He looked round at them. "Anyone wants out, then get out, no hard feelings. For I am in a mood to do some truly stupid things."

Solace coughed slightly. "Idris?"

He looked at her warily, and for a long two seconds she just met his gaze. Then she asked, "How long does it take, to get from here to Tarekuma on the Throughways?"

Kit crabwised over, presenting a reckoner on one arm-screen and highlighting the most useful routes.

"Bear with me," Idris said, checking the displays. And then: "Can't get it down to under three days, by any route."

"And if you were to pilot us from here yourself, off piste?"

"Off…? You mean deep void?" He hadn't realized the Partheni had their own term. "Somewhere between nineteen and twenty-three ship hours." Meaning the hours old Earth had used.

Rollo grunted. "You think we can charter something?" He sounded dubious and Kittering was already cautioning about expense.

"Listen," Solace told them. "I want you all to come with me, right now. I want to show you something." She stood, and after a moment Rollo did too, and then Kris. Olli and Kit were already on their various feet. Solace looked at Idris, not a challenge so much as an entreaty. He shrugged, feeling tired and vaguely anxious about whatever the woman had in mind. *Whatever it is, I'm not going to like it.*

Solace took them towards the dock levels, a ring of small private jetties. The great and the good kept their launches and yachts here. Idris bleakly enjoyed the mortified looks they received from liveried technicians and flunkies, seeing this motley mob of spacers slouching through their pristine corridors.

And then they were at a door with two Partheni myrmidons outside, in full armour and armed with accelerators. The crew shrank back as one, fearing ambush, Kittering practically disappearing behind Rollo's legs. Solace just nodded to the soldiers and the women stepped smartly aside with a mutual "Myrmidon Executor."

Olli swore faintly, as the door slid open. "What treasonous shit have we gotten ourselves into?"

"No idea," Idris lied. He was half expecting to be grabbed and bagged right here, and the rest of them shot.

There was just one ship in the bay. It was a segmented teardrop, half the size of the *Vulture God* and entirely lacking in the thrown-together look that was practically Colonial aesthetic. Its surface was silvery, and some of the jutting nodules that flanked its nose were probably weapons.

There was a column of Parsef characters on the side, along with its company badges. Kittering's screens helpfully translated its name as the *Dark Joan*.

"What's this, my child?" Rollo asked cautiously.

"Captain Rostand, I have a proposal."

"Crew to captain, or Partheni to a poor Colonial?" His moustache bristled but his eyes kept sliding back to the *Dark Joan*.

"I went to the embassy," she told them all, and abruptly there was a distance between Solace and the rest of them, a gap of status as much as physical space. "This is one of our packet transport ships. I've requisitioned it."

They stared at her, or at least their stares were split between her and the shining perfection of the ship. "You mean," Kris said slowly, "you said, 'I want this ship' and they just...let you *have* it."

"*Borrow* it," Solace agreed. Her hands were wringing at each other. Idris wondered if she realized. Maybe Partheni didn't get nervous around each other, so she'd not had his practice in hiding it.

Rollo was suddenly very sober. "My daughter," he said flatly. "The guards called you 'Executor.' What *are* you?"

"Executors are trained to go outside the Parthenon sphere and...do what must be done."

"You're an assassin," Olli said flatly.

"Olli!" Kris reproached her. "She's, what, a spy? An agent?"

"An *agent*." Solace confirmed. "So when I say I need the use of a ship, I have a ship. Which, here, means *you* have a ship. If you want it. Now Idris can get to Tarekuma ahead of the *Vulture*—so you can get your ship back."

There was a long silence in response to that. It was Rollo who put all their feelings into words. "And *why* would you do such a thing, Honoured Executor?"

Solace licked her lips. She looked a decade younger than the captain, shorter, slighter of build. Idris had to remind himself that she was even older than he was and could likely kill the lot of them with her bare hands.

"Because it's in the interests of my government that I learn everything I can about the *Oumaru*. Getting to Tarekuma—and fast—is the first step in doing that." She swallowed. "And because I think you're good people."

Olli made a disgusted noise.

"Forgive me for saying this, my friend," Rollo said, with that polite distance he put between his crew and others, "but that does not sound very Partheni to me."

Solace's brow furrowed. "What's the Parthenon, Captain?" She seemed to have reluctantly accepted that distance. "How did we come about, do you know?"

"A bunch of clever women decided that they would go grow a whole load of other women in test tubes, because they hated men?" Olli said, going from a standing start to staggeringly undiplomatic in record time. "Wasn't that it?"

Rollo shot her a look, but Solace held up a hand.

"That's how the Nativists tell it. Maybe that's how they tell it all over the Colonies." She shrugged. "The Parthenon was founded because of good people. Parsefer and her fellows looked at the way Earth had gone and saw inequality, exploitation, divisions, hatred and ignorance. They wanted to start again and do better. And if you're boosting your population through vat-parthenogenesis, it's easier just to work with the female line." Idris reckoned that was both a simplified and sanitized explanation, but perhaps it was what Solace believed.

Olli scowled but Rollo glared at her.

"One last thing before we clasp arms on any deal, my friend. Why did you pretend to join my crew?"

For a fraction of a second Idris caught real hurt on Solace's face, before she covered it with her usual martial impassivity.

"I *did* join your crew, Captain. I worked my passage. But you're right, I had another motive too." She glanced at Idris, probably wondering if he was going to spill the beans. He wouldn't, he decided.

She pressed on anyway, laying it all bare. "I was sent to

make an offer to your pilot, on behalf of the Parthenon. An offer I *still* intend to make, when I can get him to take his fingers out of his ears for long enough. No doubt he'll say no, and that will be my duty done. Now the *Oumaru* is out there too, and that changes things. I am using my discretion right now, doing what I think is best while I wait for orders to reach me. But I also want you to get your ship back, because that is fair and just. Hence this." A flip of the hand towards the *Dark Joan*. "Take it or leave it, Captain. I'm going anyway. I won't say I don't care either way, but it's your choice."

Rollo looked at his crew. Kittering was displaying "44%" which suggested he was ambivalent in the extreme and Olli was looking outright angry. Kris was nodding, though, and Idris found himself agreeing. Left with the casting vote, Rollo let out a deep breath.

"Then, my friend, we would be delighted to get our asses over to Tarekuma as fast as Idris can plot the course there. Assuming our asses will even fit in that pint pot thing of yours."

Idris felt a rush of excitement. It would be grand to steal a march on the hijackers. But he was mostly thinking that he'd never, in all his days, flown a ship as elegant as the *Dark Joan*.

PART 3
TAREKUMA

11.

Idris

Monitor Joy, the Partheni's stern diplomat, looked as though she might be Solace's aunt, though she had likely been born at least a decade afterwards. And the close-mouthed Partheni technician, who came to perform some last-minute modifications to the *Dark Joan*, might have been the Executor's younger sister. Her expression showed a marked difference, though; she didn't approve of a pack of ruffians commandeering their ship. Still, she was plainly in awe of Solace and worked for two hours to get everything flight-ready.

The Partheni packet transport was indeed short on space. There were six suspension beds in a central stack within the ring of the gravitic drive, and the pilot's seat was hard back against them. There was nowhere to be except the actual beds. Hold space was almost entirely filled by some new gear of Solace's and Olli's Scorpion frame. The packet transport was intended to lug data, after all, not goods. Idris wondered if Mordant House knew the things could be fitted out as emergency squad transport at a pinch.

"Reminds you of wartime?" Solace asked, at his elbow. "Berlenhof?"

"I think we had more space in wartime."

"*You* did. You were never in the racks. Picture something like this," she tapped the cluster of pods, "but for a hundred people at a time. Civilians had luxury accommodation."

"I never knew. Although I'd have been too busy being scared out of my mind to appreciate it." He tried to look at her properly and still couldn't, not quite. "Thank you, by the way," he mumbled.

"Hm?"

"For helping. For the ship. Getting us to... The others probably won't say it."

"I've heard all the things they say about my people across the Colonies, Idris. Probably they think I'm a monster who'll come and kill their menfolk and make regular humanity a footnote in our triumphal histories, right? Or else we're sex-starved sirens who just need to meet a good man to forswear all our Amazon ways."

"You've seen some mediotypes," he observed.

"Executor training means exposure to some weird stuff. I'd rather have stayed a simple myrmidon."

Idris cocked an eye at her, squinting sidelong. Something about her was still too much like staring into the sun, and he was worried that it was because he liked her. "Why'd you go for it, then?" And, in the blank pause that question evinced, he realized, "You didn't, did you? They just told you. Why? Not just for me?"

She shrugged. "*Probably* not just for you. The Aspirat does some pretty twisty thinking sometimes. I think it was because I'd been through the war, so I'd met people from outside the Parthenon." She was closed-up, abruptly, hugging her own arms. "Seems kind of mad that being a soldier made me right for something completely different."

"Myrmidon Executor." The technician came out of the *Dark Joan*. "Prêt à combattre." She cast what Idris could only characterize as a scandalized look towards Rollo and the crew.

Solace nodded, which turned out to be a dismissal because the younger woman left the bay immediately, ceding the field.

"It's time." Myrmidon Executor Solace turned to the crew. "Everyone on board and in the..." She stopped herself and visibly reconsidered her approach. "Captain Rostand. Your ship is ready."

Rollo's truculent expression softened by a hair. "Thank you, my good benefactor." He put his nose through the hatch, clucked at the cramped conditions. "Get yourselves to bed, my children. Not much else for it."

They filed aboard, and Kris stopped to put a strengthening hand on Idris's arm. He found a smile for her, from somewhere, and watched her pull herself up into the *Joan's* confines.

"You and her?" Solace asked him. Idris felt his expression turn wary again, but there didn't seem any hidden rocks to the question. Seeing his look, she waved away an answer. "Just thinking you'd be lucky. Definitely outranks you, that one." Her grin was natural, far too young for her—the way she'd smile with her Partheni comrades perhaps. Then she'd taken his elbow and boosted him up. He took the aid automatically, without flinching, but once in the pilot's seat a moment later, he wondered *What just happened?* Solace was already behind him, getting into one of the top pods. Then she paused and leaned over:

"You remember how it all...?" Sudden chagrin showed on her face. "Do you need me to take you through..."

"I recognize most of this from the *Pythoness*." The Partheni console had a dozen small screens, each devoted to separate metrics, and he looked them over one by one. Two were military enough that he felt he didn't need to worry about them.

"You didn't fly the *Pythoness.*"

"Who do you think got her back to *Heaven's Sword* at Berlenhof?" He felt his hands shake a little with the thought.

Solace must have seen it. "You're good, Idris?"

He was silent, staring at the controls. They were a clear evolution from those he remembered from the war, but he could do this. Eventually he said, in a small voice, "I'll be fine."

The *Dark Joan* slipped from Lung-Crow Orbital like the dreams of a fish, as the saying went. It was swift and subtle, its departure cloaked by whatever standing arrangement the Parthenon had with the kybernet. Idris checked the sleep pods' vitals and threw the gravitic drive into a low activity cycle, extending its shadow into unspace to plot out the conditions. From there, he could calculate their departure from real space.

He glanced back at the neat rack of suspension pods behind him. Four occupied, two empty, plus the incompatible aesthetics of Kit's garish red globe sticking out like a sore thumb. Then he had committed them, and the *Dark Joan* fell into the liminal void beyond the real.

It hadn't been like this on the *Pythoness.* He'd been surrounded by motion: running women performing desperate triage on the vessel's abused systems. There'd been blaring alarms and rapid orders-and-confirmations in Parsef—all as the vessel unleashed its weapons against the unthinkably vast face of the Architect. The pilot's chair had been sunk partway into the floor there too, because even a Parthenon warship held space at a premium. The body of the original Partheni pilot, and a good dozen other casualties, had been hauled away with grim efficiency. Idris had dropped into the vacant seat as though this was some bizarre dream. His elbows had been tucked in, his shoulders hunched forwards to avoid the women's booted feet. He'd been glad that he was smaller even than the average Colonial starveling. All around him the injured vessel lurched and bucked, its brachator drive clutching at the gravitic substructure of real space for purchase. And beyond their hull the colossal, invisible hand of the Architect was reaching—deforming space as it tried to remake its enemy.

The *Dark Joan* was not the *Pythoness*, of course, but her controls and the cramped pilot's seat recalled the old wartime vessel to him; the appalling chaos of their flight from the Architect, after the ship was crippled and half her crew killed. And then he was in unspace, strapped down tight and utterly alone with all those bad memories. The remembered Architect to one side, and to the other, patiently biding its time, the Presence had been waiting for him.

It was going to be a long trip through the deep void.

Kris

"You look rough." Kris was understating the case, but dealing with Idris in this kind of state was always hard. Honestly, he looked like he'd been disinterred, standing in the close-walled orbital dock outside the *Dark Joan* with his hands in his pockets and his shoulders bowed. His skin looked pallid and clammy as he used his slate as a mirror, propped against the curve of the Partheni ship's hull. He was lasering away a shadow of stubble, which would be back within a few hours.

"Where have you brought us, my boy?" Rollo stretched and rolled his shoulders. Olli was having the Scorpion lift her into its cradle.

"Some kind of Partheni channel opened up, when we quit unspace," Idris mumbled. "Set a beacon for us to dock here. I mean, Tarekuma's not the safest place to just hang about in orbit."

"This is our safehouse." Solace had unpacked new armour and was adjusting the fit of individual sections, using an interface on her slate. The gear was devoid of company badges this time. She had a new accelerator weapon, too; Tarekuma had no interest whatsoever in restricting the arms its visitors carried. "There's no embassy here, but there are groups we just about trust to do business with us."

"Even the great Parthenon gets its fingers dirty, eh?" Olli remarked. Kris shot her a look. Back when Solace had first showed, everyone had been prickly with her, but Olli seemed determined to carry on the feud, even though they were relying on Solace bending the rules for their benefit. Kris wasn't sure why, but *something* about Solace had got under the woman's skin.

The Partheni just shrugged. "From here, it's your play."

"On our own now, is it?" Rollo chewed at his moustache. "Well, you've done right by us, my friend. We owe you—"

"No," Solace broke in. "You don't understand. I will continue to back you. I just don't know what should come next. I don't know how this place works."

"Leave that to me," Kris broke in. "Me and Kit, anyway. Ready to spend some credits?"

The Hannilambra threw up some obscene human images from his library, showing exactly what he thought of that. But he displayed their Largesse account anyway. "All spending kept to a minimum!" came the translation, after some fiddling of his arms. "Do not negatively impact my retirement fund!" Which sounded funny but really was a matter of life and death to the Hanni.

They were docked at one of the elevator orbitals that ringed Tarekuma's equator. The planet's actual surface was harsh: scoured by radiation, high winds and without enough atmospheric pressure for unprotected humans. Ancient geological tumult had left Tarekuma riven with chasms, some up to five kilometres deep. The air was thicker there and conditions were more conducive to both native and visiting life. A dozen cities across the planet were built into the walls of these rifts, extending deep into the rock for vast vertical distances. Each habitation was home to millions of humans and other species, living like termites in constant close proximity. They were linked over the surface to the various elevator cables where the ground-based factions jealously controlled access to orbit. All real business had to be done planetside, no matter how inconvenient that was for anyone up above. It was just about the only thing every gang leader and petty overlord agreed upon. Orbitals that tried to cheat them were disciplined with extreme prejudice.

What Kris *could* do from here in orbit was research her quarry. She could also make some initial overtures, and for that she'd need to spend a little of Kit's "retirement fund." Nobody here was going to help her out of the goodness of their hearts. Not even Prosecutor Thrennikos, who was practically an old friend. She'd crashed out of Scintilla's Inns of Court, barely snagging her credentials as she ran out of the door. But Livvo Thrennikos hadn't even managed to qualify, after they'd caught him stuffing bribes into his pockets with both hands. However, Tarekuma didn't care about official credentials—only malign ability. The place was a weird sort of meritocracy like that. So it was that her old friend had somehow ended up here, with a hastily conferred practising certificate from a Tarekuman law school that probably hadn't existed five minutes beforehand. Then Thrennikos had been put to work to magically transform the underhand into the legitimate.

He took her comms call readily enough. She was expecting... she didn't know what, to be honest. It had been years. Would he have grown bloated and corrupt with over-fine living, or maybe have an eyepatch and a cybernetic hand? As it happened, Prosecutor Livvo Thrennikos looked far better than she expected. His long-chinned, dark face had grown prosperously fleshy without losing its strength, and he was sporting a moustache of remarkable curling richness. His eyes lit up when he saw her, which was reassuring. Maybe he wouldn't fleece them too much for his services.

"Nalsvyssnir Orbital, no less?" he exclaimed, seeing where she was transmitting from. "What brings you to my humble hemisphere, Kerry?" Because back on Scintilla they'd put the stress on the first syllable of Keristina, so the name had worn down differently on repeated use.

"Information, introductions..."

"Setting up business here?" He raised an eyebrow and flashed brilliantly white teeth.

"Would it threaten you if I did?" Despite herself, she smiled back at him. He'd always been utterly amoral, and she guessed that hadn't changed. He'd definitely been more fun than her fellow students...in a variety of interesting ways. Wouldn't bring the price down, but she found herself wondering if he'd make a nice diversion, once the current problems were sorted out?

"Come work with me," he said, apparently sincere and without hesitation. Kris found herself genuinely touched.

"Tempting," she replied. "But my ship's captain has a Tarekuman issue...and we're here to sort it out."

"That covers a lot of ground. Is this the sort of issue that leaves bodies?"

"God, I hope not," she said honestly enough. *No more than we've had already.* "We need contacts, and we need an introduction. Beyond that we'll sort ourselves out, no dirt on your doorstep, Liv. Can you help?"

"Let me look at you." And he did for a while, and she wondered about him. Was he married? With children? How much of a life could you carve out, on a planet splintered into gang territories and ruled by criminal fiefdoms? Probably quite a good one, if you were careful. At last he smiled, a little sadly. "Who are you in the shit with, Kerry?"

"Hopefully, nobody. But we need to talk to Broken Harvest."

His face went into professionally blank mode as he thought about that. Likely Thrennikos had no direct links with the Harvest, given how many factions had a stake on Tarekuma. But he'd know *someone*, or someone who knew someone. Or he'd sell Kris and her crew out to them. She was banking a lot on their old association.

"That should be possible." His professional face was still on, but he was nodding. "They're Hegemonic, which makes it hard to get to them directly. But I can scare up a minister to make the necessary introductions. That do you?"

"That would be perfect."

"There's the small matter of—"

"Our factor will liaise on the fee, both yours and this minister's."

"You're fine with coming down the line for the meeting? They like their face-to-face contact here..."

"I know," she confirmed. "It'll be good to see you again, Liv."

After that, the crew had a near-ludicrous argument about who was going to the surface. Kris said it would be just her and Kit, but Rollo said if he didn't get to save his own ship, no one was going. Then Rollo wanted Solace along in case it was a trap. Olli said that she wasn't going to just wait around with Idris. Even Idris was riled by then, and said he'd just been alone in unspace and wouldn't repeat the experience in orbit. Kris brought the whole business full circle, saying that if they appeared on Thrennikos's doorstep mob-handed he'd probably call the authorities. And given this was Tarekuma, those would basically be trigger-happy criminals. So Kris decreed that she, Rollo and Kit would go, and everyone else could loiter in the neighbourhood.

Thrennikos's offices were a quarter of the way across the planet in Coaster City, so they all piled back into the ship. Kittering took over the comms and fielded what must have been twenty different demands for ID and tolls, from whichever groups controlled individual slices of sky. Some were paid and some weren't, based on what Kit could glean about their relative status.

Thrennikos had recommended a planetside dock where they could be relatively sure the ship would still be there on their return. On arrival, Solace activated all the security the

Dark Joan had, though Kris reckoned that Tarekuma's best ship-thieves could outplay the order-loving Parthenon's locking systems. Kit grudgingly pledged some Largesse to the dock owner for added surveillance, and Olli left a camera remote on watch. Other than that, they'd just have to hope that Thrennikos was as good as his word.

On Tarekuma, the poorest districts were closest to the inhospitable surface. High-speed elevators conducted the better class of criminal into the chasm, where radiation was less of a threat and the air actually filled the lungs. So it was, in that first trip, they didn't see much of Coaster City's worst side. In fact, the law and order of the docks and the glitzy retail outlets they passed were as civilized as anything Kris had seen.

With Thrennikos vouching for them, they got to use the scenic elevator. The clear-walled car rushed them down an inertially dampened rail, on the outside of Coaster City, with a view of the local flora and fauna. Tarekuma's macro-biology flourished within the chasms, simultaneously reaching for and shrinking from the solar radiation above. What they saw looked like something from a children's story, where a gem merchant had planted his stock and found it growing in the morning. Vines crawled up the chasms' sides in a riotous profusion, budding and fruiting with faceted nodules. Leaf-like plates spread to sieve the distant sunlight, which fell in increasingly impoverished rainbows to the tiers below. Kris saw mobile life there, too—jewelled beetle-forms and lurching baubles with a spidery legspan of ten metres or more. Nothing looked familiar or even organic.

Here and there were cages, half hidden in creeping foliage that writhed visibly. Many of the governing gangs and cartels

171

liked to make a public show of their displeasure. Most of the human body couldn't be metabolized by the native life, but salt and water were potent lures. It wasn't the animals that got you, she understood, but the diamond-sharp tips of the questing vines.

What lovely places we end up visiting.

Within Livvo Thrennikos's reception rooms there was a good span of armoured glass looking onto exactly the same vista, but he was low enough down the chasm that noon outside looked like twilight, and the whole serpentine jungle glowed and glinted with a constellation of gleaming bio-luminescence. It really was very pretty, if you could forget its lethal potential.

The remaining crew had found a fairly genteel eatery where they could wait. They departed grumbling that they couldn't afford to eat there, but Kris's waspish thought was that it had been their choice to come in the first place.

The life of a Tarekuman Prosecutor agreed with Livvo, Kris had to admit. He was wearing a suit cut in the Berlenhof style, with plenty of pleating and wide sleeves. Tarekumans valued show, though, so instead of drab-yet-expensive greys, Thrennikos wore russet, with lines of gems set into lapels and cuffs. Kris would have preferred to dress up as well, but her wardrobe had gone with the rest of the *Vulture God*.

Livvo met her with a fond smile and a wrist-clasp that became a brief slapping match as each went to tug the collar of the other. An old student habit from Scintilla, where your honours grade was worn as a coloured flash at the throat. Despite his years of easy living, he actually beat her to it but paused, hand on her scarf. He was one of the few people who knew why she wore it.

She stretched up on her toes and lightly kissed his cheek. Then he ushered the three of them into his office, making sure everyone got a good gawk at another glimmering view.

A table had been set with finger-food for three humans and two Hanni. The minister they'd come to meet was already seated, one of Kit's conspecifics rolling a few nuts around the tabletop with his smaller mandibles. Kris had to stop herself staring, because this was a *rich* Hannilambra, and she hadn't seen many of those on the spacer circuit. His shell was encrusted with organic gems in complex, spiralling patterns. A half-dozen bejewelled critters, the size and shape of human thumbs, were tethered to his shield arms with gold chains. They were in constant motion across these armoured surfaces, scattering the light with their faceted backs.

"Advocate Almier," Livvo introduced Kris. "And Captain Rostand, Factor Kittering, this is Minister Shreem." And with that he had earned his payment, save for a little light hosting and pouring the wine. Kris considered that although he'd been kicked out of the Scintilla law schools, while she'd left with her dignity intact, Thrennikos had certainly landed on his feet.

Minister Shreem's legs chirped and rattled against each other, and a translator bobbing on the swag of his soft belly said, "I am, of course, delighted to make your acquaintance. I wish you all prosperous endeavours." The voice was an old man's, rich and husky with a slow, assured cadence. Kris wondered how much he'd paid for it. "Now I understand that you're desirous of an introduction."

"To Broken Harvest," Rollo broke in. "A matter of some urgency, my friend."

Shreem settled lower on his stool by a delicate rearrangement of his six legs. His quintet of eyes gazed calmly at Rollo, the spikes above them capped by a jewelled diadem. Minister Shreem, it seemed, did not wish to be hurried.

Then Kit chirped something, and the minister shifted again, leaning forwards. There was a staccato exchange, mostly shorn of any context Kris could follow. Kittering seemed to be bragging about something, or at least he was raising his shield arms. This generally meant a Hanni was establishing his credentials in some way. Then the two of them just left the table and went to play Landstep on a virtual board projected by the minister from one of his gem clusters.

Rollo and Livvo seemed equally wrong-footed by this, but the Hanni were a competitive species amongst their own kind. Kris had seen business deals concluded over wrestling matches, impenetrable puzzles and even dance-offs. The Hanni didn't wage war, funnelling all their disagreements into a myriad of contests.

That left the three humans to make small talk for an hour, as the Hanni became more and more absorbed in their tournament. Kris kept casting a worried eye over, in case Kit was wagering anything they couldn't do without. But his screens were cagily blank as he placed his tiles with rapid assurance.

Livvo dropped more than one hint that Kris could leave the spacer life for a while. Perhaps come and do business with him—or partner up in other ways...He was in a stable relationship with two other men and a woman, with three children between them, but there was always room for more. It was the sort of communal arrangement that had become common After Earth, when families had been shattered and people clung to and nurtured whoever they could find. To her surprise, Kris found the idea of settling down not quite the anathema she'd have thought. But she wasn't ready to quit spacefaring just *yet*.

"You've got a good thing going on here, Liv," she said, surprised at the envy in her voice.

"There's always a better thing." And he rested two fingers on her hand, just lightly.

Rollo coughed loudly and Kris shot him a testy look. Thankfully, at that point the game broke up. Kit's screens showed a cascade of bright colours and images that looked triumphant. Kris glanced worriedly at Shreem, in case Kittering had caused offence. The minister seemed entirely satisfied by the clash.

"A price has been agreed," Shreem's old man voice announced, and Kris assumed Kit's Landstep prowess had earned a discount. "Captain Rostand, given your urgency, is it convenient for contact to be made with the Harvest's factor immediately?"

Rollo nodded vigorously.

"You must understand that there are many layers of hierarchy within the Harvest, as with the Essiel," Shreem went on pedantically. "Navigation through lower ranks will be required before meeting some mid-grade overseer. Who might or might not have sufficient authority to make a contract. You may find the process aggravatingly drawn out." All said with grinding slowness and no apparent irony.

"All the more reason to get started," Rollo replied through clenched teeth.

Kris checked in with the others while she waited, and Rollo started to pace.

Then Minister Shreem made a surprised sound, like a string

section thrown into disarray, and scuttled in a backwards circle. It was a display of discombobulation she'd never seen in a Hanni before.

"Hold on," she told Idris over the comms. "Something's happened."

"Well?" Rollo demanded of the minister. "What, then? Some flunky will see us at his own damn leisure?"

"The matter has developed in an entirely different direction." Shreem's artificial voice sounded calm but his limbs were flurrying with agitation. "Invitation is made to the court of Aklu himself—Aklu being the title of the Harvest's undisputed ruler. You are going straight to the top."

12.

Kris

This is not going to get weird.

The word from Aklu's minions was that Rollo should bring someone to speak for him. The Hegemony firmly believed that leaders had menials to do the talking for them. Kris volunteered for the honour. It was, after all, her job. Kit handled the money, she handled the people.

There is no reason this has to be weird.

She'd sat with urbane killers in tailored shirts with ruffled fronts, who had sipped from tiny glasses and talked theatre and ballet engagements while ordering the deaths of faithless minions and minor civic functionaries. They'd liked her, overall. She knew the line they wanted women to tread.

She'd gone before a broken-nosed man whose huge frame was fifty per cent augmented artificial muscle. He'd conducted business at an arena, so he could watch his stable of gladiators tearing apart robots and sometimes each other. That had gone okay too. She knew a thing or two about the fighters' form, and that had endeared her to the man.

She'd been granted an audience by a Castigar don, Warrior caste—a segmented worm five metres long, each ring of its annular body bristling with spines. Its tentacled head had been painted with jagged symbols, suggesting violence to human eyes as eloquently as to its own kind. Each squirming arm of its crown had been capped with a chattering set of mechanized blades, mounted below the reddish bead of the eye. She had faced up to that horrifying cutlery drawer and outlined the drop-off the *Vulture God* wanted to make. She'd offered a cut of their pay cheque, and they'd made a deal. There was always a deal. Some criminals were sadists or psychopaths, but most weren't. Even the ones who *were* generally preferred Largesse to killing potential contacts. And she'd never caught any of them on a bad enough day. It had never turned weird. Yet.

The Broken Harvest was holed up in a crumbling dormitory, in the wretched upper levels of the same city where Thrennikos lived in such luxury. It was a sprawling, heavily rad-shielded eyesore of a building, erected for the first constructor crews back Before. The blocks around it were slums, filled with those who couldn't afford anywhere else. No hulking mercenaries patrolled these streets, and a thousand little gangs and fraternities formed and died there nightly. The Harvest itself was no major player on Tarekuma as far as Kris could tell. It was based within the Hegemony, a thorn in the shelly ass of the Essiel. Probably this "Aklu" was not the actual leader of the gang—or sect or suicide cult or whatever they actually were. Aklu might just be their word for a branch manager. But even if Tarekuma hosted only a fraction of their power, she soon realized that still meant something on these streets.

When she and Rollo left their taxi shuttle, one of this Aklu's people had turned up to meet them. She wore an unimpressive old tunic, bulked out with some sort of armour coating, but

Kris stiffened when she looked closer. The woman's armour was slashed down the centre of her back, revealing the articulated lobster thing rooted to her spine. Another Tothiat, like the murderous son of a bitch who'd stolen their ship. And weren't they supposed to be *rare*? And this Tothiat carried an actual *standard*, a pole with an honest-to-god flag hanging from it. It boasted a crooked black sunburst on grey or else it was a figure with many arms poised in some manner of dance. Whatever its meaning, people crossed the street or dived into alleys when they saw that flag coming. This might just be the Broken Harvest's fingertip, here on Tarekuma, but these streets were under the Society's shadow.

Their guide was Heremon, she said, and Kris recalled that their hijacker, of unfond memory, had been Mesmon. There was no other family resemblance beyond the lobster. *Still doesn't have to get weird*, she thought, as Heremon led them to that hideous concrete eyesore. Then they were inside, past a dozen humans and a couple of Hanni crowding out the atrium. They descended rough steps, still uneven and whorled where they'd been inexpertly printed, and came out into a big chamber, ranks of pillars propping up the ceiling. One wall was lined with desks of humans and Hanni at work, probably doing nothing more sinister than double-entry book-keeping. Another wall was lined with armed guards: humans, and Castigar moulted into oddly proportioned humanoid bodies. At the far end of the room, however...

Kris blinked. It *had* got weird. At her side, Rollo swore softly.

Heremon stepped forward and her voice rang from the bare concrete walls, "The Unspeakable Aklu, the Razor and the Hook."

There were actually two...entities coming forward. One was a Hiver frame like no other Kris had ever seen. Their torso was open as a birdcage, revealing the seething knot of biomechanical roaches that made up their composite being. Their head was a golden human mask, set into a contemptuous laughing expression. They walked on long digitigrade legs like a bird, waving six slender arms. The whole looked like a surrealist's take on an ancient god. None of this was what had caught Kris and Rollo's attention.

Behind the Hiver was The Unspeakable Aklu, without a doubt. It was gliding forwards on a great mechanized couch that curved in silvery wings either side of its occupant, held a half-metre off the floor by its own a-grav engine. Aklu was one of the Essiel—god-rulers of the Hegemonic cultists, lords of the Hegemony itself. And, apparently, a gangster.

Kris remembered the august Essiel diplomat sent to Huei-Cavor. It had possessed a string of titles too: revered this and wonderful that. They were human labels, she knew, but they were supposed to reflect some deep Essiel truths. So what did it mean for an Essiel to be Unspeakable, a Razor and a Hook?

Aklu was primarily shell, the two curved halves hinged at the base and overlapping for most of their three-metre height. They divided towards the top, cupping the motile parts of the creature. Its hard exterior seemed to be inscribed with complex, geometric runes, picked out in what looked like channels of mercury, constantly flowing in defiance of any native gravity A wrinkled holdfast projected from its base to wind around the couch's projections and hold the creature in place. From the top of the shell a multitude of thin arms opened like a fan, bristling with hairs and pincers. Three eyes, like red pearls, moved at the end of jointed stalks, viewing Aklu's visitors from all sides.

Kris was very afraid now and not entirely sure why. If it *was* a gangster, and the Broken Harvest a gang, this should be like any other negotiation. Except she'd never dealt with an Essiel before. Nobody she knew had. Human representatives of the Hegemony like Sathiel were the closest anybody ever came. Essiel were *not* supposed to be squatting in concrete bunkers, surrounded by desperados.

At the same time some screaming part of her was telling her—*It's a giant clam. What's the worst it could do?* Except... She'd always dismissed those cultists who fervently attributed divinity to their shelly masters. Standing in the presence of this creature now...there was *something* about it.

The Unspeakable Aklu's arms flurried through a complex sequence of postures and Kris felt a rumble through the soles of her feet, resounding back from the walls to her body without ever reaching her ears. Only in retrospect did she realize that Aklu was being conversational.

The Hiver started into motion, making an elaborate leg like a dancer, then straightening up. Kris noticed that they had two faces—one smiling gold mask facing them, and one with a downturned mouth facing away, a mask of tragedy. Then their half-dozen golden arms adopted a series of elegant poses and their bell-like voice rang out:

"So step the sanctified within our halls, who walked with eyeless tread the hidden glade. Peruse them. Linger on each page of theirs—and verdict give on how they have transgressed."

The only operative word in all of that was *transgressed* as far as Kris was concerned. She froze, ready to fight, as

Heremon came forward with some kind of device pointed right at them. For a wild moment she considered the ultimate sacrilege—leaping up on that couch with her knife, threatening oyster suppers for everyone, unless they let her and Rollo out. But what Heremon was holding didn't *look* like a gun. The symbiont woman shook her head slightly in her direction, a cue for her to be silent? Then the Hiver adopted a new posture with their many arms—briefly mirrored by their floating master—before gesticulating again.

"Sweet tones of innocence attend for these, the masters of the carrion bird, have not defiled the sanctuaries of God, nor placed a hand on that which is forbidden." The Hiver's beautiful voice rang out against the cracked and filthy walls, and a dozen armed thugs and murderers listened raptly as though it all made perfect sense.

Then Rollo nudged her, none too gently. Kris had absolutely no idea what mad etiquette held sway here but she cleared her throat.

"We are but poor supplicants to The Unspeakable Aklu. We are the, yes, the masters of the carrion bird. The crew of the *Vulture God*, the ones that recovered the *Oumaru*—"

Aklu's arms semaphored and she stopped. Speaking over the Unspeakable was probably a faux pas of epic proportions. The gilded Hiver adopted another sequence of ritualistic poses, pirouetting to again show them their frowning tragedic face.

"Our ark, our rightful casket, treasure fleet of all our dreams, explain how you, a *nithing*, with desecrating tread defiled our joy..."

Which sounded bad, however you sliced it. Kris shared a look with Rollo, then described their brief involvement with the *Oumaru*. *It was a Broken Harvest ship?* That hadn't been in the brief, but it wasn't as though most gangs made things easy for Hugh law enforcement by putting their criminal identities on the owner's manifest.

When she described the wrecked *Oumaru*'s appearance, Aklu moved again and she let her account slow. The Hiver melodiously asked her to repeat it, and then again, in more detail. And again until Kris just about ran out of ways to say the same thing.

"It had been peeled. We've all seen how it was, from the war... Melted and reformed, made into a sculpture as they do. You *know* what I mean."

"How sour false witness falls upon the ear," the Hiver remarked. Then abruptly Heremon did have a gun and it was pressed to Kris's temple. Three of the thugs tackled Rollo to the ground in a struggling heap and, in the distraction, Kris whipped out her knife and slashed Heremon's throat. Before her eyes, the shallow cut healed up. Heremon didn't seem to be remotely bothered, her gun-hand steady.

Rollo was hollering furiously, and with a herculean effort he dragged his whole tangle of aggressors half a metre closer to the couch. "I just want my *ship!*" he was howling. "My ship, you fucking barnacle! You killed my people. *You stole my ship.*"

Kris felt all possible chance of salvaging the situation falling out of the world's ass, as the saying went. She met Heremon's gaze past the glint of her knife, still at the Tothiat's throat, and saw only unfriendly disinterest. For her, exploding Kris's head with a bullet would be a mildly disagreeable task—akin to scraping something off her sandal.

Kris felt it was all over. They weren't leaving here alive. But Aklu must have had something more to say, because the

Hiver chimed, "Compounding sin with sin, bad faith with faith. To stand before th'unspoken throne and claim a right to hold the ark of the divine!"

Kris was hit with a sudden jolt of inspiration. They'd raced here *before* Aklu's people, so the gangster wouldn't know how things had gone down. And so they'd misunderstood her explanation. Hardly surprising, given its unusual nature.

"We don't mean the *Oumaru!*" she managed. "Rollo, be *still*. We *don't* lay claim to that. We want *our* ship. When your people reclaimed your property, they grabbed the *Vulture God* to transport theirs. The *Oumaru*, it wasn't going anywhere on its own, see? We just came to ask, to very respectfully ask... When The Unspeakable Aklu has reclaimed its ark, property, whatever... might we have, maybe, our own ship back?" She bit down on any further pleading and waited, body still taut as a wire.

Rollo had called the Essiel a barnacle, but nobody seemed to be shouting about that. Possibly it had been translated as something more complimentary. And she hadn't mentioned Barney or Medvig, who couldn't just be returned peaceably to them. However, right now, coming out of this alive themselves seemed a long shot.

The Unspeakable's arms waved as though in a breeze that touched nothing else, and its eyes popped up and down. Its Hiver mouthpiece was still, balanced perfectly on one foot, the other drawn up mid-pose and their fan of arms motionless. Kris guessed that it was plugged into Tarekuma's kybernet, sending out enquires to confirm her story. Then the Hiver jolted back into motion, saying, "You carry in your hearts the go-between, who stands between destroyer and destroyed..." Which could only mean Idris, the Intermediary.

Kris wondered if she was starting to get the hang of this. The arms waved again, hypnotically.

"What once the gods have seized on, none may claim, and yet divine benevolence is such that all who kneel devoutly at their feet, and hold the cup of charity aloft, may live in expectation of reward," the Hiver pronounced. Abruptly Heremon had stepped back, and the goons were allowing Rollo to stand again.

"What, my child?" the captain growled softly. "What, frankly, the fuck, did any of that mean?"

And a silence stretched out, a cue for her to answer in some way. "I *think*," Kris replied very quietly, "they mean that they've got our ship, and so it's theirs. But if we work for them, maybe we can have it back eventually? I think. And they were talking about Idris. So they want him for deep void diving?"

"Is that *all*?" She saw Rollo's face twitch with all the rage he was holding back. "And my two dead children? Do we get them back too after we've bowed and scraped and done their filthy work...? Did they say that?"

"Rollo—"

"We become their lackeys and just *forget* they murdered our people, my daughter? And if we're very, very good and kiss their shellfish ass they might just let me have my own damn ship back some day?" All said with white-hot fury, and yet still in the merest whisper. Despite everything she was impressed that he was being so restrained.

Kris cast a glance towards the motionless Hiver and their floating master. She was all too aware of the expectant killers on every side. At the desks, the clerks continued with their work, diligently defrauding, counterfeiting or whatever their duties involved.

"Say what you've got to say," Rollo ground out, and Kris took a deep breath.

"We are of course honoured by your offer to serve the Unspeakable," she declared brightly. "We will take this to the rest of the crew immediately. Thank you for your munificence." Ordinarily, she'd have been overdoing it, but right now she was in the asylum of aggrandizement and no praise could be too much. She even bowed. If she was echoing a Scintillan fencer's respect to an opponent, before somebody got cut up, nobody there was likely to recognize it.

"Consider all you will," the Hiver said, "the vulture's leash shall not be lightly shed. But we have faith that you shall come in all humility to pledge us service—and begin the path to restitution."

Kris looked sidelong at Heremon and the heavies. She was seeking confirmation, from any of them, that they found this bizarre show even a little odd. She wanted to burst, like a child calling out a naked emperor. But there was not the slightest crack in their masks of respect. She felt as though she'd fallen through the wrong side of the mirror.

Two minutes later she and Rollo were on the street, hides miraculously intact save for the odd bruise. The captain's expression was thunderous as she called the rest of the crew. Somehow Kris didn't think a long and mutually profitable partnership with the Broken Harvest was on the cards.

*

After they'd returned to the *Dark Joan*'s docking bay, Rollo sat by himself and brooded. Kris had expected him to explode. A quietly seething captain was somehow worse.

Kris had explained the situation to everyone else, especially Idris. He had a right to know that yet another unscrupulous bunch of thugs was interested in him. She half expected him to start plotting a course to anywhere but Tarekuma, but instead he kicked his heels on the ramp to the *Joan*'s cockpit and watched Rollo unhappily.

"This might be it, for us," Kris said, meaning for them as a crew, a surrogate family. "I don't imagine the Parthenon'll let us pal around in this speedster much longer."

Idris nodded, eyes still on Rollo.

"You've heard Solace out yet?"

"Not exactly," he said softly. "And to her credit, she's not pressed it. But all this, that she's done for us, it's just to sweeten me up."

"You could do worse, you know."

He glanced at her in surprise, almost betrayed, and she hurried to add, "I'm not trying to get rid of you, Idris. I'm just saying. If they made *me* a good offer, I'd go."

"Do you want to go?"

"I want to have options. And if the Parthenon want a Colonial law advocate, well, they'd be interesting employers... for a bit."

"And if it's not just for a bit? Nobody in the Parthenon is 'employed,' Kris. They don't have jobs, they have duty. And you don't get to pick and choose who you do duties for. I'm sure you don't get to say, 'Well, nice doing my duty for you— now I'm off to work for the Colonies again.'" His face twisted unhappily and he looked at his feet. "I guess I should hear her out though, then send her away."

"You like her."

"We...went through a lot in the war. We were close,

after Berlenhof, before she rejoined her unit. I needed someone, and she...I don't know what she wanted."

"Why not just the same as you?"

"I don't think Partheni are like that, are they? All that warrior spirit and selfless sacrifice...I don't think they need shoulders to cry on, like regular human beings. They edit that shit out of them in the vats. Or what's the point? What's the point of making better people, if they're still sad and afraid and lonely?"

Kris saw the signs and put her arms around him, letting him sag into her. A half-minute later and he was fine, backing away, his expression all apology. She smiled, squeezed his shoulder to show she didn't mind. It was that continuous lack of sleep, she knew. Things that the mind would normally disarm and dismantle built up inside him, and he couldn't bar the door against them forever.

Then he shifted hurriedly to one side because Rollo was coming through. He marched up the ramp into the *Joan* with such a grim purpose that Kris thought he might just fly the ship away himself and leave them all behind. To seek vengeance, to find the *Vulture*...who could guess, in his state? The others were clearly worried about him too, so when Rollo put his head back out, his whole crew was waiting.

"Right, my wastrels," he addressed them. "These pods, all this nonsense," a jab at the rack of suspension beds the Partheni technician had installed, "they come out, right? They're just bolted in there?"

Solace nodded cautiously.

Rollo grunted thoughtfully, a man stalking a mad idea through dense brush. "Idris. How long before the *Vulture* comes in-system?"

"Ah..." Idris slipped his slate out and ran a few hurried calculations. "Any time from now to twelve hours' time, depending on how tight their nav is."

"There's no Partheni embassy on Tarekuma, not a formal one," Solace started tentatively, "but I could—"

"No!" Rollo told her sharply. He pressed his lips together and went on, apologetically. "Not to disparage what you've done for us, my child, but no. This is spacer business, our business. Too much gratitude starts to look like ownership. I'm sorry."

"Understood." Although, from her expression, the Partheni plainly didn't understand. Kris considered that she came from a place where everyone was pointed in the same direction, and everyone helped everyone else. Or maybe they were all horribly competitive all the time and Kris's fond idea of Partheni life was entirely bunkum.

Rollo took a deep breath. "This you *can* do for me, though, my adopted daughter. You tell me what weapons this bird here has. Talk me through it."

Kris felt a lurch inside her. "Rollo," she said, overlapping with Olli's "*Captain...*"

"Let's call it an academic exercise, see right?" Rollo said with false joviality. Solace looked from him to the rest of them and stepped up to lean into the cockpit. "Twin accelerators here, not much against any serious defences but... good. Good for light work. Ready ammo's limited but there's a mass stripping system that'll keep them fed at the expense of... well, mass. Mass from the end-segments. There's a single narrow beam laser that can be powered from the reaction drives. I think... seven minutes' continuous burn at full power before you're dry. The gravitic drive isn't adapted for offensive deployment but it's good for shielding—and segmentation defences are built in too."

"I don't even know what that means," Rollo told her briskly. "Quite the little gunboat you've loaned us there, child. Right now, you're the favourite of my family." His smile was bleak.

"Captain, what's the plan?" Olli asked him.

He stood on the ramp, irresolute, for a few moments, and then sat at the edge of the *Joan's* hatch to confront his crew, hands clasped in his lap.

"Kris told you all the nonsense we went through down there. Crazy shellfish wants to own us, let us earn our own ship back by doing its shit work. Wants to own Idris, too. And I know how those deals go. You never *do* earn out, on a contract like that. Once owned, always owned."

Kris nodded, and everyone else was of the same mind. If you got in with the mob you didn't just walk away. Not unlike what Idris had been saying about the Parthenon, but she knew where she'd rather take her chances.

"So my *Vulture* comes in-system in a few hours, most likely, so says our Idris. Then they bring it here, repurpose it, strip it, who knows? Who knows what they want with the *Oumaru* even—which Crazy Shellfish says it owns. None of our business. We don't want it, that much I do know. But the *Vulture* is my bird and I am getting her back. Because the Parthenon, all gods help us, has given us a fighting ship."

They stared. Probably most of them had seen the direction he was pulling in, but to hear it said out loud was flat-out madness.

"Idris...you flew in the war," Rollo said. "And Solace, you were a pilot?"

"Gunnery," the Partheni said soberly. "But I can fly."

"We strip out this junk." A thumb jerked at the suspension pods. "We tool up with what we can get. We intercept the fuckers, hack the *Vulture*'s doors open, cut with the laser if we have to. We take back our ship before it hits orbit, and piss right off out of this system and never look back."

Kittering raised his shield arms urgently. "Also Broken Harvest are made enemies forever!"

"They killed Barney and Medvig," Rollo reminded him flatly. "They are no friends of ours. And—*I want my ship back*." His shoulders sagged a little. "And this is dangerous stuff, my kiddoes, my fry, nothing you signed up for. You want to make your own way, we can drop you at an orbital. Ships go from here to everywhere, every day. Kit will cash you out; you'll not go hungry. You can cash yourself out too, Kit, if that's what you want. I'll hold it against nobody. None of you told me 'pirate' when I asked you what skills you brought."

"I'm in," Olli said, almost before he'd finished. "Captain, I will cut that Tothiat bastard a new asshole. I am in."

It'll just heal up again, thought Kris, recognizing a thread of hysteria within herself. She looked at Idris, surely the least martial of all of them. He was looking back at her. They came as a pair, after all.

"Think about it," Rollo told them. "Nobody's arm gets twisted on this. No shame in walking away." Though every one of them who dropped out would be a hole below the waterline in the plan's chances of success.

There was a spacer's dive near the Castigar-patrolled dock, where they'd holed up, and Kris and Idris retreated there to mull it over. Olli stayed with the *Joan*, already ripping out the suspension beds so they'd have somewhere to muster prior to the proposed action.

"I think Kit will bail," Kris told Idris, when they'd ducked into a corner booth with beakers of acrid, fake kaffe.

He nodded, not looking at her, or at anything really, just staring into infinity in that way he did. So she continued.

"I think the Partheni...I don't know. I mean she probably trained for this sort of thing. All second nature. She, Rollo and Olli could likely do this with blood to spare. Not her fight, though. But she...I think she really wants to be one of us, you know? Which is weird, given she's basically a secret agent for a foreign government."

"She's a terrible spy," Idris said, with the ghost of a smile.

Kris took a slug of kaffe and instantly regretted it: too hot, way too nasty. "Idris...I will walk away with you. If you don't want to do this, I'll go. We're a team."

"*But...?*" He eyed her cagily.

"I don't want to walk."

She couldn't read him at all, in that moment. Then at last he said, "I thought you'd be pulling me the other way. I thought, of all of us, you'd have the good sense to have nothing to do with this. I thought we'd be having this conversation in reverse."

"You mean you—"

"I want to back up Rollo. I *want* to get closure on Barney and Medvig. I don't want to kill anyone, but I want our ship back too."

"A lifetime of trouble's going to come out of this. Aklu seemed to feel pretty strongly about this whole business."

Idris gave her a frank look. "I give not the least fuck what some renegade Essiel wants with a torn-up wreck. I just want to do right by Rollo and be back on the *Vulture*."

When Rollo returned to the bay, with a crate gliding along

behind him, he found everyone there but Kittering. The absence hit him; Kris saw it in his wry smile.

"Not bad though," he admitted, looking at the remainder of his crew. "Children, I have toys for you, dangerous toys. Not many, but it was short notice. And we need a plan of attack. Battle-daughter, you can do that for us?"

Solace tapped at her temple. "I've been working on it already, Captain."

"You are the favourite of all my brood," Rollo told her, trying for his old good nature but the sharp edges were showing through. Then there was a rapid pattering of feet and Kittering scuttled in, screens showing clashing, alarmed colours.

"Kit...?" Rollo asked.

"*Vulture* in-system!" Kittering's translator barked, and he lit up with simulations, telemetry and projections. Barely three hours had passed since Idris had made his prediction.

"Olli?" Rollo barked.

"Beds are almost out. Nearly ready." The remote specialist loomed at the hatch. She was already in her Scorpion for the heavy work, and would be taking up half the available standing room behind the pilot's seat.

"Attention!" Kit announced. "Another vessel has launched on a course for the *Vulture-Oumaru*." More lines arced across his display.

Kris took a moment to work out what she was seeing. The *Vulture* had exited unspace but it wasn't hauling its prize anywhere near Tarekuma or the orbitals. It was staying discreetly out of the way towards the system's further reaches. Aklu must be sending a ship to get whatever he wanted off his "ark"—the *Oumaru*—without the Architected wreck causing an outcry.

"Can we outstrip them?" Rollo demanded. "Olli, finish up double time. Don't worry about sharp edges or loose wires."

"They're going out full burn." Solace had taken in the figures Kit was streaming.

"We can outstrip them." Idris's voice was flat. He looked a little sick at whatever idea had just come to him. "We'll do this, Rollo. *Now*, before my nerve goes."

"Kit?" Rollo looked at the Hanni.

"Yes, my captain," Kittering confirmed. His screens displayed a sequence of complex patterns—oranges and pinks and greys—but his eloquence was beyond human comprehension this time. Then Olli had dumped the last of the beds out the hatch and backed up to give them room. With his brisk, many-legged stride Kit pattered up the ramp into the *Joan*. The rest of them followed. The game was on.

13.

Idris

"I don't like the look of it." Olli had brought up an image of the speeding Broken Harvest vessel. "Is she armed? With Hegemony ships, who the fuck knows, right?"

Rollo grunted an affirmative, then looked at Solace hopefully. She leant in to get a look at Olli's display. That put her elbow in Kris's ribs and almost ended up with her stepping on Kittering. The Partheni ship was still cosy even without the pods. Olli was being mulish about letting Solace look, but eventually gave up, and the Partheni stared at the specs sombrely.

"She's armed," Solace confirmed after a moment. The Broken Harvest ship led with a spiky eight-pointed crown, the rest of the vessel a three-lobed bulb behind it and the whole finished in dull grey, ornamented with geometric lines in gold. "I see four big accelerators. And maybe that thing front and centre is a focusing iris, for its gravitic drives."

"On a ship *that* small?" Olli demanded.

"Hegemony tech is good." Solace shrugged. "Like I say, can't be sure..."

"And I'm wondering why it even matters, given they're so far ahead of us," Rollo growled. By the time the refitted *Dark*

Joan had cleared the planet, the Harvest's interceptor had a commanding lead.

"Working on it." Idris had the maths at his fingertips, making quick and dirty calculations upon which nobody should stake a ship-worth of lives. "Almost there."

"My misbegotten son," Rollo rumbled in his ear, "I know you magicians do not like to let lesser mortals see how the trick is done. But maybe, this one time, you could show what's up your sleeve, see right?"

"Any of you ever hear the term 'stutter-jump'?" Idris asked them.

"*Oh.*" Solace had, of course. Nobody else. It wasn't a thing sane people did with a gravity drive.

And while he was thinking that, all the maths came together, perfect as a gemstone. *Yes, that will do nicely.* Except "nicely" was absolutely not the right word.

"You all need to hang on to something. Now. Not each other. Hang on and keep still."

"Idris?" Solace actually sounded worried. *I scared a Partheni. Something to cross off the life list.*

"Just close your eyes and...don't worry. We're going to drop out of the real for a very short period of time." He was mortified to discover that a tiny sliver of him was enjoying itself.

"Oh, no, no, *no*," Rollo started, but Idris had already set the gravitic drives into motion, shunting the ship into unspace. In the split second before they dropped he heard everyone start to shout at him. Then the shouts were gone and so were they. Nothing but utter quiet came from the empty space behind him, alone as he was in the little Partheni ship. *It's like a foreign country. They do things different here.*

Then he was already bringing them out again, a heartbeat later. And even in that instant he felt *something* flowing up from the appalling abyss to infest that vacancy his friends had left.

He remembered Berlenhof. He'd been on the Partheni launch *Pythoness*, like the *Dark Joan* writ large. They'd been crippled by the Architect, the surviving crew gamely discharging their weapons at the vast crystalline spears of the enemy. He'd tried to drag them away from the Architect's path, feeling its invisible grasp seeking to finish them off. In desperation, wanting to live, he had engaged the drive and just ripped the entire broken vessel into unspace. Even as he did it, he was regretting it, knowing it was a terrible idea. He tore them free, back to the real, fully expecting to find the Architect *right there* again, descending upon them. Except they had been half the distance back towards Berlenhof and clear of the enemy. He'd looked about the deck of profoundly shocked women, some doubled over, others clutching their heads at the shock of sudden transit. But alive, all of them. And if he accomplished no more than that at least he'd saved them, along with himself. Only an Intermediary's innate feel for the screwed-up spatial relationships involved had made it possible.

Idris was an old Int now, perhaps the oldest. Old but never tired of running. Only this time he was running *towards*. In the eyeblink after they ceased to objectively exist in the physical universe, they were back again. The Harvest interceptor was far behind them, still hauling its bulk across the intervening space the old-fashioned way. And ahead of them was their goal—the *Vulture* and its prey.

From behind came a chorus of complaints. Kris choking,

the staccato stridulation of Kittering making his displeasure known. Let them think on what they'd just experienced, and remember it next time they had a two-day crossing with only him awake.

"*Never* do that again, you famie bastard," Rollo hissed in his ear. "I will cut your throat one of these fine days." And he didn't mean it, probably, but there was still a jagged edge to the captain's voice. Possibly Rollo was one of those people who reacted spectacularly badly to unspace. Certainly he'd always made sure he was abed before any regular transit.

Idris found he didn't have room to be contrite just then. It had worked. "We're coming in. Five minutes. Need to be quick."

"Screw you, Idris," Olli spat, voice shaking, but she was already working, trying to establish a link to the *Vulture*'s systems. "They're still rebooting the computer. No higher systems up yet."

There was a comms ping from the console. "Hailing us," Idris noted.

"Say nothing," Rollo told him. "Olli, isolate the *God*'s hatch controls. Can we...blow our ship-jackers out into space or something?"

"Depends if they have their wits about them. We're really doing this, are we?"

"We were never going to get our ship back without lives on our conscience, my daughter. And these murderers have signed the contract for what happens to them." As he squinted at the displays, Rollo's face was hard as granite.

"Have they sent an umbilical down to the *Oumaru*?" Kris asked, over Idris's shoulder.

She was right. Apparently the hijackers hadn't just been

sitting idle after dropping from unspace. Although what they were doing with the flayed hulk was a mystery.

"Just means they're divided, distracted." Rollo's hand was on Idris's shoulder, painfully tight, as Idris pulled them closer. Their brachator drive pulled them across the fabric of space, each operation slinging them along a new line as they homed in on the *Vulture*. All smooth sailing now but if it came down to actual combat flying, they'd be rattled about like peas as Idris pushed past the dampeners' tolerance. He felt a weird, unwelcome thrill to know that the *Joan* was more than capable of that kind of nonsense.

He made the next grab and the Partheni ship abruptly flipped thirty degrees from its previous course, and hurtled towards their quarry. The comms requests were becoming more and more insistent, and then a whole new set of warnings lit up the board.

"They're *hot!*" Idris called. His memory flashed to the war, hearing the warning yelled aboard Colonial warships, or the Parsef equivalent from the lips of a Partheni officer: "*Vu khi chaud!*"

"Those going outside—helmets on." Rollo followed his own advice. A few of Kittering's small arms flicked back past his crown and dragged a clear hood forwards and all the way down until it sealed over his belly. Kit and Rollo only had standard EVA suits, although they would both be going over armed. Solace and Olli would be the vanguard.

"You two play nice now. No time for not liking each other. I'm talking to you, my daughter. Olian Timo, to *you*."

Olli looked at him rebelliously. Perhaps she'd thought her snubbing of Solace had been masterfully subtle to that point.

"After this you can tell me what the hell your problem is

anyway," the Partheni put in. She started back as Rollo rapped a gauntleted knuckle on her helm.

"No lip from you, soldier. Not so long as you're part of my crew, see right?"

"Compret, Mother," she responded automatically and Rollo managed a chuckle.

"Mother, is it? Well someone's got to look after you rabble of children."

Idris had been watching the *Vulture*'s readouts, seeing the ship's energy reserves patched through to its ailing lasers. They hadn't been used much, only really intended for debris and hull cutting. They'd still make a mess of the *Joan* if they landed a sustained hit. The scavenger's new masters had plainly decided that no comms contact meant hostile intent.

The *Vulture*'s beam split the void, reaching them before he could even register the discharge. He had to rely on the instruments to tell him that the lance of energy had curved away, splaying off in a rainbow spectrum of wasted light and heat as the *Dark Joan*'s gravitic shielding deepened the curve of space just enough.

He'd set his next bearing now. The drives were hurling the *Joan* along a heading that would bring them dangerously close to the *Vulture God*. The ship's laser stabbed out twice more, once piercing space where they should have been, the next just scattering away in impotent spectra. The near miss filled the space around them with colour.

"I have the *Vulture*'s hatch," Olli reported. "Isolated it. They're fighting for control..." But they didn't know the *Vulture*'s systems like she did.

"Open her up," Rollo directed.

Idris almost missed the fine mist of frozen atmosphere

that vented from the *Vulture*'s side. It shifted the ship slightly, beginning a tumbling roll, but one so slow that it barely affected his calculations at all. He almost missed the body, too—a human shape that pitched out into the death sentence of hard vacuum, helmetless, writhing briefly.

Murderers, he reminded himself. They were professional killers and thieves—and if their prey turned on them, it was only what they should expect.

"They've established an atmosphere bubble," Olli noted, as the surviving hijackers adjusted the *Vulture*'s gravitic envelope. If they had any sense they'd be suiting up, though; nobody should be taking a congenial atmosphere for granted right now.

He'd calculated his last two navigation points and put them into operation one after another. One moment the *Joan* was shunting sideways, skidding through space as if to broadside the *Vulture*. In the next, he'd matched speed with his target as though neither vessel was moving at all. As if they'd come to a halt alongside the *Vulture God*'s open hatch.

"Right then," Rollo said, squeezing his shoulder one more time. Then Idris had their own umbilical free and Olli took control of it—clamping its magnetic mouth over the *Vulture*'s hatch. Idris had his helmet on by then, and Kris too. They were about to match atmospheres with the *Vulture* which could be venting all its air into space in the next moment.

"*Going.*" Olli was first through, scrambling through the umbilical, using all of the Scorpion's limbs. "*Clear!*" came her voice over the comms, as she reached the far end. Solace was already following, cradling Mr. Punch in her arms. Idris hoped she didn't have to use the accelerator much, because its projectiles would go through every wall and hull plate in the *Vulture*.

That meant a *lot* of repair work, even in a best-case scenario. Then it was Rollo and Kit's turn to head through—and all Idris and Kris could do was wait for word of their triumphant victory.

Or that was the plan.

When the Hegemony interceptor erupted from unspace, spinning end-over-end and broadcasting on all channels, he almost felt his heart seize. They had stutter-jumped too—right after him. How was that even possible? The Hegemony had some few species that could navigate like an Int but he'd never expected to find any out here in service to the Broken Harvest. The *Vulture* must have signalled them the moment the *Joan* appeared, triggering a desperate lunge through unspace to intervene. It looked as though it had cost them dearly. They were here, though, and that put the steel-toed boot into all parts of Rollo's plan.

"Captain, *company!*" And Idris was sending over the nav data, even as he watched the interceptor's systems come back on line. Rollo was silent—still in-channel, but with absolutely nothing to say. Idris told him, "I'll deal with it."

"You'll *what?*" Rollo demanded. "Idris—"

"Going to have to leave you for a moment. Olli, let go of the *Joan*'s hatch controls."

"Fuck me, Idris." But she did so, and he pulled the umbilical the moment she had.

"Hang on," he told Kris. If there'd been time, he would have decanted her onto the *Vulture*, which might have been marginally safer. He twisted to look at her...Kris was wide-eyed, but there was more than fear on her face. He remembered she was a duellist, an aficionado of the fight.

He located a navigation point that tugged them away from

the *Vulture* into open space. This, even as the Harvest's own pilot aimed the bigger vessel towards them. Its tumble had morphed into smooth acceleration towards their target as its weapons powered up.

Vu khi chaud, he thought and returned the favour, diverting power to his ship's lasers and the accelerators' magnetic rails. Then he was reaching out into space, to bring them swinging past the *Oumaru*'s twisted bulk and hurtling back towards the enemy.

The enemy. He had an enemy again. He didn't like it. Loathed it, in fact. Yet an ugly little part of him was awake now, like a cold arrowhead buried deep inside his mind.

Solace

Solace had dialled her accelerator right down, to minimize possible hull and component damage to the *Vulture*. For what that was worth: given the standard of Partheni tech, even at its minimum settings the old ship likely didn't have enough walls to stop any of her shots.

When the first of the hijackers stormed into view, all on his own, she could only guess the man hadn't really understood the situation. He was suited up and carrying a bulky projectile gun. She drew Mr. Punch's muzzle across his torso and hit him with at least seven pellets—meaning she just about cut him in half. His gun went off like an afterthought as his body pitched one way whilst its erstwhile contents vomited out the other. The thunderous retort would serve as polite notice to anyone else aboard that trouble had come calling. Mr. Punch, despite the name Rollo had given the weapon, made an eerie singing sound as it ramped up more of its metal projectiles.

The door ahead of them slammed closed, as the *Vulture's* crew rushed down the short corridor from the hatch to the rest of the ship. Olli was already in the *Vulture's* system, though, fighting to get control. "Kit," the remote specialist ground between her teeth, "get that airlock shut. I'm busy."

"Confirmed. Yes confirmed." The Hanni skittered backwards and took over a terminal.

"Captain, take cover," Solace said, positioning herself in front of the main door. "Behind me and Timo, please."

Rollo, who'd obviously had dreams of leading the charge, backed off reluctantly.

"Got it," Olli said. "Door's open." Then the gravity in the corridor shut off.

Someone had tried to get clever with the gravitic drive, Solace realized. A ship's artificial grav was only a specialized function of its engine, after all. Thankfully, this was what she trained for, and none of the spacers would be strangers to it either. The hijackers might just have shot themselves in the foot.

Even as she thought it, the door hissed open to reveal a welcoming party on the other side. Their boots were clamped to the floor and they probably expected to see a group of intruders in helpless freefall. What they did do right was start shooting even as the door came up.

Three projectiles struck Solace. She felt the momentum of their impact even through the complex plastics of her combat armour. Boots fixed in place, she swayed backwards—bending at the knee to absorb the muted energy of the strikes, one hand back to push herself away from the floor.

Three hostiles, two humans and a Hanni. She was already aiming Mr. Punch one-handed, because she had a strong wrist and suddenly the weight of the weapon wasn't an issue. Of course what *she* hadn't factored into the situation was that she wasn't leading a squad of trained soldiers, who knew not to get in each other's fields of fire.

Olli's Scorpion rushed past her on the ceiling, taking up almost all the space, saw-edged tail whipping left and right. One ratcheting limb rapped Solace's helm on the way through, slamming her back against the floor. She heard another two shots from the hijackers before the remote specialist reached them. Abruptly the air was full of blood, a thousand little pellets of it, each accelerating away from the man Olli had just torn into. Solace charged up her face-plate, repelling the droplets so they spun away in every direction. The other human hijacker had a leg pinned by one of the Scorpion's heavy work limbs—it looked more broken than trapped, but he also had his gun against the clear plastic of Olli's capsule. Solace snapped off a single shot from Mr. Punch, puncturing his temple and the wall behind him. *Hope there wasn't anything essential there.* The Harvest's Hanni was retreating, sending out a wild spray of bullets from the gun clutched in its mandibles. The recoil sent the creature spinning backwards in freefall, but at the far end of the corridor, it caught itself against the wall with four or five legs and started aiming properly.

Olli was right after it, apparently believing her Scorpion frame was entirely bulletproof. When she was just halfway, a lance of fire lashed across her, severing one of the frame's legs entirely.

The Castigar was there, the big wormlike one with the

weapons-mount hood—the one that had killed Medvig. Solace put a couple of pellets through it, but Castigar tissue was dense and unspecialized. Unlike humans, they lacked discrete vital organs; accelerators weren't a good weapon against them. She settled for drilling her next three shots through the Hanni, sending its body spinning disjointedly into the top corner of the room.

The Castigar's weapons hood swung towards her and she braced herself for significant suit damage. Olli was on it in the next second, the loss of one leg barely an inconvenience. There was a great blackened furrow across the Scorpion's back, but she must have routed around the damage. She grappled fiercely with the alien, trying to bring her cutting arms and tail to bear, even as it wrapped its twisting length around the Scorpion and fought to aim its down weapons.

"Go get the others, I've got this *fucker!*" Olli shouted, even as Rollo let out a roar of fury. Solace looked up to see a suited figure sticking its head out to see what the hell was going on. The suit was one of the *Vulture's* but the face inside the helmet was none other than Mesmon the Tothiat's. Then he shut the door between them, abandoning his fellows.

Rollo was already after him, yelling at Kit to get the door open. "No—!" Solace shouted; they needed to give Olli backup. Between him and Olli, though, the captain needed her most. Solace cursed all civilians in war zones and ran after him.

Once through the door, the sudden space of the drone bay caught her by surprise. She wasn't as familiar with the *Vulture's* layout as its crew. Rollo had dived behind a tangle of pipes and was shooting at a handful of suited figures entering through the ship's remotes hatch. It was connected to the *Oumaru*, Solace realized; this was their salvage party hurrying back on board the *Vulture*. She sent a scatter of shot in that direction, pure intimidation rather than a determined attempt to kill anyone. In response three heavy impacts struck her like fists, lifting her from her feet and sending her cartwheeling across the bay into the wall. Rollo returned fire, though one of the pipes he'd been sheltering behind was now a jagged-edged stump.

"Kit, can you give me gravitic access?" Her own voice was commendably calm in her ears, even as she scrabbled for purchase against the wall. She would have been a sitting target for those shooters at the hatch. Instead, Mesmon slammed physically into her. She saw two holes in his stolen suit, evidence of Rollo's marksmanship. They hadn't slowed him down at all. His mottled face, through the cracked visor, was all eerie calm.

She clamped one boot to the wall for purchase and flipped him, slinging him across the drone bay. He somehow kept his orientation, levelling a hand-cannon at her and hitting her with another two shots. Each bullet exploded on impact. Unarmoured, she'd have been a bloody mist by now. As it was, she felt the impacts like sledgehammer blows, bruise-makers every one. Her heads-up was giving her all sorts of warnings about ablative tolerance and stress fractures. Partheni battle armour was good but there were limits.

So: return the favour. She levelled Mr. Punch and did her best to cut the Tothiat in half the hard way. One pellet did actually catch him in the leg as he bounced back from the wall, spoiling his return leap for her and spinning him away. She tried to track him, but he swung himself off in an unexpected direction, one hand hooking around the drone bay's empty control pod. Then he was speeding back at her from the other side almost faster than she could register. *Right little zero-G ballerina, aren't you?*

This time she didn't throw him off, but grabbed him when he came in, with the full intention of breaking his neck. Contrary to popular opinion, Partheni weren't superhumanly strong. Raw muscle wasn't usually needed, except, it seemed, for brawling with renegade Hegemonics. However she had the assistance of her armour's servos and decades of muscle memory.

She got a hand on his helmet and wrenched at it, yanking his head to one side. He stuck a boot to the wall behind her and used that purchase to hammer down a blow where her neck met her shoulder. *Stupid infantile move*, except she felt it, and her armour's stress warnings redoubled. She felt the first worm of worry creep in through the cracks. She could see he'd hit her so hard he'd broken his own wrist, the hand bent at a crippled angle. Even as she registered his injury, the joint snapped back into place, the damage repairing itself before her eyes. Through the rents in his mangled glove she saw skin seal and bones realign even as he came in to hit her again.

Need to update our database on Tothiat. She gave the servos all the reserve power the armour had, went for his neck, and felt something give with a satisfactory snap. When his next monstrous blow came in, she realized she'd actually heard the seal of his helmet give way. It came away in her hand, leaving his face pressed right up close to her own visor. His next blow was too much for his boots' magnetic seals, and he fell away from her, levelling his gun. She threw his own helmet at him, bouncing it off his forehead. "Gravity any time now, Kit!"

"Working working working," in her ear from the Hanni.

Mesmon's next shot blew a hole in the wall past her helmet, the propulsion sending him rocketing away from her across the room. Grimly, she lined up Mr. Punch and put a dozen pellets in him before he could change his course. The force spun him around three times, leaving a spiral of holes all over his body before it bounced him off three walls.

And now to end the others, she thought. Because surely they'd done for Rollo already, and would be coming for her next.

Yet Rollo was still over by the pipes, exchanging inaccurate fire with two hijackers while a third brought something up out of the *Oumaru*. The gangster was handling his find as gingerly as though it were a bomb rigged to blow. The other thugs moved to cover him. Despite all the fighting around them, apparently *this* was their priority.

Then Mesmon was back, notwithstanding all the holes in his hide. And she realized she had a bigger problem herself.

Idris

"Kris," Idris said. "There's a fold-out seat behind mine. Get it out, strap in."

She was already on it as she asked, "What now?"

"I'm going to push the tolerance of the ship's dampeners. I don't want you thrown around." He had the grabby drive reaching out for the universe again, dragging them at a tangent to the Harvest interceptor, which was lurching towards them in turn.

Let's see what you've got. He fired their accelerators towards the Harvest craft, burning through a hundred fist-sized pellets from the magazine, each one spun up to a speed beyond the dreams of ballistics. Their opponent was already using its drive to bend space about the vessel, so that every shot, still going subjectively straight, just swerved away. So far, so much as expected. Then the return fire was incoming, trying to track the fleet little Partheni package runner as Idris threw it through a series of abrupt changes of heading. You couldn't dodge something as fast as an accelerated round, any more than you could see a laser before it hit. But you *could* well and truly mess with your opponent's targeting. Plus the void was very big, and the *Dark Joan* was a very small target.

Idris had his own gravitic drive twisting space too, so the handful of shots that came near slingshotted around the *Joan* and were lost to the abyss. By that time he'd closed with the interceptor on a jagged course. And the interceptor's salvos continued to land everywhere the *Joan* wasn't, Idris's deft hands feeding calculations to the ship. There were gaps in their enemy's firing, too. He wasn't sure why, but his mind picked up the discontinuity. *Why not shoot back just then? Why that half a second when their guns cut out?* Malfunction or strategy?

He brought them closer yet, reaching out with the brachator to snag the universe and yank the *Dark Joan* in. Close was relative, but a hundred kilometres meant near neighbours in space. His laser flicked out and he unloaded another burst from the ship's accelerators, the high whining vibration of the weapons coming to him through the hull. The Harvest ship tried to match him, manoeuvre for manoeuvre, but its drive-to-mass ratio was far more mass than drive and he buzzed it like a fly. The Partheni console helpfully picked out all its arcs of fire and he chased the blind spots as it rolled and lurched then dropped suddenly away, trying to get him in range again. A moment later he was *too* close and the gravitic fields that had been fending off his attacks were clashing with his own. The whole fabric of the *Dark Joan* shuddered, and for a moment he lost control over where they were relative to the other ship.

He'd almost calculated a solution when the interceptor's pilot reconfigured their gravitic field and sent the *Joan* hurtling away, like a cork from a bottle. The interceptor itself was punted in the opposite direction by Newton's inescapable boot. Partheni ships had what Idris thought of as a panic pedal to generate emergency shielding. It flipped all the gravitic drive's resources towards defence, and he stomped on it then, almost closing his eyes as he waited for the *Joan* to take a hit. Then a kilometre of space around them was coursing with the angry metal bees of accelerator shot.

The missiles flowered away from them in a perfect rosette as the *Joan*'s drives took the gravitational gradient of space-time and hauled on it like a sheet. The lethal barrage of fire fell away from them, raindrops down a window. Except the window was the universe and "down" was in every direction.

Something hit them like a slap, making the inside of the *Joan* boom hollowly. Kris yelped, and for a moment Idris thought she'd been hit. But this was no laser, no punching railgun round. She was just demanding to know *What the fuck?* because she'd never been on the wrong end of a gravity hammer before.

I guess they do have one then. He really hadn't quite believed it, because serious gravitic weapons were for Partheni battle-ships and other big-ass militaria. But that was humanity. Apparently the Hegemony were just giving the damn things away, even to their apostate gangsters.

That had been a near miss, the interceptor's hammer striking the space the *Joan* was just vacating. Idris was still using the drive to ripple their gravitic shielding, eeling through the storm of shot the interceptor was sending their way. Their shielding couldn't take the concentrated gravitic force of a closer strike. Even another near miss might just flatten the spatial contours all around them, leaving them a sitting duck in a mathematically predictable volume of space.

The Harvest almost had them in the next second. Idris had the sense of being arrested in mid-leap, suddenly stationary, so the dampeners struggled and he and Kris were both rammed sideways in their seats. A moment later they were out of it and on the move. Again, the interceptor had missed its big chance to turn them into confetti. *Same thing, why stop then? What's the deal?* He let the back of his mind chew at it as he had the grabby drive sling them about a bit. Once more, he tried to exploit their blind spots, or at least minimize their attacker's lines of fire as they dodged.

"The *Oumaru!*" Kris shouted.

"What?" That part of his mind they'd monkeyed with, to make him an Int, was warning him that the gravity hammer was crushing space along their path like a raging imbecile chasing a fly.

"They don't—" Kris whooped again as the whole ship shuddered and groaned around them, "want to hit the *Oumaru.*"

It seemed ridiculous, because *something* had already hit the *Oumaru* with extreme prejudice, but Kris was absolutely right. The gaps in enemy fire occurred when that great scatter of accelerator rounds might catch the ruined freighter. *Worried about their friends on the* Vulture? But would that really warrant sending a near-as-damn-it warship after them—via a dangerous in-system jump. *What's so bloody valuable to them?*

Then the gravity hammer came down. He had a moment to appreciate that he'd screwed up and they were well and truly dead. Then he realized that he shouldn't have been allowed that moment. And now, two such moments later, he was still alive...The *Joan*'s damage console was lit up like it was some kind Partheni festival—but they were still there and the ship was responding to his commands.

Segmentation. It was Partheni tech developed at the end of the war. It had been brand new at Berlenhof, expensive as hell, and you had to build your entire ship around it. He remembered the *Pythoness* as it had come in towards the Architect, a mere mote in the face of that jagged crystal landscape. All around them, other ships had been flayed away. The unseen hands of the enemy's gravitic fields had found them and sculpted them into tatters and flowers and murderous origami. One of his Int classmates, in a ship up ahead, had been snuffed out into nothing, just gone into loose molecules and tormented strings of organic material. Then the *Pythoness* had fallen under the Architect's gravity field too, but the new tech had saved them, shunting the clenching force of the strike right down its segmented hull, focusing and concentrating that force until...

Until now, the *Dark Joan* slipped from the interceptor's grasp like a lizard leaving only its tail behind. The last five metres of the ship were just gone, sheared off and crushed into a knot of metal and plastic by the deflected force of the hammer's blow. But they were clear—and very close. He ran his calculations swiftly, taking into account Kris's revelation. He could unleash both the *Joan*'s laser and accelerators, then dart from blind spot to blind spot. He'd head for the point where all three ships lined up like a conjunction.

The interceptor pilot was pulling its ship round now, to catch them in its field of fire. He felt the judder as their gravitic shielding clashed against his own a second time. This time it was expected, all figured into his calculations. Lessons from Berlenhof again. Idris had been at ground zero, watching the *Heaven's Sword* crew play tag with the Architect. Their vast battleship was no more than an insect in the face of this enemy, as they calculated its hundreds of conflicting attempts to maul space around them.

And the *Heaven's Sword* had gone down, of course. But this time would be different.

Idris hit a blind spot and the interceptor rolled away just as he'd foreseen. He already had the *Joan*'s accelerators running hot, his barrage of fire whirled harmlessly away by the gravitic torsion of the other ship's shield. Another blind spot—and now Idris wasn't shielding but reaching out, predicting the defensive configurations of the enemy's shielding and matching them. He aligned the ships, reorienting the *Joan* to find a new *down*. The ship rolled uncomfortably around him and Kris, as he brought them swinging far too close to the enemy's hull. He'd seen Partheni Zero fighters do exactly the same as a swarm, to bring their weapons to bear on larger targets. He was no Zero pilot, but then this wasn't the war...*Make do and mend.*

The *Dark Joan* darted past the interceptor, heading into deep space; next instant the grabby drive had yanked it back, still yoked to the shifting gravitic fields of its target. Then came the moment he'd been waiting for...that heartbeat of stillness when the enemy weapons stopped, to avoid raking hellfire across the *Oumaru*'s warped hull. Even though the wreck was nothing more than a glinting dot a world away.

Idris unloaded everything they had, chewing up the *Joan*'s own mass for ammo, emptying the laser's power reserves. He used the shuddering flex of the interceptor's own gravitic field so that, when the enemy tried to twist the *Joan*'s attacks *away*, it took them into its heart instead, embraced them to its bosom like a lover.

He saw their reaction drives blow first, then their remaining fuel reserves, a constantly extinguishing fire venting out into the hunger of space. Abruptly the interceptor was spinning, turned from an arrow to a twirling baton by the force of the explosion. The *Joan*'s twin accelerators raked the length of the ship three times, automatically tracking along its length for as long as he maintained fire. His panel reported 307 discrete hits, like a proud child with a test score. But Idris was pulling away from the damaged ship, feeling abruptly sick at the surge of triumph he'd felt, the savage joy. For him, adrenaline went sour quickly.

He located the *Oumaru* and checked the *Vulture* was still attached. Then he scudded the *Joan* across the intervening kilometres at the ship's best speed, because the others would need him.

Solace

Mesmon slammed a fist into Solace's helmet, hard enough to spatter her visor with his own blood—a resource of which he seemed to have an infinite supply. She grabbed him under his arms and tried to throw him away from her, but he held on and they ended up kicking away from the wall, crashing straight into the knot of his confederates. They were all human, lightly suited for EVA duties and sheltering whatever they'd brought up from the *Oumaru* with their bodies. Her armoured knees rammed one in the back, hard enough to gash his suit. Another decided to get in on the action, grabbing her arm and giving the whole awkward tangle that was Solace/Mesmon a completely new spin. Solace gave the man a murderous glare and drove her fingers, ramrod straight, into his throat. She felt the thin suit material flex and then he was jerking away, kicking and strangling in mid-air, wrestling futilely with his helmet.

She tried the same with Mesmon, missing his neck but jamming a finger in his eye. At least it seemed to pain him, though nothing stopped the Tothiat. Then she had revolved to see the two remaining clowns by the drone hatch again, and they were pointing guns at her, trying for a clear shot. Rollo popped up and shot one dead, which served to distract his friend who—Solace now noticed—had a rather heavier weapon. It was a big laser, a cutting tool converted for anti-personnel use, and the man blazed it around at Rollo. Solace caught her breath as it made a slaggy mess of the wall and pipes. The captain himself was an old zero-G hand, though, pushing off before the beam's wielder dragged it round to him. A second later he sent enough bullets towards his enemy to drive the man into cover.

Then Kit chirped in Solace's ear, "Access! *Go go go!*"

Mesmon put a rock-shattering blow into her side, but she hardly noticed because she was no longer at the mercy of Newtonian physics. Gravity was back, and everything slammed into the floor. Everything except her: Solace had her wings again.

The drone bay was an instant mess of crates, bodies, blood and beads of molten metal. All of it abruptly remembering what "down" meant. She saw Rollo crunch onto one knee and twist over, cursing. The laser-wielder lunged for the little box they'd retrieved, only to fall back as a shot from the captain scored the floor nearby.

Mesmon had fallen, landing on his ass without dignity, then looking up to see the Angel of the Parthenon descending on him with righteous fury.

The shoulders of her armour boasted gravity handles. Olli's Scorpion had something similar. They let Solace ride the gravity fields, inside or outside a ship. They let her, in this specific circumstance, kick Mesmon very hard in the head, sending him hurtling backwards along the floor, with his neck at an unnatural angle.

She pursued, not at all surprised to see Mesmon's head snap back into place sporting a bloody-minded expression. He scrabbled for a gun but she knocked it from his hand and swung up to the ceiling to avoid his lunge. Then she flipped upside down to hit him in the neck, the jaw, the temple— pushing to see what his boosted physiology could endure. There *must* be limits to his healing, to the sheer energy his hybrid system could muster. Finally Solace darted back again and shot at him with Mr. Punch, virtually amputating one leg and scattering a handful of punctures across the rest of him.

Mesmon went down. The leg, despite all the tear-along-the-dotted-line work she'd just done, remained attached. And already, she could see the fibres and ropes of his muscles knotting together like a nest of snakes. Still, he was down and obviously in pain. She'd just have to see how many parts were too many, when it came to him reassembling himself. And whether his head would still curse her, once she'd separated it from his shoulders.

The laser caught her as she swooped down on the Tothiat, and her entire world dissolved into danger warnings and error messages. Solace aborted the attack instantly, using the gravity handles to scrabble backwards through the air, bobbing erratically. She had lost all the servos down one side, the plates of her armour half melted together by the heat. There was also a great deal of pain and blistered skin on the inside. But you could only heal from that if someone didn't kill you first, so she put it out of her mind. She swung around, trying to manage Mr. Punch one-handed, trying to find her new enemy.

She found him just as he rammed a new cell into his exhausted laser and levelled it at her, faceless behind his visor.

Damn, she thought, and Rollo shot him, shattering that plastic mask and sending the man pitching backwards.

Mesmon was already on his feet. She could barely believe it. She could also barely believe that the Hegemony hadn't just put twenty Tothiat together and taken over the goddamn universe by now. But maybe they were all inveterate criminals who only obeyed orders when it let them break laws.

She brought up her damage control. So much damage. She was half paralysed inside the crippled armour, and if she somehow got it off then her training wouldn't be enough to beat him.

The two of them faced off, or the three of them including Rollo, but Rollo and his little gun weren't a big feature of this conflict. He'd have to practically force-feed Mesmon the barrel to make much of an impression. Then Olli erupted into the drone bay, still fighting the lashing, coiling length of the Castigar.

There were two more laser scars across the Scorpion's metal hide and the wormlike bulk of the alien was gashed and ragged. It left a smear of black ichor across the plates of the floor. Even as the pair of them burst onto the scene, the Castigar's head-mounted weapon spoke again, spraying the room with a scatter of bullets and scribbling nonsense across the far wall with its energy beam. Then Olli finally secured a cutting claw about the headmount and ripped it off, taking a chunk of the creature's head with it. The clutch of tentacles still attached to the creature writhed in a frenzy and its length whipped madly back and forth. Mesmon was slammed one way and Solace the other. The thrashing was pure reflex by then, and mostly post-mortem. Warrior Castigar died hard, but they still died.

Unlike Tothiat, apparently, because Mesmon was scrambling up the Scorpion like a monkey, making straight for the cracked capsule that held Olli. One of her smaller arms snagged at his tattered EVA suit and he ripped the limb off in one smooth motion.

Solace levelled Mr. Punch but, with only one fully functional arm, the chance of shooting Olli was too high. Instead she scrabbled against the gravity field and just *flung* herself at the Tothiat. Half her body was locked rigid, yet she could still pilot herself about like a remote using her gravity handles. Mesmon was straddling Olli's capsule, one hand cocked back to strike, when she cannoned into him. She almost tore him loose altogether and got her working glove about his head, digging her fingers into his flesh as hard as she could.

With a snarl he took her wrist and tried to break it one-handed, but he couldn't quite get enough purchase. Instead, he just jerked at her arm—pulling hard enough to slam her into the nearest wall. Simultaneously, he drove his other elbow into Olli's clear plastic screen, cracking it into a webwork of crazed lines. Inside, the remote specialist's face was ashen, horrified.

Solace was fighting to recover control of her own armour, so she missed the moment when Rollo vaulted up and put his pistol to Mesmon's chest, opening a fist-sized hole. The Tothiat slammed back, one hand still hooked about the latch of Olli's lid. For just a second, Solace thought that was that—they'd finally breached the tolerance of the man's alien resilience.

There was hardly any blood, though. And Mesmon arched forwards, keening loud enough for Solace to hear even over the yelling of her armour's alarms. He abandoned Olli and threw himself on Rollo, knocking the man's gun aside and smashing him across the head. The blow was hard enough to break the captain's neck and visibly deform his skull.

Solace's own cry almost deafened her and it covered Olli's shriek. A moment later the Scorpion had three different limbs on Mesmon, driving claws and clamps into his flesh. She was pulling him taut between them as though she was going to tear him into thirds. And perhaps she would have done, but he wouldn't come apart. Solace could see the frame's servos straining, arms juddering and whining as they tried to maintain their grisly tension.

Then both doors of the drone bay airlock were grinding open to reveal a short umbilical—the one that connected the *Vulture* to the flayed, airless sculpture of the *Oumaru*. Immediately, the atmosphere started screaming out into the tunnel. Solace began skidding towards the open hatch, resisting with her gravity handles because she just didn't have enough working limbs to do it any other way. What she did manage to do was swing herself so that she had one foot on Rollo's body, even as Mesmon's dead compatriots spun or rolled past. They ragdolled bonelessly down the umbilical, into the open wound that was the *Oumaru*, before being sucked out into the wider universe.

"Kit!" she shouted, not even sure her comms were working. "Repair the envelope! Kittering!"

Something skidded past her as she tried to maintain her position. It was a plain metal box, but some part of her remembered its provenance and she grabbed it with her working hand. The thing Harvest had brought up from the *Oumaru*; the answer to why Rollo had lost his ship—and his life. Something important. Worth killing and dying for.

Then the hatch was fully open and Olli went through.

Solace had been thinking of this development as another attack by Broken Harvest people. Perhaps another troop of suited goons were coming up from the wreck? But Olli had control of the drone bay and she was going to do for Mesmon one way or another. Clinging to the rim of the open hatch with the Scorpion's four feet, she thrust him out into vacuum.

Solace stared, waiting, seeing ice form in the Tothiat's eyes and at the corners of his mouth, as well as across the cracks in Olli's capsule. He *wasn't dying*, though. He deliberately wrenched one of his arms free of the clamp that held it, leaving plenty of suit and flesh behind. In vacuum his substance flared out in a mess of sticky strings before knitting back together.

Olli shook him, holding him with just one claw now. Staring

at her through the ice, Mesmon dug his fingers into the metal of her arm, twisting it. *He wasn't going anywhere,* Solace thought. Then he was crawling up Olli's arm towards her, tearing himself from her pincer grip an inch at a time.

"I'm coming!" Solace shouted into the comm, but Olli snapped back, "No need," and detonated something at the Scorpion's shoulder joint, shooting the arm and its burden outwards, away, into the void.

Solace lost sight of Mesmon's face very quickly but she hoped he was fucking livid about this. Olli stayed at the hatch, watching to make sure he wasn't able to snag any part of the *Oumaru.* From her satisfied look, apparently he wasn't.

Then she drew back in and shut the hatch, and the *Vulture God*'s much-abused atmosphere processors began to take up the slack. Wordlessly, she stomped over to Rollo's body, her frame sparking and shuddering with the damage it had taken. Soon after, Kittering came pattering in, stopping dead when he saw his captain.

A little after that, Solace caught Idris's signal. The Harvest's interceptor was out of the fight. By then Kit had secured the *Oumaru* to the *Vulture*—and made space for Idris to dock the *Joan* and come aboard with Kris. So he could get both ships out of there; so he could hear the bad news.

As Idris ran through a scatter of hurried system checks, Solace handed the little box over to Olli so she could prise it open. She had a burning need to know what was inside. It had cost them enough.

It'll be nothing, she thought. *It'll be drugs, gems...some stupid thing a crime lord would sacrifice his minions to secure—and get good people killed in the bargain. It'll do nothing but highlight our pointless losses.*

Then Olli tripped the mechanism at last and they all stared down at the contents. They really weren't drugs or gems or any other stupid things. They were either fakes—or they were holding the fate of worlds in their hands.

14.

A tale of two colonies

The colony at Lycos had been no more than a knot of hardy ecologists and xeno-agriculturalists before the waves of refugees arrived. Life on Lycos was hard, the struggle to tame enough land to support people constant, starvation an ever-present shadow. And then, in the year 48 After, the Architect came.

It had burst from unspace without warning—back then, before the Intermediary Program, it was always without warning—and descended on the planet with unmistakable intent. Lycos had few ships. Those that had dropped off the refugees had already been deployed elsewhere. Evacuating the colony was simply impossible. The people planetside had plenty of time to understand what was about to happen to them. The Architect turned from a point of light, to a dot, to a fist, to a second satellite... whose thousand mountain-sized spines stabbed accusingly down at the planet.

And hung there. And hung there.

The science station at the heart of the colony had turned every appropriate instrument on the Architect, determined to gather and transmit what data it could before the end.

And then the Architect departed, leaving Lycos somehow whole and unmolested. For the first time in humanity's experience, the great gods of change and destruction had stayed their hand.

The scanner records showed a signal emanating from the Architect, solitary and singular as whalesong, directed at a very specific point on-planet. A flyer expedition, hastily mounted, discovered... something. Later researchers would characterize it as an outpost. There was little of it left, and what was there was buried twenty metres down in Lycos's acidic soil. The remains of three chambers, interconnected, spherical, partly flattened by long millennia of compression. Certain artefacts of uncertain purpose—rods, crooks and key-like objects, all small enough to be held in a human hand. Analysis of both ruin and rods failed to reveal how they were made, which in itself taught more than anything else. The fine structure of the materials did not conform to the rules of atomic bonds and molecular chemistry that applied to all "matter" discovered so far. Its substance was written in a language unrelated to the periodic table. Exact dating was similarly frustrated and the site interacted with the geology of Lycos in inexplicable ways.

The unknown creators were dubbed the Originators. Later research would link them to the creation of the unspace Throughways too. Right then, humanity seized on to one key idea. Whoever or whatever they had been, the Architects feared them. Even their million-year-old relics were enough to send the gargantuan destroyers away.

*

In the wake of the Lycos discovery, a survey team on Charm Prime reported finding similar relics on that barren, blasted world.

Charm Prime had been named by a real joker. The world was arid, devoid of life. The same hadn't always been true. There were signs of a thriving biosphere and some kind of civilization dating from at least a hundred thousand years before, including roads and the ground-down traces of ruins. The fate of the world and its inhabitants was unclear, but lingering areas of radiation raised some grim possibilities. However, in the midst of the largest and most intact ruin was what hazmat-suited archaeologists had labelled a shrine. It didn't seem to be made by Originators, but the contents were uncannily similar to the objects found at Lycos. They had already been old, perhaps venerated, when the Charm Prime civilization had been bombing itself and its world into oblivion.

Nobody wanted to settle Charm Prime bar one apocalyptic religious sect. However, a short Throughway linked that world to Karis, where a commune government had been taking in large numbers of refugees. Karis was a good world, able to support many fleeing humans. And when its government took possession of the Originator relics, there wasn't much the Charm Prime faithful or the archaeologists could do. Scientific research and faith both came second to saving lives.

Not long after, an Architect did come to the burgeoning world of Karis. There was little attempt at evacuation. They trusted the Originators to save them.

They were mistaken. Karis joined the ranks of reworked worlds, another planet-scale martyr to the Architects' craft.

That was how humanity learned the second lesson on Originator regalia. *You cannot move them.* Oh, on-planet, certainly. But the moment mankind took these objects into unspace they became just . . . things; useless sticks and stones. Objects of ritual significance only. Just another inexplicable mystery attached to the Originators, that hypothetical ancient civilization which raised only unanswerable questions.

Except the relics *could* be moved in a way that preserved their integrity. A few years after the loss of Karis, during the thick of the war, Colonial diplomats finally disentangled the Essiel's most important message. It was what Hegemonic representatives had been trying to communicate ever since humans first ran into them. The Hegemony was asking humans to submit to their rule, not through threats, but via a particularly potent promise.

The Essiel knew all about the Architects, from before humans had even smelted bronze. They, too, had discovered the protection these long-gone Originators could still provide. But *they* had discovered how to transport the regalia. Every single Hegemony world was protected from Architect attention. In return for the subservience and obeisance of their subjects, they offered life.

When this became clear, human worlds began to open private channels to the Essiel. The Hegemony began to acquire human subjects, one planet at a time. And what could the Colonial governments do, precisely? It wasn't as though they had a better offer, right then.

Kris

Kris had lived out of the *Vulture God* for four years. She knew it backwards. She knew its sounds too, but they had always been the sounds of other people: Barney cursing recalcitrant mechanisms, Olli clattering about in one of her frames as she worked on the remotes, the tap-tap of Kittering's many feet, Rollo's rich voice.

Alone in unspace, the ship was ghastly. Her every step, every shuffle, echoed against the metal walls. Idris had said, *be still, close your eyes* as they dropped into the void, but that wasn't an option. Without those little scuffs and rustles from her, there was only the silence...and the silence was terrible because it wasn't quite complete.

She was alone on the *Vulture God*. Or no, she *wasn't* alone.

She'd read about this, watched mediotypes: your mind populated the absence with a spurious presence. It was just sensory deprivation, operating on a hitherto unexamined sense. Pacing past the little cells of the crew cabins, Kris could sense there was *something* out there. When she moved, it moved, when she was still, it waited. A little closer every time, stalking her at its leisure.

People went mad, tried to destroy themselves, tried to destroy their ships. The alternative would be coming face to face at last with *It*...and that was literally unbearable. You'd do anything to avoid looking into that mirror.

And the fact that everyone who came out of unspace sane and hale reported the same "delusion" was not a comfort. Because Kris couldn't stop thinking, surely there was only one logical explanation to everyone having the same experience...That, despite everything, there really *was* something out there. Unspace had a single and inimitable denizen, and she was trapped in here with it.

Now she felt *It* creep closer, silent, utterly undetectable, imaginary, except that she knew it was there.

She was playing a game as she walked through the *Vulture God*, feeling that *other* take a step for every one of hers as it stalked her. She was in the *God's* command pod now, with its empty pilot's chair. *It* lurked just on the other side of the door. She knew it for certain. *For god's sake, Kris, keep it together.*

Her hand had drifted up to the door panel of its own accord. She absolutely did *not* want to see what was there. Yet her hand wanted to remove the one thin barrier between her and *It*. And she wondered: *What if this is what happens to those who end themselves? They look into Its face.*

Or what if some who come out of unspace aren't even the same people anymore? Their minds twisted by this "Other"?

Her arm twitched convulsively, pushing towards the door control.

I can't stop myself. She knew with utter horror that she was going to open the door.

Then the world dropped out from underneath her, the *Vulture God* wrenched its way out of unspace into the real— and she opened the door.

Olli was on the far side, in her Scorpion, one battered manipulator extended to do exactly the same. They shared a wide-eyed stare.

"Check in, please," came Idris's voice over the comms.

"Here," Kris confirmed, and saw Olli's lips shape the same word. Kittering and Solace followed suit, from wherever they had ended up in the ship.

What if I'd been on the same side of the door as Olli, she wondered, trembling slightly. It didn't happen, somehow. As though people, no matter how alone, retained some knowledge of what space was already occupied.

"Let's not do that again," she suggested, shipwide. They'd wanted to get clear of Tarekuma as fast as possible, and bedding down would have taken precious time. Idris hadn't liked the idea but they'd wanted him to just get them the hell out of there. *Idris doesn't ever go into suspension.* Kris felt sick at the thought—and simultaneously wretchedly grateful that someone would do this dreadful thing for her, so she'd never have to do it again.

*

Inside the wreck of the *Oumaru* they found a compartment, set into the wall of what had once been the hold. It was just large enough to hold the box the hijackers had retrieved.

Inside that box, held in some manner of suspension, was a handful of corroded, broken-ended rods and a spiked disc, all apparently made of some ancient greenish-black stone. To the untutored eye, all that was available, they looked disturbingly like Originator regalia.

"Fakes," Olli said flatly, into a silence. "Must be fakes. You can't just...lug them about. Everyone knows that."

"Hegemonics can," Solace said softly. "No one knows how, but we *know* they *can*."

They stared at the box, now resting at a slant on one of the command consoles. It was still open, displaying its impossible contents for all to see.

"This is..." Idris started, and then stopped. Kris knew why. This was *big*. They had found something literally worth a world's ransom. What wouldn't a Colonial government, a Hanni trade consortium or a Castigar world council give for this? For protection against the Architects—especially now? What wouldn't the Hegemony give too, to get these relics back? Assuming they were genuine. *No. Even if they're not. After all, how would you go about testing them? Money back if the Architects destroy your world?*

"Inestimable value here," Kittering spoke up, calculations scrolling down his arm-screens too fast to follow. "Literally inestimable. Priceless. Price, less. Invaluable. Without value."

"What are you babbling about?" Olli snapped at him. "You could sell these..." She trailed off.

"If we were Broken Harvest, maybe we could sell them for some stupid amount that was still stupidly low for what they're worth," Kris said. "But we're just *us*. And the moment we tried to put these on the market, a thousand different groups would work out we're far easier to just kill. Even if we sold them for a song."

"*Arses*," Olli breathed, staring at their newfound treasure.

"Anyway," Idris put in. "We have something else to do first."

Spacer funerals weren't elaborate. There was no grand ritual to it, no protected ceremony, fancy hangings or pretty caskets. Most of the human race simply hadn't been able to pack those old-Earth traditions when the evacuation call went out.

And so the "spacer's wake" tradition came about.

"Captain Rollo Rostand," Olli announced. They were in the *Vulture's* drone bay, because there was more room there. It was a novelty for spacers to have a physical body present. Not knowing what else to do, Kris had printed out Rollo a fresh set of shipboard clothes and dressed him in his father's old jacket. He had newly printed sandals on his cold, dead feet and they were slightly askew. Kris kept wanting to adjust them, as though Rollo might get blisters wherever he was going.

Olli took a deep breath. "Born 73 After, on Orbital Nexus Seven over Tormaline," she said, and looked around at the others.

"Terrible gambler," Kris put in dutifully, staring down at the man's body. He had been by far the best captain she and Idris had signed on with, despite his flaws. Because of his flaws. No slave-driver, no profit-chaser, no margin-cutter, and so never quite the successful man of business some of his peers were. But a far better captain to work under, for all that.

"Too quick with his fists, by half," Idris said faintly. He looked to Kittering but the Hanni was tilted forwards, screens dark and arms motionless.

The silence stretched out until Kris elbowed Solace. Olli looked as though she would object to the Partheni getting a word in, but then scowled and subsided.

"No sense of delegation." And to her credit, Solace looked as upset as any of them, despite only having known Rollo for a short time. Kris wondered what they'd taught her to expect of a Colony man with a command position. Nothing good, probably, so maybe meeting Rollo had shaken her preconceptions.

Olli sighed. "Our father, he was, our grandfather, our uncle, a captain of his own ship. Loyal to his crew and safe hands. Died in space where we all die, where he belonged. One of ours, he was."

Kris mumbled the last few words along with her, adding

this grief to the others stored up inside her, the way spacers did. And some time in the future there'd be somewhere to drink, some place that didn't need clear minds and constant maintenance to keep it together, and then the grief would get a round bought for it, and more than one, and have its edges dulled.

"This is not…not not correct," Kittering's translator piped up. "Observation of set protocols is recognized and observed but…But no, not for him. Grand tragedy of a lost nurse demands pledges of furtherance and dedication."

They stared at him. Kris glanced to Olli, finding the same lack of understanding there.

"He produced zero offspring in continuation of his germ line," Kittering's translator rattled, turning Hanni concepts into their nearest human equivalents. "He dedicated himself to the nurturing of others, of us, of we. He nursed us. He was our teacher. Our *teacher*." And there were nuances of meaning that just weren't coming through. "I pledge to him that when I give up myself to continuation, he shall be added to the pool of names. I dedicate nineteen eggs to Captain Rollo Rostand."

Later, Kris slept on this, and on what she knew of the Hannilambra, and thought she understood. Right then, none of it had made sense—save that the little alien was as upset as any of them and needed to express this in his own way, beyond the stripped-down envelope of a spacer's funeral. Before they sent Rollo off to roam the universe on his last, eternal voyage.

*

And after that: there was the box. It was still on the *Vulture*'s command console, open and waiting for them, its contents shimmering within a field Olli had not been able to analyse.

"Some kind of gravitic interaction," was all she could say for certain. "No idea how there's any kind of generator in that little box. And you don't feel any push or pull, even when holding the case."

"Open it up," Kris suggested. "See how it's done." When the drone specialist looked at her, she shrugged. "If we find out, the information alone would be worth..."

"Every Tothiat assassin in the Hegemony after us," Idris suggested wryly.

"It's Hegemony tech..." Olli squinted at the box as though trying to see into its substance. "You ever hear of Transient Component Engines? The high-level Essiel stuff—not the toys they give to their underlings. They generate ghost fields in fluids, so that the substrate springs into the shapes they need. Infinitely reconfigurable tech...you need a toaster, it's a toaster; you need a cutting torch, it's a cutting torch."

"They need a lot of toasters in the Hegemony?" Kris asked, intentionally trying to keep things light now the funeral was done.

"Means if you take it apart, the gubbins just splats out the bottom of the box and you've got nothing. Even with top-flight lab equipment, nobody's been able to learn much from Hegemony tech. And you can bet they protect this particular golden nugget with a *lot* of failsafes."

"Question," from Kit, and his screens flashed up. "Aklu's equivalence to Hegemony."

"I guess its not officially Hegemony." Idris shrugged. "But... what do the Essiel think about one of their own going renegade for a life of crime? Same as for anything. Nobody knows."

"We can't just *sit* on this," said Solace. It was her first contribution since the funeral.

"Sure you've got a load of suggestions," Olli growled.

"If these *are* real, we have the tools to save a planet," Solace said. Idris glanced at her warily, sensing a slight distance that hadn't been there before.

"Query as to which planet," Kit chirped.

"You don't understand. We have the tools to save *any* planet. If we can ship it out in time, the next planet an Architect shows up at can be saved—just by getting this box ground-side," Solace went on implacably. "Assuming these relics are genuine, which they may not be."

"Assuming the field holding them lasts indefinitely, which it may not," Kris added. "Aklu might have been desperate to get them back because it's about to run out of battery."

"Even so," Solace said, "we have a duty—"

"Let me guess," Olli broke in loudly. "This comes down to giving it over to the Parthenon. Slice it thin as you want, that's what this is about, no?"

"You want to give it to Hugh?" Solace wasn't backing down this time, meeting Olli's angry stare. "Or maybe the Hegemony? Some Magdan Boyar with deep pockets? Kittering, you've a buyer lined up?"

The Hanni's screens displayed bafflement, not following the subtext.

"We will sell the damn thing back to the Essiel before it goes to *your* lot," Olli said flatly.

"Now wait—" Kris started, but Olli sent her such a murderous glower that she bit the words back.

Solace, face absolutely calm, gave that a moment to hang in the air before saying, "I know that in the Colonies they say a lot of things about my people. I've seen the Hugh propaganda too. We're warmongers, we're man-haters, we're unnatural, born in a lab, indoctrinated, Programmed like machines. All that, I've heard. And nobody remembers we died for the Colonies, above a hundred worlds, during the war. We were the *line*." And the softer edges of her voice were ablating off, revealing only steel beneath. Kris belatedly remembered this wasn't just third-generation ancestral pride; Solace had *been* there. She had fought in the war, faced the Architects.

"We were the shield and sword of the Colonies," the Partheni went on. "And then, when the war was over, you started asking why we had to keep on being *different* to you. Why couldn't we just come back and be your wives and daughters again? You really think we quit Hugh because we had some designs on your planets? Because we wanted to line all your menfolk up against a wall, and make everyone else like us? We left because you *hated* us and would have used your laws to break us if we'd stayed." She stood, jabbing a finger at Olli. "All we *ever did* was put our lives on the line for you. And you still hate us for it."

"That," Olli spat back, "is *not* why I hate your bloody kind." And Kris blinked, because she'd noted the friction between the two, the scowls and frowns from Olli. She'd taken it for a clash of personalities, the rigid soldier against the prickly spacer.

"*Look* at me, Myrmidon Executor Solace." Olli twisted in the capsule of her walking frame, stump arms and stump leg shifting. "Your precious eugenics wouldn't ever have made *me*, would it? You see a thing like *me* growing in your vats, you'd flush the contents out into space. Not fit for your perfect society, am I?"

Kris saw anger twist Solace's face, rage there for a moment like a trapped beast, then just...go, leaving a hollow expression on her face. The Partheni sat down abruptly.

"I...what do you think we'd...? Well, no, but..." Solace's eyes were fixed on Olli, and everyone else was silent. Eventually she said, in quite a small voice, "I don't know what to say. I mean...you're probably right. It would be before you were *you*, but...with the fleet's resources we could... I mean..."

Kris waited for Olli to go on the attack again, exploiting the breach. But the drone specialist had sagged back in her capsule, looking unhappy. "Listen, there will be a war between us, some day, maybe even when I'm alive to see it. Your side don't want it, Hugh sure as fuck doesn't want it, but it'll happen."

"There won't—" Solace started, but Olli just rolled over her words.

"A war," she repeated. "And you'll win, probably. You have the best ships. But we Colonials, we're awkward buggers, we won't just behave ourselves. So you'll have to make us better people, won't you? Just like your Parthenon is full of better people than us. And you know what better people means? It means that people who aren't like you don't have a future, if you win. So the Parthenon doesn't get this box."

Solace took a deep breath. "That wouldn't happen. We don't want to change people."

"You said yourself, we hate you," Olli told her quietly. "That's a real grand high horse. You can look down from on high, knowing that you're hated by dumb, regular, inferior humans. Gives you the moral right to do all sorts of things for the greater good. You going to straight up swear to me that there's no chance, none at all, it'd go like that?"

There was quite a silence, after that. Probably Solace should have been advancing all sorts of guarantees about the future intentions of her government. But Kris reckoned she was a fundamentally honest person.

"I am actually starting to hope these things *are* fake," Idris dropped in, when the quiet had become unbearable.

"Overwhelming possibility," agreed Kit. Kris watched the tilt of his mandibles as they whittled against one another. There was a language to the angles there: you could tell something of his mood—not Hanni moods in general but Kittering in particular. Because he'd been around humans for years and had taken something of them into himself. Right now he was unhappy, plain enough.

"Then let's focus on that. If we have the real deal or not," Solace suggested.

"Oh, right, I'll get my artefact verification tools out, shall I?" Olli snapped, then looked away. "Fine. Okay. Not constructive."

"It's all right." Solace pressed her hands to her face, briefly. Then she was abruptly bright, businesslike, everything else pushed away. "If you do want to check their veracity first, I have a suggestion. And it's not, 'Take them to a Partheni assessor,' before you ask. Idris, do you remember Trine?"

Idris twitched at his name, then frowned. "Do I...? Wait... you mean the research hive? That Trine?"

Kris looked from one to the other as Solace nodded, sensing the submerged weight of their unspoken memories.

"But they...can't still be around. They'd have gone back to the Assembly, surely. Whatever Trine is now..." Idris stuttered to a halt.

"The longest-instanced Hiver consciousness, ever. Almost as old as we are," Solace said drily.

"How...?"

"An expert's an expert. I was sent to consult with them, years back. They've been working on dig sites across multiple jurisdictions ever since the war. I can find out where they are now. We can go there...If that's what people want."

"Explain," Olli pressed.

"This was—"

"Back in the war, sure," Olli agreed. "Who or what is Trine? A Hiver?"

"After Lycos, studying Originators became top priority," Idris explained. "They set up a whole war department to find out how their relics repelled the Architects. Needless to say, that's not something anyone ever found out. Then there was Karis, when we realized we knew even less than we thought. They flew a team from one site to the next, gathering data, late on in the war. Partheni ships, because they could get out of trouble best; Int pilots, because we cut corners fastest. I hadn't thought any of those guys were still around but... Trine was a Hiver. Or, back then, Trine was just an asset of the archaeology team, because Hivers weren't people. But they talked like a person. They curated all the data for the others, which meant they basically knew more than anyone. I...it's hard to believe that instance of them is still around, honestly."

"I think Trine intends to go on until the work's done," Solace said. "Which could well be forever."

"And they can tell us if these things are real?" Olli pressed.

"If anyone can," Solace confirmed. "There is literally no greater expert on Originator relics outside the Hegemony. And I don't think we want to head that way, right?"

15.

Havaer

The relationship between Tarekuma and the wider Council of Human Interests was a complicated one. And from Havaer Mundy's point of view, it was entirely unsatisfactory. Officially, the system was in the heart of the Colonies; it even had a seat on the Council. In practice it was what was called a "Ward Borough," along with perhaps a score of other worlds. Tiny outposts, science stations, terraforming operations or planets that had no interest in engaging with Hugh but needed to be looked after anyway. Then there were worlds like Tarekuma where there were plenty of people but no legitimate authority. Every year, some councillor or other said that Hugh should move in on Tarekuma, root out the gangs, lift the standard of living. There would be a study, the appalling cost of the operation would be duly reported, and the project would end up shelved until next time—when those same figures could be updated and re-presented.

Havaer knew full well that people in his line of work had a use for places like Tarekuma. He himself had arranged clandestine meetings there, received covert information via its informants and hired operatives who wouldn't ever appear on the books. Some of his colleagues were completely at ease with that side of the job. He didn't judge them, nor did it escape his notice that several had ended up kicked out of the service after becoming a little too...personally involved. That was the problem with associating with criminals. It led to Newtonian espionage. Each action produced an equal and opposite reaction and you couldn't use without being used in turn.

Tarekuma was the worst den of villainy that Hugh oversaw. Its position at a nexus of Throughways had brought many sinners together inside one atmosphere, and Havaer was bleakly aware that some of their dirty money stuck to the hands of high-up people in Hugh. Another reason it would never see reform.

There was a Hugh station in orbit hosting a reasonably equipped Mordant House sub-office. The department's formal name—the Intervention Board—was a bit of a joke in these parts. Nobody was *intervening* on Tarekuma. Heading up the Tarekuma office required someone who was simultaneously unambitious and grimly devoted to the service. Such was Albas Solier, who came to meet Havaer at the dock.

"You're after *Vulture God* and the *Oumaru?*" she said, without even a hello or a formal introduction: a broad, very dark woman ten years Havaer's senior at least.

"You've got them?" Havaer guessed that was too good to be true.

"They've been through here. Some fireworks, some raised eyebrows, some very angry people down below. Interesting friends you've got, Agent Mundy."

"You've a dossier?"

"I've all the rumour and fiction you could wish. As to what we actually know, well, step into my office."

Albas grew plants for a hobby, or at least Havaer assumed the spiky, faceted things were plants. Decorative enough, so long as you didn't end up cutting yourself on them. He drew up a stool as she misted them with something that smelled faintly of burning hair. Nothing about Tarekuma was nice.

An aide came in with a slate: the promised dossier. He opened it up idly; there was a timeline, a cache of contacts, incident reports and a longer and woollier file of perhaps and maybe.

"Let me summarize what we *do* know," Albas said, turning from her plants. "The *Oumaru* and *Vulture God* turned up in-system a couple of days ago, far enough out that we almost missed them. A Partheni packet ship went after them the moment they appeared, as did a marauder-type vessel from one of the local docks. They fought and the Partheni won out—meaning the girls were punching *way* over their weight class, frankly. They docked at the *Vulture-Oumaru* and then jumped out of system. The marauder limped back later with casualties."

"Who's the marauder registered to?"

"Do you honestly think that information is of any practical use?" She had linked to his slate and pulled up the relevant documents for him: some shell company registered in Scintilla, where a million meaningless puppet enterprises had a fictional existence.

"Track back," he directed, and she walked him through the chain of events, layering the evidence on his slate as she spoke. He took it in, but the spectre of a Partheni military action within the Colonial Sphere was looming large in his mind. Then one detail snagged in his brain and he said, "Wait, they visited a *what?*"

"A lawyer, of all things." Albas showed him the Partheni packet runner parked up in expensive surroundings. "A dock rented by a Prosecutor Livvo Thrennikos, ex-Scintilla dropout. One of the standard sorts of leechfat in these parts."

Havaer sat back. The same Partheni packet runner had left Lung-Crow, and according to his information, the *Vulture's* crew had been on it. So *was* the whole thing a Parthenon operation? And if so, what did *they* know about the Architects? He tried to get a gut-sense of just how big this mess was, and failed. Everything was just ghosts in the mist.

"I'll need to get a packet ready, encrypted, for the next runner going anywhere."

"Facilities at your disposal," Albas confirmed. "And?"

"Book me an appointment with this Thrennikos," Havaer said. He'd planned to go planetside in his mediotypist persona, but right now he reckoned there were better ways to crack the nut. "Tell the son of a bitch we want to talk about his tax returns."

*

There were no local requirements to file returns. However, people in Thrennikos's position did business off-world too, which gave Havaer a cover. He couldn't say for sure that Prosecutor Livvo Thrennikos had some skeletons filed away inside his tax returns, but something definitely had the man on edge.

"Nice view." Havaer had deliberately come dressed in Berlenhof-standard clothes printed at the Mordant local office. As always, they hadn't been able to properly tailor for his odd shoulders and wrong-sized feet, so nothing quite fit. Thrennikos himself was dressed in a manner Havaer recognized as "Glittery Business Pimp." It made Havaer proud to be a little unkempt. *Shows my Polyaspora roots.* Stupid, but the thought gave him a little glow.

"It's better in the first few weeks of summer." Thrennikos cleared his throat, which sounded pleasingly dry. "There's a, hm, migration, of some of the local wildlife."

Havaer was supremely uninterested. "Prosecutor Thrennikos..." he started, emphasizing the title with some irony. Sure as hell nobody on Tarekuma ever got prosecuted for anything.

"You wanted to check something?" Thrennikos had the fiction of his tax documents up on a virtual screen. He waved at them, nervously. "I'm aware that the entertainment expenses for my Amaryllis trip were somewhat high, but that's just how they..."

"Prosecutor, I'm not averse to twisting your arm over..." Havaer consulted Albas's notes, "what looks like nineteen solid hours of brothel time. I mean, I could refer it for investigation, recommend a fine, or I could just assume that Amaryllis is a fun place and your clients like being put at their ease. However, if you answer a few innocuous questions, we can pretend I never spotted your epic brothel-a-thon."

Thrennikos was observing him, still very nervous but not the nerves of your typical tax evader or even someone with a weird fetish they didn't want raked up. "Can you put into plain language what you mean, Officer Mundy?"

Havaer checked the surveillance readings on his slate and raised his interference field. He didn't want this business recorded.

Thrennikos watched this, then said "Mordant House?"

Havaer nodded.

"Thank god for that."

"That's an unusually enlightened attitude to take, Prosecutor. Most people aren't too happy to see us."

Thrennikos finally dropped into his chair. "Better than actually having to go through the tax stuff." He was trying to be cool, now, but Havaer could still see the tension in him.

"I need to talk to you about some visitors..."

"Oh, I know exactly who you're here about," Thrennikos told him. "And if I'd known just how much trouble they were going to be, I'd have said no. Just an introduction—that was all they wanted. Who knew it would end with space piracy? I assure you, Officer, I was acting entirely in good faith, a favour for an old friend, even, if you can believe that."

Havaer found it within the bounds of credibility. "You met with...?"

"Kerry Almier, plus some shabby spacer and a Hanni factor." Thrennikos glanced at the slate Havaer showed him, picked out the face of Rollo Rostand and the shell pattern of Kittering. "Like I say, all above board, just an introduction... You probably won't believe this, Officer, but just about everything that goes through this office is sunny side up. When my clients come to me it's for the legitimate side of things. They've got the crooked stuff covered."

"Introduction to whom?" Havaer pressed. He was getting

twitchy himself now, seeing the man's nerves just keep mounting. *It's not me he's worried about, so...?*

That was the point when the office door burst open and four thugs came in. Havaer whipped a gun out, a magnetic pistol that wasn't quite an accelerator because it was hard to fit a metre of barrel in a concealed holster. Three of the intruders were human—a woman and two men in rough ship-style clothes with reinforced jackets. All armed, all tough-looking, and there was something about the woman that suggested *Not entirely human*. The fourth, leading the way, was a squat Hiver frame, four-legged and headless, their chest sporting three serpentine manipulator cables and what he could only describe as a rotary cannon.

Thrennikos was very still and not at all surprised. "Officer, these are my new clients, representing the Broken Harvest Society. They share your interest in my earlier visitors. And in anyone asking questions about them."

"And the currency your new clients are paying you in is...?"

"Not skinning me and wearing me like a cloak, yes," the lawyer said. "Like I said, if I'd known the kind of trouble Kerry was bringing to my door...but I *didn't*. I had *no idea*." Words spoken very clearly for the benefit of the newcomers. Especially the woman who was coming forward now, studying Havaer.

"Government man," she said. "My name is Heremon, herald of The Unspeakable Aklu, the Razor and the Hook. I am sent to tender you the most cordial invitation to confer with my liege and master concerning a commercial shipping matter, specifically the freighter *Oumaru*, which has been stolen from us."

"What a cordial invitation." Havaer sat on the edge of Thrennikos's desk and had his internal dispenser calm his heart. His gun was directed right at her chest, but Heremon didn't seem to care. Her own weapon just dangled loose in her hand. Of course, the Hiver's piece was basically light artillery that would turn the whole office into an exercise in Brownian motion if it spun up, so maybe she felt she didn't need to ram a pistol up his nose to make the point.

Heremon smiled. It wasn't a nice smile but there was at least a spark of humour there. "We *do* hope you'll accept," she told him, making a fair attempt at a high-class Berlenhof accent. Havaer wondered whether to double down on the government card. To say Hugh writ ran thin on Tarekuma was something of an understatement, though. Besides, all that string of titles was a Hegemony thing, which put them even further from caring a damn about his precious authority.

"Well I'd be churlish to say no, then, wouldn't I?" He scratched at his jaw, activating his locator beacon and sending a message through his slate to Thrennikos's linked desk system. When he left the room, it would send Albas his personal recording of this conversation. Or that would be the ideal result, if nobody out-finagled him.

Heremon actually swept a bow, like something out of a cod-historical mediotype. Havaer caught a glimpse of the segmented louse-roach-looking thing melded to her spine. *Oh, right.* He'd heard of the Tothiat, but that was as far as it went.

"This is it, right?" Thrennikos burst in, trying very hard to keep his voice steady. "We're clear now? Your boss is okay with me?"

The Tothiat woman gave him a level look. "I'm sure we'll be in touch, Prosecutor. Now, Menheer, if you'd be so kind?" She offered him her arm. The Hiver took three metal steps back as he took it, keeping him in sight of their gun. The fact that it would chew Heremon to pieces too, if the weapon fired, didn't seem to upset the woman at all.

*

They took him to a service port at the edge of the vertical city, and for a moment Havaer thought they were just going to throw him down the chasm. His career might not have survived that. But there was an a-grav platform waiting there, a hovering disc three metres across with a profoundly inadequate railing. He stepped aboard brightly enough, sending a signal to his metabolic balance to up his coordination and response times in case this became acrobatic.

"Mind telling me what this is about?" he asked Heremon, as they ascended up the chasm—and downwards through the social strata of Coaster City. "The Prosecutor and I were just discussing some taxation matters, so..." He gave her a sidelong look, staked his life on his character judgement, and went on, "If you need some help filling in forms."

He received the slightest twitch of a smile, which was reassuring. He didn't know how human Tothiat were, but a sense of humour seemed a good start. Then she said, "Don't do jokes at our meeting, Hugh-man. My master is not in the mood to be amused."

"This Aklu?"

"The Unspeakable Aklu, the Razor and the Hook," she

recited in full, with a hard look at him. "My master is not casual about his honours."

Which means precisely what the hell, exactly? Havaer wondered. Matters had suddenly gone sideways, as far as he was concerned. "What does he want *me* for?"

"It's enough that he wants you." Heremon looked away and that, apparently, was that.

There were another three toughs waiting at a higher platform. The atmosphere was thinner here, and the sunlight a hot glare against his skin. His medical monitor cautioned him about exposure times. He had no way to explain to it that the shit he was in counted as mitigating circumstances.

His comms implant received a ping telling him the local office had his position. Havaer didn't particularly want to become the focus of a firefight, but he was starting to feel curious now the initial shock had worn off. He scratched at his jaw again, casual as anything, sending the command: *Hold till my signal.*

Just hope I don't regret it.

Not quite a prisoner but far from a free man, he was cordially escorted to some concrete dump of a place, cracked and pitted and bleached by too much solar glare. Inside he was brought into a scene of utter carnage.

He missed the main feature of the room for some time, because the bloody foreground had his full attention. A couple of humaniform Castigar and a dozen humans were standing around watching someone get flayed alive.

Havaer just stopped, eyes bulging. He uttered a sound that he'd thought a career at Mordant House had ironed out of him. They had some luckless bastard strung up by his wrists from an a-grav frame while a six-armed golden Hiver with a sad metal face vivisected the poor sod. They'd pinned back his chest and abdomen, opening up the ribs and holding them in place with clamps and vices. The victim's intestines and various other organs were spread out in an eerie halo about his body, floating in the a-grav field. He was somehow still alive, his blunt face locked in a savage grimace. His blood, and there was a lot of it, was also suspended in droplets. The nimble, darting arms of the Hiver were gathering them to draw designs in the air—a sanguine litany of alien art. The most terrifying thing about this barbaric, alien spectacle was that it wasn't quite barbaric or alien enough that Havaer couldn't see the pattern. It reminded him of nothing so much as what the Architects did to worlds. There was old history between the Hegemony and the Architects, wasn't there? The clam bastards had suffered and lost worlds for an age before they worked out their trick with the Originator toys. Didn't it make sense, then, that the trauma of those cataclysmic days had wormed its way into their psyches and their art? But this...

The victim groaned and gasped, and the Hiver took hold of his elbows and spun him gently. His array of innards— though they were no longer *in*—rippled like serpents around him. The blood patterns undulated and formed new arrangements, a message that Havaer was grateful he couldn't read. Then he saw the black and yellow arthropod thing melded to the man's back and understood. Another Tothiat. He wasn't watching an *execution*, but a punishment for failure.

Then he looked past the display and realized he had been in the presence of "The Unspeakable" all this time. There was an actual real live Essiel *right there*, hovering in its couch, watching its will be done.

The Hiver stepped away from their work and daintily shook their arms, the skin of blood sloughing off them into the a-grav field, leaving their hands gleaming and clean. At some signal, a couple of watchers stepped forwards gingerly, queasily even, and slid the victim away. His wounds were trying to heal, Havaer saw, but the a-grav field and clamps prevented the man's bloody-minded resilience from doing its job. It must, he reflected, really, really hurt.

A tortured groaning sound shook the room and the Essiel's array of arms flurried. The Hiver took a light step forwards and regarded him with their frowning gold mask.

"Crows gather yet the shadow of the vulture passed above us, crossing past the bound of the horizon. Know this, mordant man: seek now to dip your beak, and you will meet the fury of our wings."

Havaer blinked at them, then at the enigmatic bulk of the Essiel, Aklu. There were no crows, no birds of any sort, on the Essiel homeworld. They were an Earth thing, long extinct save where some planet had resurrected or transplanted them. The words were an attempt to give a human gloss to alien sentiments and he translated all that flowery doggerel as *Hands off, it's mine.*

And *"mordant man."* His tax officer ID wasn't fooling anyone. Or likely the Broken Harvest had access to some back-channel, which had "made him" even as he entered the system. Or else the divine Essiel could read minds? *I mean who actually knows for sure?*

"Well," and he addressed the bivalve master, not the cyborg servant, "it is of course an honour to be in the presence. You'll forgive me for not knowing the proper etiquette, but let's take the awe and respect as read, if we could?"

Another basso rumble from the creature, joined by a tortured groan from the flayed Tothiat. Havaer was proud that his voice had been steady, devoid of either fear or awe. Before the Hiver could start their rigmarole again he added, "You were talking about something belonging to you that my people have no claim upon? I hope I'm not here to discuss that. I'm on Tarekuma for information. I came from Mordant House, as you say, because some spacers dragged a ship here recently—one that had been wrecked by Architects. I imagine you appreciate why that's of interest to us."

The Hiver took three precise steps at an angle to him, arms spread in a fan that mimicked the rayed figure on the thugs' banners. "The drivers of destruction that have brought demise to worlds are of no interest here. We seek what's ours. And let not Hugh or Mordant—nor the lords of the Hegemony itself—step in between us and our treasure."

"No interest?" Havaer echoed. "The Architects' return is of no *interest*?" He looked around at the audience of thugs and monsters. "You wouldn't raise an eyebrow if one of *them* arrived in the sky over Tarekuma?"

They still seemed profoundly unimpressed, which was either criminal *sang froid par excellence* or just utterly inward-looking stupidity. Unless this Aklu carted around its own Originator defence kit.

"Well look, I don't know what you're seeking. But it doesn't sound like it's anything to do with us. I'm after bigger fish."

The Unspeakable Aklu actually shifted slightly in its couch, and he saw the whole assemblage hinge and flex beneath its weight. The trio of red globe eyes spread wider, as though trying to find a crack through which to weigh his soul. A long, slow vibration built through the room until the walls shook, and everyone around him tensed. He saw hands go to knives, to guns…Heremon, the other Tothiat, stepped into a fighting stance and Havaer found himself matching her. He was ready to go down swinging, if that was all that was left to him. *Died for the honour of Mordant House. Lousy thing to go on your permanent record.*

"Know this," the Hiver chimed, their bell-like voice clashing with the mood in the room. "Not all the nations of the worlds may stand between the Razor and its mark. We do not fear the tyranny of state nor brook the bite of laws. What we shall do is that which we decree."

"You're not afraid of us, right, I get that." *Goddamn gangster's facing down the whole Colonial government, apparently, while hiding in a bomb shelter on an armpit world.* "You'll do what you need to, to get whatever it is that's been taken from you. I get that. Like I say, it's the prospect of Architects destroying whole worlds that has *us* all flustered." On the basis that he was as screwed as he was likely to get, he wagged a finger in the Hiver's face. "You put that in a respectful way, you hear? Because I do not know the dance steps around here."

To his surprise the golden head revolved, giving him a moment of smiling regard from their other, benevolent face before returning to the exaggerated frown. They paced through a half-dozen stylized attitudes, strutting before Aklu like a peacock—arms folding and fanning repeatedly. The Essiel thrummed and belched, its own myriad limbs fluttering like a debutante's fan.

"The compact is agreed, and reverence given," the Hiver announced. Then everyone relaxed, just like that. Everyone except the tortured Tothiat, anyway, who didn't really have the option. Havaer didn't like the sound of the words, which implied he'd just signed up to something—possibly as a representative of the entirety of Hugh and the Colonies—but that ship had left dock and gone into the void. He'd just have to live with whatever misunderstanding had been perpetrated. *Maybe I agreed to give them back their drug shipment if we get to the* Oumaru *first. Well, we'll see.* Other heads would handle that. And that could actually happen, if someone felt the Broken Harvest would make a useful tool in some other Mordant House gambit. A back door into the Hegemony was no small thing, even one that might slam shut on your leg without warning.

*

Back at the local office, safely in orbit, he completed his report and fed back to Albas. It was her bailiwick and she probably needed to know.

"An actual *Essiel*?" She shook her head, already updating the records on her slate.

"Right? Who knew?" They were eating "Colonial style," which meant working at the same time. Back on settled Colonies like Berlenhof and Magda, people made a big show of sitting down just to eat. But this was the true Colonial custom and Havaer preferred it.

"Who knows how rogue this Aklu is," Albas considered, "or maybe going rogue is just like a mid-life crisis for them. Or it's pathologically insane, or ill, or...something we don't even have a word for."

"Well it's doing a damn good job of playing gangster right now," Havaer said. "And there was some damn thing those spacers took that it was really pissed to lose. Which backs up why they'd send a whole pocket warship to go meet the *Oumaru*. I mean, there's a basic law of resources here, no matter who or what you are. And that's a considerable investment. Damn me, I mean how many Tarekuman factions actually have military-grade ships to throw around?"

"Oh, enough," Albas said, with the air of someone who's reported the problem on multiple occasions, to no avail. "What's your next step? How can we help you?"

"The *Vulture* crew has an Int so they could have gone to spread panic anywhere with that damn Architected wreck. And right now the only way I can get news is via the packet trade—so I'll have to sit tight until I hear where they've docked, or..."

"Or?"

"Or we hear some other ship has been found turned inside out. Or—if we're really lucky—it won't be a ship, but a planet."

*

In the end he almost missed it. However, Albas's data crawlers were particularly thorough. He'd been looking for the *Oumaru*, assuming nobody could miss something like *that* turning up on their doorstep. But the *Vulture God* crew had just ditched the wreck instead, stashing the thing in the deep void. Doubtless until they could auction it to the highest bidder, if that was their plan. Although just what their plan was had become a wide-open field: they certainly hadn't shown up anywhere Havaer would peg as a hub of intergalactic intrigue or commerce.

"I need you to send a priority packet ship. I'm going to

need an Int pilot, sworn to Mordant House, if I'm going to keep up with these famies," he told Albas. The old insult for starving spacer pirates seemed particularly appropriate for the maverick *Vulture God* crew.

Then he sat down to work out why in all hells the *Vulture* had just arrived at Jericho.

PART 4
JERICHO

16.

Kris

Kittering's quarters were away from the human crew, a little bubble of the Hannilambra homeworld. Here he could admix the atmosphere to his own tastes, adding trace elements he didn't *need*, that humans wouldn't appreciate, but that would remind him of home. Dull reddish lighting soothed his eyes. And, whenever he wanted, he could play the staccato yattering and rapid percussion that was Hanni music. However, when Kris signalled him she couldn't hear any music. And when his door irised open, there was almost nothing of him to be seen there at all, his things packed away in a row of plastic canisters.

"I was wondering," she said, "if you'd stay or not."

"This question is also being asked of myself," came the bland voice of his translator, in response to the rapid fiddling of his mouthparts. "The skirling of home is to be heard. Some day soon there is potential to fulfil, or else never to be fulfilled."

Where his software had got the word "skirling" from, Kris had no idea. "Home and settle down?" she asked numbly. "That sounds nice."

"The mournful and the joyous occasion," Kit confirmed. "The loss of a nurse recalls duty. Wealth enough exists for this."

"Yes, you've made your pile," Kris agreed. Kit received a

percentage of every pay packet he clawed in for the crew. On top of that, he had his Landstep winnings and even the pocket change he made renting out his shell as a billboard. People who didn't understand them said the Hanni were greedy, but what the Hanni really obsessed about was giving their kids the best start in life. Hanni biology meant they didn't survive to see their offspring. A nest-egg to pay for a good nurse was all they could provide. Kit had considered Rollo the *Vulture's* own nurse; no higher honour to a Hanni. She couldn't quite get her head around it, but she knew she was touching the surface of a deep friendship. A meaningful relationship between human and alien, on a level seldom reached. Kit and Rollo had been together for a long time before the current crew had met either of them.

"I understand. Everyone will," she told the Hanni. "If it's time for you..." Some human part of her kicked in then, as she thought, *But you'll die. Don't go. Don't do it.* Yet that was a human interpretation. Kit was the product of a different world and culture.

Kittering was still and quiet for a while, his arms moving about one another without touching. His screens were a lucent grey that steadily lightened, as though a dawn was coming.

"Soon," he said. "Soon-ness is relative. It is unsatisfactory to leave behind more questions than answers. When there are answers, perhaps then it will be the time."

Kris was surprised at the sudden spike of happiness she felt, that Kit wouldn't be leaving them just yet.

They were out in the deep void now, and at that very moment Olli was cutting the *Oumaru* loose. It was, after all, the most recognizable piece of space junk in the Colonies right now. Olli would mark its position, so they could come back for it if necessary. In the infinite wastes of vacuum, away from the Throughways, the odds of anyone locating it here were infinitesimal.

*

"Jericho is out on a limb, location-wise," Idris told them. "Only one Throughway goes to it, kind of the opposite to Tarekuma. Even if I took us direct, it's a long jump." They were gathered in the command pod again, all five of them, and he looked from face to face. "This is what we all want, is it?"

Kris touched his arm lightly, for a little solidarity. "This Trine is an old friend of yours, aren't they?"

"Acquaintance. Maybe. It was a long time ago...You know Hivers. But Solace says they never re-instanced."

"For, what, fifty years or more?" Olli frowned. "You'd think they'd go nuts or something."

"They're something of a test case." Solace was being careful around Olli after their previous clash, speaking softly, not facing her head-on. Kris was surprised how shaken the Partheni had been by it all. Not what you expected from the genetically engineered elite.

"What have you told your people?" Idris asked Solace frankly.

"That I'm following up a lead that may be of great import to us—connected to the wreck of the *Oumaru*." Solace didn't meet anyone's eyes. "I have *not* mentioned the regalia. I don't like the omission, and I am going to have to report this properly, but right now they might be fake, and then...what would be the point in stirring things up? If Trine confirms the provenance then I *have* to tell them. I have a duty. I'm sorry." She looked around defensively.

"Great talks are required between us in that case," put in Kittering. "Parthenon has deep pockets, *see right?*" The last two words were given Rollo's exact bantering spin and Kris felt a catch of loss in her chest.

"The wreck's disengaged. And the *Joan's* secured to us," Olli put in. "If we're going to Jericho, then let's go."

*

The first thing Kris knew, Idris was triggering her pod's emergency wake-up protocol. They'd dropped into the Jericho system and were being hailed by a Hugh military frigate, demanding to know their business. It was, they were being told, not the best time to visit the system.

Jericho was the last habitable world to be found by explorers from Earth, before there was no longer an Earth to be from. A survey team exploring a dead-end Throughway burst into a virgin system. They found a planet a little closer than Earth to a sun a little cooler than Earth's. Then they found a biosphere crammed full of riotous life whose biochemistry overlapped with Earth by at least forty per cent. *An Eden!* surveyors crowed. Then the planet's biochemistry ate two of the landing party and they quickly revised their estimate to *A monstrous death world!* But there were still scientific grants for that, and a permanent research presence was established only months before an Architect appeared over the skies of Earth. That research team was intended to be the sole presence on Jericho: an opportunity to conduct pure research into a thriving alien ecology, untouched by humanity save for the luckless surveyors.

Then Earth fell, the Polyaspora began, and Jericho received its shipments of refugees—same as everywhere else. Establishing a colony on-planet was not the nature-red-in-tooth-and-claw experience everyone had expected. Desperate humans in need of a home could tooth-and-claw right back, and twice as hard. Soon enough, settlers and scientists were developing crops for the Jericho soil and curing all the problems caused when the local life messed up human bodies. The planetary population climbed to about a hundred thousand, concentrated around the city that had by then given the planet its name. "Jericho" seemed fitting, because the first thing people had focused on—given the ravenous nature outside—was walls.

Then Originator ruins were discovered.

The original survey hadn't picked them up, because Jericho was covered in a dense quasi-jungle and the local life generated its own electromagnetic interference. Both factors made it a hard world to survey. But eventually, settlers had started bringing back stories of strange things from the interior and the discovery was made. It didn't seem a priority, until Originator relics thwarted the Architect attack on Lycos, and suddenly life on Jericho seemed much more appealing. Hostile wildlife beat having your world torn apart by a moon-sized alien.

Eventually the war ended and Jericho's scientists, backed by the newly formed Hugh, asked everyone to please vacate so they could get on with their work. The Jerichan settlers refused to be thrown out of their new homes, thank you very much. This led to the creation of the Jerichan Resettlement Board, and the ongoing attempt to relocate its colonists. This led in turn to the Nativist movement's Jericho Chapter, formed to protect the colonists' "rights." And to make plenty of other trouble besides.

Idris had burst into real space at what he fondly imagined was a discreet distance from Jericho. However, its entire system was buzzing with traffic. It seemed someone had turned the trouble up to eleven.

The colony planet itself should have been the crew's main priority, but the *Vulture God* crew's attention was caught by one of the outer planets. It was being pulverized into an asteroid field, and its debris trailed along the curve of its old orbit for over a hundred thousand kilometres. Idris brought up images: the planet was swarming with vast factory-machines like city-sized flatworms. Past the ravaged curve of its horizon loomed a great bristling lump of mutilated-looking technology. This was a Naeromathi Locust Ark, the Jericho system's very unwelcome visitor.

Humans ran into the Naeromathi almost half a century before Earth fell. The creatures roamed the Throughways with an apparently insensate hunger, breaking apart worlds for raw materials and ignoring any requests to stop. For the next few decades, humans and Naeromathi would clash repeatedly. Nobody had any idea where the Naeromathi homeworld was located or even if they had a governing body. They just turned up, devoured and built more arks.

So it went, until something even bigger than the Naeromathi came along. The joint human–Castigar colony of Amraji were fending off one of the species' vast Locust Arks, when an Architect arrived to make the whole business moot. When the Naeromathi attacked the Architect, that established the first common ground between the species. The Naeromathi *really* hated the Architects, and the

Architects were why nobody had ever found the Naeromathi homeworld. Which didn't mean finding a Locust Ark chewing up planets in the Jericho system was a terribly comforting thing. Current détente suggested that they wouldn't proceed to munch on Jericho itself, but they were a strange, lost species and there were no certainties. All of which seemed beyond the pay grade of Jericho's lone military vessel, the tired old cruiser *Samphire*, which looked as though it hadn't had an upgrade since the war. As if to compensate for its impotence against the Locusts, the *Samphire* was bombarding the *Vulture God* with demands instead.

Olli had set them up with a cover ID as the *Jenny Kite*, in case people were watching for the *Vulture God*. It was only meant to fool a cursory inspection, not a full-on military inquisition. Kris spent a few fraught minutes liaising with a suspicious navy lieutenant who couldn't work out why a deep-space salvage vessel would be touting for work out here—and he had a point. She'd eventually sold him on the story that, as there was so much damn junk floating about in-system, the *Jenny Kite* was here to scavenge crumbs from the Naeromathi's table. She had a feeling their details would be on the next military packet ship out of there.

"They think we're in league with the Locusts?" Olli demanded disgustedly. "I mean, why all the suspicion?"

"They think we're Nativists," Solace put in simply. All eyes turned to her.

"Why...?" Kris asked, and the Partheni gave her an odd look.

"Seriously? Jericho is on the Parthenon's red list. We don't come here. It's prime Nativist recruiting territory."

Apparently nobody else had known this. Kris herself had only just learnt the potted history of Jericho, and as far as she was concerned, the place was a backwater armpit.

"Well, it wasn't the Nativists who stole our ship or killed our friends," Olli said flatly. "Wasn't them came to steal our *pilot*, either."

"Enough of that," Idris said sharply, or at least as sharply as he said anything.

"The Salvation Orbital's kybernet is calling," Kris noted. "We're docking there?"

"It's closest to the dig." Idris had found some survey maps, which showed various arboreal topologies: lowland forests, upland forests, supermarine forests, polar forests. And although "forest" was a human term, it seemed fairly appropriate here. "There's an elevator planetside there. It's probably the closest we can get. Direct orbit-to-surface flight isn't advised because there's a craptonne of interference within the atmosphere. Partly the local lifeforms, partly the Originator ruins, they think. These are the biggest anyone ever found, except they're all buried under the jungle, so no one's quite sure how big."

"What sort of interference?" Olli obviously didn't like the sound of that.

"Weird sorts," Idris said unhelpfully, but then sent over the data. Apparently the native life was constantly shifting the EM bandwidths they put out. Scientists reckoned they were competing to drown one another out or to locate their prey. But for this reason, the survey teams had recommended switching between algorithms to maintain communications.

"Why can't we ever go anywhere nice?" the drone

specialist complained. "You know, maybe this time I'll stick in orbit. Where I won't suddenly lose contact with my fucking legs."

*

There were plenty of ships at Salvation Orbital. The elevator terminus was ninety per cent dock, ten per cent a rat run of doors and compartments surrounding the elevator. A single thronging establishment was ostensibly an eatery but seemed to be doubling up as a drug den, gambling emporium and synthetic brothel. The hub was crowded, all elbows and shoulders and the stink of unwashed bodies. Usually, Kris gathered, it was a ghost town. Right now, there were off-duty military and the crews of twenty ships all jostling for room. She saw the blue and white badge of the Nativists proudly displayed on collars, on chests, even tattooed across the bare back of one scrawny, drunken spacer.

"This can't just be down to the Locusts," Kris hissed at the others, as they pushed through the crowd. She had her slate out and was skipping through the mediotype channels, searching the news. "Blessed equity, there's timing for you," she spat. "A Hegemony diplomat turned up at Berlenhof a few days ago suggesting that Hugh should *cede* Jericho. It should make good on its promises to evict everyone and hand the planet over."

"And *why?*" Idris asked, incredulous.

"It's the Originator stuff. The Essiel claim to be the old guys' heirs, or that's how it translates, and I guess Jericho's got ruins big enough to impress even them." Kris shook her head. "Look, I need to get us passage down to the surface. Solace, I don't suppose your lot have any secret back way in?"

"So now you're *happy* to be working with the Parthenon?"

Kris cocked an eye at her. "Look, that was all Olli, and she's not here."

"Olli had a point though," Solace said shortly. "How we came about, maybe how we could end up. And jokers like this..." A wave at three tables of Nativist spacers, voices raised in a drunken chorus of *The Green We Lost, The Fields of Home*. "They spit on us, and it drives us further towards *becoming* that thing. I...I don't know what to say to her, Kris."

That made two of them, because Kris didn't know what to say either. Except: "Wait, so you're saying there *is* a secret Partheni handshake?"

"I have made contact with Trine and they will authorize our descent."

"They can do that?"

"They are senior researcher on the dig. They..." Solace actually looked shifty, which was a new one. "I think they're in some trouble of their own. You know Nativists and Hivers."

Kris had seen plenty of anti-Hiver propaganda in her time. Boots stomping on knots of squirming bugs. Discontent about the hive intelligences winning free from their creators. Nobody wanted their appliances demanding independence. Or that was the Nativist message.

"So are we just walking into more trouble, if we head down there?"

Idris barked out a mirthless laugh. "You *know* what we've got on the ship. I mean, trouble? Us? Who'd have thought it?" There was a distinctly hysterical tremble to his voice.

Kris put a hand on his arm. "You want to wait on the ship? It's no bother, Solace and I can..."

"No, no. I'm sorry." He shook his head, embarrassed. "Be good to see Trine again. Old times, hm?"

Kris's slate pinged to say they had access to the elevator. She wondered who'd just been bumped, and hoped it was either a Betrayed activist or some pompous cult hierograve.

They ended up sharing the elevator car with a real slice of the planet's current turbulent life. Biologists, Hegemony cultists, Hugh military, Colonial agriculturalists and Nativists. No guns were permitted in the elevator, but this was a wild, frontier-type planet. Kris knew there would be plenty in the luggage compartment.

"Pills, people," Kris reminded the others as they descended, and popped her own. Most colony planets had their own version—a vaccination and antidote combination. Otherwise, a world could start killing you the moment you stepped onto the surface.

"Why's that guy looking at you?" Solace asked Idris, making him jump.

"What guy?"

"Don't look."

"Then how can I—?"

Kris scanned the room from the corner of her eye, catching who Solace meant on the second pass. Half a head taller than the rest and of decidedly healthier physique than the average Colonial. His lips moved as he stared at Idris, talking into a communicator in his lapel. He wore a shapeless poncho that failed to hide the broadness of his frame, but Kris caught a glimpse of bottle-green fabric at his neck. *Where have I seen that colour? Ah, right.*

"I don't want to alarm anyone, but he's Voyenni. Like the clowns who snatched Idris back on Roshu?" she murmured.

"Can't be," Solace said. "What are the odds?"

"Their chief was spouting a lot of that 'good of humanity' business when he was leaning on me," Idris pointed out. "Right out of the Nativist playbook."

It made a depressing kind of sense, Kris thought. The Magda Boyarin were the acceptable face of Nativism—and Jericho was prime recruiting territory for the movement right now.

"We can only hope they have bigger fish to fry," Kris decided, nodding at the Hegemony's cult members. She just hoped the Betrayed and the cultists could keep their knives to themselves, at least until they escaped the elevator.

17.

Solace

Jericho's Anchortown was laid out in concentric rings, each showing the limit of a generation's ambition before the next influx of refugees arrived. Beyond the walls and the surrounding fields, the native plant life stretched away in clashing shades of yellow and indigo-blue. Those "trees" moved, Solace knew. The fences kept up a modulated electromagnetic babble that repelled the local life, but the forest still made the odd slow rush for the barricades, overwhelming the fences until the farmers retaliated with chainsaws and flamethrowers. Even the trees were at war with people on Jericho.

Then they were dropping the last ten metres, the elevator car folding open so the bitter-scented alien air washed over them. Cargo crews were already descending on the elevator's freight compartments, using loading frames and a-grav to haul out the supplies, scientific equipment and luxuries that had come down the wire.

People were staring at Solace's armour but she wasn't going to be down here without it. She made a big show of going to the luggage compartment and bringing out Mr. Punch. She'd had the name printed onto the accelerator's barrel, a little personal nod to Rollo's memory.

The inhabitants of Anchortown looked a hardy lot, whose fashion ran to long sleeves, heavy boots to the knee and high closed collars. Sensible, given the wildlife, and a world away from shipboard clothes.

"Get some new clothes," Solace advised Kris and Idris. "Lots of things here to bite and sting and get under your skin."

That meant a visit to the printers while Solace soaked up the atmosphere outside, scowling at anyone who looked at her twice. There were Hugh military on the streets, and she saw them arrest one local at gunpoint. Nobody liked it; nobody stepped in. This close to the anchor point, Hugh still had its colony in hand. Likely towards the outskirts it was a different story. And of course those Hugh personnel looked at her just as hard as the locals did, and didn't look away as quickly. She was happy to see Kris and Idris emerge. Idris had purchased the drabbest, saddest long coat and boots she'd ever seen but Kris had made an effort, sporting explorer chic and a new blue and yellow scarf to match the alien foliage.

"I can't make contact with Trine," she told them. She'd been fitfully trying her comms since they got here, without any joy.

"Can we not just go to their office?" Kris asked. Solace thought back and realized she might not have explained everything.

"They're on a dig," she said. "I told you that."

"I thought you meant...you know, some project..." Waving a hand vaguely at the city around them, a gesture that slowed as Kris realized her mistake. "They're out in the *wilds?*"

"That's where the ruins are. We'll need to arrange passage.

And I need to call Trine somehow and tell them we're coming."

"Is that even possible?" Idris asked. He had a crinkle of discomfort about his eyes. Solace wondered if the planet's EM chatter was impinging on his Int senses somehow.

"They use the mother of all transmitter stations," Kris recalled from her research. "They cut through the background buzz via main force. I guess we go pay to put a call out."

There was a transmitter office close enough to the anchor, beside a handful of seedy-looking shacks that claimed they could arrange expeditions into the wilds for you—though Solace assumed game-hunting and smuggling eclipsed sorties for scientific research.

Solace had kept in touch with Trine after the war, across the decades, when she wasn't in the freezer herself. Each time she'd woken assuming that the Hiver would have re-instanced, that the intelligence she contacted wouldn't be her old correspondent. Each time she discovered that Trine had clung on, still the same. And now they were going to meet, and she had one hell of a surprise for the old academic.

The transmitter station managed to establish a link on the third try, then lost connection twice while she was waiting for someone to find Trine.

"Can't you just lay cable or something?" she asked the acned operator, who shrugged.

"They eat it. Anything in the ground gets et," he said.

"This planet..."

"Oh, tell me about it."

And then they had the line again and a crisp, slightly fuzzy-sounding voice was saying, "Gold City Dig to Anchortown, are you receiving me, over?"

"Gold City this is Anchortown," Solace said obediently. "Communication for Asset Trine, over."

"*Delegate* Trine is speaking, Anchortown," the voice said, notably frosty. And she knew it was her old acquaintance, for all the voice was unfamiliar. A Hiver voice was a matter of what software they plugged in, after all.

"Delegate Trine, this is Myrmidon *Executor* Solace, over." She found herself smiling.

"Well, then we've both had a promotion," came that precise voice. "Congratulations to everyone. You can't see me right now, but I've put on a tiny festive hat and am blowing on a little streamer." Then static fuzzed up and she lost the connection for a handful of frustrating seconds until their voice faded back in: "Repeat, over?"

"Repeat yourself, over," she pressed.

Fuzz, hiss, buzz, "...saying you didn't come all this way for a party. Can it be the Parthenon has remembered me after all this time?"

"Trine, I've a matter befitting your expertise, something special. Face-to-face discussion only. Can I come to you, over?"

"Can you fly in?"

"I'm told it's not advisable?"

"But you have a ship? Repeating: you have a *ship*, yes?"

Solace frowned uneasily. "I do, over."

"Better than nothing. Base of the elevator..." Fuzz, buzz, hiss, "...Don't leave it longer, est-ce compris?"

"Compris, Delegate."

"Then done, over, out, whatever," and then the static rose like a tide and ended the connection for good.

Solace stepped back from the transmitter, frowning, because there was obviously something else going on. You couldn't sift a Hiver's tone for emotional cues, but either something was worrying Trine or the Hiver was having long-term instantiation issues.

I don't want to bring yet more trouble to the others, she thought. Yet as she stepped out of the transmitter station, she saw they could find their own trouble. Kris and Idris had been cornered by none other than the Boyarin Piter Tchever Uskaro and a couple of his bottle-green Voyenni.

As Solace strode over, she heard the Boyarin say, "What else is a man to think, finding the Int here, but that he's had a change of heart? That he wants to do best by his species after all?"

"Step away, please," Solace grated out, not quite pointing Mr. Punch his way.

Piter Uskaro glanced about him, and Solace saw plenty of black looks sent her way by those rubbernecking nearby.

"Should I call those Hugh marines over, Patho?" he asked. "Who will they back, do you think? I'm a citizen of the Colonies with diplomatic credentials. You, on the other hand, are a foreign agent—and not even *human*."

Solace blanked. It wasn't his words alone, but the fact the crowd were plainly in agreement. She was surrounded by angry faces, who probably believed all the anti-Parthenon propaganda. That sisters bore male children but murdered them at birth; that they poisoned water supplies to make men sterile, all the usual.

However, she *had* shifted Uskaro slightly away from the pair, and the lawyer took full advantage, shoving Idris forward with a brisk, "Enough, we're going."

"I've not done with you—" The Boyarin reached out and hooked Kris by the scarf, pulling the garment half off. Solace moved to club the man and his goons if she had to, but he'd frozen. The Voyenni hovered in confusion.

Solace couldn't see what had happened. A moment later, she realized Kris had a knife out. But the Boyarin had stopped before he'd seen it, his fingers still caught in the scarf.

"Well?" Kris asked him. He'd gone pale, and the artful scar on his face twitched. Solace had no idea what question he was being asked. And it seemed Uskaro didn't know how to answer.

"I can quote official protocols, so everyone can hear," Kris said, calmly, quietly. "But then we're committed, *Messernbruder.*"

The Boyarin stepped back, finally releasing her scarf. Solace magnified her field of vision through her visor and caught a glimpse of the pinkish line that encircled almost half the woman's neck. It was a thin cut, just like the blazon on the man's face. A very particular type of duelling scar.

"Mesdam," Uskaro said coldly. "Our next meeting..." But Solace saw a faint glimmer of sweat on his forehead, despite the Jerichan climate.

"The *hell?*" Idris exclaimed as the man marched off. People were still staring at Solace, and suddenly facing down Colonial scorn didn't seem much fun anymore.

"Just come on." Kris had her scarf arranged again, hiding the scar. Solace wondered what sort of a bloody mess that duel had been, to give her such a trophy. Not the mannered little game of blades that the Boyarin played. *Messernbruder.* Knife-brother.

"You—" she started, but Kris just brushed past, angrily.

"I've arranged transport. We've got a land-car to catch, being as that's the only way to get to this damn dig site of yours. If we miss it I really will end up having to knife somebody."

"Would you have actually—?"

Kris turned on her heel, and Solace decided that she'd never doubt the woman's readiness to take up her blade again. As they left, someone bounced a rock off Solace's shoulder-guard. Better that than face up to an angry Kris.

*

"Can you configure that thing for chain shot?" the biologist asked Solace, once they were past the last fence.

"Why would I need to?" She eyed him, clutching Mr. Punch protectively.

He was a wiry man named Robbelin, with dyed-blonde hair and a strong accent that said he came from Somewhere Else far away from Jericho. "Your 'celerator," he drawled, "won't matter piss to the locals. Their fucking flesh is this viscous goop and you've never seen the like...Bastards. You send a pellet into 'em, just comes out the other side with its energy intact. Doesn't do a king's piss of a damage. Hereabouts we use these fuckers." He showed her a chunky weapon with a barrel his fist would have fit inside. "Pops 'em with a bean bag, just about subsonic. Doesn't kill the bastards, but it makes a mess of them and they don't like it, you get me?"

"Chain shot, right..." Solace nodded. She made the necessary adjustments to Mr. Punch and glanced at the jungle—looming far too close on either side of the trail. A tracked ground car wasn't her preferred way of getting anywhere but the locals wouldn't trust much else. Not between the planet's EM chaos and the way a-grav systems attracted aerial predators like some kind of mating call.

"Mockery of an ecosystem, this bloody place," Robellin went

on easily. "There's no actual *species* here on this godforsaken world, you know that? Just *things* that have a shape. And if that shape ain't working for them, they start shifting into something else. These trees're only going to stay trees as long as it works for 'em. Bastards'll morph into fucking balls of teeth and attitude the moment the soil gets too poor." Abruptly he had his "beanbagger" levelled in both hands, staring suspiciously into the jungle, or perhaps at the trees themselves.

"Anything intelligent here?" Idris asked faintly.

"Official answer?" Robellin queried. "Fuck knows, mate."

There were six others in the car besides Solace, Idris and Kris—their guide Yon Robellin, four new dig staff and an academic. They'd started out around midday and had driven through the night, then all the following day, before they set up a camp. The day after that, back on the trail, a thing like a tree had hoisted a junior archaeologist out of the car. Kris and a couple of others hung on to the victim's legs in a grim tug of war, while Robellin went for the attacker with a chainsaw. Eventually, Solace scythed down seven entire trees with Mr. Punch. Presumably one of these had been the perpetrator. It felt like an identity parade gone horribly wrong, but at least their archaeologist was recovered intact.

"That," Robellin reflected later, "is just bloody typical of this place. Whole new way of fucking you over since I was last out here."

"They learn?" Solace asked. "The creatures here? From the human presence on the planet?"

"Sure wish they didn't but yes—learn and evolve," was his response. "Give 'em another ten years, they'll be turning up wearing clothes and speaking Colvul. And then eating people because they'll still be the same nasty fuckers."

The next time they stopped to sleep, Solace got to see a groppler—not a specific species, Robellin said, but a predatory shape the locals took on. It came right into camp and, though it wasn't dressed or making conversation, its apparent arrogance seemed to fit with the biologist's gloomy predictions. One moment they were bedding down and setting out the proximity alarms. The next moment, this thing, half the size of the vehicle itself, had just sauntered into their midst. It was three metres tall and walked on two columnar legs, ending in thorned pads with jagged clutches of talons. Most of the front of it was mouth, easily big enough to slurp up any one of them, and it had a dozen tentacles like a beard reaching to the ground, all of them lined with vicious hooks. Its hide was a mottled blue-white that interacted weirdly with the yellow and azure foliage around it, making it leap out one moment, blend in the next. On either side of the mouth there were big circular organs, probably not actually eyes.

"Fuck," said Robellin. He had his beanbag gun to hand, but the thing was right there in the middle of them, an invitation for friendly-fire accidents.

A gurgling rumble came from the creature's innards. Its body language now spoke of someone who'd stepped into a neighbour's hotel room by mistake, almost abashed. Then Idris shifted and something about his furtive, prey-like movement caught the groppler's attention.

"Idris," Solace cautioned. "You stay very still now."

Idris was staring into that cavernous mouth. The tentacles swayed on a non-existent breeze, tasting the air.

"Any hot takes from the biology department?" Kris hissed.

Robellin's eyes were narrowed. "Fuckers've never done this before, far as I know." He had his weapon levelled but seemed reluctant to shoot. "If I sting it and it goes on a rampage, that'll go bloody badly for us, I can tell you."

Solace brought her accelerator to her shoulder. "I am going to cut this creature in half now."

"Hold," said Idris hoarsely. He was staring at the groppler, and although it didn't seem to have anything to stare back at him with, its attention was increasingly fixed on him.

"Mate, I'd move back now if I were you," Robellin advised Idris lightly.

"Hold," he said again. His narrow face had lost all expression and Solace had a sudden chilling flashback. *Seen this before.* She almost pulled the trigger then and there, out of sheer reflex. Berlenhof, the Ints trying to reach the Architects with their minds. Idris with his face utterly slack, nobody home because his mind was *out there* flying across the face of a moon-sized alien intelligence.

Everyone was very silent now, watching the Intermediary face the monster. The groppler stamped again, and its tentacles knotted and twitched as though it was wringing its hands in embarrassment. Solace half expected Idris to reach out a hand and touch the monster's sagging skin, tame the thing, arrive at the dig riding a groppler in fulfilment of some bizarre local prophecy.

"Mate, seriously," Robellin whispered. "I don't know what you're about but that bastard will fucking eat you and crap out the bits it can't digest."

"There's something...Oh. Hell." Idris sat down suddenly. It seemed to surprise the groppler as much as anyone, because it took a skittish step away from him. "You...ever get Ints here, Menheer Robellin?"

"In this armpit place? Not bloody likely."

Then the groppler shook itself like a man remembering a prior appointment, lurched sideways, to general alarm, and stamped off into the jungle.

"Idris, what was *that*?" Kris demanded, sounding furious with him, though Solace could tell it was mostly adrenaline.

The Intermediary held his head in his hands, as though to physically hold it together. "Yon said the life here *adapted*."

"All the bloody time," Robellin confirmed. "Listen, mate, like the lady says, what *was* that?"

"Originators," Idris said weakly. "The ruins here. I bet the local wildlife keeps clear of the sites, right?"

"The big fuckers, sure." The biologist nodded warily.

"They don't like them." Idris was abruptly running with sweat, despite the cool air. He looked absolutely wrung-out with fatigue and nerves. "Don't know why. But they know *how* to detect them sure enough. They're...on the same channel."

"As what?" Robellin asked, but Idris had clammed up and wouldn't say more. Solace knew what he'd left unsaid. The "Originator channel" carried some indefinable signal—one that telegraphed the location of *anything* from that ancient civilization, even a handful of leftover junk. It broadcast so that even a moon-sized planet destroyer, up in high orbit, could detect its presence and would rather flee than risk a confrontation. It was the same channel that Ints like Idris could access, that had let them touch the inhuman sentience of the Architects and send them away. This planet hosted the most extensive set of Originator ruins any human had ever seen. And here, the entire ecosphere was plugged right into that same channel and was listening.

Two of Jericho's brief day-and-nights later, the trail finally

283

led their grinding, complaining car to the dig site. They lurched abruptly over a rise and into a bowl-like crater, at least a kilometre across. As they did so, the dense foliage thinned out a little. The group was silent as they descended the incline. Laid out below, like the bones of time itself, was all that the Originators had left behind.

18.

Idris

In an eerie echo of the nearby human settlement, the Originators had certainly liked their concentric circles when it came to architecture. Or maybe it was something to do with their technology—or something else entirely. Whatever their purpose, those circles were the last remnants of what might have been a city. Maybe. They were visible as striations in the grey, ashy soil of Jericho where the plantlife had been cut back. Or they could be spotted beneath odd swathes of off-colour vegetation. Each circle enclosed a weird mazework of buried foundations. It was as though the whole site was composed of a series of nested labyrinths—each only large enough for a five-year-old to comfortably navigate. Idris could see where the archaeology team had been working, because a whole slice of the ruins had been exposed. The excavation currently extended down two metres, and Idris considered how much further down it might go. The thought of a half-mile of cramped, subterranean labyrinth lurking beneath them made his insides twist. And yet somehow he felt it was there.

The ruins seemed to be formed of eroded stone. Perhaps the chewing of the elements over countless centuries had given those structures their toothy, irregular texture. Yet the stonework of the exposed lower levels was no smoother. *Maybe it's just what the stuff is supposed to look like?* By this time the ground car was winding around the outer circle, careful not to crush any priceless archaeological rubbish. Idris spotted some large dome tents nearby—big ones, with individual chambers podding out from the centre on spokes. They were lit up from within, now the sun was on its way down. The sunken basin, surrounded by tall forest, must mean night came suddenly to the dig site.

"What," Kris asked Robellin, "keeps the damn gropplers and the rest from just...chowing down on you all?"

"Half our generator power goes into creating big-ass EM static," the biologist told them. "Fucks with our comms all right, but it's like shouting into the ears of any bastard that wants to come at us." His grin slipped. "Still, it's like your mate was saying. Nothing much big does come down there. They don't like it."

"Do the ruins put out their own EM frequencies?"

"That'd be a tidy bloody piece of explanation, wouldn't it? No such luck. We've tested everything, and they're dead. They've been dead for hundreds of thousands of years—conservative estimate. You wouldn't expect them to have left the fucking oven on or something."

Idris stopped listening because he was looking at the ruins—no, *feeling* the ruins. He could sense them in the same way that he could sense the Throughways and the nodes of unspace. Something *was* active there. It was a tugging at the edge of his mind, like someone plucking at his sleeve. There was a metaphysical weight to the whole area. It was baked in to the structure, the shape, the weird maze-like arrangements and the materials that nobody had ever been able to satisfactorily analyse or duplicate.

"Has the site ever had an Intermediary here, working on the Originator ruins?" he asked.

"An Int? Don't think so, mate. Not that I heard, anyway." Robellin spread his hands. "I mean, you fellers are pretty few and thin, right? Not as if there's a bundle of you at the careers bureau, wondering what you can do with your time."

Idris fell silent, wondering if he had a duty to tell someone about this—the Liaison Board, maybe. It would be a cushy job for some of their forced-conscript Ints to work in archaeology, rather than brave the trauma of unspace travel. But when the leashes were signed, even Originator archaeology lost out to interstellar trade, espionage and military transport. There was probably no point.

A handful of people were coming out from the tents to welcome the land car, and they eyed Solace warily. Probably no Nativist hostility out here, but you wouldn't expect to find a battle-ready Partheni soldier on Jericho. Then the staff began unloading the car and hauling crates away—and Idris saw what must be Trine limping out to greet them.

The Trine of his memory had been shiny and new, instanced into a frame that was broadly humanoid, faceless and just about identical to their Hive-built siblings. Back in the war, this had been standard for Hivers who interacted with humans. Once they were free to quit Hugh and humanity, Hivers had started diversifying. This Trine's frame had two legs, thin and jointed like a bird's, and their torso was a barrel shape above a box pelvis, opening onto a whole cutlery drawer of folding limbs. Trine's head was a silvery bowl containing a projected face. It was human, androgynous, middle-aged and cheery-looking, and a trick of the projection made it appear to be looking straight at you, no matter what angle you were at.

The other thing Idris noticed about Trine's frame was how old and battered it was. Any polish was most definitely gone, and the metal body was covered in dents and spot repairs, off-colour panels cannibalized from other machinery. One leg was slightly shorter than the other. Only that array of arms had been kept polished and perfect.

"Subtlety was never the Parthenon's strong point." The precise, amused-sounding voice issued from somewhere within Trine's torso. "Myrmidon Executor Solace, as I live and fail to breathe. No Partheni task force behind you, about to take possession of the Gold City dig site?" Everyone could hear his comments, and Trine received a number of awkward looks from their colleagues.

"This is purely for self-defence, Delegate." Solace also raised her voice, to confirm to the camp that she wasn't a one-woman invasion. Mr. Punch currently rested on one shoulder, muzzle only threatening the first faint stars. "And that seems a necessity on this planet of yours."

"Oh yes." Idris had never heard a Hiver snicker before, but Trine had apparently felt it necessary to install the facility. "Our neighbours."

"About our new friends," Yon Robellin broke in, coming back for another crate. "Your feller here, the skinny one, he's a surprising fucker. Groppler wrangler. May just have opened up a whole bloody can of research on us. Tell y'about it when we've got stuff put away."

The Hiver's attention now focused on Idris. "Menheer Idris Telemmier...?" The statement trailed off questioningly. They might not think like humans, but as a product of human technology, Hivers were good at putting on a nuanced show.

"None other," Idris confirmed weakly, knowing that Trine would be performing a compare-and-contrast with the young Intermediary they'd known during the war, and finding far too few differences. "Long story."

"Evidently," Trine agreed. "But, now, let us step over here and speak of matters utterly innocent and unconnected with subterfuge." They took several canted steps towards the perimeter, beckoning with some of their arms.

"You mentioned *subtlety*," Solace pointed out, when they'd put ten metres or so between them and the ground car.

"Well you did rather push that ship out and burn it," Trine remarked tartly. "When is *your* ship due, may I ask?"

Solace exchanged a glance with Idris. "It...isn't. The EM interference, they said we couldn't fly because of it..."

"You *said* you had a ship," Trine pressed, their ghostly face tight-lipped and disapproving. "I specifically enquired as to whether you had a ship. You equally specifically confirmed that, yes, a ship was what you had."

"We do have a ship. In orbit," Idris put in.

"I am not sure why you imagine that would be of any immediate use, Menheer Telemmier," Trine told him sharply. "Solace, my dear, my love, friend of my youth, et cetera. Did you not consider that, when I was asking about your ship, I meant that I might have need of one?"

"Trine," Solace said, with obvious patience, "what's going on?" Idris could almost read her mind: *Have they gone crazy?* After all, nobody knew how long a Hiver could stay separate and instanced, without rejoining the whole.

"I have had two attempts on my life, these being the specific circumstances to which I am alluding," Trine said shortly. The holographic face made a big show of looking suspiciously left and right. "I don't know what you saw in Anchortown, but the politics there have taken a very marked downturn in the last year."

"Nativist recruiting drive," Solace agreed. "We saw some of it."

Trine made a dismissive sound. "Oh, it has always been thus, my good, dear friend of my heart. But Nativists are an empty hand, all they can do is a little light slapping. I refer to those hands that carry a knife. You know the ones, dear heart?"

"The Betrayed?" Idris asked. "I mean, they've got enough people to hate without bringing archaeology into it, haven't they?"

"You'd think, but no," Trine insisted. "According to them, of course regular humans could have *won* the war. But then Ints came along and made contact with the Architects—and made some nefarious deal with them, plus a bunch of aliens and the Partheni...the usual suspects." Trine's chest-arms waved about in mockery. "But even the Betrayed can't get round the fact that *alien* artefacts saved millions, because Architects won't touch Originator sites with a long pole from orbit. As a result, the Betrayed are starting to claim that Originators were the ur-humans—mankind's mystical space-parents or some such ridiculous supposition. They also claim that various 'traitor factions' are even now pillaging Originator sites, and selling everything to the aliens, the Hegemony or whoever. There's no Originator site bigger than this one, so the Betrayed have been trickling into Jericho for a year at least. They hold the sincere belief that we at the dig are all traitors in need of a good knifing. And I, my dear, am both the sole non-human academic here and the highest-profile Originator expert. Or, as we call it here, I'm 'a target.' We found a bomb in a crate of instruments I'd ordered. Someone spotted the tampering, thankfully. And a few months ago, someone came to our camp and *shot my leg off.* Which was inconvenient."

"Why are you still here then?" Solace demanded.

"*Because* my good old former boon companion Myrmidon Executor Solace didn't bring her ship with her," Trine hissed. "Look you, my dear. I can't just leave. I'm not going to walk through the streets of Anchortown alone or jump into an elevator car with who knows what company. Which was why, my old comrade-in-arms, I rather hoped *you* were bringing your *ship.*"

"They said you couldn't fly out here!" Solace almost shouted at them.

"Well you *almost* can't!" Trine snapped right back. "But if you time it right, you just about can—if you have a very good pilot."

"We have a very good pilot," Solace insisted, then grimaced. "Who's here with me and not on our ship."

"Well," Trine said, "with all apologies to your doubtless excellent piloting skills, Menheer Telemmier, that's not a great deal of use, is it?"

"Can we raise Olli?" Idris put in. "What are your comms here?"

"As of now, zero. They've put the night screen up to keep out the gropplers," Trine explained. "Once the sun's up, we can negotiate for a gap in the EM noise to try and get a signal out. We'll have to route it to the transmitter station at Anchortown. They can send it up the cable to your vessel. It's an inexact science."

"You'd think they'd just put in a focused beam signaller or something," Solace said. "Blink tight-light from Anchortown to here. I mean, it doesn't *have* to be radio."

"Oh they tried. Just because we're not Partheni doesn't mean we're completely impractical," Trine said. "Originator ruins do something to the light, my dear. Something interferes with the signal. Most of my colleagues said what they received was hopelessly corrupted, devoid of information."

"What did the rest say?" Idris asked automatically, suspecting correctly that he wouldn't like the answer.

"That a message did get through, it just wasn't the one we'd sent. We got through a beam receiver a month. The *nightmares*, you know." Trine's face waggled its eyebrows alarmingly, wide-eyed, and Idris decided he could have done without that.

*

As Idris didn't sleep, he found himself on his own once the camp had settled in for the night. Without the others distracting him, he couldn't blot out the sensation anymore. He'd felt it the moment they came in sight of the ruins—perhaps even since he set foot on-world. There was a *presence* to the Originator site. It wasn't dead, though surely it had once been something far grander and was now just a worn-down stub. Whatever had made this place what it was, whatever struck fear into the Architects, it was still here. The silence he felt was the silence of something standing close, making no sound—not simply an absence of sound. *And nobody knows this, except me.*

Perhaps there was a whole covert research program on the subject, run out of Mordant House. But he thought not. There weren't enough Ints, not enough Originator sites. Nobody to join the dots... except him. He felt as though he was on the edge of a colossal revelation—wondrous or terrible, he couldn't say. And because no more understanding came, he just stayed on that edge. An exhaustion of suspense kept him strung out for hours, while dark turned back into dawn and then headed towards dark again. The camp, he discovered, worked for one day-night cycle and then rested for the next one. It wasn't something that fitted well with human diurnal rhythms but, since Idris had shed those, maybe he was better suited to Jericho than anyone else.

*

"Basically, unless it's an emergency, we put the EM down for an hour every two days—so's people can call their loved ones. Or their pimps and bookies," Robellin explained. "Also, we need to upload and download the science, y'know. Order supplies, get the news medios, all that. So it's usually chocker, is what I'm saying. You getting a channel for your pilot, whether you can dodge the interference or not, wouldn't normally happen."

"Is that right?" Solace said. The tilt of her jaw suggested that Mr. Punch might have something to say about that.

" 'Cept obviously we know Trine's in a spot, and this is for him. And also..." The biologist shot a sly look Idris's way. "Your mate here, he's made a discovery. Something we never guessed was even there to be discovered, eh? Shows what a shower of fucking amateurs we are. Give us another bout of free and frank with him—then when we take the generators offline, you get first go on the transmitter. Deal?"

"Idris?" And at least she was asking and not ordering.

"I don't know what I can tell you," Idris said to Robellin, "but sure." Then Robellin gathered an audience of geologists, biologists and Trine's dig team, and his interrogation began. They asked him all manner of questions: about his Int senses, how he reacted to the Originator site, and on and on. True to his predictions he had precious little he could tell them, the same odd guesses and failures of description getting hopelessly mangled between mind and mouth.

"Look," he explained at last, "it's what being an Int is, see? There's a place you feel, and you go to, in here." Poking himself hard in the side of the head. "Saint Xavienne was born like this, and they made the rest of us like her. As best they could." Seeing too many blank looks on young faces he snapped out, "Surgery and implants and chemotherapy and most of the time it kills you, you understand. We're not meant to happen. You wreck people's brains, trying to make something like me." Seeing their flinches or disapproving expressions and thinking, *How is it you don't even know this? Kids, they're just kids. There was a war on, so of course they'd try anything.*

He reined himself in, before he started going all crazy old man on them. "Those of us that lived... There's this sense we have, here inside, it lets us do what we do in unspace. But most of all, it let us talk to Architects, right? To say, 'Hey, we're here. Stop doing that. You're...'" He let out a little laugh that sounded dangerously hysterical, even to him.

"'You're killing us. Stop killing us,' basically." Staring out bleakly at their uncomfortable faces. "These ruins you've got here, they're speaking into that same space. And your gropplers and things, they hear it too. So yes, I can hear this place doing its thing, just by being here. That's what the Architects hear too, I guess—when they come to these places? But I don't know why I'm hearing this. Nobody knows why. If we did, we wouldn't have to kill so many people to make a freak like me."

He could tell they were disappointed and it made him ashamed to be so useless, so ignorant of his own workings. Then Robellin was there, putting a hand on his shoulder. Not a spacer's usual quick tug for attention, but an attempt to give comfort.

"It's okay, mate," the man said, and Idris realized he'd been shivering like a hypothermic. "Fuck me, I just thought Ints went through a secret training thing, or..."

"I'm sorry." Idris actually sniffled, like a child who couldn't do his homework. "I wish I could tell you more about it."

"Look, it's good. Just the idea that the site works that bloody way at all, mate," Robellin said. "I'll make sure you get your comms time..."

Idris just felt more wretched with every word, as though the comms was a consolation prize. A trophy for turning up, no matter how dismally he'd performed. Desperately, he burst out, "If it's any use, I can show you where the other ruins are."

There was a loaded silence, and then one of the archaeologists asked, "You...can...what now?"

"The rest of the ruins. Unless you've found them, but just haven't got to them yet?"

"Menheer Telemmier, my old acquaintance, what precisely are you offering to impart?" Trine asked, stalking over.

"Only, when I met the groppler, there was a moment," Idris went on awkwardly. "I just felt...like a radar pulse went out from us. It sent a wave across the planet, and pings came back, mapping out...For example, there's a long avenue that way." He pointed, knowing the direction without needing to think. "And there's another place at the end of it. Must be... a hundred and nineteen klicks that way. And...look, is there a map, a satellite map?"

An hour later, and he'd drawn what he thought might be out there. If they could get a geophysics scanner working or even manage a flight over the jungle, then they'd see the truth of it. And he still couldn't say *how* he knew it. In the Intermediary Program's labs, they'd used every damn instrument invented to search for how the information flowed from the universe into their heads. Nothing had worked. What they did was happening on some unknowable other level, just like unspace.

After this revelation, the dig staff told Solace she could take as much time as she wanted on their comms channel, and she set about hailing Olli up on the *Vulture God*. For the first fifteen minutes she was just shouting into the staticky void; frustrating for her but downright chilling to Idris. Because, sitting at her feet in the comms tent, he felt like he could hear the whole planet listening, breathing down the open channel.

The EM interference that was screwing with their transmissions was just the visible portion of a shifting buzz of chatter. The cacophony tugged at the edges of his mind, the local life exploiting the channels opened to it by the Originator presence. He wondered about the uniquely plastic form of life that had been evolving around these ruins for millions of years, supremely able to exploit its environment. Jerichan biology might be more unique than even Robellin had thought...It might be the only known biosphere that had developed to exploit unspace on a local level.

"Let me help." He pulled himself to his feet and Solace moved away from the transmitter, annoyed by her failure. He skimmed the frequencies, trying to ride a conflicting tide of EM babble from the jungle—tree shouting over tree, monster over monster, tiny bugs screaming at each other and a trillion other calls. There was a path through it, he knew, though it kept shifting. Solace had to fumble for it, blindfold. But if he just let his hands do their thing on the transmitter, without his conscious mind intruding...

"Anchortown to Gold City, receiving, over." It was the distorted voice of the transmitter operator, tiny and far away. Solace lunged in to speak, as Idris did his best to keep the connection open. She almost asked that they be put up the wire to the *Vulture God* before remembering their *Jenny Kite* alias. A few touch-and-go moments later and they had Olli's voice on a slight delay.

"About time!" the drone specialist snapped the moment she had them. "What the fuck are you doing down there?" There was more but she cut out for a moment before Idris retrieved her.

"*Jenny Kite*, this is Gold City. We have Trine but need evac, over," Solace said, as clearly and carefully as she could.

"Yeah you sure do," came Olli's static-mushed voice. "Look, guess who Kit and I found docked right here. Remember the *Raptorid*? Belongs to that Magdan bastard who got Idris and the captain arrested."

"Yes, he's here, on-planet," Solace broke in. The interruption resulted in them losing the link for five whole minutes. Then they heard Anchortown station's tremulous tones again and were patched back through.

"Look, you're not the only one who can do spy stuff, Patho," Olli asserted belligerently, apparently as part of a tirade that had been going on for some time.

Solace was gritting her teeth. "Gold City to *Jenny Kite*, repeat, over."

"Repeat what? Would you stop with the—" and they lost Olli for another moment. Solace kept on patiently asking her to repeat until her voice phased back in.

"...I said that Kit hacked the *Raptorid*'s comms. All that shit on-planet means Uskaro's not using encryption."

"Olli, we are losing you every few seconds. What do we need to know, over?"

"Oh. Right." Idris pictured the specialist swallowing her annoyance. "Did you get the bit where I said they were coming for you?"

"No," said Solace with some restraint. "No, I did not."

"They think you're here to grab this Trine character," Olli said, static rising and falling behind her voice like surf on a shore. "They think you're stealing Originator secrets or some damn thing. Were waiting in town for the Hiver to come to them, but you taking off for the dig kicked them into gear and they're on their way after you. Maybe twenty hours behind you."

Solace blinked, and Idris could see her doing the maths. He reckoned that meant *Any time now*, if Uskaro's people had commandeered the same type of transport.

"Olli, we need evac, over. We need to get out of here with

Trine." Solace met Idris's look. They both knew that wasn't likely to happen, given local atmospheric conditions.

Olli apparently had a different take on things. "Well obviously," she said sharply. "Been working on it since I knew you were in the shit. Sit tight. I will be with you as soon as I've finished refitting the *Joan*'s shielding."

"Wait, what do you—"

"Seriously, the longer we're jawing here, the less time I'm spending saving your ass, Patho girl." And then Olli had cut the line, leaving Solace staring angrily at nothing.

The pair of them bundled outside and grabbed Kris. "We're getting company," she announced to Trine, Robellin and the dig staff. "Armed Nativists from Anchortown, coming for Trine."

Everyone stared at her, Kris included.

"We're going to need a defensive perimeter," she said. "Just as well the jungle's just stubble close to the dig or..."

"Solace, mate," Robellin put in awkwardly. "We're...you do understand we're not soldiers, right?"

She blinked at him.

"You're serious about this? There's a squad of bloody gunmen on their way?" he pressed.

"So I'm told. They've tried to kill Trine before, right?"

Idris looked from face to ashen face. "Solace," he said hollowly, "we can't stay here."

"It's not the most defensible position," she agreed, not quite understanding his point. "But this is where Olli'll come looking for us."

"If we stay here, people are going to get hurt. It's not their fight. We've just screwed them over by turning up."

"Not entirely true, mate," Robellin said. "I mean, Trine's

one of ours, right, and they'd have come sooner or later, I reckon. But…beanbag shooters aren't going to be a whole lot of fucking good if these clowns have real guns."

"They will." Solace stood very still, and Idris imagined her mind working like a military machine, breaking down the problem. How much weight did the Parthenon give to civilian lives, exactly? Colonial civilian lives, at that.

"I hear vehicles…" someone called, voice twisted in panic. "They're coming!"

"Kris, Idris, Trine," Solace said. "With me. We're going to head up the trail, and then into the jungle. We'll break their advance and then fall back. We'll hope to lose them in the trees and circle back in time to meet the *Joan*, if Olli can get it down here. Compris?"

They nodded, although Idris felt it was anything but *Compris*. As plans went it was a series of unknowns tied together with string.

"These guys, they're likely Voyenni, house guards for a Magdan Boyarin," Kris told Robellin. "They'll be all very pushy, arrogant…Probably won't just go mad with bloodlust though. So give way and tug your forelocks. It's us they're after."

"With luck, they'll just leave you alone," the Partheni added. "I'm sorry. That's all I can give you."

19.

Idris

Solace settled them two metres into the trees, where they could get a glimpse of the Anchortown trail from cover. Kris was plainly unhappy being even that far in. After all, they'd seen Jerichan trees in action. Idris himself was strangely calm. He didn't feel he had some magic rapport with the planet's unpleasant ecology and one abortive groppler attack didn't make him the Archdruid of Jericho. He knew they were very close to the buried avenue he'd felt stretching from Gold City to the next Originator site, and was really hoping the Originator construction would keep away the nastier predators. He might be wrong, though, which might make them dead.

What Trine thought of this development was anyone's guess. They'd turned their face off so its glimmer wouldn't give away their position.

The sound of oncoming engines had grown steadily louder in fits and starts. It sounded to Idris as though the vehicles were trying to make best speed but falling foul of the vegetation. He could distantly hear a shouted argument. Maybe the bad guys were more concerned with each other than a potential ambush.

He had lost sight of Solace completely.

Then three vehicles came into view along the trail, two open-cabined cars on balloon tyres and a big enclosed truck behind them. The lead vehicle had four men hanging on to it. The second had traded half its crew for a significant toothy gash in its flank, suggesting some manner of groppler had put the vehicle on the menu. The men seemed a mix of local mercenaries and Voyenni thugs.

Idris had assumed that Solace would pull some kind of highwayman stunt. She'd step out, point Mr. Punch in their direction and they'd surrender in the face of her sheer panache. Instead she opened by just shooting up the lead vehicle and its occupants. She still had the accelerator set for chain shot, and it made a hell of a mess of the car's hull, tearing through metal and plastic and just about slicing both engine and driver in half.

The rear end of their vehicle flipped over the front and hit the dirt. The two Voyenni who'd been reclining back there were flung forwards, which put them out of Solace's eyeline and likely saved their lives. The second vehicle, damaged as it was, was going slowly enough to steer clear of the wreck and its crew jumped and hit the ground running. Solace began potshotting at them from the trees, individual pellets punching clean through the skewed car they were trying to hide behind.

Then men began to pile from the big vehicle at the back. There were at least half a dozen in the first wave, and they started shooting into the trees indiscriminately. Idris kept low, glancing back to check that the others were doing the same. Trine was crouching with their humanoid legs uncomfortably akimbo, chest close to the ground and propped up on their arms. The local mercs had projectile launchers and beanbag guns, but the Voyenni had magnetics and a couple of true accelerators. They would cut through Solace's armour as easily as flesh.

Even as a particularly savage salvo shredded the native life over Idris's head, Solace was suddenly kneeling by him.

"Come on," she said. "Fall back."

"But we can't," Kris objected. "The dig crew—"

"Not to the dig, not yet. We'll go further in. Hope we lose them. Come on." Solace gestured emphatically then raised Mr. Punch again. As Idris scrambled in the direction she'd indicated, he heard the weapon's high, ringing voice toll three times. He hauled himself over a rise, slipped and rolled helplessly down the other side until Kris caught him.

"Ow."

"I was concerned that I would be the most inept fugitive here, old comrade," Trine observed acidly. "Thank you for sparing me that." Despite their limp they were keeping pace well enough.

Solace slung herself back over the ridge towards them, turning to send another few shots back towards the pursuers. As soon as the pellets had left Mr. Punch, she was already moving. She dropped into cover of the ridge before the answering salvo could shred the leathery foliage where she'd been. Then they were stumbling deeper into the forest, squeezing between close-grown trees, tripping over roots that twitched and writhed beneath them. *Not trees, remember? Just monsters who've got a good tree thing going on right now.* He hoped the Voyenni ran into some trees that were considering an aggressive change of lifestyle.

He heard shouts behind them. Solace turned and sent a handful of shot back that way and shoved him onwards.

"Disappointed," he panted over his shoulder, "with the Parthenon war machine. Aren't you supposed to be as good as a hundred Colonials, or something?"

He couldn't see the expression behind her visor. "Low on ammo," she said curtly. "All that chain shot. Don't want to get down to fists."

A moment later and he thought he'd lost track of Kris and Trine entirely, but it was him going off course. Solace had to snag his arm and haul him back on track. Then Kris yelled out a warning and there was gunfire dead ahead, whickering through the crowded spaces between trunks and hacking out explosive splinters of not-quite-wood.

Solace forged past and he saw two scars appear on her armour, the force of the impact sending her stumbling left. Just projectile shot, nothing that would cut through her protection, but worse could come next.

"Go!" she ordered the three of them. "Go, keep going. I'll catch up."

Kris looked rebellious but she had literally brought a knife to a gunfight and it wasn't enough. Another yell from Solace sent them plunging deeper into the jungle, struggling up a rise using twisting roots as a ladder and startling a pack of metre-long hopping things. The air whined with tiny specks of life, swarming in glittering helices wherever the sunlight broke through the canopy. And all around them the locals were ramping it up, a cacophony of clattering and booming as various monsters registered their displeasure.

"Idris, where are you *going?*" Kris shouted, and he realized he'd just gone off again. He'd veered to the top of a rise, stubbled with trees standing out like hairs on a fright wig. He slithered halfway back down, whacking his knee hard on a trunk he swore had lurched into his path. *This damned planet.* Kris and Trine were waiting for him. From somewhere behind he heard a scream and then sobbing: a man's voice, not Solace.

"My old acquaintance, my fellow veteran, would you just *not?*" Trine demanded testily. They had abandoned an upright posture entirely for the rough going, using all their arms to skitter about, legs arched high like a grasshopper's. And then Idris's lips moved and he said, "This way." The words came from the part of him he wasn't quite on speaking terms with, the same part that knew unspace and had touched the mind of a destructive god.

"What?" Kris looked up the rise. "No way. We need to stay low."

His mind filled with attempts at explanation, but he didn't have the words and they didn't have the time. "Just...this way." And then he was off, trusting that she'd follow him and Trine wouldn't want to be left alone. Trusting that Solace would find them. Trusting...trusting himself, which was a hard thing to do at the best of times. *Ints go mad, everyone knows that.* And nobody knew it better than an Int.

When Idris reached the top of the next rise he risked a look back and saw movement below. Solace had spotted them and was running their way—pausing for a moment to send a single shot back then picking up the pace again. Off to her right a sudden fit shook a couple of the trees as return fire lashed at them. Then he was scrabbling past the rise and running too, flat out running over the treacherous ground, Kris and Trine following behind him. Something had a hook in his mind and he battered through the clutching foliage, bounced off spiny trunks and fell headlong. He wrenched himself up from roots that tried to find out what he was made of and whether they could eat it. *It'll be real funny if there's just a monster at the end of this with its mouth open, waiting for me.*

Hilarious.

Then he saw a shadow through the trees: huge and grey. For a moment he thought it really was a monster, but he was pelting headlong, too fast to put the brakes on. He ended up slamming into a rough, overgrown wall and sitting down hard. Beside him, Trine scuttled to a halt, with Kris a dozen paces behind and gasping for breath.

"What have you found?" Trine's clipped voice issued from their torso. "Menheer Telemmier, you creature of remarkable surprises, what's this?"

"Defence," he got out. "Walls." And then Solace was coming, virtually scooping up Kris on her way.

It was an Originator site, just a single structure—but it was *tall*, not just buried foundations. It reminded Idris of the abandoned shell of some marine mollusc. He could make out three concentric sets of walls with random holes in them, ending in jagged rock teeth about three metres up. The jungle had overcome its Originator squeamishness here, and trees had grown up close to the walls. Vines snaked over their pitted substance as though questing for meaning.

"This'll do," Solace decided. "In."

"The scientist in me," remarked Trine, "protests against using a once-in-a-lifetime discovery as a defence against gunfire. But not too much." And they were hurrying themselves inside even as they said it.

Solace found a breach in the wall at around the right height and was ready when the first of their pursuers could be glimpsed through the trees. She sent off three pellets one after another, the retorts hanging in the air.

"How many of them left?" Kris asked.

"At least seven." Solace sighted, but didn't shoot. "You hear a ship out there?"

"Not yet. And even if Olli can get the *Joan* down here through the EM, she'd go for the dig site."

"We can find some way to signal her. We can set fire to the jungle?"

"Jerichan substances don't burn, my friend. They desiccate without even smoke," Trine remarked.

"This planet really is good for absolutely nothing," Solace growled. She sent out one more shot and was rewarded by some alarmed shouting. "Well, they have us pinned here. The walls are good, but not a permanent solution."

"Wait, listen," Kris was saying. To Idris, it seemed as though she was receding. Not physically, but along some other axis entirely... they all were. Which meant, of course, it was him not them. Something to do with the structure around them was screwing with his head, expanding his consciousness and he wasn't comfortable with that at all. He sat down, back sliding down the abrasive structure of the wall, ripping up his tunic. None of the others noticed.

"Is that the *Joan* now?" Kris was saying. "I wish all these fucking monsters would shut up for a second."

They shut up.

Idris whimpered, because *he'd* done that. Not intentionally. But Kris's demand had passed through his brain, into the building around them and then out—into the world. He'd somehow turned it into a shout, and every single bloody denizen of this monstrous jungle had stopped in mid-croak, mid-bellow, mid-shrill...because it wanted to know what he was and precisely how edible.

"Um..." Kris started. But the Voyenni had taken the quiet as the cue for an attack. In response, they were now rushing through the last few metres of tree cover, shooting as they came. Solace drilled one through the head, then dropped Mr. Punch because a big Voyenni had surprised them. He'd ducked around the wall with a magnetic pistol raised before him. Solace went for the barrel, twisting it from his hand with servo-enhanced strength. He picked her up and slammed her against the wall; he was tall and broad enough that she looked like a toy in his grip. Then she rammed an armoured knee into his sternum and chopped at his neck with the blade of her hand. He dropped her but another man was behind him, then another. Idris stared down the barrel of a massive projectile gun and literally couldn't move. His body was frozen with fear, his mind away with a multitude of horrible alien fairies.

Kris knifed the gunman in the hand and the gun went off— bullet ricocheting back and forth within the walls before spanging off Trine's body, its momentum almost spent. Then the knifed Voyenni had his own blade out, something closer to a machete, and hacked murderously down at Kris. She dodged in the limited space, feinting at his face to keep him back.

Idris felt as though he was watching a mediotype of unlikely events, things that had happened to someone else. His mind was filled with a thousand living things, linked through the broken tower to the whole electromagnetic life of the jungle. The jungle was like a brain, he thought, but a brain at war with itself, fighting for dominance, neuron against neuron. *Feels like my brain, then.*

This forested brain wouldn't do what he wanted though. It had its own business, after all. Except this tower was something like a transmitter station. Not in any way the operator back at Anchortown would have recognized, but it had been raised to boost and send signals. And right now the only signal was him.

Perhaps there were ways that his wishes and the drives of the biosphere outside might coincide.

Hold them off, he tried to say to it, but knew that no words had escaped his clamped-tight jaws. Solace had sent her opponent into Kris's Voyenni, then swept the pair of them out of the entryway. They were coming right back in with reinforcements, but she was keeping them out. Idris could only wonder at the economy of her movements. The Voyenni were trained thugs, the products of expensive schools in brutality and intimidation. Solace had been engineered as a soldier, mind and body. She was also encased in top-flight Partheni armour and trained from childhood to fight. There were too many of them for her to go on the offensive, but she was holding, holding.

Someone howled outside, a human voice in mortal terror. Idris felt vomit rise in his throat, because in some way *he* was outside too, breeding that terror. It was his fault. Someone else howled, and then it stopped, because a mouth that was half tentacles and half hooked teeth had closed and ripped its target in half—grinding the remains down a gullet lined with backwards-curving blades. Now there were more shouts and shooting—not aimed at the tower this time. Idris was carried along helplessly, linked to the monster he'd found. He moved from victim to victim as his champion took one horrifyingly long stride after another, hunting this intriguing

309

new prey. He didn't even know the nature of this beast. His connection was from the inside to inside. He just caught flashes of the various horrifying parts of it, without grasping its doubtless equally horrifying whole.

Solace had her back to the wall, waiting for the next opponent, but they'd spotted something else to worry about. Kris caught sight of it first and recoiled from the opening. Later she'd tell Idris about something with a sack of a body suspended on too many tall skeletal legs, stilting along as though jerked with strings. It was high up in the canopy, its leg-span stretching between the trees. And it was plucking up human shapes and shearing them apart, then picking over what was left as though trying to read a future in the entrails.

"The *Joan!*" Solace shouted suddenly. And Idris, sightless within the ruin, was nonetheless aware of the new intruder in the sky. He felt the biosphere bend towards it, a great roaring chorus of EM wash out, only to meet the ship's gravitic shielding. Olli was flying the vessel without instruments, without anything. She had the hatch open, he realized in horror. Their would-be saviour was sitting in her Scorpion frame at the hatch, looking out, wired into the pilot's station, flying the whole circus by wire and guesswork. And she couldn't see them, buried as they were in the jungle.

But she *would* have a comms channel open, he knew. He'd *heard* her signalling the dig site, hoping to cut through to reach them. Perhaps she even received brief moments of Robellin swearing at her, telling her that her crew wasn't at the dig, that they'd...

"I don't know what's going on out there, but the mercs won't hold off forever," Solace said. "We need to signal the

Joan and simply hope she can get low enough for us to get aboard."

We need to signal. That's why we came to a signalling station. At this point the thoughts were just sliding about his head like unsecured junk on a ship's deck. He had no idea what he'd known before coming here, or what he knew now. Communion with the outside world, with the jungle, was eating up all his mental capacity.

A broken, millions-of-years-old signalling station, the bulk of it buried beneath him. Its intricate, shell-like structure extended into the earth for half a kilometre. And it wasn't dead, because Originator tech couldn't die. Every part of it cast a shadow outside the real, even the little trinkets and rods the Hegemony carted about and used to claim whole planets. The very construction and substance of this ancient tech pointed to its function and meaning. There was a world locked away inside this stuff that nobody had ever guessed at.

This is a signalling station. So signal. It was such a trivial use of what he'd found, but it was the only thing he actually needed from it. And like any unknowable demon power, it was best not to ask for too much. *Be careful what you wish for.*

He signalled Olli, flagging their location in the clearest way he possible could. That was all he did. The forest exalted in that moment for a hundred metres in every direction, every monster, tree and buzzing thing shrieking, howling and trumpeting, but that was incidental. The whole EM babble around them became one single message, for just that second: a means to an end, burning their location into the *Joan's* flight computer.

The last remaining Voyenni took potshots at the *Joan* when

she came lurching down, veering and hovering clear of the trees while Olli lowered a chain-link ladder. Solace returned fire, burning the last of Mr. Punch's ammo. She stayed ground-side until Kris and Trine had scrambled up the ladder. Then she threw Idris over her shoulder and put a foot on the ladder so Olli could retract it. Idris sure as hell wasn't in any position to climb up on his own.

Kris

"So," Olli yelled as her frame fought with the closing hatch. "Idris good to take over for me?"

Kris risked a look at the pilot and saw that his skin was waxy, his face wild-eyed as if he was on a really bad trip. "I don't think Idris is going to be doing anything useful for a while."

"Okay, *fine*." Olli shouldered past her and Solace and set her frame to crouch in the centre of the passenger compartment. It took up most of the available space. "I'll just keep doing his job as well as mine, shall I?"

"That's not fair," Solace objected.

"Didn't ask your opinion." Olli looked wiped-out herself. Her Scorpion was physically wired to the pilot's console with heavily insulated cables, and the inside of the *Dark Joan* fairly crackled with electromagnetic fields. Kris guessed that she'd jury-rigged the packet runner's gravitic engine to run interference with Jericho's natural EM field, but she'd still had to somehow keep basic ship operations going. It obviously wasn't exactly a barrel of laughs keeping on top of it.

"Bloody Patho tech doesn't help. You don't make it to be monkeyed with," Olli added, sending Solace another filthy look. The Partheni didn't rise to it. "This your Hiver friend, are they?"

"And hello to you too," Trine said. They were looking woefully at their damaged leg, which was bent at an awkward-looking angle. "May I at least assume your vessel has an adequate workshop?"

"Medvig's tools'll be good enough for you," Olli said curtly. Then the *Joan* had cut free from Jericho's atmosphere and they were heading for the beacon of the *Vulture God*. "Kit'll be panicking," the specialist predicted. "Been out of all contact for way too long. *Vulture,* this is *Joan.* We're coming in."

The last faint vestiges of the upper atmosphere burned about them as Olli accelerated the packet runner to a respectable speed, clipping around the planet's curvature. Kris glanced at the nav console and decoded the readouts there.

"We're not going to the elevator hub?"

"Look, we were getting some attention there," Olli told her. "And then there was the stuff Kit scavved from the *Raptorid's* comms. We could have sat tight and hoped the *Jenny Kite* ID would cover us. But who knows whether that Magdan turd hired someone with two good eyes and half a brain? So we reckoned we wouldn't want to fuck about with permits when time came to scoot. Didn't know who might be beating on the hatch, see right?"

"Right," Kris agreed.

"*Vulture,* this is *Joan.* Kit, tell me something useful." Olli let herself sag back in the frame, flying the ship with her eyes closed now her sensors and instruments were clear of interference.

"If he's dodged round the planet, the EM will mess with our signal," Solace suggested.

313

"Yeah, maybe." The specialist sounded unconvinced. "Kit, you crab bastard, speak to me."

"You can't say that," Kris told her, knee-jerk.

"He doesn't care."

"You don't know that, and just don't. And knock off the 'Patho' stuff while you're at it."

Olli stared at her, obviously working up to an acidic comment, then just as visibly she backed down. "Fine. Can I just call him a Hanni bastard then...oh god *damn*."

They'd picked up the *Vulture*. Hunched over it like a predatory bat was the sleek double-pronged shape of the *Raptorid*. They could see that it was clamped to the salvage vessel and there was an umbilical connecting the two.

"We have comms contact," Olli noted tonelessly. "Turdwagon's hailing us."

"Open it up," Kris suggested. "Give it to me. I'll talk."

"Give it nothing until we've heard from Kit."

"I know." She stepped over the part-folded limbs of the Scorpion and dropped into the pilot's seat. After the chase and fight through that carnivorous forest, she didn't need any of this.

"Good day to you, crew of the *Vulture God*. I assume we don't need to bother with your false alias?"

"It's a real alias," Kris said, "just a false name." Pedantry wasn't going to win her any diplomacy awards but she wasn't in the mood for niceties. "Identify yourself."

"I think you recognize my *Raptorid*," She recognized the voice now, too, though she wouldn't give the Boyarin the satisfaction of showing it. "And you are the attorney. I remember you. We were having such a pleasant exchange before your warrior-dyke broke in. You have the honour of speaking to the Boyarin Piter Tchever Uskaro. I, on the other hand, am unfortunate enough to be addressing a crew of wanted criminals."

He doesn't half like the sound of his own voice, Kris thought.

"Now, I'm going to suggest that you divert course and come dock with me, Mesdam attorney. Bring your Int client too. Otherwise your carrion bird is going to take a long dive down the gravity well."

"I'm not entering any manner of negotiations until we've spoken to our crew on the *Vulture*," Kris said. "If you think the ship is leverage enough, think again."

There was a pause, then Uskaro broadcast on an open channel, "*Vulture*, you may speak."

They received a frenzied babble of scritching and scraping through the comms, together with a great dump of text and images. That certainly looked like Kittering's handiwork. Olli sorted through it quickly, decoding a long complaint to find the hidden details Kit had secreted within the message. It was an old Hanni game.

"Two guys with him. Hauled him over and locked weapons on him before he could do anything. He's not exactly a pilot, poor bastard. Still alive, though."

"So what do we do?" Kris asked. "I don't see Solace fighting her way over to the *Raptorid* and ending the lot of them. Idris?"

She looked back to see the Intermediary sitting with his back to the hull, looking ill. "Anyone we can hail?" he croaked.

"No friends hereabouts," Olli said.

"We could fight. I'm full on ammunition now," Solace said quietly. "We suit up in case we're hit. I shoot their hull full of holes, take out some key systems."

"That's how you'd do it in the Parthenon, is it?" Kris asked her frankly.

"In the Parthenon I'd have at least three others with the same kit and training as me. And then, yes, we'd go in and do exactly that, with full confidence. Right now, with just me, maybe not ideal. But the man wants to enslave Idris and he's hardly going to let the rest of us go, given the trouble we've caused him. You have other ideas?"

"Yes," Kris insisted. "There's always other options... Let's give talking a chance. The Boyarin likes to talk. And if they take Idris intact and we leave this alive too, we can spring him some time. We work out a rendezvous, Idris can take whatever damn ship they put him on there, and we'll have pirates waiting. We know some pirates." She faced up to Solace's raised eyebrow. "Well, we *do*. Alive is better, is all I'm saying. Give me a chance to talk to them."

"We talk, we've lost our best chance of fighting it out," Solace said, but in a tone that said she was knuckling under.

"*Raptorid*, we are coming in," Olli reported in venomous tones.

"Of course you are," Uskaro said, vastly pleased with himself. "I will hand *you* over to one of my people, while *I* take care of the bigger picture."

"Small people for small matters. Right." The specialist's face looked like thunder.

"Idris?" Kris asked. He looked at her without much expression.

"Pick a system," Solace encouraged him. "I'll have a team there on standby for as long as it takes. The moment they give you free access to a ship's controls..."

"And then I'm yours, rather than theirs," he murmured.

Solace looked away. Kris searched for anger, frustration, even guilt on her face. She found none of it. Instead there was an unexpected misery.

"By that point...I don't think I could ask my people to go to those lengths, including attacking a Colonial ship, to then come away with nothing. But isn't the Parthenon better? Better us than the Magdans, surely?"

"*We'll* go get him," Olli said bluntly. "Us...we might use pirates, crooks, whatever. But we wouldn't be starting a fucking war."

"Solace, old comrade-in-arms," Trine put in, "I am less than enthused by these developments."

"As for you—!" Olli started, but then Kris barked out, "*Hold!* Who's this?" She'd been keeping an eye on the pilot's board— and the *Joan* had some eager early warning systems.

"What now?" Olli turned her attention to the piloting feed and caught up. "Someone else is out there. Some other ship."

"Friends, I don't suppose?" Trine asked hopefully.

"You *don't suppose* correct. We've got no fucking friends round here," Olli told them. "They're hailing the *Raptorid*— oh, bless your skittering little feet, Kit. He's still hacked into their deck, even though they're looking over his shoulder. He's sending us the traffic. Listen up."

"*Raptorid*," came a thin, slightly nasal accent. Kris reckoned it came from somewhere central and settled in the Colonies. "This is *Mordant's Hammer* requesting an address with the respected Boyarin Uskaro of Fief Yachellow."

Idris jolted to his feet hard enough to crack his head on the curved side of the hull. "That's got to be a very poor joke," he got out.

"Isn't Mordant..." Kris started uncertainly.

"They're saying they're the secret police," he said, and when that didn't seem to make much sense even to himself, he added, "The *blatant* secret police. When Mordant House throws its weight around, they show it in the names of their ships."

Over the comms came the sound of the operator, sounding cagey. "*Mordant's Hammer* this is *Raptorid*. The noble Boyarin would ask for your credentials and to what he owes the pleasure of your presence?"

"Nativist bastard's a little leery when the actual authorities turn up," Olli muttered. "I guess the whole of Hugh doesn't *quite* belong to them yet, then."

"There's some kind of ID coming through. Looks... genuine? Idris?"

"I'm no expert. If you think it's sound, probably it's sound. Mordant House. Damn me." He looked sick with the thought. "They're here for *me*."

"You somehow failed to mention that the Hugh spook squad were after you, ever," Kris noted, guessing that at least half of this was his normal paranoia.

Sure enough, he hesitated. "Well..."

"I mean, it's not like we haven't gotten mixed up in a whole world of *other* pain recently," she pointed out calmly. "Maybe it's not all about you."

"*Raptorid*, this is Agent Havaer Mundy of the Intervention Board. I claim eminent domain of the vessel you are detaining and all of its crew. I appreciate your assistance in holding them, but kindly repatriate any you might have taken aboard and decouple. Your cooperation is noted—and Mordant House always remembers." The words came over without much inflection, all business and no threat, until you read between them. *Oh he's got our man Uskaro's number all right.*

"Hailing us now," Olli said, and that same calm voice came to them.

"Partheni packet runner *Dark Joan*, it is my sincere belief that you are not carrying diplomatic personnel or restricted data that places you outside jurisdiction. Therefore I am requesting that you follow your original course and dock with the *Vulture God*, which I am taking under my control. Please do not deviate from that course."

Kris brought up an image of the *Hammer*, which was cruising in at some speed. It was a blunt-nosed vessel with a heavy head and a bulky torus body. As close as you could get to being a light fighting ship without painting her up in navy colours. Kris could even see two banks of heavy accelerators ready to shred any ship that didn't fall into line.

"How are the *Joan's* shields. Could we survive *that*?" she asked, indicating the weaponry.

"For a short period of time," Solace confirmed. "But we're massively outclassed here—and the *Vulture* can't handle that kind of firepower at all."

"The *Raptorid's* backing off," Olli noted. "They don't fancy it either, and they're tougher than we are."

"They don't want to be on the Mordant shit list. And neither do we," Kris said hollowly.

"We already are. Look at the fucker they sent after us!"

"Think about what we've been involved in recently. You think Hugh didn't sit up and take notice the moment word came that we'd hauled an Architect-touched ship into Lung-Crow?" Kris demanded. "This doesn't have to be *our* trouble. We just need to be frank and honest and not assume they're going to screw us."

"They *are* going to screw us," Olli insisted. "But I don't see what we can do other than bend over. Kit's out there and he's not even a Colonial citizen. He's utterly fucked if we just hightail it away."

A glance was exchanged: Olli to Idris, Idris to Solace, Solace to Kris. Trine's holographic face just gurned through a series of frustrated expressions, looking at all of them at once.

"*Hammer*, this is the *Dark Joan*. We're coming in," Kris confirmed. *Better than being at the mercy of the Magdans. Maybe. Possibly.*

20.

Havaer

"Havaer Mundy?" asked Keristina Soolin Almier. "Wait, like the Ragman? The 'Travelled Opinions' guy?"

Havaer stared at her. It wasn't often someone managed to wrong-foot him at the very start of an interview, but here he was. And that was the drawback of having a public ID under the same tagline as his spook work, certainly, but it was rare his two worlds clashed when he wasn't personally bringing them together.

"I moonlight," he said. "You can assume I'm wearing my other hat here."

"Oh, right." The woman still seemed entirely at ease, chatty, eager to help. "I like your stuff."

"That's very kind of you," Havaer said automatically, shaking off a touch of the surreal. It was just the two of them and the recording rig, here in the heart of the *Mordant's Hammer*. The interrogation room was intentionally spare, just metal frame furniture and bare walls adorned with only a little tracery of machinery. Enough to suggest the room might have other purposes than hosting a friendly chat. Almier didn't seem to have noticed.

"Mesdam Almier, you can imagine what I'm here to discuss. I'd hoped to talk to Captain Rostand, but I understand..."

"Broken Harvest killed him."

"Yes. While you were retaking your ship from them. Some might say that was a little out of the league of a salvage crew."

"Some didn't know Rollo," she told him with a hard smile. "Also, some might not have had a Partheni ship and soldier to hand."

Havaer had the irrational impulse to school her in how to behave under interrogation. *Play down the Parthenon involvement, or at least make me work for it.* And she was a lawyer, wasn't she? Accredited out of Scintilla, of all places. A very odd start, when you ended up working the spacer circuit. And he'd read her file, read all of their files—where they existed. Almier had more detail in hers than the rest, coming from a settled background rather than being born to the spacer life. A nasty business for her there, at the end. Expensive blood she'd ended up shedding, even if it was all legal under Scintilla's ridiculous duelling codes.

"What happened to the *Oumaru*?"

"We stowed it. In the deep void. I mean, you could talk Idris into taking you there? Or we could nip back in the *Vulture*, and bring the whole thing back to you...?"

"We have our own Intermediary navigator," he said. *So don't think you can just vanish.* He was trying hard to be the bad guy interrogator, the looming shadow of Mordant House, but she seemed blithely unaware of it. He'd been minded to go in heavy-handed—with accusations of them selling out Hugh to the Parthenon, all of that. But it was hard to put the screws on when she was being so damned cooperative. Easier right now just to keep a regular police hat on and let her talk, see what spilled out on the table.

"So why were this Broken Harvest mob involved?" Something he had a personal stake in finding out, given the unpleasant interview he'd just managed to survive.

"Said the *Oumaru* was their ship, or was carrying their cargo." She shrugged. "Or—maybe, I mean, just the wreck itself has a price, right? Who wouldn't want the chance to go over an Architect's leavings? That's why we picked up Delegate Trine, after all. We wanted to know just what we had, now we had it."

"Recoup your losses?"

Her mildly reproving look actually made him feel bad about the words. "Our *losses* are three dead friends, Menheer Mundy. But we still have to make a living, and if we could sell the thing, to you, to the Parthenon, to some Hanni consortium? I mean, Architects are everyone's problem, right? Even the Hegemony would be interested. Probably that's where Aklu the Hook's buyers are."

He let himself blink at her without any sign of recognition. "Who?"

"Oh, well." She flexed her fingers enthusiastically. "Agent, let me tell you about the Broken Harvest's top dog, because that is *really* worth an opinion piece..."

*

He had tried to interrogate the Hanni, whose Colonial trade permits transliterated his name as Kr'k'ctahrr—although his human colleagues referred to him as Kit or Kittering. Havaer suspected strongly that the alien was leaning heavily on the species communications barrier to frustrate any kind of questioning. And although Mordant kept a few Hanni on the payroll, he hadn't had time to requisition any. So: one useless suspect.

Delegate Trine turned out to be another dead-end. Not even a member of the *Vulture* crew, but an academic with a list of Colonial qualifications as long as a human arm. The problem was the "delegate" in front of their name. Hiver Assets would have been fair game, under the reciprocal agreements between Hugh and the Hiver Assembly. Delegates were a different matter—a rank awarded sparingly by the Hivers, and only conferred upon individuals of particular significance and knowledge. Hugh had agreed not to prod one without going through slow official channels. This in return for the Hivers respecting Hugh's own diplomats and, not to put too fine a point on it, their spies. It turned out that the *Dark Joan* really *had* been transporting someone with diplomatic immunity, but their credentials had been Hiver Assembly rather than Parthenon.

Olian "Olli" Timo was another matter. They'd got her out of the Castigar engineering frame by a careful mix of reason and veiled threat, although it hadn't done much to take the fight out of *her*. She turned up in a six-legged walker instead. Havaer's crew had done their best to scan it for hidden weapons, but the thing was a mess of clashing parts and incompatible tech, and spacers were so damn ingenious with their jury-rigging... For all they knew, the whole thing could have been a bomb or a home-made accelerator cannon.

"Well?" she demanded. "What, then?" Her finger stumps

flexed and the feet of the walker scraped on the metal floor like fingernails on a board.

I will have some carpet put down when we hit dock, Havaer vowed, hiding the way the sound wormed into his head. "Mesdam Timo, you know why we're here..."

"I'm saying nothing."

"You're a Colonial citizen, Mesdam. You resent your government taking an interest, when it looks like the war's back on?" Meeting her bluntness with bluntness was probably the best tactic.

"Not *my* government. You know spacers get no say in what goes on in Berlenhof."

"Tell me about the *Oumaru*."

"I'm telling you nothing. Not one word. On advice of my lawyer."

"Mesdam Timo," Havaer said calmly, "I have just had a perfectly pleasant and informative conversation with your lawyer."

"Then you don't need me, do you."

"Let's change topic then. Tell me about the Broken Harvest."

"Those fuckers," she said, forgetting instantly that she wasn't telling him anything. She proceeded to describe the cartel, their Essiel leader, their Tothiat enforcers and a great deal more without any real prompting from him. *I suppose it was this "Mesmon" who was taking part in the anatomy lesson, when I was there.*

"So, fine. You don't like them," he concluded for her. "I've had my own run-in with them—as it happens—while on your trail. This Mesmon, who killed your captain..."

"We did for *him*, the bastard."

"You didn't." And he saw her face go still and then clench

like a fist. He told her what he'd seen, the way that The Unspeakable Aklu punished failure in its more durable servants. She didn't like Mesmon being alive, but he could see she didn't mind him being alive and *flayed*—and she appreciated both the warning and the mental image of the Tothiat's torture.

"So, tell me about the Parthenon."

"Those eugenicist fuckers?" she snapped. "Oh, that's what's got your panties twisted, is it? That figures." She hunkered forwards in her walker with a twitch of her limb stumps. "Let me tell you exactly what I think of those turds…"

*

Which led him onto what he reckoned was going to be the toughest interview.

They had not persuaded the Partheni to take off her armour. She wasn't quite under arrest, although Havaer had broad powers when it came to foreign operatives in Colonial Space. Her ID was good on the surface too, but stank of espionage the moment he turned a spook's practised gaze on it. He had three marines in with him, also armoured and all with accelerators. If anything kicked off, they would end up riddling the *Hammer's* hull with holes, and also anyone who got in their way. Havaer's pessimistic assessment of anything kicking off included himself being used as a human shield, and he was, as a rule, averse to death by friendly fire. *It's never that friendly, let's face it.*

At least she'd agreed to leave her own gun on the *Vulture*.

Sitting down, he opened with, "Well now, Myrmidon. You're a long way from home."

She nodded, watching him. Everyone told you how impossible Partheni were to read, but it wasn't true. The warrior angels were humans too, perhaps their biggest secret. They really weren't machines or perfectly bioengineered superwomen, although both Nativists and the Parthenon had unintentionally colluded to hide these facts. Right now this one, Solace, was tense, a little antagonistic. But he could tell she was worried, too. Worried for herself? Concerned about Partheni interests? He didn't think so.

"I'm anticipating that this interview is going to consist mostly of belligerent silence, Myrmidon." He'd half expected her to deny the rank; claim she was renegade, freelance, some other fiction. She just let it go by, though. "But, look... you'll understand that your mere presence has put your fellows in even more trouble. My superiors see a possible Architect presence, and then they see the Parthenon in its shadow. You don't need me to tell *you* that relations between Hugh and the Parthenon are in a particularly fragile state right now. Half my friends in the Colonial reserves were on stand-by for active duty—even before your friends pulled their stunt at Lung-Crow. Your government is making a lot of demands on Hugh right now, Myrmidon. And we both know there are plenty in mine who are reaching for their guns too."

No denial that the Parthenon was still her government. No protestations of having gone rogue. She was trying to be impassive, but he'd seen the twitch when he talked about the others being in deeper shit just because she was around.

"I'm no Nativist," he told her. "I don't automatically assume anything the Parthenon does is inimical to human interests. Because we're all human, right?"

The tiniest nod, small enough that maybe she didn't realize she'd made it. And the Parthenon had its own Nativist equivalents, its hardliners, and so maybe Solace wasn't one of them. Always preferable to deal with non-fanatics.

"This is where you give me at least the cover story of why you linked up with these reprobates."

She smiled, so unexpectedly that he was slightly taken aback. "That's a good word for them."

"And the cover story? Only I was expecting you to go long on how the Parthenon was our front line against the Architects. Always had been. And that's how you ended up involved?"

A blink. "The information about the Architect came out later. As you're probably aware. And I won't deny my government's interested in it *now*. Of course we are. Who wouldn't be? It's a problem for all of us." She took a deep breath. "I'm Myrmidon Executor Solace, Heaven's Sword Sorority, Basilisk Company." And, after a beat, "Angels of Punching You in the Face."

"Huh." He assimilated that. "Quite a salad of competences going on there. Basilisk is a mass loom gunner, isn't it?"

She looked surprised that he knew, nodded shortly.

"From soldier to spy is quite a jump."

"I'm not a spy. I'm just tasked with working outside our territory. That's all Executor means."

"But you didn't bring your mass loom..."

"Aren't you glad?" Hugh hadn't managed to replicate the Partheni's huge gravitic weapons, and that still smarted.

"So why *are* you here, if not to prep for the next Architect invasion?" And he was too confident now; he'd let something slip, because:

"You know that already. You've talked to Olli and she's told you."

Havaer smiled, not quite sure what had given it away. "Well, you've got me there. And?"

"And Idris is a free man. It's *his* choice." Real feeling now, in her voice. "My people would rather I twisted his arm: guilted him, forced him, kidnapped him, even. And I haven't. It wouldn't be right. But *you've* no right to stand in his way, if he decides to work for us. He's free to make that choice."

"He's a military asset," Havaer told her automatically and, having been frank, decided that frankness was the way to go. "I can seek authority to detain him to keep him out of the hands of a foreign power, one we may well be at war with in the near future. That is literally something I can do as an agent of Hugh and Mordant House. In the same way that your own heads of staff would slam the door the moment one of your weapons techs decided that a luxury apartment on the Berlenhof Archipelago sounded like a cushy retirement option. Est-ce compris?"

She nodded sharply, hating him but understanding him. Maybe she hated herself a little too. Because the pair of them knew damn well that her next order might be to cut loose from the *Vulture*'s crew and take Idris with her. Whether he wanted it or not.

*

Havaer took a break then: grabbed some kaffe, ordered his notes. Between Kris and Olli, at least, he had a good idea of what had gone on with the *Oumaru* and the Architects. And nobody had reported any planets missing recently, so maybe the *Oumaru* was a one-off event. Except his racing heart didn't believe that.

It's what everyone will tell each other. That one fluke doesn't mean they're back. They'll tell that to each other, and nobody will believe the news is true. He was trying to imagine the wave of panic spreading across the Colonies, once elusive rumour became hard evidence in the form of a wrecked *Oumaru*. Mass evacuations, worlds defecting pell-mell to the Hegemony, apocalyptic cults and survivalist brotherhoods and—yes—the goddamn Nativists would find some way to capitalize on it as well. *Betrayed!* they'd shout, and get in the way just when Hugh needed unity. To Havaer, as a professional agent, the thought of the paperwork alone filled him with dread.

And he knew the Parthenon wanted their own pet Int, too— not exactly hard to guess, even if Olli and Solace hadn't independently confirmed it. And right now, if the Architects *were* back, the Parthenon would be even more determined to get an Int on their side.

Which only left one interview to go.

Idris Telemmier was slumped in his seat. He had the same shadow of stubble Havaer remembered from Lung-Crow, the same inward-looking, flinching manner. Stripped of his friends, he looked as though he was waiting to be beaten with hoses or have wires clipped to his nipples.

"Hell, man," Havaer said, sitting down across from him. "This doesn't have to be *that* sort of conversation."

"*You . . .*" Telemmier stared at him bleakly. "I said all I wanted to say to you on Lung-Crow. I don't want anything to do with Hugh anymore. I did my bit. Nobody can say I didn't."

"Look, Menheer—"

330

"*I stopped the war!*" Telemmier burst out suddenly, eyes wide. "I went into the mind of an Architect, me and the others. We stopped the war. We saved everyone. *You. Cannot. Imagine—*" He clearly had more to say, but his teeth were clamped together now and he couldn't get the words out. His wrists were pressed to the arms of the chair as though, in his head, he was shackled to it.

"Menheer Telemmier. Idris." Havaer kept his voice very calm. "*This...*" he indicated the interview room, "isn't even about you."

"Sure it isn't." Drawn-wire tension was pulling every part of the man taut.

"You found the wreck of a goddamn *Architect* attack!" Havaer snapped. "Why is it nobody's focusing on that, exactly? We could get an Architect over Magda or Lief or even Berlenhof any moment. As we sit here, it may already have *happened*. Packet trade to Jericho space is pretty damn slow after all. A few billion people maybe just got offed, while I'm goose-chasing after your crew to ask some questions. Help me out here, maybe?"

And *that* was the right approach, yanking the man out of his self-made misery hole. "It's not my fault," Telemmier told him. Aggrieved, but that was better than self-pitying.

"Nobody's saying it is," Havaer said. "Look, I'm not even starting on the whole Parthenon thing. Why you have a pet soldier aboard your ship." *Not yet, anyway, though that is definitely on the menu for interview two.* "Just tell me what you know about the *Oumaru* and what happened to it. I've got the facts from the others. Give me anything that'll only have come to *you*."

"I mean, why would they?" Idris burst out, the non sequitur

taking Havaer's train of thought and shunting it into a siding. "They attacked *one ship*. One Hegemony freighter. Since when was that how Architects did things? They take out planets. And even then, only ones we're actually *living* on. A thousand rocks out in the void, and none of them gets special treatment. Only places that are someone's home."

"The *Oumaru* had a crew, and *they* called their ship home," Havaer suggested.

"But...it's wrong. It's not how they work." Because the war had been all kinds of trauma, for the Ints, but at least they'd thought they knew how the enemy operated. "And yet, and yet, we all saw the *Oumaru* had been just...*Architected*. And you're asking why's nobody focusing on that fact? Because the *Oumaru* was too small a disaster and people need something *big* to make them understand, Menheer Mundy. Everyone's built new lives for themselves in the last forty years. I watched them do it." Shaking his head wildly at the foolishness of it. "At first, people were terrified to put down roots. They still had their bags packed and every ship had spare pods to carry refugees. You're too young. You wouldn't know. But year by year, when the Architects *stayed* gone... I saw people begin to realize they could live again. Build, settle, invest, have families. And now if they're *back*, all that goes away. We go back to being *doomed* every day of our lives. So take it from me, nobody'll focus on this goddamn fact—until some colony somewhere gets an extra moon all of a sudden, and then gets worked over." His shoulders hunched further. "*I* don't want to believe it. I saw the wreck up close and I don't."

"And so you came here to get confirmation, from this expert you knew from way back?"

"What? Yes."

The story's still not right. He had the maddening sense of a missing piece, but they'd all told the same tale so far. If he wanted the hard truth that meant harsh methods—actual arrests, solitary confinement, serious interrogation at a secure Mordant facility. It also meant paperwork, expense and having to justify it to his bosses. Given the stakes, it wouldn't take much justification, but still...

Do your job, man. No place for a soft heart in Mordant House. But he'd always fought against becoming the sort of man who reached for extreme measures as a matter of course. *Which means maybe I'm not the right man for the job anymore.*

The soft touch first, he told himself. *Time later for the rest. If it's necessary.* He had done it before, when he had to. He had never *liked* it. It was the crumbling cliff-edge of decency he clung to.

"Menheer Telemmier..." he tried again.

"The Presence has shifted."

Havaer went cold. "You mean...the *thing* in unspace. The thing people feel, that isn't really there?"

Idris just stared at him. "Is it not, though?"

"What," Havaer said hoarsely, "do you even mean, 'shifted'?"

"I don't have the words for it. Your own Int, what does she say?"

How does he know our Int is female? No disguising his surprise and suddenly it was Telemmier with the level and knowing stare, and Havaer was shifting uneasily. "She hasn't said anything."

"You haven't asked her. But she's on a leash, one of the new class out of the Liaison Board, right? When the Board took over from the old Int Program they went for quantity.

333

She hasn't been doing it as long as me. I've been in and out of unspace fifty years, Menheer Mundy. *Something's* changed. Maybe they are back. Maybe they're practising on the small things before they take on a planet again, Maybe they're rusty."

*

Havaer let them go back to the *Vulture,* because they demanded it and he was getting enough cooperation to make the open-handed approach worthwhile. And he wouldn't call any of this crew traitors or criminals, exactly. Spacers didn't like to feel they lived in a universe that could tell them what to do, and he could work with that. Worst came to worst, he could pledge some of the budget because it was amazing how quickly most spacers could be bought, once they felt they were making a deal rather than knuckling under.

He composed his report, letting the spacers stew. The *Hammer* was still clamped to the *Vulture,* because he wasn't done with them and their secrets. Most likely they were hiding a little light smuggling, customs evasion or something similar— and he would drop some heavy hints that he didn't care an iota of Largesse about that sort of thing. But if it *was* something else, maybe Almier would talk the rest into coming clean. Or if it really was funny business with the Parthenon, Timo might give up the goods on that front?

But what if it's Hegemony stuff? If *that* was the case, then he had a problem on his hands. Hegemony, Parthenon and an Intermediary all in the same small boat. With a rumoured Architect out there too. That wasn't the sort of mix Mordant House was going to like.

He rubbed at his forehead, hoping sincerely that nothing of the sort was going on. After all, spacers constituted a good thirty per cent of the human population, and they were traditionally sanguine about doing business with anyone they chose—though Nativist sentiments were starting to change that.

Not my job. Just a servant. Focus on the greater good. He felt that familiar, baseline unhappiness of someone who would be judged entirely according to moral decisions made by others.

Then his comm implant went off and Captain Khefi, who'd been sangfroid itself when facing down the Boyarin, was shouting at him. Havaer activated his ready room's viewscreen and saw an Essiel ship bearing down on them.

"How long have you been keeping *that* to yourself?" Havaer demanded, and Khefi assured him that, no, the newcomer had come out of unspace practically on top of them.

"Hail them, full colours, standard codes for Hegemony vessels," Havaer directed, on his way to the bridge already. His implant would keep him in the loop but he had a need to be there, in the same place physically as his crew. "Signal the *Samphire* for backup." Although the antiquated navy picket ship wasn't going to be much help if this turned into a shooting war.

Standard codes for Hegemony vessels. Because there wasn't any mistaking the ship design, and what the hell did it mean, to meet an Essiel ship so far from anywhere they'd claimed as their own? Except Jericho housed extensive Originator ruins, and Hegemony cultists had been whining about gaining access since forever. Dealing with that hot potato was absolutely *not* Havaer's job, but maybe he'd become a new first line of defence.

The vessel had come out of unspace in a slow tumble, a thing like a twisted silver rose. Hegemony ships tended to adopt multi-petalled forms, yet this one looked different, less geometric than usual. There were fewer straight lines— every frond and flange shaped to follow a rippling curve. It was as though a transformative wave had frozen as it rippled through the ship's substance. It made Havaer's eyes ache to look at it.

Talking with the Hegemony was a pain at the best of times, unless they had some of their pet humans aboard to translate. Even then you never quite knew if you were getting the alien masters' intended meaning. They weren't hasty, though. They loved their pomp and posturing, as befitted a species that had evolved sitting on its fundament.

"Their guns are *hot!*" one of Khefi's people was shouting as Havaer hit the bridge. "They're not slowing."

The hell? "Are they responding to hails?" Havaer demanded. The central screen showed a model of objects in near-space buzzing with trajectory lines and a host of numbers. The left screen showed an image of the newcomer, enlarged and cleaned up in all its disturbing glory. The right panel displayed technical data—including the fact that those twisted petals hid a dozen heavy-duty accelerator cannon. All of these were currently spiking the Hegemony ship's gravitic field.

Is this it? Did we go to war with the Hegemony and this is the first news we've had of it?

"Hail incoming, in Colvul," the comms officer reported, sounding calmer than Havaer felt.

"Let's hear it."

Over the comms came a bell-like voice. For some reason

it sounded familiar as it declaimed, "Take flight, O villains crouching so to shield the right inheritor of all our wrath. Begone, lest all our fury fall upon you like your namesake."

"The fuck...?" Khefi muttered, at Havaer's elbow.

"Ship name is *Broken Harvest*," the comms officer confirmed. And Havaer sighed in a weird relief. It was the Essiel from the concrete bunker. Not war then. Not yet, anyway.

"Stall them, something ritual, respectful, basically time-wasting," he directed. "Tell them we're taking them seriously and are convening our most important people to prepare a fitting response."

"What is this, Agent?" Khefi demanded.

"Believe it or not, they're a crime syndicate."

"That is one hell of a big ship for gangsters."

"Don't I know it. What do we think they can do?" And Havaer could only goggle at the *Broken Harvest* as it came at them. Was it named after the gang, or did the ship come first? It wasn't a full-on Hegemony diplomatic barge, but it was still twice the size of the *Mordant's Hammer*. Scans showed superior firepower and what looked to be some advanced gravitic shielding. On the other side of Jericho, the old *Samphire* was getting underway from dock. However, the *Hammer* could have run rings about the antique warship, and the *Harvest* could take them both.

"What do they want?" Khefi demanded.

"They want the *Vulture*," he said. "Can we run?"

"Not and take the salvage ship with us," Khefi said. "The *Vulture* could actually run faster if *she* carried *us*. But we'd still both be slower than that thing."

"Can we sync drives?"

"Not in the time we've got." Because you really didn't want

to hit unspace in two locked ships, where one drive wasn't perfectly aligned with the other. Havaer had seen the result one time, and it had started a brief panic about the return of the Architects.

"They're hailing us again," the comms officer said.

"Hegemony don't shoot first," Khefi muttered. "They bluster, and they defend themselves, but they don't..."

"This one will," Havaer decided. "It's renegade...mad maybe." *The Unspeakable Aklu, the Razor and the Hook.* And perhaps it wasn't even madness. Perhaps Essiel society threw up outliers like Aklu to fill a pro-active void that would otherwise remain empty, and was occasionally useful?

"Orders, Agent?"

He'd made his decision, he realized. It was a bittersweet one, but today was not the day to die for a good cause, not even for Mordant House.

"Get me the *Vulture*," he said.

Idris

The crew of the *Vulture* had been desperately trying to get the *Hammer* on comms. The sudden arrival of a Hegemony maybe-warship hadn't gone unnoticed by them either. And when Havaer's voice finally came through, as they crowded around the captain's chair, the release of tension was an almost physical shock.

"Some old friends of yours," Havaer told them. *"Broken Harvest.* Demanding we give you up."

"And are you going to?" Kris demanded.

"Telemmier there?"

"What?" Idris demanded, leaning in beside Kris. "Why *me*?"

"Get to your pilot's station, Telemmier," Havaer told him shortly. "This is how it's going to go. We're pulling back, but not as fast as their ship's coming on. And it's a full-on Hegemony fighting ship, which means my little sloop won't hold her off for long."

"So what now?" Kris demanded, as Idris squeezed past Trine's metal body to get to his seat.

"So I'm decoupling you. I want you to fall into unspace as quickly as you can, just jump right out and we'll do the same. Telemmier, I'll link you to my navigator. Make sure we don't end up clashing."

"So we stutter-jump together, in-system?" Idris asked politely. He was already calculating a course to the deep void, but felt the illusion of cooperation was worth maintaining.

"We *both* know you'll go on the lam straight off." The knowing edge in Havaer's voice cut deep. "Maybe that's best for now. And once you're clear of us, I know full well that I've got no hold on you. I'm Hugh, and you spacers will take every chance to buck authority."

"Not entirely fair," Kris protested, although Olli shouting, "Damn right!" over her probably didn't help.

"It's like this," Havaer's voice went on. They could hear the faint babble of his crew behind him, as they readied ship systems to face the *Broken Harvest*. "Mordant House is only interested in the Architects—this isn't about *you*. And I know you all have very different loyalties, but this is way bigger than any one government. If the Architects are back, everyone needs to know. I am therefore *pleading* with you to get your ship to Berlenhof—with or without the *Oumaru*. Berlenhof has embassies for every major galactic power. And specifically for Executor Solace, you should know that the *Heaven's Sword*—your own damn sorority ship—is there right now along with the *Thunderchild*, in the most overt display of gunboat diplomacy I ever saw. All because of even the first sniff of Architect involvement. If you value anything beyond your own skins and profits, come testify there. You'll be heroes. And once this is all out and public, you'll be safe."

Idris wondered how much of that the man believed.

"We need to discuss it," Idris told Havaer over the comms.

"Just think about it," came the reply, and then, "Right, they're on us. Decoupling you." The umbilical had already withdrawn and Idris's board showed him a warning that the *Hammer's* clamps were retracting.

"Ready," Idris replied. He coaxed a drachm of force from the *Vulture's* reaction drives, to push them away from the *Hammer* the moment they were free.

Perhaps the *Broken Harvest* assumed they were fulfilling its demands, as it changed course to intercept the smaller vessel while keeping its weapons targeted on Havaer's ship. Idris let the *Vulture* tumble as though drifting away from the *Hammer*, while calculating the space between the vessels. Mass screwed with gravity, so a complex gravitic operation like entering unspace wasn't wise when in another ship's shadow. Especially if that ship was already plotting its own jump.

He had a weird sense, then, as if the universe really was a sheet and three fingers were pressing dimples into it. Here *he* was, here was the *Hammer's* leash-contracted navigator, and there was the alien mind that guided the *Broken Harvest*. Ogdru, the species was called. He pictured it like a predatory whale, vast bulk, long jaws.

The others weren't all in suspension pods yet, but they'd

just have to go through the final motions on the other side. Even as the *Harvest* swooped in, he activated the *Vulture's* gravitic drive and yanked them into unspace. And they fell away from the Jericho system into the deep abyss.

21.

Idris

Or that was the plan.

Something seared like a knife into Idris's skull. Space around the *Vulture God* abruptly contained vast volumes more than it should, every axis of distance receding away from them. Including that vital step from *here* to *there* that would remove the ship from the real and place it within unspace. The salvage ship's gravitic drives were clawing at the substance of the universe, running at full power as they went absolutely nowhere.

An angry rainbow of warning lights spread across his board and all that power had to go somewhere: use it, lose it or it would tear the ship in two. He remembered how the Broken Harvest's interceptor had been so careful not to shoot at the *Oumaru*. Possibly the hoods thought the relics were still hidden aboard that wreck, because apparently the *Vulture God* didn't warrant the same kind of deference. Or maybe they had given the relics up for lost and were avenging the utmost heresy.

Gravitic interdiction was theoretical tech. He knew Colonial scientists had a model around the end of the war but had got nowhere with it. He didn't think the Parthenon had it either. Apparently the Hegemony did, though. Apparently even rogue Hegemony *gangsters* had it. War with the Hegemony had always been a possibility should the Colonies decide not to allow one of their worlds to secede to the alien empire. Fighting the force of the Hegemony gravity net, Idris had a really bad feeling about how that fight might go, because just maybe the Essiel's non-confrontational manner didn't stem from their not being able to put the boot in when they needed to. Havaer Mundy would doubtless have some interesting reports to file—if he escaped this mess.

Right now, Idris felt space stretching to infinity on all sides, making the mere idea of travel in any direction laughable. Behind it, he sensed the mind of the Hegemony pilot, the Ogdru. It was like an arrowhead, a killer. There was no real sentience there, just an animal hunger—a predator whose environment was space, both real and otherwise. Unspace would hold no horrors for this creature; it didn't have brain enough for existential dread. And the Essiel had given it access to ship systems so it could hold prey in its net as it stalked them.

Yet the net wasn't perfect. There was a gradient to it, as though the *Vulture* was caught in a bag full of water with a leak in one corner. Perhaps it simply wasn't possible to isolate space perfectly. A maze, then.

Idris closed his eyes and cut himself off from his senses, searching. The hunter was undulating towards him like some vast underwater thing. His imagination cast it with a thousand eyes, tentacles, toothy jaws—all the sea monsters that had ever troubled human dreams. It was a shadow beneath him, rising from the depths, opening out like the rose petal structure of its own vessel, seeking to engulf ...

And while his conscious mind shrank from the horrors he'd concocted, the rest of him had taken that gradient, analysed and followed it. He'd found the flaw in the trap and instinctively solved the proofs required to exploit it. Any human catching a ball must solve complex three-dimensional equations of space and velocity without conscious thought. And for Idris, this wasn't much different.

The *Vulture God* twisted, tangled in reality, halfway between everywhere and nowhere. It was both real and unreal all at once. Idris felt a terrible wrench in his mind, which resonated equally in the keening ring of the ship's drives, and then they were gone. They'd skidded sideways out of reality and into the underlying mechanics of the universe.

There was a moment when Idris wasn't sure they'd survived it. Instead of the transition into the familiar nothingness of unspace, what greeted him was too bright, too unfocused. The ship around him seemed to exist in five or six different slightly out-of-phase versions. And he thought: *We're lost, we're coming apart.* He felt they were suffering a loss of integrity, not physically but philosophically. Perhaps only his own waning belief was holding the ship to this side of existence.

He faced this doubt by screaming at it, there in unspace where nobody would ever hear. Just a mad animal bellow of *I am here!* The ship shuddered around him, then came sharply back together in a way that owed nothing to material sensation. Finally the glare turned into the dead-screen radiance of unspace. He felt his heart slamming painfully against the cage of his ribs. His lungs burned as though he'd been breathing something other than air. His splitting headache was like an axe to the skull.

Idris Telemmier sagged in his seat, weeping. He wished

more than anything that he could let *go*, just let himself lose consciousness like any sane human being. Who even cared if they were all lost to unspace? Just a moment's peace, a moment's rest. But he was denied that release. It just wasn't in him anymore. The Intermediary Program had taken that part of his mind out. He'd signed a waiver for it and everything. The Program had affected all of them differently, but this was why he was such a good Int. Even when he wanted to give in to the darkness, he couldn't.

He threw calculations together, hasty and slipshod, sending the *Vulture* out beyond the Throughways, off beyond everything—and who cared where? Just *away* for now. Away into the void where nobody would ever find them. There was always more void. It was the universe's greatest resource and you could mine it forever and never run out.

Twenty minutes and he drove them back into real space. He'd sunk even lower in his seat, pale and sweating, thinking: *Why do I do this? Why would anybody do this? But what else could I do?* Then he ordered the ship's higher systems to reassemble themselves, and woke everyone up.

*

"You look like shit," was Olli's considered response.

"Good." Idris tried for a smile but barely felt his lips twitch, "Hate false advertising."

None of them looked particularly perky, he thought. Having to get yourself into suspension *after* hitting unspace would do that. Nobody seemed to have noticed the whole we-almost-ceased-to-exist thing either. That particular struggle must have only been apparent to someone with Int senses.

"Seriously, though," Kris pressed. "What the hell happened there?"

"The *Broken Harvest* had countermeasures," was all he said. No point spooking people more.

"Unspace *countermeasures*?" Solace's look confirmed she was aware of the theory, and plainly the Parthenon didn't have the tech yet either.

"Feel free to tell your bosses next time you check in." It seemed the maverick actions of one Essiel hood could do more to prime the galaxy for war with the Hegemony than decades of regular contact.

"Oh, I will." And of all of them, Solace looked the least hit. Even Kit's body language said he was suffering: with unsteady legs and many twitches of the mandibles. His screens broadcast jagged bands of static. Solace, though, looked as though she could get back in her armour and fight the Colonial navy at a moment's notice.

For Idris, that thought brought their whole political crisis roaring back. If they really *did* have mobile Originator relics, who the hell should end up with them? The crew all had their own separate loyalties. Unless the things *weren't* genuine, of course.

"What about these trinkets, then?" he asked the cabin at large. "Now we have Trine."

The Hiver's ghostly face raised its eyebrows. "Well apparently you've got me," they noted. "And I appreciate your collective arrival at Jericho was not some magical gift from the universe, responding to my distress at people trying to kill me. So: what service might this humble academic perform?"

"We have some Originator relics—and we need you to look at them," Olli told him flatly.

Trine's false face didn't bat an eyelid. "Of course you have. Provenance?"

"No idea. Just…found them."

As patronizing expressions went, Trine's was no less effective for being insubstantial. "You are of course aware, my nomadic naifs, that just taking a *souvenir* robs the object of practical value? Its functionality ceases the moment it goes off-planet. And without an idea of its source, its scholarly value is similarly negligible…"

"It's in some sort of Hegemony suitcase thing," Olli said, deadpan, watching. "In suspension. You know, that trick they do that nobody ever saw."

Trine's face froze. Their voice, abruptly disconnected from its lips, said, "Excuse me. You have…what, exactly?"

"Just *show* them," Solace said. Olli scowled at her but went to retrieve the relics. They had all agreed this was the one thing they wouldn't mention to Havaer Mundy, because there was not a hope in hell they'd be allowed to keep them if Mordant House got so much as a *sniff* at their existence.

"We need you to analyse them," Solace explained, as Trine bent over the floating rods and parts. They looked like so much dusty detritus, broken things the Originators would doubtless have binned had they still been around. Detritus that could save a world from destruction. "Analyse without disturbing them, obviously. Just let us know if they're the real thing. And there's something else." She nipped into her quarters and came back with a corkscrewed piece of hull metal. "I cut this from the *Oumaru*. I know Architects have a signature, and that there's a registry of each one still, from the war. This came from a ship taken by one. Recently. I want to know anything that can be known—is this a new Architect that isn't up to speed with the war being over? Is it an old one that's come back...? Can you do that too?"

Trine's face blinked mildly. "Well you put quite a price on my rescue, old friend, old soldier. But I put quite a price on my continued instantiation, so we can call it quits. Yes, I can perform both analyses. It's a low-level plod, that kind of work, but it will take my units considerable time. I'll set aside a portion of myself for rote functionality and we'll get the results in due course."

Solace understood that. Part of the colony that was Trine would become a non-sentient cluster, performing the legwork. Then Trine would "know" the results when this cluster rejoined the whole. As Trine themself would be reduced while divided, it wasn't something Hivers did on a whim.

Kit sorted out some food then, printing a selection. They all sat together in the drone bay to eat as the *Vulture God* drifted, hidden in the cloak of deep space. A little food seemed to take the edge off the superspatial nausea Idris had been feeling, made him feel human again. The company helped, too. Olli and Solace were being civil to one another and nobody was mentioning the thunderhead of the future. Kit had some music on, some of that string-and-percussion-sounding stuff that was his favourite. Idris even found his foot tapping along to the shifting beat as he started to relax.

Then he felt...

He stood up, spilling his tray, unable to form words. He could *feel* the universe skewing sideways, the underlying layer of unspace shifting, even as real space stayed still. Everyone else was staring at him. Kris was at his elbow, calling for a medical kit. Possibly she thought he was having a stroke.

"Beds, everyone!" he got out. "Suspension! Beds! *Now!*" For a moment he couldn't get his body to work, then he was rushing towards the command capsule, sandals skidding as he ran.

"Idris, what?" They weren't taking him seriously, because *another* impossible thing was happening and he couldn't articulate it properly. Even as he hurtled headlong into the pilot's station the proximity alarm went off and another ship was right there. No, *the* other ship. The *Broken Harvest*, with its hungry predator's mind at the helm. The Ogdru had tracked them, tracked *him*. They'd followed his trail through unspace.

This time, wise to it, he could actually see them building the unspace net beneath real space, trying to box him in. He had no time.

"Get to your beds!" he hollered into the comms. "Whatever happens, get to your *beds!*" And he had the engines charging up, killing every safety and failsafe there was, to plunge the *Vulture* into the abyss before the trap could close on them.

They fell away from the real, and he felt the Ogdru's anger. No, not anger—it was enjoying this. The chase was something it lived for, buried deep in its species' evolutionary history. *One more reason never to meet an Ogdru.* It would be after him as swiftly as the technology that encased it allowed. He imagined it straining at the leash that was the *Harvest*'s technical specs.

Somewhere, the *Vulture God* would be in chaos, every member of the crew alone and plunged into the nightmare of unspace. They'd be stumbling for their couches, feeling the yawning hunger of the place just beyond each wall, behind every door, at every shoulder. He hoped they'd just focus, get themselves bedded down and in suspension. As if they were children—and pulling the covers over their heads meant the monster couldn't get them.

He had no covers. Whatever monster was out there could absolutely get him.

He had dropped into unspace with no course, but it wasn't the first time. He found another deep void point and let the ship fall towards it through a series of incremental calculations. He was bargaining with the devil to take them from *here* to *there*, shortcutting twenty light years in a matter of minutes. The headache was back and his stomach was trying to return everything he'd eaten, with a side order of acid reflux, but he fought it down. *Nothing I've not felt before.*

But the Ogdru was breathing down his neck, if it even breathed. He could imagine the questing dart of its head as it sought his trail. In its mind it swam an endless ocean, navigating rip tides that translated into working the *Broken Harvest*'s gravitic drives. The complex maths that challenged Idris's conscious mind was effortless instinct to this creature. He'd always thought he was at home in unspace, but he saw he was a clumsy intruder.

They roared out of unspace together, and Idris jumped immediately—borrowing energy from the interstice between real and real. Then the *Vulture* was falling away again, and again, and again...making a series of short jumps from space to space, zigzagging back and forth within the cube of a single light year. In, out, back, forth. Each transition frayed Idris's nerves a little more. His hands were shaking at the controls. This wasn't how you did space travel. This was how you drove yourself mad. There were now too many maps of the universe, real and unreal, overlaying one another inside his mind. He *heard* the Ogdru. In his head it was like angry whalesong, a deep, long cry dripping with murder. Idris slung them into real space again.

There was a planet there, a star, a whole system. He had a sight of pale ice, of blue about the equator, browns and greens. He caught a buzz of electromagnetism that could have been natural or artificial. He had no time to analyse it because he had to drop *again*, hands weaving a new course at random, far away across the galaxy from this unknown sun and its unknown world. Maybe he could find it again, maybe not.

They skidded into unspace once more, spiralling away like a bird with a clipped wing. He was losing track of how many jumps he'd made. He was...

Lost.

His mind went completely blank. He was lost. He didn't know where he was. And he *always* knew where he was. That was the thing about unspace. It was connected to points in real space. That was the essence of it. That was what people used it for.

They were falling through unspace and he had lost all connection to where they'd been or where they were going. The Ogdru was gone, outfoxed, howling *somewhere* because it didn't know where its prey had gone. But its prey was just as clueless.

Idris clutched the board, trying to find... a beacon, a landmark. Except unspace had none. Unspace only had...

The Presence moved, within the ship. In all the panic he'd been almost oblivious to it, but now it had his full attention. It had been waiting patiently for him to pause. Now he felt it had coughed politely, just to show it was there. And, yes, he knew all the caveats about the Presence being a trick of the mind. Except Idris had no doubt *whatsoever* that there was

351

something out there in unspace. Perhaps the sole real thing in all of that notional realm.

He fixed his attention on the board. Usually the Presence at least started off outside the ship. Usually it didn't try to confront him—he was just aware it was there. Until the very dread of existing in the same space was enough to make him want to tear his own face off. Right now, though, it...

Was in the command capsule with him. He felt it precisely as he would have been aware of another person. Not the sound of breath, the scuff of sandals, but some subconscious certainty. *Something is at my back, in this room.* A shadow seemed to flicker at the corner of his vision and he stared straight ahead, at the board, through the board. He reached out into unspace in the hope of finding some way out into the real. But they had no origin point and no destination, and that meant they were going to be here forever.

He all but felt its breath on the back of his neck.

"You're *not* real," he told the board. "You're just the universal response of a—a conscious mind to the peculiar parameters of a non-material space." It took him three tries to get the words out without stammering.

"You know it's all coming back, Idris."

The slightest whimper escaped him.

"You know *why* you don't want to admit it to yourself."

A pleasant enough voice, gender-neutral, familiar.

"You've felt those big battalions on the move, deep within unspace. Like great old blocks of stone being shunted down there; like locomotive engines." The owner of that voice had always been fond of old-Earth images. They'd had a whole library of salvaged ancient film: non-interactional pre-mediotype stuff. It was Lois T'Sanko, a classmate out of the first Intermediary Program. They'd gone out with him in the vanguard at Berlenhof, had Lois, and had vanished into unspace, never to be seen again.

"Not real, no one's there..." *It's just a ghost. But what happens to people who die in unspace? What if the usual rules don't apply?* But then the Presence was leaning right over his shoulder. He screwed his eyes up to avoid seeing it, and its voice was Rollo's now.

"Your problem, my child, is that if you admit the bastard Architects *are* back—then what was the point? What was the point of anything *you* did? All that war, just to buy a little breather? Hardly worth it, see right?"

Abstractly, he wondered if he was undergoing some kind of breakdown: brain death, stroke, some unspace-specific malady... All around him, the featureless plain of nothing extended forever, a prospect too awful for the human mind to grasp. He'd failed all of them. Better if the Ogdru had caught him.

Except...

And a shadow was indeed passing through the depths of unspace. A dread shadow he thought he'd left behind decades ago, but that some part of him had always looked out for. *It's true then. The* Oumaru *was just the start. The Architects are back and we're lost.*

Except...

Something caught at his mind, a texture within the absence of everything, a scar. Impossible, obviously, because unspace didn't really exist. And no matter what you did, you couldn't *mark* it. You couldn't create any persistent landmarks here, in the absence of everything. But it *was* there.

"Intermediary Telemmier." The voice was deep, human-sounding but not human. The voice of the Harbinger, Ash, who had first warned humanity of the Architect threat. And *it* wasn't dead, insofar as Idris knew. "You should be more at home here," Ash told him. "Don't buckle now."

"What do you know about it?" Idris demanded through clenched teeth.

"You think *I* don't know about *this?*" Ash could always do any kind of human tone it wanted. Right now it was bantering, punchy. "You think I got to Earth by *walking*? What, you're going to just let your crew die here? Come on, Telemmier. Pull yourself together."

"Screw you." But that scar, that *scar*. It was like an asteroid impact, the shock of its landing written into the deep crystalline structure of the rock. Something *cataclysmic* had happened to create that scar. Something of appalling scale. It wasn't the only such mark in all the universe but there were few, very few. And he knew it. He'd seen this one *created*.

*

The Presence was looming behind him and to both sides, far too close. And now it was shorn of personality again, no T'Sanko, no Rollo, no Ash. Just that incredible hunger, that distant curiosity. *What is this human mind and how can I break it?* Idris wasn't breathing, wasn't even able to blink as he fed the computations in. Gave the ship a course, a direction, a vector back to reality.

"You're not real," he whispered to the universe.

It laid a hand on his shoulder and he screamed and passed out.

*

Kris

Kris jerked awake to the echo of alarms, sound and vibration from another room, a catastrophe happening to someone else.

She was in her suspension pod, and she had been a spacer long enough to recognize the shuddering aftershock of a sudden wake-up, without the cushioning chemical cocktail that usually transitioned her to wakefulness.

"Hello?" she called, but comms had nothing but ghosting static for her, and the lid of her pod wasn't opening. She rapped on it hopefully, in case Solace or Olli were just on the other side. But a creeping dread had been stealing up on her. Something was terribly wrong.

She hit the emergency release and the pod popped open, retracting its medical paraphernalia so that she could sit up. The inside of the suspension bay was empty. Olli had bedded down in her bubble in the drone bay. Kit had his own pod in his quarters. Her only neighbour was Solace. And the Partheni was...

Not there.

"Hello, Kris to anyone, what's shaking?" she asked to ship-wide comms. Maybe Solace had just woken up already. Maybe everyone was waiting for her. Somewhere. Utterly silent and not responding to her calls. Then she knew.

We're still in unspace.

"Idris?" she called to comms. "Idris, what's going on?" But that was wasted effort because they were in *unspace*. Meaning no Idris, no Solace, no any of them. Just her and the vast chasming universe.

Something's gone wrong. Some failsafe had tripped and the

ship must have known to wake her. Probably it had woken everyone ... But that didn't help, because there was no "everyone" in unspace. Just Keristina Soolin Almier, who didn't know how to fix spaceships.

Get to command. She stumbled out of the suspension bay, feeling the dimensions of the ship around her all subtly wrong— too big, too small, receding off into unexpected, nameless directions. And empty, so very empty.

Not entirely empty.

Kris knew this was how it went, but knowing didn't help. Her shoulders itched, sensing that *thing* somewhere on the ship, somewhere close ... intolerable. Human myth was full of creatures that were anathema to the sane mind. Look upon them and you'd die, meet their gaze and be turned to stone. Had some ancient sage somehow touched unspace, in an age before humans had ever climbed up out of the gravity well? Because that was the Presence in a nutshell.

As Kris crept through the vacant chambers of the *Vulture God* she felt it closing on her, matching her step for step. But its paces were longer, so it grew fractionally closer every time she moved. It was every shame, nightmare and rejection she'd ever had. It was all these things given teeth and claws, weaponized to be her ultimate nemesis. She slipped her knife from her sleeve, thinking, *Well I have something for you too, nemesis.*

Then she was through into Command, seeing the captain's chair, the pilot's board. She tried diagnostics, but the ship systems were all stripped down to the minimum. It couldn't tell her what was wrong. It didn't seem to know why it had woken her. According to the ship, everything was absolutely fine. Peachy even. Why was she asking?

Everything was *not* fine. Kris had a cold feeling in the pit of her stomach. She needed to...

Something scraped, a long rasping sound, outside the command capsule.

She gripped the back of the captain's chair, almost losing hold of her knife. *I couldn't have heard that.* There were no other physical presences aboard. Nothing long and disjointed, dragging along the wall outside Command. She stared at the minimal ship display, seeing but not processing. *It* had moved, it was right outside. Kris could sense it reaching, fumbling its way along like a blind man. There was one precise moment when its search paused, and she knew it had become aware of her.

No, no, come on, there must be something here. What's going on? She called up all the information the ship could give her. *Why am I awake?* There were no mechanical errors, nothing was flagged, except...she was awake because an order had been sent to wake her. Emergency codes, overriding the failsafes that would normally keep her under.

Idris...? But what if it hadn't been Idris? What if Idris was blithely doing his thing, and instead *something else* had woken her? Sprung her into this vacant, insubstantial vessel so it could hunt her down?

And it was *there*, in Command with her, right behind her. The Inimical, the thing she couldn't ever see. The horror of it flooded her, fingers digging into the back of the captain's chair like claws.

Kris lifted her knife, catching a glimpse of her reflection in its gleaming blade. She looked away hurriedly, in case she saw something over her own shoulder. The knife, yes. The knife—that would be no use whatsoever against the *other*, but she could still use it. She could sever the ties binding her to this place. She could rob the Presence of its prey.

It loomed closer: worse than pain, worse than death, the incarnation of All Bad Things. She brought up the knife.

The ship fell from unspace with a sudden wrench. There was no physical shock but Kris stumbled anyway. She found herself a metre from where she'd thought she was, with Solace's elbow in her face. In that moment of reflexive surprise, she almost cut her own throat. She locked eyes with the Partheni over the poised edge of her knife and allowed Solace to take her hand and gently push it away.

"What...?"

"Here, attend!" Kit was crouching on the pilot's board. There was a peculiar yellowish foam about his small limbs that Kris had never seen from a Hanni before, and his six feet were rattling back and forth erratically. *He* had brought them out of unspace, she realized, done it manually using Idris's console.

"Sound *off*," Solace snapped into the comms. "Olian? Trine?"

Kris pulled herself together, checking the readouts. "Both still under. The general wake-up order only went to the suspension beds. Olli's in the drone bay and Trine just put themselves under standing up. Idris, why'd you wake us?" Kris blinked. "Idris?"

The pilot was slumped in his seat, staring, a trickle of blood running from the corner of his mouth. For a terrible moment she thought he was dead. Solace tried to take his pulse the old-fashioned way, but Kris grabbed Command's ancient medalyser from its niche by the door. It established he was still with them, but blood pressure, respiration and brain activity were all flagged as problems. Kris felt panic clutch inside her. Idris was out, and he was *never* out. He didn't even *sleep*. But right now, there was nobody behind those staring eyes and his brain was burning up.

"We need help, medical help. Unless you...?" She looked hopefully at Solace but the Partheni just shook her head.

"This goes beyond battlefield trauma. Where even *are* we?" Her words created a silence that rippled out as Kris just stared at her. Because if they'd exited unspace in the deep void then that was *it*. Unless they could get Idris back, none of them could get the ship anywhere. Nobody would ever find them again, a grain of sand in the immensity of an empty universe.

"Kittering, when you brought us out...?" Solace started slowly.

"Zero navigational data was available," the Hanni's translator confirmed. Figures flashed up on its arm-screens. According to the computers they'd been going from nowhere to nowhere with a pilot catatonic at the helm. Jumping them out into the real was the only thing Kit could have done.

Kris thought about the doomed freighter *Gamin*, which had ended up in the deep void and died there in desperation and madness. Unless they could get Idris awake and able to fly, then...

"Wait," Solace said. "We have transmissions. I'm getting... news mediotypes, entertainment? A rewatch of last cycle's *Heirs of Space*...what?"

"Trash," said Kris, who secretly enjoyed it. "Terrible, terrible slush." She had never been happier to stumble upon bad media in her whole life. "Origin?"

"We're..." Solace tapped at the screens. "Huh."

"What?" Kris craned past her to see what their rebooting computer was showing them, as it reformed its map of local space. "Holy equity...did *Idris* do this?"

They were still a long way out, far further than any normal exit from unspace would have deposited them. But there *was* an inhabited world out there. A familiar one, well travelled and populous. Berlenhof, heart of the Colonial Sphere.

PART 5
BERLENHOF

22.

Idris

In the seventy-eighth year of the war, an Architect came to Berlenhof.

Idris had put out in the *Pythoness*. All the Intermediaries at Berlenhof had been deployed, sent out in separate ships on an eggs and baskets basis. All of them, bending their minds towards the Architect. Motes in the eye of its vast crystalline grandeur.

A bulk like a moon, its near half a crazed mountain range of gleaming crystal spines a hundred kilometres long. The light of Berlenhof's star touched them and gave back rainbows, cut apart into its constituent frequencies. The dark side of the Architect was a faceted hemisphere, semi-translucent, monstrous suggestions of form all the way down. A machine or a rogue world or a force of nature; no mere human could fathom it.

Saint Xavienne had seen further than most, though. There was a singular mind at the heart of all that crystal, a consciousness as vast as oceans. The Architect possessed a will and the ability to inflict that will upon the universe. And it was one of many. Only one had come to Berlenhof—only one had ever been seen at once—but human science had already discovered distinct flourishes attributable to individuals, at the macro and molecular level. They were not a lone threat, but a crusade.

The *Pythoness* arrowed in under the direction of its Partheni crew, dodging back and forth. A little ship trying to get Idris close, without that awful invisible hand turning them into artfully refigured scrap. And somewhere out there, Idris's classmates had been dying.

The Partheni crew, Solace's sisters, handled the little launch adroitly. They were following patterns—hard-learned from ships that had evaded Architect notice for just long enough to get away. Except this time they weren't trying to get away.

And Idris was young and a fool and thought he wanted to fight.

"*Elsinore* reports contact…" an officer was translating Partheni chatter for him. "*Ching Shi* reports contact. *Ocasio* in contact." She was listing the other Int-carriers that had engaged the Architect.

"Whenever you're ready, Menheer Telemmier," said the *Pythoness*'s captain in heavily accented Colvul, as she flicked his shoulder. Idris realized he'd been holding back. He opened his senses, his expensive, ruinous new senses, and found the Architect.

He had expected to feel a point, a single seat of reason deep in the crystal depths of the behemoth. Instead it was *all* mind, the entire multi-million-tonne edifice. Or maybe its mind and its substance had no meaningful division. He met a will like God, as amenable to his fighting it as the physical vastness would be if the *Pythoness* had turned its little weapons against those jagged mountains of crystal. He was peripherally aware of the efforts of his fellows. They were grappling for purchase against the smooth wall of its intellect, beating their mental fists against it. Trying for that moment Saint Xavienne had achieved—when she had touched the mind of God and stopped leviathan in its tracks.

And for one brief moment, he *had it*. He'd made himself not vaster, but smaller. He'd shrunk his image of himself until he could somehow slide himself into that mind. As subtle as a card slipped beneath a door, inviting himself, making the entity "Idris Telemmier of the Intermediary Program" nothing but data. He was a virus bearing a message: *We're here. Notice us!*

There was a shout in impenetrable Parsef, followed for his benefit by, "It's making a two-degree deflection, Menheer!" Words came to his ears from somewhere far off. The Architect *had* changed its course slightly. He had found some lever within it. Perhaps it was just a machine? Perhaps he could hack it with his mind, find the steering systems, find the self-destruct...

More rapid discussion, and then the translation came, urgent and hurried. "Registering disruption across its surface. Is that *damage*?" Partheni were rock calm, everyone knew. They bred them without emotions, the perfect soldier-angels. Except there was excitement in those words, elation even. They were having an *effect*. They were wrestling with Lucifer, about to cast him down.

And yet, even once he was *in*, Idris was aware he had not struck the target. There was indeed a *self* there, the thing that Xavienne had brushed, but he could wander the maze of its mind for a thousand years and never find it. Even getting as far as any human ever had, they had failed. They had pricked

365

it, discomfited it, but it was no more than a momentary jab, a thorn to the hide of an elephant.

He felt the shudder build up within it, and he was trying to warn them, opening his mouth wide to vomit the words out, still lost somewhere between *I* and *It*...when the Architect took space between its sightless hands and wrung it.

He came to himself in the aftermath. All he heard were groans and whimpers, because the Partheni did not scream when someone else's orders needed to be heard. Survivors on all sides were trying to save those caught in the gravitational focus of the Architect's brute swipe. They were loosing their weapons, accelerators and gravity cannon. The second in command was barking orders in Parsef as tears ran down her face. Half the crew were dead, one side of the bridge a sparking, mangled ruin. And as they hauled the pilot's body from her seat, Idris dropped in to take her place. He could sense the angry grasping of the Architect as it swatted and crushed in unconscious irritation at these gnats that had troubled it.

And he got them out. Without even considering the impossibility of it, he jumped them away from the crushing mass-shadow of the Architect. Jumped in-system, the thing you never did.

He limped them back to the *Heaven's Sword*. He was vaguely amazed that not one of the warrior-elite had objected to him commandeering their ship. They'd just taken his participation in their stride, accepting his help without a word.

There had been no peace on the *Heaven's Sword* either. It'd been Solace marching him to the bridge the moment he was on board. All of Berlenhof's defenders were rushing forwards to meet the Architect. Somewhere out there the battered Naeromathi Locust Ark was gouting out fleets of constructor drones and factory ships converted into one-shot massdrivers. Hiver orbital frames vented clouds of little killers into space like swarming bees. Refitted Castigar freighters and crescent-shaped Hanni merchant venturers were about to live out their final moments as unlikely warships, their alien crews bound to this desperate purpose by fellow feeling or quid pro quo. A hundred separate human vessels were being flung out in a mad suicide bid to buy the evacuation another few minutes.

Then there was the pride of the Parthenon—the big battalions, the warrior angels come to save humanity from extinction. *Heaven's Sword, Ascending Mother, Cataphracta*: the most advanced warships ever made by human hands. They'd been fitted with outsize gravitic drives to shield them against the Architects and power the colossal new mass looms meant to do to the enemy what the enemy did to the rest of the universe.

"Menheer Intermediary!" one of the officers called to him the moment he arrived on the bridge. "Front and centre, if you please—snap snap!" Her Colvul was sharply accented and—

"Compret, mother." Solace was there at his elbow, moving him to a quartet of screens at the bridge's heart. Each was screeding information about the Architect or modelling relative positions in space.

"What am I supposed—?" he managed to say.

"Whatever you can do," that same officer told him sternly, "do. Once we see what that breeds, we can work with it." She sounded as though she didn't believe in him, which he'd have sympathized with an hour before. Now he had met the enemy. Now he knew he actually *could* do.

Solace, that younger Solace without the Executor to her name, gave him a tight smile.

The bridge was busy with fast-flowing Parsef, reports and orders, efficient and regulated as percussion. The vanguard of the planetary defence had already reached the Architect, and he began to see its hand extend across them, points of animation with nametags winking out, too many for anyone to remark. Colonial ramshackles and swift Hanni raiders coursing into attack runs they were never able to complete. A long, elegant Castigar ranger taken and twisted as a child might a stick. Hiver spaceframes wrecked, their colonies spilling out into space, all ruined parts and extinguished composite minds. Then the *Cataphracta* had focused its mass loom. It bent the force of its gravitic drives to clench ten square kilometres of substance within the very heart of the Architect.

And nothing. The thing had seemingly shrugged the weapon away. But then the scanner teams were calling out fractures within its substance. The *Heaven's Sword* targeting computers were throwing up best options. Something roared through the warship's hull like angelic voices declaiming the end of the universe. Idris realized it was their own loom speaking, unleashing a wave of stresses that sent their every bulkhead and strut complaining in eerily beautiful harmony.

And he *had it*. He wasn't even the first Int to the breach, but he had it. He remembered how he had reached into the Architect's mind before. He folded himself small, like a letter, like a needle, like an idea, and pried his mind into that incandescent mass of angry thought. And it *was* angry. It did not know him, did not know any of them, yet it perceived an environment that was resisting it. Making its life difficult, impeding the creation of its apocalyptic art form. Idris screamed, entering the outer reaches of the Architect's consciousness as though he was entering the photosphere of a star.

He felt it stumble, just for a moment. No more than a man slipping on ice for a second before catching himself, but in a knife-fight that could be fatal. The *Sword*'s mass loom spoke again and again, counting twenty seconds of recharge between each attack. The whole substance of the ship was shrieking with the strain. Around him, half the Partheni had their hands over their ears.

Between blasts he heard a tightly controlled shout. He caught the ship name *Cataphracta* and knew one of the *Sword*'s sisters had been ripped apart. On the screens he saw the vast Locust Ark just unravel. It was shredded across fifty kilometres of space: into wire, into artfully warped metal peelings, into frozen smears of organic material.

Idris was weeping now and his head felt as though it would explode. Elsewhere, one of his classmates just died, simply dropped dead; heart, brain and organs all failing from the biofeedback of touching minds with a god. But Idris held on. He held on and he fought for purchase, even as the Architect's consciousness cast around for *him*, unable to quite conceive of anything so tiny, a giant hunting a mouse.

Each explosive detonation of the mass looms lit the way for the next. The Partheni computers bounced EM pulses off the Architect's jagged surfaces, reading the stress patterns and damage and spitting out fresh targeting solutions. The most powerful weapons ever made by human hands, being wielded with the precision of scalpels.

Then the Architect *reached* for them. Idris felt it, and tried to oppose it, to deflect that space-wringing attention that would make them no more than a filigreed monument to their own stupidity. The *Heaven's Sword* shuddered and groaned, the sound blending into the bitter scream of the next mass loom detonation. Damage reports poured in from every part of the ship. But Idris was transfixed. He didn't care. His own mortality was so small a thing compared to what he was seeing.

The *Ascending Mother* was still loosing attacks, upping the ship's fire rate despite the damage they were inflicting on their own hull. The Colonials, the Hanni, the Hivers, every vessel out there was unleashing whatever weapons they had, from accelerated shot to towed asteroids. All were being guided by the targeting telemetry the Partheni were broadcasting. And Idris, with his privileged front-row seat on the inside, was watching the Architect come apart.

It was still at least partly within unspace, he realized. It was even bigger than the physical manifestation that intruded into the real. But the damage done to it was cascading backwards, rippling through its entire substance. The fractures the Partheni spotters were reporting were the least of it. The mass loom attacks had been driving a chisel deeper and deeper into the creature, and now it was shearing into pieces.

Idris felt the Architect know death and trembled in anticipation of the rage and grief that must surely attend that thought. Yet it was not so. What it felt was mostly nothing a human mind could comprehend. But when others demanded he put a word to it later, he would say *acceptance*.

The Architect died. And, dying, its final energies lashed out across space, destroying a score of vessels and taking the

Sword from merely "crippled" to breaking apart. And this was where Solace would bundle him into the escape pod, because the Partheni took their duty seriously. This was where he would find himself in a medical camp on Berlenhof after the last period of non-consciousness he would know for fifty years. Except for Idris now—lost in the mad flight of the *Vulture God*—it didn't happen. No Solace, no escape pod, just the eternally drawn-out moment of the *Heaven's Sword* dying and the Architect dying with it, in an event so traumatic to the universe that it left a permanent scar on the substance of unspace, a persistent landmark in an infinitely transient medium. A beacon that he had found from across the galaxy, the one landmark in the featureless void.

23.

Havaer

"Questions have already been raised about how you handled this one," Chief Laery said. She'd called Havaer in during her exercises. This was something she only did when she was displeased, because of how discomfiting it was. Her a-grav chair was tilted back, and a mechanical frame had one of her arms in three well-padded grips. Currents shocked the atrophied muscles of the limb and a trio of clear tubes fed urine-coloured liquids into her: high-protein muscle-builders to fight a battle her body had already given up on. The young Laery had spent a long time at deep-space listening posts without any grav tech. She'd subsisted on even less than the usual poor Colonial nutrition of the day. A combination of factors had resulted in most of her muscle mass just giving up and going away. A return to more wholesome living habits hadn't done much to reverse the loss, and every handful of days she underwent treatments like this to try and stave off the end. Half-naked, she looked like someone who'd died of starvation a week before.

"I had to make a judgement call," he told her. "I needed to keep our witnesses out of the hands of criminal elements." He had been frank and exhaustive in his earlier report about the Broken Harvest and its rogue Essiel ruler. Just as well he had, or he'd be in a hole twice as deep around now.

"You should have brought the crew aboard the *Hammer* and abandoned their ship," Laery told him.

"I didn't think I had the time. And I didn't need a shooting war with some spacers and a one-woman Parthenon army just as this Essiel reached us, to be honest."

"At the very least you should have held the Intermediary."

"I had no grounds."

Her eyes narrowed. "You have standing special powers, Havaer." A hiss escaped her as the medical frame tracked round to her other arm. "Threats to the Colonies. Especially from the damn Parthenon."

"I made a judgement call."

"A bad one."

He nodded. "The problem with judgement calls is that they're only ever good or bad in retrospect."

"Make sure you say that at your inquest," Laery snapped. Then, after a deliberate pause, "If there is one. It's under deliberation."

"What's my current status?"

"Active until told otherwise. We're too short-handed to put you on ice. On a separate subject, your information regarding this Broken Harvest organization has potential."

"How is that a separate subject?" he asked mildly.

"Since it makes us look good. Whereas your 'judgement call' looks a hell of a lot like a mistake. In *retrospect*. Because your damn spacers aren't turning up at our doorstep any time soon, of that you can be sure."

"We've not reached 'retrospect' on that one yet," he said, still measured.

"You want to wait until the first Partheni warship stutter-jumps here? Hopping past Berlenhof's orbital defences with a brand new Int Angel at the helm?"

Glib answers fell away. "Does it look *that* bad?" he asked.

Chief Laery regarded him from beneath hooded lids with reptile animosity. "Two Partheni warships are in orbit over Berlenhof right now. That look bad enough to you, Havaer? You can probably just about see the *Thunderchild* from my window."

"Sabre-rattling, surely..."

"When they send two big new battleships to cast their shadows over Hugh's planetside offices, it's pretty much swords drawn." She waved her unoccupied hand idly. "Of course, they did bring some actual diplomats. So currently ours and theirs are working their way through lists of all the usual rubbish: trade tariffs, joint action against rogue elements and the like. But you can bet the Partheni keep pressing for the Liaison Board's raw data. Now the Architects might be back, they're really upping their game. '*Oh, we'd love to come save your worlds again, but we seem to be lacking a key anti-Architect weapon.*' They avoid mentioning that the Ints will be our only advantage over them, if—or should I say when—we finally engage in a shooting war."

Havaer took a deep breath. "Permission to speak my mind on this one, Chief."

"Oh, do enlighten me," she said acidly.

"If it comes to that, the Parthenon can put Castigar navigators on their ships. They could even go to the Hegemony for the creature-things that they use. Our Ints are good unspace pilots, maybe even the best, but they're not unique."

"If it comes to that," Chief Laery replied, "the Castigar know we'll pay more for them to do nothing than the Partheni can pay for them to put their Savants in harm's way. Parthenon's gun rich but trade poor. Give us any field of combat other than actual *combat* and we can beat the Partheni hands down. And we all just have to hope the Hegemony won't get involved. Which is another damn headache right about now." She clicked her fingers, the sound like a dry twig snapping, dismissing the topic. "This one, face like a pederastic uncle, you spoke to him?"

She called up an image of a genial-looking white-bearded man, the high collar of a Hegemonic cult robe arching over his bald head.

"Hierograve, on Huei-Cavor. He'd been trying to get hold of the *Oumaru* when Broken Harvest stole it," Havaer recalled. "Sathiel, isn't it?"

Laery nodded, birdlike. "His crowd is just one more breed of parasite we've picked up in-system. For some reason, a whole sect of them is descending on us claiming to be delegates from the Hegemony. May or may not be true, because nobody ever got a straight answer out of the Essiel. This jolly old grandpa has quite the record, you know?" The names of half a dozen systems appeared by Sathiel's image, ending with Huei-Cavor. "I mean, the Hegemony doesn't have hatchet-men, but if it did... This Sathiel's game-plan is to turn up and take over the local cult chapter or whatever. Then he starts agitating, spreading rumours, schmoozing people in power, talking up the benefits of cosying with the clams. You know he's flipped three whole systems? And as for ones he didn't, let's just say Mordant kept a finger on the scales. To make sure people were exercising their free choice as freely as they were supposed to."

Havaer nodded without comment. He remembered his fake interview with the hierograve. The man had *seemed* genuine, but that came with the job, so no great surprises there. Sathiel had wanted to use the *Oumaru* to highlight the benefits of Hegemony protection. But again, that was to be expected. "We know he's not in cahoots with the Harvest mob. Or he wasn't back then."

"He wasn't back then," Laery echoed him. "What accommodations they might have reached since, we don't know. At least *nobody* has the damn *Oumaru* now. That was the one thing your pet spacers did right. But it won't stay lost forever." She sighed. "If by some miracle we do find the *Vulture* again, you can goddamn convince them to tell you the location of that wreck. Then we can blow it to pieces and forget it ever existed." She met his gaze challengingly. *"What?"*

"You don't think, if the Architects are really…"

"The Architects are far away, ruining the day of some other civilization. You think we wouldn't know by now, if they were actually *back*? You think they'd scrap one luckless freighter and then go on sick leave for a month? Right now we have problems with the Parthenon and the Hegemony. They're both using the *Oumaru*: to get Ints; to convert more worlds. And so, if we never hear of that wreck again, maybe both of those problems might just fade away." There was a grim finality in her voice. Hearing it, Havaer wondered what would happen if the *Vulture God* did reappear. It would be a shame if their galaxy-hopping ways came to an abrupt and secret end. But such thoughts were above his pay grade and it wasn't as though there was anything he could do. He wasn't likely to get another chance at making a "judgement call" concerning them, after all.

*

Solace

Trine's automated splinter units were still working, and had been throughout their breakneck chase through unspace. So it was that, after an hour loitering at the edge of the Berlenhof system, Trine declared they were ready to reveal some preliminary findings.

"Firstly," the Hiver announced, "I would like to thank you all, especially my old comrade-in-arms Myrmidon Executor Solace, for giving me this opportunity. It's not often that I get such a chance to supplement and expand the boundaries of my knowledge."

"Trine," said that same comrade-in-arms, "the point, please. Are they or aren't they?"

Delegate Trine's spectral face adopted an expression of arch dissatisfaction. "Would you believe that the opportunities for proper showmanship in academia are limited, old companion?"

"Trine, *please*."

"It's not as though we get to reveal murderers, or such entertaining frivolities."

"Trine!" Although she couldn't help a quirk of the lips at that, because the damn Hiver had been mad for old-Earth detective stories from way back.

Trine gave a pained sigh, a sound entirely voluntary and artificial. "My friends and co-motional fellows, I believe these are indeed authentic Originator relics held in some manner of suspensory stasis with which I am unfamiliar. My investigator units will continue a cautious analysis. Although I am obviously unwilling to take any steps that may interfere with their preservation."

"But do they have the juice?" Kris asked. "The . . . whatever it is, that makes them do what they do?"

"An unscientifically phrased query, my new associate, and the answer is 'I have not the first idea.' We don't actually know what it is that changes in Originator regalia, when taken off-planet by any other than Hegemonic hands. And the Essiel, curse them, do not respond when we invite them to symposia. Hence my earlier expressed gratitude—because nobody of my profession has ever been able to study such preserved regalia in transit. What are you going to do with the things, exactly? I need to know whose centres of higher learning I should be making nice to, in order to secure a transfer." Another ostentatious sigh. "And I had been considering packing it all in and returning to the Assembly, but apparently my work is not done."

"And the other thing, the Architect wreckage?" Solace prompted.

"Under investigation," Trine confirmed. "But, let's face it, old friend, not quite as high priority."

After that, Solace went to her assigned quarters and wrestled with her loyalties for perhaps seven minutes. She wasn't sure whether the conclusion she came to was a win or a loss. If Idris hadn't been lying comatose in one of the suspension pods, perhaps she might have come to another decision. Right now the liking and respect she had for the crew couldn't outweigh the fact that she was a soldier of the Parthenon. Her sisters were in-system with two massive Partheni warships. She had a duty.

She checked where the others were stationed. Kris had command and was keeping a fretful eye on the boards. Trine was devoting most of their energy to the investigation, and probably wouldn't have objected anyway. And Olli and Kittering were monopolizing the ship's printers with some private piece of business. At first, Solace thought Olli was printing medicines. Most people who spent that much time jacked into machinery ended up with all sorts of chronic pain and neurological imbalances. To her surprise, Solace discovered a comms connection from Olli's current station by the printers, artfully bounced off a series of satellites to obscure its origin point. Olli was definitely exchanging information with someone around Berlenhof. For a cold moment Solace's mind was racing. *Is she Hugh? Is she already ahead of me?* As carefully as she could she tried to get a sense of what the pair of them were doing, without alerting them.

The electronic misdirection was nicely done but short on encryption. So, not spy work. It looked as though Olli was querying library databases for information about pharmacology and xenobiology. Solace isolated some of her search terms, but the requests seemed haphazard rather than targeted. All very mysterious, but probably not germane to Solace's current problems. However, if she was deft herself, she could use their comms as a carrier wave to conceal her own traffic.

Solace wasn't a tech, but you didn't grow up on a Partheni fleet without a fair amount of cross-training. In the drone bay, given that Olli was actually out of it for once, she accessed the ship's main systems. Then she began inserting her own callsign as a hidden layer beneath the ongoing research dialogue.

She set up her code and sent it off, flagged so that the Parthenon ships out there would pick it up. No material data yet, in case of interception, just a string of handshakes and ID. After that it was down to waiting, and flinching guiltily when Kris left her post to go use the head. *I am doing my duty*, she told herself. And yet she felt wretched and furtive, an absurd situation for a Partheni myrmidon.

The response came promptly, although she'd felt every dragging minute of delay as the signal tracked the long way to Berlenhof and back. Olli and Kit continued their work, alternating library queries with commands to the printer. They were trying to coax some unfamiliar concoction from it for some reason. If it was drugs they were after, they were going a long way for their next fix.

Then the next data packet from Berlenhof had a rider for her; compressed data hidden in the handshake codes that bracketed each exchange like telomeres. She read *Monitor Superior Tact responding to Myrmidon Executor Solace*, along with all the expected assurances to let Solace know that was who she was dealing with. Then came *Do you have the Intermediary?*

Tact: the superior who'd set her after Idris in the first place. On the one hand, Solace didn't have to waste time introducing herself or dealing with some obstructive mid-rank. On the other hand it meant the fate of Idris was suddenly front and centre and that wasn't what she was calling about.

Shift of priorities. Ship's crew in possession of live Originator regalia, certified genuine, believed still active despite transit. Hegemonic containment in place. And send.

She put her back to the wall, cool against the thin weave of her bodysleeve. *I am not betraying anybody*, she insisted to herself. *This is for the best.* After all, what would the Colonies *do* with the things? Waste them, use them to prop up some planet like Magda or Berlenhof, where their rich lived? Whereas the Parthenon would take that tech and analyse it. They'd discover its secrets and save many worlds—or the universe. That was what she told herself.

Send location immediately. Team being prepped.

Solace bit her lip. Of course she must send their location and heading. Direct intervention was the only way, except...

Request crew not harmed; reimbursed for service to Parthenon.

Passed to Bursary Tribunal. I'm sure there will be something. Location didn't come through. Please re-send.

That middle sentence. Monitor Superior Tact's own words, not a clipped standard message. *There will be something.* Not a threat, like Uskaro or the Essiel gangster might have made, but a genuine promise of reward. Solace believed it.

Then: *Also confirm Int status for simultaneous collection.*

Solace stared at the line. Idris was lying like a dead man, just a room away. And Idris needed help, without doubt. Help he might get from Hugh. Help he could also get from the Parthenon, with fewer strings... Except...

Team ready. Location please.

She prepared the data, hesitated, discovering the unwelcome truth that she was going to hate herself no matter what. The mechanical back and forth of Olli's convenient library queries continued shuttling through its network of blinds and satellites. Still, Solace could almost feel Tact's razor-sharp attention on her, even from where *Heaven's Sword* orbited Berlenhof.

"Son of a bitch, I *knew* it!" The voice was Olli's. It was amplified by the speakers of her Scorpion frame until her words shook every loose piece of kit in the drone bay. Because of course Kittering could continue sending queries quite happily while Olian Timo went snooping to see who was messing with her signal.

Solace twitched and her hand sent the message, not sure whether it would actually go anywhere or whether Olli had already blocked her. She stood up—unarmoured, unarmed—wondering if Olli was just going to go for her. Given the frame's shears, pincers and saws, she didn't think she could do much about that.

"Not so tough now, soldier?" The specialist leant forward in her capsule at the frame's heart. She'd reinforced it since the fight with Mesmon, Solace saw: less clear plastic, more armour. Her face was simultaneously wrathful and gleeful—someone finally given an excuse to let loose. "What's it going to be?"

"You tell me," Solace said, standing very still. Her mind was racing through countermeasures, for if Olli just lunged at her. The drone bay was the biggest space in the ship, but with all its limbs and tail extended, the Scorpion could cover just about all of it.

"Everyone get in here!" Olli's voice roared from the ship's comms, and Solace heard a yelp from Kris over in command. A moment later she came running, expecting who knew what and finding the pair of them facing off. Kittering tapped in a moment later, Trine last of all.

"This is really not conducive to—" the Hiver academic started.

"You, shut up," Olli told them. "You're not one of us."

"Olli, what *is* this?" Kris asked.

"Warrior angel has been phoning home," the specialist revealed. "Piggybacking on my own call and thought Kit wouldn't track her down."

Kris's eyes flicked over. If Solace had thought to see sympathy there, she was disappointed. "What did she tell them?"

"All in code, but I'll give you three guesses."

"Did you sell Idris to them?" Kris asked. Solace saw her fingers twitch at the sleeve where she kept her knife.

"I am not selling anyone to anything," she said, as calmly as possible.

"It's the relics," Olli spat. "Of course it's the relics."

"Well what were *you* going to do with them?" Solace demanded. "Trade them for Largesse? So some Boyarin can keep his holiday planet safe, when the galaxy burns? Or you want Hugh to unravel them for secrets? Even assuming they don't screw it up and just render the whole thing useless, what then? Who's been causing trouble for us? The Parthenon? No. Who hunted us across Jericho? Was that the Parthenon? Who grabbed Kittering and the *Vulture*? Not us. And was it my people who arrested and interrogated us after that?"

"Oh, the Parthenon have been our problem all this time," Olli told her, "just from *inside*. Just sneakier. Pretending to be one of us. And I fucking *knew* it would come to this."

"I told them to pay you!" Solace tried desperately. She heard a catch in her voice, because Olli's barb had caught. Because she *had* felt like one of them, and here she was, just a spy in their midst—an outsider, a traitor. *Fuck.*

"Reward without contract is an unacceptable standard of business," came Kittering's strident translation.

"And you *knew* they'd take Idris. Especially in the state he is now, when he can't say no," Kris added.

"Look, he needs help. We can *help*."

"And after *helping*, you'd let him go? I'm sorry, Solace." And

Kris's eyes glittered with hurt. "Maybe you even believe it's for the best, but no. Just...no."

Solace's fists clenched. "The Architects are coming back," she said. "Who will save you, who will save *everyone*, if not us? That is what we do. That is what we are *for*."

"You and your people would let us all burn if you knew you'd be safe," Olli's voice boomed from her Scorpion. "Everyone not born perfect out of your fucking vats."

"That's not true!" And Solace surged forward, well within the arc of those lethal arms. All her training abandoned for one stupid moment, because the woman was being so *unfair*. Olli just brandished a stump at her—a clutch of stubby fingers jutting from what would have been her truncated elbow. And of course her words weren't fair, it *wasn't* fair. Yet on another level it was something the woman absolutely had the right to say.

"Do we call Hugh then?" Kris asked. Solace's heart plunged, seeing that she had just flipped the whole situation to the exact and precise worst-case scenario. But in this, Olli became an unlikely ally.

"Fuck Hugh," the specialist decided. "What would they do for us? Nothing. We plot a course out of here, regular-like— take some Throughway to somewhere we can hide out. I can do it. We can't go deep void, but we can just find a current and flow with it. We hide, we find a buyer, we set up a deal."

"Idris needs help. *Now*," Kris said. "We can get help on Berlenhof."

"We can also get arrested, disappeared, snatched by Partheni," Olli countered. "Look—"

The scream of proximity alerts swallowed up whatever she might have said next, and Olli's eyes snapped to Solace.

Her expression was abruptly pure murder. "Bitch told them where we were!" howled from her speakers. Then the Scorpion was in motion, three arms snapping out for her.

Solace leapt straight up, using one lunging claw as a stepping stone to get to the frame's shoulder. She was shouting that it *wasn't* her, the Parthenon couldn't possibly have got to them this quickly. Except it was standard practice to have a few picket craft running silent in-system, so maybe...

The alarms shut off abruptly and a mechanical voice snapped out, "Stop fighting, being boarded. Stop it. Stop it. Stop!" It was Kittering, patching himself into the drone bay comms for volume. Solace had frozen, staring at the savage-looking stinger spike Olli had installed on the Scorpion's tail. It had halted a metre from her face. All around them the *Vulture* shuddered and rocked as a vessel grappled it. Something big. Far larger than any little Partheni picket vessel.

The readouts on the drone bay hatch began cycling. Someone was coming in. Olli swore and backed off, spreading her metal limbs, Solace still riding her shoulder.

The hatch grated open, overridden from the other side. The man who strode through wore an armoured suit. Solace would bet it had been modified at the back to fit the carapace of his wasp-coloured symbiote.

Mesmon gave them all a bright, glass-sharp smile. There were others at his back: humans with guns and a headless Hiver frame built around some kind of cannon.

"I have a fucking grievance," he said to Olli in particular. "I can resolve it right now, and leave you with even fewer fucking limbs than you currently have. Alternatively, you can slip into something more comfortable, and then the lot of you doomed sods can come for an audience with my boss."

24.

Kris

They'd forced Olli out of the Scorpion. Mesmon in particular would remember exactly how she could use it. Solace went to help her, and the specialist gave her a look as though she'd actually bite if the Partheni came close. It was left to Kris and Kit to get her into the walker frame, under the increasingly impatient gaze of the Tothiat.

That done, Mesmon looked at the inert Scorpion. "I am having that," he said, meeting Olli's murderous, impotent glower. "I have a fondness for trophies. Something to remember you by." He leant in close to her. "After I've returned certain favours."

"All the way back to Tarekuma, is it?" Kris asked bleakly.

Mesmon's expression was mocking. "Oh, stupid bitch," he told her, "who doesn't understand just how *personally* the Unspeakable Razor takes all of this. Believe me, it is a matter that has pierced within the shell." Translated from the Essiel no doubt, but the meaning was quite clear enough. "You are all cordially invited to your own fucking executions, and my lord and master will watch."

They were prodded out of the drone bay, down an umbilical and onto the Hegemonic ship. The gravitic mismatch set them stumbling, as the *Harvest* pulled off at around forty-five degrees to the *Vulture*. Mesmon was watching, and Kris guessed he'd been hoping for someone to face-plant. Experienced spacers wouldn't be caught by simple gravity tricks; she felt obscurely proud at how well they were all handling their impending demise. Then Trine's bad leg folded underneath them and they ended up measuring their full length down the nacreous substance of the docking bay floor. Kris helped them up, looking daggers at Mesmon's people.

Delegate Trine sighed and their nest of arms made a disdainful little gesture, as though brushing dust off imaginary robes. "Thank you, fellow condemned. Good to see that politeness is not dead."

One of Mesmon's people brought up the rear, and Kris saw he held the unassuming grey case which had been hidden in the wreck of the *Oumaru*. Aklu was reclaiming his precious regalia.

Whilst exacting his revenge on those who made off with them.

The interior of the *Broken Harvest* was a curious piece of engineering. In a human-built ship, tightly stacked rooms would take up all the space not occupied by machinery. Here were branching, round-sectioned tunnels, shafts heading off at odd angles that suggested the a-grav wasn't always pointed in the same direction. Everything seemed to be made of mother-of-pearl, gleaming white with a rainbow sheen. Golden geometric traceries bloomed at random points, extended and flourished, then atrophied and died even as Kris watched, reabsorbed back into the matrix of the walls. Messages, warnings or readouts? Or just art? Impossible to know.

Then they were half walking, half skidding down a slope,

entering a room shaped like a flattened oval with scalloped edges. More armed men clustered here, with a couple of the humanoid Castigar that Kris remembered. She also noted Heremon, the Tothiat woman, wearing a robe thrown over a light armour coat. The sunburst figure that was Aklu's heraldry was displayed on her chest, and the back was slit so her lobstery passenger could take the air.

The Unspeakable itself was at the room's centre, still set into its ornamented a-grav couch. It remained a figure of awe, just this side of supernatural. *It's just a barnacle!* Kris wanted to yell at the gunmen. *Just a whelk with delusions of grandeur.* And yet, stood before the gaze of those stalked red eyes, it was more than that. She had no idea how the Essiel had claimed so much of the known galaxy, but for sure they had something up their notional sleeves.

The prancing Hiver major-domo stood beside the throne, as fancy as ever. Their two-faced head was turned to suggest the next few moments would involve more tragedy than comedy. Within their latticed body, insect-like elements chased one another around its core.

"Have you redeemed yourself, my wayward son?" their bell tones chimed, as they took a birdlike step towards Mesmon. "Or have your failures bowed your borrowed back, so that you lose all use to the Unspeakable?"

"See for yourself," Mesmon growled, plainly not fond of being the butt of the thing's odd wit. He gave an angry gesture, and the man with the case marched forward, presenting it for the Hiver's inspection. The creature made no attempt to open the case, but their head tilted a little, as though listening. On its floating throne, Aklu made a flurry of sharp gestures.

"Oh, Mesmon, once again you disappoint." The Hiver took a step sideways, arms unfolding a pair at a time into a whole family of open-handed poses. The man who'd carried the case fell sideways and a gout of blood shot along the iridescent floor. It didn't pool or flow in any one direction but separated out into individual tendrils, forming curlicues and arabesques of dark red. Kris blinked. She'd not even seen the Hiver with a blade, but one of those formal gestures had signified murder.

The case fell from nerveless hands and broke open when it hit the floor. It was empty.

Mesmon let out a grunt. It was a remarkably small sound really, to contain the vast amount of rage visible on his face. Then he was lunging for them and Kris knew he was going to rip someone's head off their shoulders. And that was just for starters.

Solace tried to get in his way and took an elbow to the temple that sent her tumbling aside. Even as she fell, Olli rammed her walking frame into Mesmon's groin. It didn't seem to inconvenience him much; apparently those parts were as resilient as all the rest of him. With a snarl of frustration he reached down and just picked up the entire frame, its legs kicking madly, about to dash Olli and her conveyance to pieces on the floor.

"Hold," the Hiver said. "Stay your hand." They had taken one more step, and Aklu's couch shifted too, the Essiel's several eyes craning.

"It may well come to pass," the Hiver continued carefully, as though working extra hard to translate the gestures and rumbles of their master, "that we shall have our fill of broken bones. That truth must be extracted from these few like corks from bottles: in we drive the point, and out the rush of ruptured fluid comes. Not yet, not this one, cousin that she is. The Hook admires her."

Mesmon replaced Olli and stepped back. His expression suggested his bloodlust was undiminished. For her part, the specialist looked more alarmed at Aklu's forbearance than at the violence. *Cousin?*

"The wreck of the *Oumaru* is not here," the Hiver tolled. "Our sacred relics likewise are astray. To take the knot of any of their lives, and pull it taut, might be to cut the string that leads us to our treasure, might it not? They shall give up the one who knows, and know that if they fail then we shall start with toes, with fingers, faces, eyes and all the parts a man may part with long before he dies."

One of the gilded thing's gestures apparently included a command, because the guards were closing in. Mesmon's purpling face hovered around the outskirts, as though he wouldn't trust himself to stay his hand if within arm's reach of them again. Then a grinding rumble came from the throne like the shifting of tectonic plates. Everyone froze, glancing at the golden Hiver for translation.

The major-domo took a half-step back. Six arms made an elaborate genuflection that indicated Olli, Aklu and the space between them.

"Approach," it intoned, "O favoured one."

Olli sent Kris a wild look, but all eyes were on her. She manoeuvred the walker frame, stepping cautiously out of the ring of thugs until she was level with the Hiver. Aklu's eyes twitched and shifted position, examining her as its pipe-thin arms flicked and flurried.

"You, we will save till last," the major-domo said softly,

barely audible to Kris. "For we approve of those born bound who yet refuse to be."

Olli swallowed and nodded, leaning back in her frame as she stared up at the Unspeakable. She was stared at in turn.

Then it was evidently time to go. And while the guards laid hands on everyone else, Olli got to walk unescorted. Kris wondered, in fact, what would have happened if she'd just stayed in the throne room. Had the whole thing been a veiled attempt at recruitment?

*

She'd been expecting to be dumped in the hold, but the *Broken Harvest* apparently took prisoners often enough to have dedicated facilities. These were spherical rooms budding off a central hub at different angles and heights—a bunch of grapes in negative. The captives were prodded into a cluster of adjoining cells sealed with energy barriers: Solace first, then Kris, Kit and Trine. Finally, Olli was allowed to choose her residence of the moment, still being treated with baffled respect by the guards. As soon as Aklu's people had gone, she burst out, "I'm not a Hegemonic! Or a gangster! I'm not their *plant*!"

"Nobody thinks you are," Kris said, although she'd had a moment's unworthy suspicion.

"I don't know *what* they want from me," Olli went on, sounding almost frantic. "These fucking Essiel are crazy. And this one's crazy even for an Essiel, right?"

"Wait," Solace snapped. Olli glowered at her, though not without a touch of gratitude for having something comprehensible on which to focus her ire. "Trine," the Partheni went on. "Static."

"Ugh," the Hiver archaeologist said, a buzzing grunt from within their casing. "Really?"

"Just do it."

Trine's face displayed a burlesque of petulance as they started putting out a sound like a dentist's drill at the very edge of hearing. Kris's teeth twinged at the sound—more the feel—of it.

Olli doubtless wanted to make some caustic comment about things being bad enough already, but she was a professional at heart. "Blocker?" she asked cautiously.

"My fellow incarcerates, electronic listening devices are now having a very bad day." Trine's voice rose like clashing music from within that tooth-jarring sound. "Pass comment upon our captors all you wish."

"What do we say about Idris?" Kris put in quickly. "Olli, you're not with them, fine, we get that. But Idris…He's still on the *Vulture*, unless they brought him out separately. What if they jettison the ship or something?"

"On the other hand, if they don't know he's there, maybe that'll work for us," Olli suggested.

"Rescue mounted by Idris resurgent?" Kit piped up. His screens were grey, fuzzing with vague patterns that seemed to echo Trine's low buzz. "Unconvincing. Further priorities are suggested. Where are the coveted objects now, please?"

"Ah, the…things, yes." Kris agreed. Despite Trine's alleged cover, speaking of the Originator regalia openly still seemed difficult. "They'll be searching the *Vulture* from top to bottom right now, I guess. They'll find Idris anyway."

"Great consideration towards the potency of such objects removed from their resting place. Is that not the point?" Kit pressed.

"Fuck, he's right," Olli agreed. "You can't just pocket the damn things. So did they just...fall out of the crate or something? Who had them last?"

One by one they all ended up looking at Trine.

"Analysis continues. Kindly remove such accusatory expressions from your features, my fellow stalwarts, old friends and new," the Hiver said.

"*Trine*," Solace said warningly.

"I cannot imagine under what circumstances this suspicion has come to fall on me," they protested.

"Wait..." Olli looked between them. "You...were *stealing* the things? Like, from *us*?"

"That is an entirely unwarranted suggestion," Trine said weakly. "However, someone must think of the benefit to *science* of such irreplaceable objects. They must not simply be sold to the highest bidder. Fellow cognoscenti, I am sure you appreciate this."

From their expressions, nobody seemed to appreciate it. Not even Solace.

"Objects where precisely? Elaborate please," Kit asked urgently. "Life-death level of import hangs on this."

"Science demurs," Trine told them flatly.

"Science will not stop them from taking you from your frame, and murdering you piece by piece," Solace snapped. "*Trine*, will you just—"

The Hiver pointedly turned their face off, and stopped the juddering hum. Presumably this made any further conversation vulnerable to outside surveillance. Everyone lapsed into silence.

They heard movement, on and off; the business of the ship going on about them. Even gangsters needed maintenance crews and duty rosters, Kris supposed. But every sound raised the spectre of Mesmon and the guards coming to haul them all out, or maybe just one of them, never to be seen again. If Solace was expecting some grand Partheni cavalry charge, that didn't seem to be happening. The *Harvest* hadn't dropped back into unspace and tortured them all that way, that was the only positive. Presumably Aklu wanted to secure his toys first.

Then they had a visitor. She heard the sound of sandals scuffing at the rounded floors and straightened up, hissing at the others. Someone came into their suite of cells, garbed in bright red and purple. Kris had to blink at this vision in Hegemonic livery a few times, before quite accepting he was there.

It was Sathiel, the hierograve from Lung-Crow—just as mild and avuncular as before. A handful of cultists clustered at the doorway, possibly keeping Aklu's people out and giving their leader privacy. Unless...

"You were working with *it* all this time?" she demanded. "You and Aklu?"

Sathiel shook his head. "I'm afraid not, or we would be meeting in more comfortable circumstances. When your captain and I made our contract to free the *Oumaru* and your ship I had no idea the Unspeakable was involved. My people died too, when the Hook stole the *Vulture*." He sighed, shaking his head. "It's all very distressing."

"How are you even here?" Olli demanded. The others were just watching, waiting to see whether this might be their break, somehow.

"A diplomatic courtesy," Sathiel explained. "The Hegemony has many formalities that may seem curious to outsiders."

"But Aklu isn't *in* the Hegemony any more, right? It's gone rogue. Isn't that the point of the whole 'Unspeakable Razor' thing?" the specialist pressed.

"Ah, well…" said Sathiel, and Kris knew a lecturing tone when she heard one. "The mistake is to characterize Hegemonic systems as if they were human ones. The Essiel have been ruling a vast and diverse empire for centuries. They have persisted because they have a system for everything. That is how they work. They prefer not to have to *react*. Instead, they *foresee*. This applies even to aberrations within their own species. Perhaps some of you are students of religion?"

"Among other things," Trine put in, sounding mulish. "Who is this greybeard and what relevance has he to our predicament?"

"Many religions have an antagonist figure, a Devil, or perhaps a whole class of demons whose job it is to tempt and torment us poor mortals," Sathiel explained, speaking over Trine. "And yet, these adversaries remain part of the system they mock. They act as an example of what *not* to do, a foil to higher powers. As such, Aklu has a place within the Hegemonic firmament. So, when the Razor and the Hook comes to a system, it announces its arrival to any Hegemonic presence there. Which in this case is myself, here to represent my masters in the negotiations regarding the Architects' return."

"You've gone up in the world then," Kris noted acidly.

"A sign of the times," Sathiel agreed. "However, all to your benefit, as I may be able to help. Under normal circumstances, your position here would be bleak. You've taken something belonging to the Unspeakable. Examples would be made. But perhaps I can intercede, as one part of the Hegemonic system to another. For old times' sake. You'd have to return the regalia, obviously."

"Obviously," said Kris, with a venomous look at Trine, who contrived not to notice her.

"Specify your rates and remuneration, please," Kit piped up.

"Ah, well." Sathiel spread his hands benevolently. "As you might imagine, what *should* be talks focused on the Architects' return have degenerated. The Council of Human Interests and the Parthenon are engaged in mutual finger pointing." He sighed. "We need something to refocus them on the truly important things."

"You want the *Oumaru*," Kris divined.

"I'm sure you've done the sensible thing and hidden it," Sathiel said. "A very wise precaution. However, if it was retrieved by my people and displayed above Berlenhof, the great powers might just abandon their brinkmanship. Then we can start dealing with the key issues at stake."

"And that's your price for putting a word in?" Olli asked.

"I regret the necessity of being so mercenary, but yes," Sathiel agreed. "Millions, billions of lives are at stake, and I have a sacred duty."

"We'll think about it," the specialist said.

"Olli—" Kris started.

"I *said* we'll think about it, discuss it maybe, free and frank exchange of views."

Sathiel sighed. "I will be called before Aklu shortly, to reaffirm the disdain and rejection of the Hegemony towards the Unspeakable," he said. "There are proper diplomatic and ceremonial forms to these things, you understand. I will suggest you be brought out to witness this, and then most likely Aklu will make a start on you. You are aware, of course, that a great deal of Essiel cultural form is coloured by their early contact with the Architects. By which I mean that the proper behaviour of the Unspeakable is to make ruin an art form. Please let me help you."

"We'll think about it," Olli repeated firmly, and just stared at the man until he'd taken his cultists and gone.

"Well we could do worse," Kris said, after Trine had reluctantly reinstated their jamming field.

"Question as regards the credibility of his contractual consideration," Kit's translator spat emphatically.

"Yeah, I reckon all the help we'd get from that quarter is a little hand-wringing and a 'Well I asked him not to torture you, but...'" Olli agreed. "We keep all our leverage close, and..." But she didn't have an "and," not really.

"Excuse me, but can someone at least explain to me who that even was," Trine complained. Kris gave them the potted history, including the Architected *Oumaru*, the *Vulture* being taken at Lung-Crow and their first clash with the Broken Harvest. At the end of it, Trine's phantom face was staring at all of them simultaneously with an expression of exasperation.

"You needed me a long time ago, my companions in adversity."

"We *need* you to tell us where the things are," Olli growled. "Or I will use whatever weird-ass influence I have with the Hook to have him do you first and make it slow."

Trine manufactured a vast sigh. "If it comes to threats, my somewhat obstreperous cellmates, then know that sometimes the greatest treasures are to be found *within oneself*."

Kris blinked. "Seriously?" She stared at the Hiver's barrel body. "And they're still...potent? You cracked the containment system?"

"Not exactly. I simply discovered that it was independent of the casing," Trine admitted. "But if it comes to blood, I will give these things up, despite the loss to science. In the hope it will soften the blow. Although you were the ones who robbed an Essiel gangster of a priceless treasure, so I don't feel this is on my head."

*

Soon after that, they were back in Aklu's presence. True to his word, Sathiel had driven a wedge of cultists into the heart of the court. They were standing there, robes bright and regal, as though they'd turned up for a party everyone else had heard was cancelled. Aklu's people didn't seem to know quite what to make of the interlopers. The pack of thugs and heavies were probably not connoisseurs of Hegemonic theology. However, they *were* keen weathervanes for the mood of their boss, and the Essiel seemed to accept the cultists with equanimity, like some kind of ineffectual judgement on its ways.

The gilded Hiver spread their many arms towards the crew, in a gesture that eloquently conveyed *Well?* Kris glanced at her companions, because now they *did* know the location of the regalia. For a fragile moment, they retained a defiant camaraderie. Then Heremon appeared, pushing a simple six-by-four scaffold with obvious bindings for wrists and ankles, and a whole host of hooks and pins on jointed arms. You couldn't have said for definite how those arms might be deployed, but they gave the imagination plenty to chew on.

Kris looked to Solace, whose face was set in a stubborn expression. She was determined not to betray her companions to anyone *else*. Olli was being bloody-minded, too. And probably Kit had worked out that a Hanni wouldn't fit on that frame: it was a nastiness designed for a human physique.

"Damn it," she muttered, because apparently it came down to her, but then Trine stepped forward. Despite their oft-repaired leg, they managed a halfway decent parody of the major-domo's elegant dance.

"I would—how does this go?—I would address the most Unspeakable from my position here of abject dread. How's that, does that work?" Their fake face beamed genially at all and sundry.

"Show first the relics," the major-domo cautioned.

"Gladly shall I so," and Trine's torso just folded outwards. Within the hollow canister of Trine's body, a honeycomb hosted a seething nest of thumb-sized insects. Slotted in front of them were the precious Originator regalia. The rods and fragments hovered there without obvious support, as though they were visuals projected from some hidden lens. Despite her life being on the line, Kris still found herself wondering, *How? Where does the power come from, for the a-grav?* She hoped Trine knew, because those relics would become trash in a blink if they lost their mystical provenance.

Trine's arms spread out and the regalia drifted out from the confines of their body. All eyes tracked the fragments, as they danced in the air above their many hands. "Behold the treasure of an elder age," the archaeologist murmured. "May I now speak, 'fore sentence is pronounced?"

A deep, pained sound ground out from Aklu, but apparently it was positive because the major-domo said, "Be brief."

"Whoever'd think such enemies would cosy up," Trine declared, in rough mimicry of the other Hiver's rhythms. Their nest of arms spread and curled inwards, perhaps conveying something cutting to an Essiel, save that it brought the relics closer to their open body again. "Who'd think to find such daggers sheathed that formerly'd been drawn? Or something like that." They abandoned the pose and forced metre for a moment, rolling ghostly eyes at all the room as though mortally embarrassed. "Or I mistake myself, but these robed dullards set themselves against your divine majesty." The room was very quiet when he'd finished, and he gurned at them all. "Did I not do it right? Well excuse me, O my captors, but that's the best you'll get from me. *They are enemies*, is my meaning. The clown with the beard and his robed loons."

Sathiel sighed. "You misunderstand, my friend. We are foes, yes, but on an abstract, philosophical level—"

"No. I'm talking about the *Oumaru*. That was the name of the ship, wasn't it, old Hierograve, old sect-captain?" Trine swung back to face the Essiel. "For lo! The vessel 'pon which you had placed your treasures, all secured against the world, has foundered! Who'da thunk it'd go that way?"

Nobody seemed to know what was going on. Mesmon was obviously waiting for the signal to shut the Hiver up, but Aklu just watched, fidgeting without giving any apparent order. The major-domo paused, then pulled their limbs in, steepling all six hands together.

"The Architect of our misfortune came..." they tried, a questioning tone to their golden voice.

"I can't be bothered with this nonsense talk," Trine snapped. "Just tell your boss I am the foremost expert of the age... Or rather, I am the greatest scholar on Originator lore this side of the Hegemonic Sphere, and I used to analyse Architected wreckage for the war effort. Tell it that. I've gone over pieces of your *Oumaru* and I can tell you this for free. It wasn't Architected."

"You fucking *what*?" Olli barked out, wide-eyed.

"No Architect!" Trine declared. "Someone mangled it with a gravitic drive and a complex program. The subatomic signature you'd expect is completely absent. This was someone's shoddy forgery. Someone who had no idea what the freighter contained. Because let's face it, the one thing we *do* know about Architects is that they won't go near Originator gubbins. Whoever perpetrated this little scam must have been hoping for unquestioning panic at the return of the Bad Times, so they would surely have picked another ship to ruin, if they'd known. Isn't that the case, Menheer Hierograve Sathiel?" And their rack of arms made a rippling gesture towards Sathiel.

"You're accusing *me*?" the cultist demanded. And Kris read his expression of outrage and knew for certain that Trine had landed it.

"It all makes sense, doesn't it?" she spoke up. "*You* were the one desperate to get the *Oumaru* into the public arena. You probably told station admin about the missing ship. Then, when they hid the *Oumaru*, you manipulated *us* to break it out into the open. What were you trying to do? Get the Colonies falling over each other to sign up with your masters? And was that the Hegemony's idea or just yours? Just a way of scoring points with your bosses?"

Sathiel's face was completely composed now. For a moment the whole universe seemed to be hanging on his response. In the end, all he said was, "This doesn't need to change anything."

"*Excuse me?*" Kris felt outraged beyond all reason. "You're not even *pretending* you weren't behind this?"

"Why do you care?" Sathiel asked, maddeningly nonchalant still. "Surely whether worlds join the Hegemony or not is a little beyond your usual level of engagement with the universe? I've heard you talk, you and yours. You're not Nativists or even Colonial loyalists. I'll intervene on your behalf here, in return for the wreck's location. That offer still stands and it's all that matters to you, surely? Let the politics take care of itself. Joining the Hegemony *is* for the best, you know. You haven't lived under their rule. Peace, harmony, a place for everyone, nobody goes hungry or cold. It's *better*."

"Except for the *Oumaru*'s crew, right?" Olli demanded. "I guess you just had to murder them all. Or they might have mentioned something inconvenient, next time they made port."

"Listen to me," Sathiel insisted. "This can still go very well for you. When you're clear of Berlenhof, I'll make sure you want for nothing. You do remember that you're for hire, yes?"

"I..." Kris said slowly. For a mad moment she'd imagined a triumphal confrontation with malefactors brought to justice, like an old-Earth murder story. But the only authority here was a criminal alien, and why would it care?

Solace took two steps, ending up standing protectively by Kris and Kittering.

"You *intervene?*" The clear voice of Aklu's Hiver rang into the silence. "There are no *words* for those who meddle with the corpus of the gods. Such hubris!" For a moment, nobody seemed to understand what the proclamation meant. Then Sathiel's calm facade cracked.

"Unspeakable...Razor and Hook...there was never any intent to act against *you*. I merely sought to advance the agenda of the Essiel. An action in *everyone's* best interests." His eyes swivelled to the prisoners, as though to recruit them as allies.

"Ready yourself," Solace murmured in Kris's ear, making her shiver. Then the whole ship shuddered around them. A low moaning seemed to issue from all the white walls at once, gleaming patterns chasing each other back and forth in shifting hues. Kris just stood there dumbly, but Aklu's people were abruptly in motion. Heremon was shouting orders, and the bulk of the pirate court abruptly dashed out of every available exit. Somewhere on the ship, a musical voice was announcing an alert in perfect couplets.

The ship was under attack, Kris realized numbly. There was a shuddering detonation and she felt the distinct shift to the air that meant a breach somewhere. *Boarding?* Almost immediately the sound of weapons fire came to them: the high searing song of accelerators, the rattle and bang of projectile guns. Someone was crashing Aklu's court with extreme prejudice.

25.

Solace

Solace had heard, through her implant, a harsh *tck-tck*. It wasn't repeated and it was easy enough to mistake for static, had anyone been listening in. Long conditioning set her pulse racing. The rescue party had arrived.

Monitor Superior Tact had said they were putting a team together; there must have been a picket ship closer than she'd thought. Now she sent out her own recognition code, just a stuttering of ticks, receiving bounce-back from two separate infiltrations. The ships would have ghosted up to the *Broken Harvest* under dead momentum, gravitic drives stilled so as to dampen any ripples that might alert the target. Everyone was so reliant on the wonders of gravitic sensor arrays. People forgot there were old-fashioned ways to do things.

Then the fun would have begun, cutting into the bigger vessel's hull the moment they were clamped to it, knowing discovery would be inevitable and soon. She had no idea how many of her sisters had come for her, but likely it wasn't much more than half a dozen.

Solace was shoving Kris even as the gangsters became aware of the infiltration, pushing the woman towards the closest signal. She tried to scoot Kit along with a foot, too, but the Hanni skittered away from her. They were unaware of what was going on and, reasonably enough, didn't trust her judgement.

"Trine!" she shouted. "Here!" Her voice was almost lost in the general commotion, but the Hiver picked it from the air and limped towards her. They still had the regalia, Solace saw, their arms carefully folding the pieces back into their body.

"Go! That way!" Solace shoved Kris onwards, seeing the next few moments unfold in her mind. Heremon had gone to order the defence but Mesmon was right there and off the leash. He was going for Trine to get back their precious relics, punching down an out-of-place cultist and shoving one of his own people aside to do so. Solace, unarmoured, unarmed, went for him anyway. A human gangster got in the way and turned a magnetic pistol on her. Or offered it to her, as far as she was concerned, because he was far too close and a knife would have served him better. She got a hand on the barrel and twisted it against his thumb until he wasn't holding it anymore, then slammed a shoulder to his chest and a heel onto his instep, knocking him onto his back as she turned the gun on an incoming Castigar. She was also too close to really be relying on ranged weaponry, but she was just quick enough to chew the thing's blockish head off with half a dozen high velocity flechettes. All of which left her too late to help Trine.

Trine was still coming, though. Solace saw that Olli had rammed Mesmon with her walking frame again, hard enough to stagger him. Even as he recovered, glaring murder at her, the specialist yelled some kind of war cry. A section of her frame shot forwards, turned into a makeshift metal javelin. It lanced through Mesmon's chest and pinned him to the far wall, writhing and howling. For a moment Solace dared to hope that it might have destroyed the symbiote at his back. Then of course he was working his way off the shaft, bloody foam at the corners of his mouth. She put seven flechettes into him to slow him down, but reckoned their effect would be minimal.

"Solace!" It was Kris's voice, and she glanced over to see the woman standing by an armoured Partheni myrmidon.

"Trine, that way!" The Hiver had already gathered as much and was hobbling towards Kris accordingly. Solace looked about for Kit, but the Hannilambra was nowhere to be seen. "Olli—!"

The specialist was already scurrying in the other direction. She cast a baleful glance over her shoulder as she yelled *"No!"* A gunman tried to get in her way and she rammed the tip of one of her walker's legs into the man's knee. Solace heard the crunch from across the room.

"Olli... Timo, *please.*" Solace ran after her. "We'll get to the *Vulture.* We'll get Idris." Solace glanced about, seeing that the throne room was almost empty, though she could still hear shots outside. A group of thugs had formed up around Aklu to escort the Essiel elsewhere. Sathiel and the cult had already left by another route. The chief remaining threat was Mesmon, still nearby and almost free. She shot him another three times just for the hell of it, emptying the magazine, then took up the projectile rifle dropped by the man with the smashed knee. She headed after Olli at a run.

"Just leave me alone, Patho." Olli had taken one of the circular corridors out, following some indicator on the walker's board. She wasn't headed towards the *Vulture.* "I've business to take care of here. Something of mine to get back."

"Is it your *suit*?" Solace demanded. "Olli, it's not worth your life." *And it's not worth mine and I should leave her to it. She hates me anyway.* Yet Solace carried on running, barely able to keep up with the skittering of the walker. At least Kris and Trine were with her sisters.

"You wouldn't understand," Olli shouted over her shoulder. One of the *Harvest*'s crew crossed her path, perhaps just some perfectly innocent technician on his way to repair something. Olli ran the man over, trampled him and barely slowed. "You don't know how long it took me to make it mine." She looked at her instruments and took a sudden left-then-up, the walker scrabbling at the gradient, slipping a little. It gave Solace the chance to catch her. And then they had broken out into a spherical room. Someone's quarters, no need to guess whose.

There was a bed suspended in a-grav in the room's centre. A big one, too, suggesting that Mesmon either liked company or was a very restless sleeper. Several tanks and hoses were set into one wall, some concession to his hybrid biology. Maybe the symbiote liked to detach and go for a swim every so often. And there was the Scorpion, already mounted on one wall with its arms spread. Plenty of room for it, here; Mesmon's quarters were bigger than the *Vulture*'s drone bay. He wanted a trophy, he'd said. And, despite all the Scorpion's threat and power, here it was no more than a specimen pinned to a card.

The rest of the room was a mosaic of faces, and that was what had stopped Olli just inside the doorway.

They were virtual images, larger than life-size. Probably there were more than a hundred, though Solace had no wish to count them. They were almost all twisted in pain, fear or desperation, where those emotions applied. Most were human: men and women both, and at least a handful of Partheni. There were some Hanni too, a few knots of eye-tipped Castigar tentacles and a beautiful metal mask, probably from a Hiver frame. And all these beings were dead, Solace knew. She knew because she saw Rollo's likeness there, his last moments from Mesmon's point of view. The Tothiat apparently liked to record mementos of his work. They were standing within his resumé.

She heard Mesmon coming just then, the soft scuff of him as he loped into the room behind them like a beast. He still managed to throw a solid punch into her ribs and took the gun from her, sending her tumbling down into the shadow of the floating bed. Olli spun the walker to face him but he just flipped her over, rolling the frame onto its side and half spilling her out of it.

"I should be killing your friends now," he told Solace flatly. "But my sister will deal with the mess. She's the homebody. I'm the *people* person."

He stepped down into the curve of the room, the gun held loosely in his hand. "I will be made to suffer, for my failures. The Razor will cut me for how I've handled things. But I will remember then how I made you two bitches suffer, and that will warm me when my guts are out on wires again."

Solace went for him before he'd finished speaking and he looked gratifyingly put out at that, a man who liked his own monologues. She slapped the gun barrel aside so he couldn't just shoot her, then her thumb went into his eye. She struck hard enough to hook the rim of his socket and rammed his face into the hard plastic of the bed.

He grabbed her throat with one hand. His un-gouged eye stared at her, wide and mad. He grinned.

"They don't tell you about the pain," he explained conversationally, incrementally tightening his fingers. "When the blessing comes to live within your flesh, you know you'll live forever, but they don't tell you how these cuts and bruises still hurt. But the Unspeakable understands. He hurts you until nothing hurts anymore. Then you can really reach your full potential." He tried to snap at her fingers with his teeth where her hand gripped his skull, and she yanked it away, trailing blood and viscous jelly. She could look into the ruined pit of his socket and see the tissues busily mending themselves. But not for long, because there were black spots dotting her own vision and her breath was failing.

"One day a legion of my people will make your precious angels extinct," he told her. "We are better than you'll ever be."

The sound of the Scorpion wrenching itself off the wall and crashing down behind him was like thunder.

Mesmon threw Solace across the room but she bounced off the bed, landing up against the rounded wall, surrounded by the faces of the dead. *How did Olli climb up to her frame?* she wondered. But of course Olli was still lying in the overturned walker, eyes closed as she linked into the Scorpion's systems remotely. Mesmon came to the same conclusion and went for her, but the big frame caught him with one boathook arm and slung him across the room. He hit hard enough to crack the nacreous wall on the far side, extinguishing a dozen dead faces. Blood, tears and nameless alien ichor ran down his face as he straightened up.

"It won't help," he barked. He raised the gun to shoot at Olli past the Scorpion. Two bullets sparked from its casing, then Solace tackled him and grabbed the weapon. She kicked away from the Tothiat and shot him in the arm, an event he barely deigned to notice.

"Kit, you there?" Olli said. It would have been a non sequitur, except Solace saw she was speaking into the walker. "Kit, come on now!"

The Scorpion went for Mesmon, who did his best to vault over it. Blades and drills made a mess of the wall he'd fallen against. Then the tail clotheslined him across the chest, knocking him sideways. The frame tried to pounce and pin him, but he rolled out from beneath it. Instantly he was up again and made it to the fallen walker, ripping it aside to get at its passenger. Olli was desperately shrugging her way backwards across the floor, face locked in a snarl.

Solace rushed Mesmon again, kicking at his knee. She felt it grind, saw it snap back into shape a moment later. She rammed an elbow into the centre of his back, the articulated spine that was the symbiote. Maybe it didn't share in the unnatural resilience with which it had gifted him?

It was like striking stone and she felt something fracture in her own arm, a shock of pain up to the shoulder that startled a scream out of her. Mesmon, never one to miss a chance, had that arm in his hands a moment later, using it as a lever to throw Solace at the oncoming Scorpion. She bounced off it, narrowly avoiding being impaled on its drill. It reached Mesmon a heartbeat before he could stomp on Olli, half severing one arm with its cutting claws and impaling him on its hook.

Using his other hand, the Tothiat took hold of the Scorpion's pincer arm at its base and twisted. One foot on the frame for purchase, he contorted his whole body, muscle against muscle. With a convulsive heave he ripped the

Scorpion's limb clean out of its socket, leaving it dangling from a handful of cords and ducts, the claw still snapping feebly. He went for the bubble next, finding the catch and wrenching it open before casting the armoured casing aside. Olli was screaming in rage and Solace staggered over to try and haul him off it. She took a foot to her solar plexus for her trouble and sat down, abruptly unable to breathe.

She couldn't have said when Kittering actually made his appearance. The little Hanni was abruptly there on the Scorpion's back, clinging tight with his six legs. The Scorpion's tail arched over him, until its tip was within range of his reaching mouthparts. Mesmon spotted him a moment later and lost a valuable moment staring, not sure what was going on. Then he decided it was nothing he wanted to permit and swatted Kit off the frame, sending the Hanni tumbling across the room.

"Now," he said, and reached into the Scorpion's opened bubble, taking hold of the control board there. "Let's neuter your bastard pet."

The Scorpion's tail lashed forwards, driving its tip deep into Mesmon's shoulder. He barely shifted, just shrugging with the impact. "Is that really all you've got left?" he asked, and ripped out the entire control board in a visceral tangle of severed wires and conduits. For a moment Solace thought Olli could keep on puppeteering the thing remotely, but the entire frame spasmed and then went still, utterly dead.

"Ha," said Mesmon. "Ha . . ." He smacked his lips and Solace saw a greenish residue leaking from them. Abruptly he shuddered from head to toe, swaying alarmingly until he was leaning on the bed. "The fuck?" he demanded. "The exact fuck *what*?" He seemed to have forgotten they were there.

Something clattered to the ground at his heels. A long

black and yellow lobster-looking thing, arching and flailing. Its underside was raw, red with human blood, bristling with contorting cilia.

"Oh," said Mesmon, and more stuff was seeping from his mouth, nose and eyes. "Oh. Oh *no*." Then he jack-knifed forwards, vomiting. What came out looked a lot like the sort of anatomical details people preferred to keep inside. That done, he stared down at what he'd voided, then fell onto his face and was still.

Solace made a sound. It mostly conveyed disgust, but was at least partly impressed. "You found a poison?" Olli had been researching, she remembered. At the time it had just seemed a convenient cover for Solace's own message home, but Olli and Kit had been scouring the xenobiology databases of Berlenhof's academia. And monopolizing the *Vulture God*'s printers for something chemically complex.

"Kit?" Solace called, suddenly aware that the Hanni hadn't resurfaced. She found him lying on his front, the screen on his back cracked and dead. His limbs were twitching and she had no idea if that meant he was stunned or if he was dying. She could carry him, of course, but could she carry him *and* Olli...?

Looking around, Solace saw that the specialist had dragged herself back to the walker. She'd prised a hatch open and was sorting through the tools spilling from it. Sensing her gaze, Olli looked daggers back.

"I guess this is where you tell me how much better the Pathos are, for not getting themselves into trouble like this." Her face was wet with tears of pain and fatigue. "Just *go*, Patho. Go back to your friends. Get Kit and Kris and the Hiver out. Get Idris."

"What are you trying to do?"

"Why do *you* care?"

"Olli, we don't have time for this. Please, just tell me."

The woman scowled at her. "Walker board's compatible with Scorpion board. Link them and I can use it to replace what that fucker tore out."

"Then show me. Direct me," Solace said. "I'm not a tech but I know enough to get things done." *I hope.*

"Fuck you," Olli replied, barely able to get her words out past all the anger. "Fine, then. Why, though? Why put off the inevitable? We all know the Pathos are coming for us, to remake us all in your image, right? You're seriously going to tell me you're all real angels and that would never happen?"

Solace started to work, disconnecting the board from the walker as swiftly as she could, letting Olli's clipped directions guide her hands. She composed what she wanted to say in the moments of quiet in between. What she'd been thinking, ever since her first clash with the specialist. *And why do I care what she thinks? Not like it'll change anything.* But Solace did care. Olli's accusations stung because they could so easily have been true.

"You know the biggest topic of discussion in the Parthenon, since the start?" she asked. As Olli sure as hell wasn't going to ask her to elaborate, she continued, "We asked ourselves what Doctor Parsefer actually wanted, when she created us? She designed our society, coded our genome range, picked what she liked from a dozen Earth ethnicities and cultures. She even had a personal hand in a lot of our early tech. She was a polymath, smartest woman there ever was."

"Hate her already," Olli responded, then said, "Not that, the other one, with the yellow tape around it."

"And yet we still don't know what she wanted," Solace went on, following each terse instruction. "This was before the Architects, you know? Did the Doctor want to come back to Earth, kill every boy-child and institute the Tyranny of Mothers? Or did she just want some part of humanity to develop that wasn't...fucked up, in so many ways, and she thought parthenogenesis was the best way to make that happen? She wrote a whole load of science manuals, but no sociology at all. Then the war came and nobody had to decide. We were humanity's estranged sister, returning to the fold when we were most needed. We were the warrior angels and everyone loved us."

The walker's board came free, because Colonial tech was designed to be taken apart and cannibalized at a moment's notice. She dragged it over to the Scorpion, feeling her injured elbow every step of the way. Then Olli talked her through what to keep and what to discard. She was expecting more of Mesmon's crewmates any moment and the sound of gunfire still rattled from elsewhere in the ship. But she was working quickly, and Olli's instructions were clear and to the point. It had only been minutes.

"Then the war was over," she went on, prising at a bent plate, "and step by step things went sour. You know that already. It's in your historio-types too. Eventually it was so bad we just left Hugh outright. And then we started talking again, about what Doctor Parsefer meant. You ever hear of the War Party?"

"Sounds like a riot," Olli said weakly.

"It started in response to the Nativists. It had one message: *They will come for us, so we have to go for them first.* Generals, scientists, philosophers. They were mobilizing the fleet to swing right around and come back to Hugh, only not for talks. You ever hear that?"

"Only a matter of time, right?" Olli grunted. "Start connecting, now, if you're going to. Patch me in."

"But one day, the entire War Party leadership was found dead," Solace said grimly. "All five of them, all in different ships, different star systems. All shot dead."

"Fuck…" said Olli, despite herself. "What, you're going to tell me that was you or something?"

"Me? I was in suspension. Only heard about it next time they woke me up. A lot had changed by then. And nobody knows who did it, to this day. But the cabal that took over, they made it plain: *that is not us*. The Parthenon will *not* become what you people fear. And the War Party died because we were *so close* to becoming that very thing. Do you understand? We have the best ships, the best weapons. We come from the vat ready to fight, quicker to learn, just… better."

"Fuck you."

"Yes, yes." Solace's hands were anticipating Olli's guidance now. She was getting the hang of this mishmash Colonial tech. "But we made a decision that we were going to use our skills to be the shield and not the sword. Who knows? That decision might get made again, differently, in the future. But anyone trying to do that's going to think about the War Party." She laughed, half bitterly, half embarrassed. "You know what mediotypes do the rounds, back home? There are things we're not supposed to see but everyone has a bootleg copy. Stuff that students smuggle into the dorms? The—" She stopped suddenly. "Actually, I won't—"

"Oh no, you better finish that thought. What?"

"*Sách vé faim.*" Solace said. "Means, 'stories of the starving.' Stories about your people, the Colonials."

"I can't begin to tell you how offensive that is," Olli told her.

"I know. I'm sorry. But they're mostly...there's always some Colonial girl, and she's born to a hard life, with no food, on a hostile planet. She makes it to one of your military academies and has rivals and friends and...it's like our life, but different. More different. She's brave and has adventures and probably falls in love with a girl, or even a boy. Or both, and..."

The Scorpion groaned and lurched sideways. For a moment it seemed about to fall on Solace and crush her, but then it caught its balance.

"I'm *in*," Olli said. Then there was a long silence as Solace contemplated all the killing implements she had just made available to the woman.

"I still don't like you," the specialist said tiredly. "Or your people. And if you think that finding out you all love reading goddamn school stories, about all those military academies we don't have, makes me like you any better, then..." She hacked out a sound that was part cough and part laugh. "That was the dumbest thing I ever heard—what you just said. You know that, right?"

Solace shrugged and stepped back from the Scorpion. "I am *not* a diplomat," she said with feeling. "I'm a soldier. I love the Parthenon. But that doesn't mean I want everyone to be like us. The *Sách vé faim*, they're stories that...celebrate difference. They're all about teaching us to love the Colonies, despite everything. So the War Party won't happen again. So we won't be like *that*, whether Doctor Parsefer wanted it or not."

Olli had bared her teeth in frustration, as she clearly needed help for the next stage. At Solace's awkward look, she merely waved her truncated arms irritably. Solace picked her up, cradling her as best she could, and fumbled her into the Scorpion's torn cockpit.

"Ow. Bitch," Olli yelped. "Are you—*crying?*" She had one eye on Solace, one on her board, where the displays were lighting up with unhappy colours. "You get real sad about these starve-y stories?"

"I think my arm is broken," Solace said, truthfully enough. Although it wasn't just that.

"That so?"

"My blockers aren't keeping on top of the pain anymore."

"Blockers. Right," Olli said. "Forgot you were better than the rest of us for a moment there. Humblest apologies."

Solace waited for her to say that was a joke, but apparently it wasn't a joke. Things had perhaps reached a détente between them and maybe that was as much as she could hope for.

"Where are your lot at?" the specialist asked, taking a few careful steps in the Scorpion, working around its busted leg.

"Kris and Trine are already on the *Corday*—that's the Partheni ship." Solace had been trying to keep track of the coded transmissions. "You and Kit should—"

"Will be getting out of here on the *Vulture,*" Olli told her. "You take your chances—with us, or with your people—but we are *not* losing the ship. And we're keeping Idris, for that matter."

"Fine." *And I'm not in a position to argue, between my injured arm and the frame I've just got you into.* "You bring Kit."

Olli led the way, the Hanni held with surprisingly gentleness in two of the Scorpion's arms. The remaining limbs all worked together to send her lurching crabwise down the corridors of the *Broken Harvest*. They ran into a couple of Aklu's people almost immediately, tough-looking men with guns. They took one look at Olli and the Scorpion and ran in the opposite direction. Distant shooting came from elsewhere on the ship.

"You even know where to go?" Solace asked the specialist.

"Sonar pulse," Olli said shortly. "Bounces like a beauty down all these tunnels. Got a big room up ahead that isn't where we were...Hope it's a docking bay, hold, somewhere else with access to the outside." There were two bodies ahead, tumbled into one another at a conjunction of tunnels. The Scorpion stepped over them and Solace followed. The pain in her arm was only mounting, all that mechanic work having pushed the fracture past the point where she could ignore it. The injury ate into her combat readiness, chewing at the edges of her concentration.

Then Olli was moving downhill, at first scuttling, then galloping, and at last simply sliding because the corridor became a shaft. Solace was right on her metal heels, trying to slow herself because she could really do without a broken leg as well.

The Scorpion landed on three legs and two arms, one of which buckled. Kit's curled form was still held protectively close. Then, even as Solace dropped down to join them, Olli was tilting the frame to avoid a scatter of magnetic shot that drilled holes into the frame's body. Solace ducked behind her, seeing a couple of Aklu's people running past. They were rushing down a much broader thoroughfare, heading elsewhere. And in their wake came...

Aklu itself. The Unspeakable Aklu, the Razor and the Hook. The Essiel glided into view, still perched on its a-grav couch as though part of a procession and just wondering where the cheering crowds had got to. Its gilded Hiver major-domo marched to one side, two holes punched in their tragedic face but otherwise none the worse for wear. On the other side was Heremon, the Tothiat woman. She called for her boss to hurry and began shooting at the Scorpion. Olli cried out, hunched as low as she could get in the horribly exposed cockpit. With a bizarre feeling of sacrilege, Solace returned fire. She emptied the gun at the whole pack of them, knocking Heremon back with a hole in her chest, for all the good it would do.

Then she saw what was coming and yelled at Olli to get back, get down...except there was no back nor down to be had. The four-legged Hiver with the rotary cannon stalked into view and levelled their entire body at the Scorpion. Solace wasn't sure what ordnance it was packing, but surely enough to turn the frame into scrap—and her, Olli and Kit into bloody shreds.

"Shoot it!" the specialist shouted at Solace.

"No ammo!"

"Some fucking soldier!" And then a line of accelerator shot tore the Hiver apart, even as the cannon spun up. It clipped off the Hiver's leg and a slick of frantic metal insects spilled out like living intestines. Another lashing barrage came, almost invisible save for its effects. It tore away one of the gilded major-domo's arms before shearing through Aklu's couch. With a scream of overstressed machinery and failing gravity engines, the whole stately conveyance sagged to one side and ploughed into the corridor wall, tearing up the mother-of-pearl inlay and leaving a blackened gouge of fried circuitry.

A pair of Partheni in full armour ran into view, trying to shoot past the downed couch at Heremon, who they'd obviously identified as the real threat. Olli ran the Scorpion forwards, tail high, to serve the woman the same way as she had Mesmon. The Unspeakable didn't look as though it would be razoring or hooking anyone in the immediate future. Or perhaps forever, if the Partheni finished the creature off.

Then Aklu began to move.

Olli skidded to a sudden halt and began backing away. Her eyes were wide as plates, and perhaps some smidgeon of that was respect—from one enthusiast of the mechanical arts to another.

The bulk of the broken couch was left behind, as Aklu unfolded a body out of it like a deep sea monster forcing itself from a crevice. It rose up on a frame that was mostly segmented metal tentacles, black ringed with gold at the annular joints. In moments, the Essiel was borne aloft once more, the shimmer of a gravitic shield about its body. One limb lashed out like a whip and slapped down a Partheni myrmidon, hard enough to send cracks crazing across the plates of her armour.

"We *go, now*," Solace told Olli. She'd been told her sisters would hold here and draw the enemy off. She was to get herself and any other civilians out. "Do you know where they attached the *Vulture* to this ship? Your sonar good for that?"

"On it." Olli closed her eyes to prioritize the frame's artificial senses. "Fuck me, though, did you see that?" She sounded more impressed than Solace would have liked.

"I'm still seeing it." Aklu was retreating down the broader

tunnel, with Heremon and the major-domo running interference. The mass of tentacles undulated beneath and around it, finding purchase on walls and ceiling. It carried the whole assemblage along faster than Solace could have run.

"Got to get me one of those someday," Olli said. For her part, Solace was remembering the odd respect the Essiel had shown the specialist, and now perhaps she understood. *And is that what made it a renegade? The desire to move under its own power? Does that count as incurable insanity, amongst a species that's supposed to just take root?* Some weird part of her was trying to feel sympathy towards the alien gangster. A convenient anthropomorphic narrative that likely didn't get anywhere near a truth the Essiel would recognize.

Then they dropped another level into a smaller corridor, mercifully away from where Aklu had been heading, and Olli had found a hatch.

"I can't access ship's systems," she complained. "Hegemony tech is not goddamn cooperating. I've got the *Vulture* linked in, though. It's either right past here, or it's right past the next hatch along and this goes into hard vacuum. How lucky d'you feel? Hey, don't fall over on me. I'm not carrying you *and* Kit."

"I'm fine." Solace felt anything but fine, but she'd be damned if she was going to admit it. "Go for it."

Olli set the Scorpion's drill arm to the hatch and selected the smallest bit she had. She made a hole a little thicker than a human hair and there was no instant loss of pressure, no fog of water crystals as the air froze. Solace took that as a good sign, as Olli employed three separate arms to wrench the stubborn hatch open. Then finally, they were looking at the umbilical that led into the *Vulture's* drone bay.

They piled into the scavenger ship and Olli went straight for command and began working on detaching them. Solace took Kit to the Hanni's little room and decanted him into his suspension pod. He didn't seem to have anything else that resembled a bed. Then she went for the human suspension pods—and Idris.

He was still there, and Solace breathed a huge sigh of relief. However, the bed's rudimentary readouts showed his condition had only deteriorated. Now would have been a really good time for him to have woken up, ready to take control of the ship. But he looked so fragile, a hollowed-out Colonial with big ears and a thin face. Even unconscious he seemed somehow frightened—and with good cause, she supposed. He faced the void for a living and everyone thought that meant that Ints were just inured to it, naturally resistant to its horrors. Except he'd told her, way back in the Berlenhof medical camp, that it wasn't like that. They could navigate the void, but it didn't make it any less monstrous to them. It just condemned them to face it.

The ship shuddered around her and for a moment there was no internal gravity at all. Then it snapped back, wrenching her arm—and all the other bruised and abused parts of her. She heard Olli shout over the comms.

"We're away!" Then, on its heels came, "Fuck me, *everyone's* away. What's the hurry?"

"What now?" Solace forced herself not to sit down and pass out. Instead, she hustled over to the nearby drone bay, where she could raise some working screens. She found herself looking at the petalled mass of the *Broken Harvest*—although from their perspective it was upside down. The *Vulture's* instruments had caught the *Corday* as it sped off, and Solace hoped her sisters had all made it out alive with Kris and Trine. Another ship was underway further out—a blocky Colonial wedge a little bigger than the *Vulture God*. She enlarged the image to see it was covered in arcane-looking patterns in gold, red and purple—marking it as Sathiel and company making good their escape. Then she saw what Olli must have spotted, which had triggered the exodus. The *Harvest*'s gravitic drives were powering up, reaching for unspace.

"We're too close!" she said, as Olli did her best to haul them as far from the bigger ship as possible.

"Good luck to you, you bastard," came Olli's voice. "We are going to have trouble with the ol' Unspeakable again, you realize that?"

"Yes," Solace agreed tightly.

"But still..." Olli went on, then the *Vulture*'s instruments froze briefly, refusing to process the space around them in any meaningful way. Perhaps they were throwing up major philosophical objections to the universe bending out of shape. Then they unlocked, reporting that the *Broken Harvest* had vanished itself away.

In its wake, the *Corday* was hailing them. Before Olli could create a major diplomatic incident and demand Kris's return, Solace patched into their comms from the drone bay.

"*Corday* to *Vulture* and Myrmidon Executor Solace," came the crisp voice of one of her sisters. "Myrmidon Executor Grace speaking. We are for the *Heaven's Sword*. Follow us in. Welcome home, sister."

On another channel, one that excluded the *Corday*, Olli's voice came in calm and flat. "It's like that, is it? And I bet you're already in your shiny tin suit with that hole-maker in your hands, right?"

"That would have been a good idea." The thought of getting into her armour seemed so logistically exhausting that Solace found herself swaying. "What's your plan, Olli? Idris needs help. Kit needs help. I know absolutely nothing about Hanni med. My people can help. And do you really trust Hugh anymore?"

She'd expected a barrage of expletives, but Olli was quiet, thinking, the channel still open between them. "I can see you now," she said at last. "You really haven't tooled up, have you, you dumbass? I could just open the hatch on you. You're practically standing on it."

"I appreciate that I'm not making the best tactical decisions at the moment," Solace said.

Olli made a disgusted sound. "I wouldn't just abandon Kris to your lot, would I?" But there was less venom in her tone than her words might have suggested. "Tell the executioner we're on our way to the scaffold."

Solace wanted to correct her: *Executor, one who does. It's not about killing people.* But "*does*" implied a wide remit, and killing was in there somewhere. Olli wasn't going to let her off that hook so easily.

"*Vulture* to *Corday*," she told the other ship. "Lead on, sister. We'll follow."

26.

Idris

In Idris's memories, the Architect died. And in dying, its final energies lashed out across space. The gravitic convulsion whiplashed through the *Heaven's Sword*, shattering bulkheads, opening compartments to space, rupturing its gravitic drive. The colossal mass loom—which had done so much damage— was caught as it prepared for another salvo, the frustrated energy it had harvested from unspace set catastrophically free. Then the front third of the ship was smeared into a spray of fragments, each worked into a filigreed caltrop as unique as a snowflake. Abruptly, the ship was dying, dealt a single all-consuming blow its shielding had been unable to deflect.

Idris's mind was ripped from the dying Architect and he had a moment of utter revelation. Infinite clarity where the universe extended away from him, forever, and he was so insignificant that he lost himself in the midst of it.

Even as Solace pulled him away he could still feel the Architect's mind, the last dregs of it, surrendering to oblivion. Did it call out to its fellows? He felt that it did. Not to whip up vengeance or summon help, but just so that they knew. So that the gargantuan world-breaker did not die alone. He lost consciousness too when it finally let go, the spark of it winking out like the extinction of a star.

When he woke, Solace was holding his hand still. Or, in retrospect, again. Because several days had passed, and presumably she hadn't just been glued to his side like someone's pining pet. But she'd stayed there, this random Partheni soldier who'd been told to look after him. All around them the beds had stretched away, a camp of the injured and dying too big to station in orbit. The shockwave of the Architect's death had crippled half the fleet and ruptured a dozen orbitals too. The sheer fallout of their triumph had bred more wounded than the actual battle. Architects didn't normally leave many injured in their wake.

"Hi," he croaked and squeezed her hand. She must have been half dozing herself because she jumped and yelped. Then she stared down at him, a slow smile spreading across her face.

They were in the camp together for two weeks. Solace was fully recovered long before he was, but there just weren't enough ships to take the wounded away. Of the pride of the Partheni, only the *Ascending Mother* still existed as anything other than scrap, and she was already overcapacity with survivors from the *Cataphracta* and *Heaven's Sword*. More vessels were on the way but, until they arrived, everyone had more leisure time than the war had ever allowed. Idris even found himself forgotten by the Intervention Program for a blessed while. So he became an honorary Partheni, playing Landstep and Go and Two Worlds with Solace and her sisters. He lay beside her at night, tucked into the warmth of her body, just two veterans given a moment of peace.

*

He opened his eyes. Here. Now. She was still holding his hand. She hadn't really aged since Berlenhof, but then neither had he, for other reasons. The only change was the infirmary, which was a big open room in Partheni blue and grey. For a nasty moment, he thought this was still his memories bleeding into one another, because the insignia on the wall was the familiar winged blade of the *Heaven's Sword*, and that ship had very definitely *not* survived the Battle of Berlenhof. Except now he recalled they'd just reused the name, honouring the fallen by giving it to the next ship of the same class to come out of the yards. *Heaven's Sword II*, then. And, for some reason, he was aboard it.

"Hi," he croaked, and just like before Solace jumped. She looked about as beaten-up as last time, too. Badly bruised and with a thin medical sleeve over one arm.

"Medic!" she snapped. "He's awake!" She kept hold of his hand, though. And again he felt it was as much for her benefit as his.

The doctor who hurried over wasn't Partheni—a lean, hawk-faced man in white, his hollow cheeks scruffy with salt-and-pepper stubble. His clothes looked Hugh-issue, something governmental.

"Menheer Telemmier," he said, his voice severe. "Your readings are still slightly outside what I'm comfortable with. I'd advise you not to think too hard about anything—but it's probably unavoidable, under the circumstances." He seemed somehow distant, dismissive, as though dealing with a commodity not a person.

Idris was about to thank him when the clothes and manner threw up an unpleasant suggestion. "You're Liaison Board, aren't you?" The body that had taken over from the old

Intervention Program when Hugh decided it needed a corps of Peacetime Ints and didn't much care about how it got them.

The doctor stared at him with faint outrage. Maybe he wasn't used to being addressed by experimental subjects. Solace squeezed his hand again.

"We had to reach out to them," she said flatly. "Who else knew Int neurology?"

"So...what does it mean?" Idris asked weakly, still eyeballing the doctor. "We're on one of your ships but there's... a Hugh medical team or...?"

"Not just a medical team," she confirmed. "Because you and the others are here, and Trine and the regalia, that means *everyone's* here. Hugh diplomats, Hegemonic cult, everyone."

"Aklu?"

"Well, not quite everyone, then," she admitted. "Thankfully. Look, people are going to want to talk to you. If you're up to it?"

"I want to talk to people. Let's have all the people. Let's just get this over with."

"Idris—"

"Thank you."

She blinked. "What?"

"For sticking with me. Then and now." He closed his eyes. "We're over Berlenhof, right? That was where I was trying to get us. That was the only landmark...Because of what we did back in the war. Well good. Let's get it done. Let's open the diplomatic bag."

Solace went to pass that on. But of course, the united diplomatic staffs of the major galactic powers weren't going to assemble at Idris's personal request. So that left him in the infirmary, sampling the Partheni a-grav, which always seemed a hair stronger than Colonial standard.

"The others will want to know you're awake," Solace said when she came back. "Kris has been frantic."

"What happened, exactly?" He was asking Solace, but the Liaison Board doctor was suddenly at his elbow, running a rod-like instrument over his head like a magician.

"You suffered a recursive loop from too many subordinate layers," the man told him. "How many sequential jumps, precisely?"

"Lost count. I was being hunted." Idris glared mulishly at the man.

"The sensation of a predatory presence is entirely the human mind's reaction to the peculiar properties of unspace," the doctor told him. "The modern literature is fully in agreement."

"That's what you tell your convicts is it? Before you screw with their brains?" Idris asked, smiling pleasantly. "I was being hunted by an Ogdru navigator. They can track a mind through unspace. Who knew?"

"That is *entirely* impossible," the doctor told him, spreading condescension like a rich man with butter.

"You'd better hope we don't really end up in a war, because we're so screwed with people like you in charge." Idris was maintaining his smile, though he felt it was tearing at the edges.

That saw off the doctor, but not Solace's judging expression.

"They *did* bring you back," she pointed out. "I don't even know what a recursive subordinate loop layer is."

"Neither do I," Idris admitted. "I think they imported all the long words after my time. He blinked at her. "You haven't been sitting there all this time, have you?"

"Sometimes it was Olli. Sometimes Kris. Kit's been in a tank most of this time, but he was on his feet today. Came round to look at you. So there's a Hanni mercenary-surgeon on board too, by the way. On the Parthenon's tab, all of this, in case you were wondering."

"Well, I hope they're not saving my friends' lives just to bribe me." He smiled weakly, but it was far more genuine than what he'd offered the doctor. Solace's expression, though, told him that might be exactly what was happening here. And that the Partheni's offer was going to come up sooner rather than later—probably delivered direct from her superiors.

She went off to get him something to eat and fetch the others. In her absence, he tried to work out how he felt about her. It was about time he did. After all, he'd woken up precisely twice in the last six decades and she'd been there both times. Had to mean something. It wasn't as though he'd fallen madly in love with the beautiful warrior angel, like some mediotype. But they'd been forged in that same thirty minutes of fire, and she'd got him out. They'd lived when so many hadn't. And when she'd come back into his life, even with her ulterior motive, he'd felt *something*. Perhaps she had too. He didn't know what to do with any of it. His life hadn't exactly equipped him for this kind of thing.

As he lay there, introspecting, a squad of soldiers walked into the infirmary. These weren't Partheni but Colonial navy men. He tensed, expecting Mordant House, the Liaison Board, some kind of trouble. Seeing who it was, though, he blinked, mouth suddenly dry.

"Hi, Big Sis."

Not his actual sister of course. She'd died in the Polyaspora when he was very small indeed. But all of that first class out of the Intermediary Program had ended up using that nickname. She was the one woman who'd gone ahead of them, the original, the proof of concept. Xavienne Torino, known to the post-war Colonies as Saint Xavienne.

She was a few years his senior. At the time of the "Miracle at Forthbridge" she'd been fifteen, just a barefoot girl on the freighter *Samark*. She'd faced up to an Architect and sent it away, saved her ship, saved a planet. Saved humanity because suddenly there was *hope*. Idris had first met her when the Intermediary Program reached the human subject stage, eight years later. This was after the scientific establishment had finally accepted that Xavienne's mind really *did* interact with unspace in unique ways. Then they'd taken over three hundred volunteers like Idris and killed ninety per cent of them trying to replicate the effect. Nobody had stopped them. Idris didn't even hold it against them. The times had been desperate; each Architect attack killed millions at a stroke. And the experiment had worked.

She was seventy years old now, he reckoned, give or take. And unlike him, she'd aged. Seventy was old for a Colonial. Most spacers and frontier locals wouldn't look as healthy or whole by that age, especially those who'd grown up on the refugee transports. Idris remembered her toughing it out with everyone else during the war: a thin, dark woman in outsize military surplus and cheap printed sandals, eyes huge and bright in her lean face. She'd been everyone on the Program's big sister—the only person in all the universe a budding Int could go to with their fears. She'd wept for the dead, like they all had. Yet she'd gone on working, nobody harder. Then, after the war, everyone had wanted to know her story; she'd been the public face of victory. People had her on posters, medallions, mass-produced commemorative plates that somehow reproduced her likeness without any of that starveling look about the eyes. Eventually she went into seclusion, finding her own private retreat away from the supplicants and the pilgrims and the occasional death threats. Idris wondered if the Parthenon had ever dared to woo her. Though surely they couldn't bring their match to *that* powder keg, not unless they really were serious about a war with Hugh.

And here she was, on a Partheni battleship no less. But would her military escort really be enough? Would it stop some of the local high-ups considering just how much they wanted their own Intermediaries right now...?

"Idris." She sat where Solace had been, lowering herself carefully.

"What are you even...? I mean, it's so good to see you, but..." He hadn't ever thought he would see her again, not once the war was done. Idris Telemmier had just wanted to disappear.

"They needed this old brain again." Her face was lined, a map of all the triumphs and cares that had brought her this far. The unruly explosion of curly hair he remembered was grey-white now. The patterned robe she wore wasn't from a printer. Someone's hands had made that, and serious money had paid for it. He felt a stab of vicarious pleasure that she'd done well for herself, over those past years. If anyone deserved it, it was Saint Xavienne.

"The Partheni asked for you?"

"Doctor Justinian did," she corrected. "The Liaison Board don't deal with 'originals' these days. They needed to reference my scans as a baseline, and so I came out of retirement one more time."

"You talk to the Board much?" He almost asked: *Do you know what they're doing, in your name?* But that wouldn't be fair.

"As little as possible. But for one of my little brothers... You're almost the only one left, you know that? Demi Ulo's with the Cartography Corps still, and Chassan's on Berlenhof with Hugh. But they're old, both of them, just like me. You'll outlive all of us... unless you keep pulling stunts like that."

"No promises."

She regarded him then, expecting something and seeing he plainly didn't know what. At last she said, "You don't have any message for me?"

"For you?" He frowned. "I didn't even know I was going to run into you. What—?"

"I was told... At the planetside elevator link, when we were waiting for the car. An old friend turned up, said you'd have something to say."

"I have no idea what you mean," he confessed. "I... Old friend? But not one of the 'family'?"

She nodded, eyes flicking to her escort.

He made a little dumbshow for her, two hands up, one with fingers spread, one making a "talk-talk" gesture with fingers and thumb. A mime for an alien of a particular shape. *Ash, the Harbinger.*

Xavienne's nod was all he needed. Abruptly his fragile sense of wellbeing was entirely gone. His hallucination of the Harbinger in unspace had been quite enough. He didn't want Ash, of all things, to be paying him any heed. *Just want to disappear, get back into space, move on before anyone catches up with me.* Except events had well and truly headed him off at the pass, and here he was.

"Nothing you haven't already heard," he told her, and then there was a babble of voices from outside—he recognized Olli's strident tones—and Xavienne stood suddenly.

"We'll talk again," she said. "*Think*, Idris. There must be something." Then she was gone, and her escort with her, just before the others piled in. Idris caught Kris looking back as though to say, *Wasn't that...?* But the rest were more concerned with making sure their navigator was in full working order.

"Well, look at you. Awake and everything." Olli was in a motorized wheelchair, presumably of Partheni issue. He expected there'd been a fight about whether or not she could walk around in the Scorpion. The very thought was exhausting. Idris was glad he'd been dying right then.

The others looked well. Kris was beaming from ear to ear. Kittering's arm-screens were advertising what looked like some kind of Hanni pharmaceutical, so possibly he'd cut a deal with his physician. Solace hung back and let them have their moment, shifting aside to let Trine duck in too.

Idris nodded at the academic. "I'd have thought you'd have abandoned us by now."

"We've putting on a unified front," Kris said firmly. "Trine, us. I think even Solace is being coy with her bosses." Snickering at the Partheni's expression. "We were waiting for you and Kit to wake up, so we've said just about nothing."

"We've still got the ... the *things*?" Idris asked, wide-eyed.

"Ah, no, not exactly. The Partheni have the *things*." Kris shot a look at Trine.

"What precisely was I supposed to do?" the archaeologist demanded tartly. "They knew what I was carrying. I couldn't just pretend to have lost them down the back of my internal backups, could I?"

"Well they're not our problem then," Idris said, feeling weirdly relieved. "Was there any money in it?"

"Now we have Kit back we are damn well going to try for it," Kris assured him. "If for no other reason than the *Vulture* needs fixing up. But first ... Solace was saying something about a hearing?"

"A hearing?" Idris looked blankly at her, then at the Partheni beyond. "That wasn't what I ...?"

"Not a disciplinary or something criminal, but ..." Solace spread her hands. "A lot's happened. Everyone wants to hear from all of you, and they want to hear it together. Because right now, there's not a lot of trust going round. So, yes. A hearing. You speak, they hear. And then you can get paid and ... go."

She'll stay, of course, because she's a good soldier. Idris was surprised at the stab of unhappiness he felt at that—and when he met Solace's eyes, he reckoned she shared it. She'd liked being a freelance spacer. There was even an off-chance she'd liked meeting up with him again. The universe was big enough for such slender possibilities. He wondered if she'd go back on ice now, or if they'd have some other mission for her. *Get paid and go, remember. No more war work messing with your head.* Except it seemed peace work could do that just as well. He realized he'd been staring at Solace for long enough that everyone was shifting awkwardly.

"Someone tell me what's happened, then," he said. "Apparently I jumped us to Berlenhof but I get the impression all hell broke loose soon after that."

"Ah, well," and Kris had obviously prepared quite the spiel for this very occasion. Yet even as she put her hands behind her back and stepped forward in her best leading counsel stance, a Partheni officer turned up at the door.

"Myrmidon Executor," she addressed Solace. "Pret?"

"Pret, Mother." Solace turned wide eyes on the others. "They're ready for us."

"They can wait," Olli growled.

"'*They*' are humanity's combined diplomatic staff," Kris pointed out. "Once you've cat-herded them into one room, you can't expect them to just twiddle their expensive thumbs. Idris, how are you doing?"

He swung his legs over the side of the bed, took to his feet and would have gone face first into the floor if Kris hadn't caught him.

"They got another of those chairs?" he asked Olli.

*

"That's Monitor Superior Tact," Kris identified for him, pointing out a severe-looking older Partheni. "Don't you love their names, by the way? Sounds like they're laughing behind your back half the time, doesn't it?" Although she was grinning when she said it.

"Kris, please." Idris said. He found the lights in the big

circular chamber over-bright. He was sitting lopsided in the motorized chair, leaning on one arm. He hadn't been able to drive it properly, juddering and scraping the walls. The frustration it had engendered in him had been out of all proportion to the inconvenience. He was a navigator of starships. A goddamn wheelchair shouldn't be beyond him. Instead he'd ground and rammed and drifted while Olli had surged on ahead with enviable skill. Now they were here, the lot of them, taking up one third of this conference chamber. The other thirds were for the Parthenon and the Colonies respectively.

"Okay," Kris said. "So Tact is a diplomat. And if she's taking the lead, that tells you how they're playing it . . . I think the woman behind her is Fleet Exemplar Hope."

Hope looked like Tact's younger sister, and not much like her name. If Idris had been asked, he'd have guessed at "Suspicion." There were half a dozen other Partheni behind them, younger, all with variations on the same features. The same ashy-coloured skin and strong cheekbones, a factory-line beauty made uncanny by repetition. Kris didn't have names for them, just adding, "Hope's a full-on fighter—but you'd expect her to be present, given we're on her ship. Tact is Aspirat, dirty tricks and espionage. And, from the look I caught, I reckon she's Solace's boss."

Idris nodded tiredly.

"Now over there . . . that's Lucef Borodin. He's out of the High Diplomatic Service Office, here on Berlenhof." Kris was indicating Tact's opposite number. Borodin was stocky, greying, a match for Tact in age, but with twenty centimetres on her in height and thirty kilograms in weight. He had a flat, open face and had turned to smile at the lean woman behind him. The smile was still in place when he faced forward again, but it didn't reach anywhere near his eyes.

"Lady at his back is Elphine Stoel. She's supposed to be DipSO too, but I think she's really Threat Analysis. You know, the sort Hugh keeps around to predict what the other big powers might do next." Stoel was regarding the Partheni with a fixed intensity. A half-dozen younger diplomats were at her back in turn, along with a familiar face—Havaer Mundy of the Intervention Board, looking like his wife had left him.

"One of the others is probably covert Mordant House too," Kris noted. "Mundy's here because he's met us, has a handle on us maybe. And I guess you know Herself there, beside him."

Saint Xavienne, of course, watching Idris and nobody else. He managed a faint nod to her.

"You'll note no military from Hugh, just civvies," Kris added.

"That good?"

"Interesting question. You might think yes, but Borodin's out of Magda. So though he's not exactly shilling for the Nativists, maybe he's skewed that way? Also, maybe *not* sending a soldier to the Parthenon is a kind of veiled insult or something? I don't know."

"Some help you are."

"That's the spirit."

"Why are we even here?"

Before Kris could answer that, Monitor Superior Tact finished listening to one of her subordinates and opened proceedings. "Menheer Borodin, thank you for joining us." She directed a bright smile across the room at the Colonials.

"I trust our reception has been to your satisfaction."

"Impeccable as always," Borodin countered warmly. Nobody was looking at the *Vulture* crew. Yet. "And I appreciate your efficiency in setting this meeting. I'm glad the Parthenon are treating this matter as seriously as we are."

Idris gave Kris an odd look. "But they didn't have much choice, surely? Now they know the Architects are back..." But Kris was listening intently, a slight frown on her face.

"Perhaps we could commence with the *Oumaru* wreck and its location, as it remains unaccounted for?" Tact proposed. "As per your request, we've left any questions for the *Vulture God*'s crew to this meeting." *Except for debriefing Solace*, Idris guessed. Because surely they'd done *that*. Had Solace noted where they'd ditched the freighter's corpse?

"Actually," Borodin put in, sounding apologetic. "I have some preliminary business we need to clear up. Specifically, Hugh requires that the Parthenon repatriates our citizens currently held aboard this vessel."

Kris twitched, and Olli leant towards her, demanding, "That us?" in a whisper that could probably be heard across the room.

"Menheer Borodin..." Tact said flatly.

"The Council understands *entirely* the circumstances under which they came into your hands," Borodin said, conciliatory now, spreading his hands a little. "We appreciate you letting our medical personnel aboard to give urgent care where required. But a swift repatriation really is necessary now. No doubt you've seen the tensions we're facing planetside—and indeed across the human sphere. We very much want to avoid suggestions from certain elements that anything like a hostage situation is brewing up here." Again that reasonable smile, conveying I-too-can't-believe-we-have-to-deal-with-this-nonsense.

"*Your* citizens…?" Tact echoed, profoundly unimpressed, and Kris murmured, "Welp, this has gone some places fast."

"Olian Timo, Keristina Soolin Almier and Idris Telemmier." Borodin was not looking at the crew, as though their names existed only as a bureaucratic exercise. "I am aware there is a Hannilambra aboard, operating under Accredited Commercial Traveller status. There is also a Delegate registered to the Second Assembly. They or their governments will need to make separate arrangements."

Tact leant back a little. "And the Hegemonic regalia…?"

"Obviously custody of the regalia is the primary concern, for all of us. I've just been asked to deal with this bookkeeping first and foremost, which will allow us all to avoid, as I said, any suggestion of Partheni duress." Borodin nodded very seriously.

"Do we get a say?" Kris's voice vanished into the space and she looked up for the ceiling mic that apparently wasn't on. A moment later there was a loud buzz of static. The Partheni delegation twitched, almost as one. Idris guessed Olli had patched into their electronics with her implants. Must have given their electronic security department kittens.

"Why don't you try again?" the specialist said to Kris, her voice loud and clear over the speakers. "I don't think they heard you." At least someone was enjoying themselves.

"I said—" Kris started, but Tact and Borodin virtually trod on each other's words to drown them out. Idris heard, "If you'll allow me, as your representative—" from him, and "When you're called upon to speak—" from her.

"I am my own representative," Kris stated. However, the

collective diplomatic glower was too much for her and she subsided.

"We would *prefer* to leave such matters to the addendum," Tact said firmly. "Menheer, I'll be blunt. We were on the point of dispatching the regalia for analysis when your communiqué reached us. Because certain *inferences* were contained therein, concerning how such Partheni actions might be construed, we put this on hold. I had very much hoped that Hugh was here to propose cross-border scientific efforts. After all, this represents a chance for both the Parthenon and the Council of Human Interests to attain parity with the Essiel Hegemony in the field of safely trans-porting Originator relics. Delegate Trine has already volunteered to head up this research."

"That research is, of course, the main event," Borodin agreed smoothly. "But our people are being held against their will on a military vessel. Until this is resolved, we cannot be expected to enter such delicate negotiations."

"Ah crap," Idris said, low as he could to avoid it being picked up. "This is about *me*, isn't it. Me and the damn Int Program."

"Well I hope to fuck so," Olli said. And either the Parthenon had locked her out, or she'd flicked the speakers off herself. "Because I don't want any government caring this much about where the fuck *I* end up."

"So, what do you want?" Kris asked him.

"What? *Me?*" Idris looked at her, at Kittering's array of amber eyes and Olli's exasperated face. Past them, he could see Solace's unhappy expression and the benevolent beam of Trine's projected visage.

"You want to go to Berlenhof planetside, or stay with the angels? Or get on the *Vulture*—see if we can just take off and leave them bickering?" Kris shrugged. "I'm your lawyer. Tell me what you want and I'll see what I can throw together."

"This is insane," Idris whispered. "Why is this even happening?"

"Seriously, Idris," Kris pressed. "Just make the call."

"No, look." Idris tried to stand up, felt a wave of nausea and sat back down. "Olli, give me a voice, please." That last word rang out across the room, and suddenly everyone was looking at him.

"Look—" he started, as Borodin shook his head urgently.

"I am sure we all appreciate, niceties of diplomatic language aside, just what Menheer Telemmier represents," the man spoke over him. "I'll be frank, shall I?"

"No, look—" Idris tried again.

"Perhaps you should," Tact agreed, seamlessly squeezing him out of the conversation. Idris wondered wildly whether the Parthenon actually *had* a Monitor Frank somewhere in its ranks.

"The Council cannot contemplate one of its Intermediaries, a veteran of the original Board, being in the Parthenon's hands," Borodin set out. "I'm sure you'll deny that you've taken samples of Menheer Telemmier's genetic material— and we can play the usual games over just what has and hasn't been done. But our Intermediary has to be repatriated immediately."

"Wow," Olli remarked. "Guess it's just as well it's *her* who's called Tact, right?"

All these years, Idris thought numbly, *thinking I was out from under*. But now he was here, over Berlenhof, in the spotlight. He was here because of the damned *Oumaru* and suddenly *everyone* cared what he did. In the worst way possible.

He could see that a quiet life was no longer an option, not anymore, perhaps not ever. Events had made him a commodity for governments to wrestle over. And abruptly he couldn't handle it, couldn't listen to it.

"You're both *crazy!*" he shouted, his voice battering about the room from the speakers. "You know what happened to the *Oumaru*! The damn *Architects* are back, and *this* is what you're arguing about?"

There was a profoundly awkward silence. But he didn't see the shame he'd hoped to provoke. If anything, he sensed they were embarrassed for *him*. For his outburst.

"What?" he asked awkwardly.

"Er... Trine did their thing," Olli put in, her own voice starting too loud then dropping as she fought the Partheni electronics. "They said the *Oumaru* wasn't, ah... wasn't Architects. That old boy, the cultist, he faked it. He wanted to scare people into joining the Hegemony... right?"

Idris looked to Trine, wide-eyed. "Say what now?" he managed, very aware that a roomful of diplomats were impatient to get on with their agenda.

"This is the startling truth of the matter, my old friend and co-credulator," Trine confirmed, with appallingly inappropriate cheer. "A hoax all along! Who, as they say, would have thunk?"

Idris looked across the room until he met Xavienne's curious gaze. He felt sick, physically sick. *Something to tell me,* she said, and he'd thought she must already know. Of course Xavienne knew all about the Architect threat. *Everyone* knew. The evidence had been mediotyped across the whole Human Sphere and beyond.

Except it had been faked. But that fakery didn't change the truth.

"But, no, listen," he said hoarsely. "*Listen* to me. That's not it, not at all. They really *are* back. The Architects are moving out there. I felt them, in unspace, like it was the war. It's all happening again."

27.

Havaer

Panic. Screaming. Entreaties to a divinity or imprecations against an uncaring universe. Was that what Telemmier had been expecting? If so, he was going to be disappointed. Although if he'd been hoping for dumbfounded silence, at least he had that.

Havaer could see that the *Vulture God*'s crew had also been caught on the hop. They were goggling at their navigator, and the lawyer, Almier, was whispering something. Surely something like, *No, seriously, what?*

"Menheer Telemmier." Monitor Superior Tact recovered first. "Perhaps you would like to elaborate?"

"They're *back*. They were there, in unspace." Idris waved his hands, clutching at something that Colvul had no good words for. "I *felt* them."

"It's understandable that Architects were on your mind, given what you found," said Borodin sympathetically. "You survived the war, we understand that. But we have Delegate Trine's report on the *Oumaru*, and our own technicians concur with their interpretation of the data. It was a deftly managed hoax."

"It's true, Idris," Olian Timo added. She looked disgruntled about having to agree with Borodin, or perhaps with anyone. "That son of a bitch said he'd done it. All for the greater good or some bollocks, you know how they talk."

Idris was holding hard to the arms of his chair, shaking. *That's some powerful PTSD*, Mundy thought. *God, someone should just get him out of here.*

"You. Don't. Understand," he said. Each word forced out between clenched teeth. "In unspace, when I was dodging the *Broken Harvest*, I had to go so deep, to escape. I could feel their pilot's mind hunting me. Like a beast." He shuddered. "And...I'd gone so far to get away, cut off from every Throughway." He swallowed, hard. "And they were there, moving in the deep, *coming back*. Like a wave across the universe."

"Menheer Telemmier, perhaps you should collect your thoughts in...appropriate quarters," Tact said. Not "in the infirmary," which Mundy reckoned was what got cut off. *Why make the poor bastard sound any more mad than he already is?*

"Our requirements regarding our citizens have not changed," Borodin said flatly. "Monitor, we know how convenient it would be, if some fiction of the Architects' return spread across the Colonies. Convenient for the Hegemonic cult, yes, but also for the Parthenon."

"Are you accusing us of having any hand in this hoax?"

"No, emphatically no," Borodin said, dismissing her suggestion. "However, I know full well that I'd be making what hay I could out of it, if it helped me. A wave of panic about the Architects would give you a great deal of leverage at the table. The warrior angels here to protect us all, isn't that right? We'll debrief Telemmier back on Berlenhof and share the results with you."

"Appropriately redacted, of course," Tact noted.

"Of course."

Havaer watched the *Vulture God* crew arguing inaudibly, because they'd turned their mic off again. Seeing the utter certainty on the Int's face, he felt a worm of worry inside him. Obviously Lucef Borodin was walking the appropriate party line, but...

Tact had leant back to listen to the officer behind her and now she nodded sharply. "Your solution is unacceptable," she told Borodin. "The stakes have just become too high to simply let this crew vanish into Hugh custody."

"With all respect to Menheer Telemmier," Borodin said patiently, "The stakes have not changed at all—"

"Listen to me," the Intermediary burst in again, now twice as loud because their tech was having fun with the sound system. "Both of you...Why are you still having this conversation?"

"Menheer Telemmier, please," Borodin said, exasperated. "I am a representative of your government attempting to free you from the hands of a hos—of a foreign power. Will you just—"

"What if we don't want to go?" Almier put in.

Havaer Mundy was close enough to see Borodin tense in anger, and marvelled at how little of it made its way into his voice. "Mesdam Almier, the legal implications of such a... defection are rather complex. You and your fellows were involved in a series of criminal actions aboard Lung-Crow station, followed by an act of piracy over Tarekuma. You are now in possession of sensitive information and resources at a time of diplomatic crisis. And you are suggesting you might join a military rival—"

"Lung-Crow was under Hegemonic jurisdiction at all relevant times," Almier continued. "Good luck bringing the Broken Harvest to the dock to give evidence on how we got *our* ship back from *them*. And I will fight you in any court you care to name about our right to freedom of association and movement, Menheer Borodin. But we are not defecting to the Parthenon. Nor are we meekly going to accompany you, either. Mostly because Idris thinks you'll give him to the Liaison Board and he really doesn't want to have anything to do with 'those butchers.'"

"I appreciate that courtroom theatrics are your stock in trade," Borodin crowbarred in, "but you appear to have reasoned yourself into a corner. So you're not going with us, or them. What's next?"

"We are placing ourselves in the neutral hands of the Hiver Assembly," Almier declared brightly. "Specifically, as represented by Delegate Trine. For the time being we'll sit in our ship. And our ship can sit right here in the bay of the *Heaven's Sword*. Unless you'd rather we took the *Vulture God* to Berlenhof's Hiver diplomatic orbital? If we remain here, under Trine's auspices, we all know it's basically a fiction to keep us out of anyone's hands. Whereas if we actually go to the Hiver embassy, the Hivers are likely to have questions, don't you think? So I suggest you allow us to stay here and talk to whoever we want. You can both keep an eye on us that way—to make sure the other party doesn't just bundle us in a bag and cart us off, see right?"

Havaer was working hard to keep a straight face. Borodin and Tact were just staring. Tact recovered first.

"Well, then. As a temporary measure that will be acceptable."

There was more but Havaer was distracted by Telemmier, as the man stared across the room at him. *At me? Man, this is out of my hands...* But Havaer wasn't the focus of Telemmier's gaze. Saint Xavienne was sitting beside him, and Havaer saw she was staring right back. Some communication passed between the Intermediaries, some *I told you so* from one Int to the mother of them all. And she looked ten years older for it, as though she might collapse at any moment. The diplomats were still wrangling, but it was more for form's sake than anything else now, and at least they had a plan to follow.

Minutes after they had filed out of the room, Havaer was talking to Mordant House about the urgent need for him to go see the new asylum seekers.

*

Getting to visit them involved the usual fun and games, but Havaer had all the right Hugh clearances. Both sets of guards outside the *Vulture God* still stared at him, though. He expected he cut an odd figure in his scarecrow way, but he reckoned he'd do better than Borodin, in his expensively tailored suit. That would get right up the nose of any spacer, and this lot were punchier than most.

He was met by Kittering, the Hannilambra—because why not bring yet another citizenry into play? The alien's shield arms bore screens displaying a complex pattern of silver lines on black.

"What's that?" Havaer couldn't help but ask.

"Behold the flag of the Hiver Assembly!" the Hanni's translator declared proudly.

Havaer suspected they were making a fool of him. "When did they get one, exactly?"

"For purpose of entering into contract with my kinsmen. Heraldry is always appreciated." Kittering made a show of examining Havaer's unornamented black clothes. "Eyes are wasted on humans sometimes."

"I consider myself properly told," Havaer said. "Look, you probably think I'm here to put the screws on for Mordant House? Offer you something that serves Hugh and fucks the Partheni, that kind of thing?"

"All the lights!" Kittering exclaimed. The figure of speech was opaque but the artificial tone suggested agreement. And not friendly agreement.

"I just want to talk to Telemmier," Havaer said. "I'm actually not part of the official delegation. I'm following a hunch…" It struck him that his own figure of speech might not translate well, to a species without shoulders. "Don't have to meet him alone. Everyone's invited. I have one question, really. That's all it is."

Soon after, he found himself in the *Vulture God*'s drone bay, perhaps the only room big enough to contain them all. The actual drones had been moved to the walls to make space, resting near a remarkable mess of disconnected wires and general mechanical gubbins. Someone had printed out a set of the cheapest plastic chairs he'd ever seen. Almier and Telemmier were sitting on two of them, side by side like they were going to give a prepared statement. She was sleekly elegant in a new gold scarf and formal suit. Telemmier still wore his drab spacer's clothes, looking small and unwell. A man at the fulcrum of events who wasn't prospering under the attention. Solace stood behind the Int's chair with her actual accelerator in her hands. She'd left off the armour, but the weapon could shoot someone three rooms away. Once again, Havaer considered himself properly told.

"I'm not an assassin, by the way," Havaer started. "I appreciate that's also what an assassin would say...but just to clear the air."

Timo entered at that point, in a damaged-looking walker frame that still had half its panels off. "You again," she observed.

"Hi."

She shook her head. "Just don't take too long. I need to work in here." Then she left, apparently not at all interested in whatever he had to say. Kittering had scrambled up onto another chair and was perched there precariously.

Havaer found a smile hard to put off. "You know, I do get to go to embassy functions now and then," he told them, lowering himself into a seat and hearing the cheap plastic creak. "I know just the sort of well-dressed backs you're trying to put out, with this sort of carnival. *Make do and mend*, right? Spacer diplomacy."

Almier sent a complicit look towards Kittering, face too deadpan. And then the Hiver, Trine, came in with a tray. The aroma of something like biscuits gusted in with them, just off enough to suggest the *Vulture's* food printer needed looking at. Trine bent low before Havaer, proffering the tray in a lattice of their chest-mounted arms.

"As I am now apparently some manner of ambassador, my honoured guest, it is only appropriate that I extend what hospitality I may," the Hiver announced. Their translucent face bore an expression of snooty disdain. "Have a cookie."

Havaer took one. "Please tell me you'll put on this same

show for Borodin and Tact. Let me have a mediotype of it, in fact. So I can watch them rupture their etiquette."

"Indubitably," Trine assured him. "Now, you'll be wanting some manner of electronic privacy?"

"Actually...this isn't even gov business, not even spy business," Havaer said. "This is just me with my police hat on, trying to tie off an investigation. Just me trying to get my report square before I hand it in and go off the case."

That had their attention. They'd only put on this act to put unwelcome visitors' noses out of joint. It was only Telemmier who wasn't enjoying their five minutes of fame.

"Go ahead..." Almier said cautiously.

"Why'd you come to Berlenhof?" he asked, flat out.

"When we met, *you* said we should come here and—" Almier began. Havaer was only looking at Telemmier but he answered her anyway.

"I *know* I said you should come here. But even when I did, I thought why the hell would you? With a whole universe at your fingertips, why would you suddenly get a dose of the law-abiding and hand yourselves in? Since when did you people do anything anyone told you to without a contract?"

"You're excluding simple patriotism?" the lawyer suggested.

"You know what? I absolutely am," he agreed. "Menheer Telemmier, was it your decision?"

"Yes." The Int was staring at his own toes.

"So tell me why. Did you decide you wanted to do the right thing? Or was it chance, even, that you ended up here?" Havaer pressed. "I want to understand."

"Berlenhof was like a beacon," came Telemmier's quiet, worn voice. "Could see it from across the universe. The grave marker of the Architect we killed here." Solace put a hand on his shoulder, and he unconsciously covered it with his own. "And we were lost, by then. Too many jumps, too far out. But that marker I could follow— What?"

Havaer had jumped to his feet. They were all staring at him, these ragged diplomats, as though *he* was the strange one.

"What is it?" Almier pressed. "Agent Mundy?"

In his mind he heard the Int's voice at the hearing, telling of the storm coming from the deeps, the great fleet of the Architects returning from the unthinkable vast places they had retreated to.

It was like a beacon...

"You've been very helpful," he managed, dry-throated. Then, from sheer force of habit, he added, "We'll be in touch."

*

He did not, in fact, return to Borodin and Stoel to help them plan their negotiation. Instead it was time to call home. Chief Laery didn't make him wait, which suggested either it was a slow day for spying or she was also having some worried thoughts about the whole business herself.

"So the Int believes his story?" she asked him.

"For what it's worth, yes. I mean we both know they do burn out, go scatty. And this one's been around as long as any, aside from Saint Xav herself. But it's not some scam they're running, that's for certain. Despite how the *Oumaru* turned out, he's absolutely convinced."

"And?"

"And Saint Xav looked like she was taking him very seriously."

"The Saint dodged her handlers recently," Laery said sourly. "But our data suggests she met with the Harbinger." She rolled her eyes. "Saints, Harbingers... Our predecessors could have been less fucking messianic with their naming conventions." At his raised eyebrows, her image waved an emaciated hand. "Forgive me, not been sleeping well since forever. It's just that Ash has been poking around, making his own enquiries into this business. I have never liked or trusted that creature." Ash had been an established appendage of the Colonial government since long before Laery was born. Mordant House's successive directors had never appreciated the ancient alien's meddling. "We don't know how it knows what it knows," she complained. "And I do not believe in magic or seeing the future."

"Nobody believed in unspace once," Havaer said. Unwisely, to judge from her expression. "Chief, I don't know the truth of it, but I don't think Telemmier's fooling around here, is all. Unscientific as it is, my gut feeling says we're in trouble." He swallowed. "How unhappy would I be if I asked about the evacuation protocols for Berlenhof?"

Laery stared at him, stony-faced. "I am glad," she said, "that this is a heavily encrypted channel. Because we couldn't have realistically evacuated ten per cent of the planet even during the war. Since which time the population has increased four-fold and nobody has their go-bag and a map to their closest evac centre. So let's not say things like that in earshot of anyone prone to panic, shall we?"

He wanted to say, "But what if...?" but she'd told him the *What If*. Simply put, there was no *What If*—any more than there had been with Earth. And, just as with Ash's warning to Earth, nobody was going to completely dismantle the heart of the Human Sphere just because of a crazy prophet. Except...

"He said Berlenhof was a beacon."

"Telemmier?"

"He said he could see it from right across unspace."

"And nobody else has noticed this?" Laery demanded.

"There aren't that many Ints. Almost none left who were at that final battle. And maybe it's like city lights obscuring the stars...you need to get further out into the countryside before you can see them clearly. Or some damn thing." Havaer grimaced. "I have bad feelings, Chief," and she nodded soberly.

*

He slept on it, or tried to. The Partheni had given over a whole student dorm to Hugh's negotiating team. There were forty beds and just a handful of occupants, but the sparse Partheni design robbed the space of any sense of luxury. *Spartan* was the appropriate term, on a variety of levels. Havaer reflected gloomily that it was the Colonies who were supposed to be poor, but Colonial spaces were never plain. If you were rich you showed it through having stuff that people could see. If you were poor, everything was patched and home-made and botched together.

Being taller than the average Partheni, he ended up sleeping folded up in a weird position, so that something hidden down the side of the plastic mattress jabbed at his side. It turned out to be a mediotype nib, just a thumb-sized datastore. Filled with hopes of discovering Partheni secrets, he cracked it open, only to find it was crammed with episodes of some mediotype. It was prose and animation and voice drama, all about

455

some girl from the Colonies during the war. She was living on a ship, learning to be a pilot. But mostly she was arguing with rivals and having unrequited crushes on classmates of both genders. It was possibly the least historically accurate thing Havaer had ever seen. He ended up watching it for three hours solid, feeling a weird connection to whatever Partheni naval student's life he'd just invaded by finding her stash of cod-Colonial drama. And then he heard the alarms; his comms alerts lit up like fireworks and he knew *it* had happened.

Architects over Berlenhof? He wouldn't have been at all surprised, but what had actually happened was the first ships had come in from Far Lux.

Far Lux?

The small packet runners had fled the system first, bringing urgent requests for emergency refugee facilities. And there were many more ships on the way—every ship the mining colony could get into space, and several that shouldn't have tried it. And Far Lux had quite the population these days.

An Architect had come out of unspace in the Far Lux system and begun cruising towards the defenceless colony planet. People had crammed every ship they could find. Far more had been left behind to watch that vast crystal moon approach, then witness the end of it all.

But why Far Lux? Despite Telemmier's dire warnings about Berlenhof being a beacon, it was some far-flung colony making history. It was insignificant, except for one thing. Far Lux was where the peace had happened, where humanity's Intermediaries had finally reached out and touched the universe's destructive gods. Three Intermediaries—and one had been Idris Telemmier.

Idris

They had spread the Ints wide, after Berlenhof, to try and protect the Human Sphere. The battle had at least proved that Intermediaries could affect the Architects' movements. Even slowing an attack would mean thousands more evacuated. And the Intermediary Program itself was constantly brainstorming, thinking up strategies, welcoming new ideas... Saint Xavienne, her Ints and the Program's researchers were working from first principles, assembling a patchwork science of suppositions and second guesses. Xavienne was even discussing the unthinkable—making contact with their enemy. Idris had no idea if this was a Colonial initiative or if she was off on her own. It wasn't as if anyone was qualified to oversee her. And her Ints would have done anything for her. After all, they had been born from pain and madness with her as their midwife.

And Idris had gone to Far Lux along with Olumu Garrison and Tess Mangolign. And if their Partheni captain had rankled a little at letting these three Colonials take turns in the pilot's chair, dragging her vessel hither and yon across the Human Sphere, well, that was tinted with the superstitious awe people had back then for the Ints.

One thing Xavienne had wanted was an early warning system. Ints were sensitive to the impending arrival of an Architect. Idris remembered that from Berlenhof. He believed you could tell where they were going to arrive, plenty of Ints did, although the actual hit rate of their predictions was too low to be useful. Still, his instincts had brought the three of them to the small mining colony in the little Partheni runner *Yennenga*. They'd found it peaceful, going about its business.

Idris had half felt that the appearance of the *Yennenga* in their skies should have been like a comet in the olden times, chaos and panic and portents of the end of days.

And the Ints had delivered their warning, but the frightened Colonials had just been angry at the false alarm. They'd chewed out the scaremongering Ints over the comms, because what were they supposed to do? Just pack up and leave, because three crazy people told them it was the end of the world?

Then all three Ints had gone dead silent, staggering as though the ship's a-grav had faltered. Two minutes later the Architect had torn its way into the system. It tumbled out of unspace and righted itself, its million serried spines directed at the planet.

Olumu was a small, dark man, older than Idris-as-was. He'd die two years later, in space as a spacer should, when the freighter he was piloting suffered a catastrophic systems failure at the exact moment it opened a path to unspace. Tess was an angular woman, starveling-thin, half her face a tinted plastic mask because she wouldn't get her reconstructive surgery until after the war. Ints were too valuable to take out of circulation for that long. She'd join the Cartography Corps and bow out of Colonial history that way. Vanished into unspace, searching for new Throughways and planetary systems, fate unknown but not coming back.

But they would live to die later. All three of them would live, as would every soul aboard the *Yennenga*, and the entire population of Far Lux. For this was the day the war ended.

There was no fleet gathered at Far Lux that day, no valiant holding action planned to buy time for an evacuation. Everyone planetside was simply running for the ships, for the landing fields. The orbitals' personnel were clearing out already, all except for a skeleton staff who stayed at their posts to coordinate the escape effort below. Idris had thought of them as the *Yennenga* moved forwards, a solitary mote against the immensity that was descending on the planet. Bureaucrats, data-pushers, planners and accountants—they were all giving their lives to save just a few more families of miners and factory workers.

Numb, he'd felt numb then. He'd been living through the holocaust of war all his life. And he couldn't remember a single moment of security; always the Architects ridding the galaxy of humanity one world at a time. He'd spent his childhood crammed into the hold of one ship after another, his family lost long ago. Maybe they were dead, or just scattered by too many losses and too much stress. Then as soon as he was old enough, he'd gone for active service. Because what else was there? The war didn't spare civilians anyway, so why not? As soon as he'd heard about the new Intermediary Program, he'd signed up for that too. He'd been chosen due to some arcane criteria he never understood. And he'd survived it, when most volunteers hadn't. He'd been remade into something else inside his head, something not quite human. Then he'd gone to war. He'd been at Berlenhof. He'd touched the mind of the enemy.

And so it was war he wanted to bring. The three of them were a living spearhead, and they were going to stab into the brain of the oncoming Architect. What else was there? Nobody thought they'd win, not anymore. Perhaps they'd manage a nomadic existence like the Naeromathi, limping from system to system. Stripping worlds to build more ships, so they could limp some more. Or perhaps they'd be gone, like Harbinger Ash's people. No doubt there were many other races they'd never know, because they had been so thoroughly and comprehensively removed from the universe.

The Partheni captain knew they were courting death. She didn't hesitate, though. Idris and the others wanted to fly straight into the teeth of the Architect, and so they went. They were a tiny fleck of dust against that barbed landscape as it readied itself to turn Far Lux into another barren sculpture.

Idris imagined his mind like origami, *small, so small.* All the complexity of it folded down to a point, so he could drive it deep into the vastness of the Architect. They'd learned that whole expanse was the entity's mind, as well as its substance. He could feel Olumu and Tess making the same preparations. They couldn't coordinate, not quite, but they struck almost simultaneously. Their minds ranged across the outer reaches of the enemy, prying for a way in, becoming ever smaller, smaller...until they could slip their consciousnesses into the radiant labyrinth of its being. Then they could chase through the canals of its thoughts, looking for something to break, something to tear.

The voices of the Partheni crew were in his ears, reporting and receiving orders. Every slight variance within the Architect was measured and broadcast back to the planet. So that the data could travel with the refugees and get back to the Program. Because there was always another battle to prepare for, another lesson to learn. Nobody knew this would be the end.

Idris struck. His mind was a lance, driven as far as it would go into his enemy. He sought vulnerable tissue, baffled by the sheer scale of it. As well try to stab a man to death with a needle an atom wide. He clawed at it. He screamed in the halls of its brain, beat his fists against the walls of its mind, and it didn't sense him. It felt the intrusion, but didn't understand what he *was*. He was turbulence, interference, static. A bad dream. But he was nothing it recognized in any meaningful way. The Architect trembled ever so slightly as the three Intermediaries tried to break it, and just shouldered on. Then the *Yennenga* fell back as the nightmare accelerated towards Far Lux. It had singled out the system's inhabited world, as Architects always did. Because they must have their art, and their art demanded death.

No Architect ever reworked a lifeless desert world into a planet-sized sculpture. Idris knew they understood the teeming lives they snuffed out, and he hated them for it. In that moment something in him broke and he made himself big again, inside its mind. He unfolded all that careful origami, shattered that needle point, pressed himself against every wall at once, inside his mind, inside its mind... and he *pushed* outwards.

On the bridge of the *Yennenga* he'd been screaming, lying on the floor with the captain shouting for a medic. He'd been rigid, muscles wrenching at bones so that he'd ache for a solid month after. Idris's face had been awash with tears from clenched-shut eyes, blood flowed from his nose, spittle from his locked-open mouth.

And Idris had been there. With *it*. All that maze of complexity within the Architect had focused, in that moment, into a single consciousness. This was an entity with the power to reshape worlds, and he had its attention. Not a mote of dust in its eye, not a pebble beneath its foot or a thorn pricking its thumb. He had a mind, as it had a mind. He was a thing that, minuscule as he was, it saw as *real*.

He'd roared in: hating, angry, terrified. He'd driven into the Architect's mind on a flame of negative emotions, knowing only that it was the executioner of worlds. And now he touched the truth of it. He understood that until now no human—perhaps no denizen of any planet it had ruined, in its millennia of life—had ever existed for it. At his/its back was the world of Far Lux. And Idris could see through its senses that the planet was mottled with a kind of rot, a disfiguring decay that the Architect needed to clear away. That rot was *thought*, the collected minds of all the people living there. They exerted a pressure on the fabric of space that the Architect, for reasons Idris had never grasped, felt the need to release.

For a measureless time he and the Architect had confronted one another. He had sampled the immensity of its mind and it had taken a magnifying lens and studied him, as a human might examine a microbe. A thing so small that it might as well not be there at all. He had no anger left, at that point. There was nothing of the white-hot fire that had taken him so far. Such emotions withered and died in the face of that godlike scrutiny. How foolish it was to rage over the deaths of so many microbes, the extermination of something almost invisible.

Yet it saw him and understood him. Perhaps it unfolded the page of his mind to its fullest extent, ironing flat the crenulations of his brain until he was spread so thin and wide that he finally became visible to it. His past and present and all the complexities of his being, all exposed for study as never before—and still the most insignificant thing the Architect had ever been called upon to recognize.

He'd stopped screaming then. He stared sightlessly towards

the ceiling of the *Yennenga*'s bridge as the medics restarted his heart and used machines to keep his lungs working.

There was a moment he recognized as regret. He was never sure if he'd felt the being's regret over all its kind had done. Or if this was some perverse personal response to the Architects departing, now they wouldn't be continuing their work. For they would not, he understood. For now, at least, and who knew what "now" meant to beings so vast. Perhaps they would go and think about what they'd done for a hundred million years, before coming back to pick up where they'd left off. Perhaps they'd wait until the suns had all gone out and the universe was cold.

The Architect had fallen back into unspace and not returned. And that was the last anyone saw of them. That day was the last day of the war, although it was months before anyone dared suggest it was so.

*

Decades later, in diplomatic isolation aboard the *Vulture God*, Idris caught the news out of Far Lux and felt as though someone had taken his guts out. *It was all for nothing*, he thought, but of course that wasn't true. Humanity had been given fifty years to consolidate and grow; people who would have died had been given decades to live. It had been his achievement—him and Tess and Olumu, and he the only survivor of the three. He had ended the war, there at Far Lux, and on the back of that, he tried to become irrelevant. Just be Idris Telemmier on a succession of crappy ships towards the outskirts of the Human Sphere. He'd had his fill of making history.

Now, sections of the Hugh administration on Berlenhof were being yanked out of decades-old mothballs. The next unspace shipment from Far Lux would be a wave of refugees. Everyone was scrambling to set up camps, kitchens, shelter, medical supplies. And at the same time, less savoury engines were turning their wheels.

"There's Sathiel, the *fucker*," Olli said, jabbing a finger at the screen. They'd all crammed into Command, where the *Vulture* was displaying rolling news. "We should've had a sweepstake on it."

They could see the cult hierograve's benevolent white-bearded face. It was as if he'd never committed the biggest fraud of the last forty years. Instead, he was talking animatedly about the protection the Essiel would be only too happy to extend—and for such a small price. Idris waited for the interviewer to mention the *Oumaru*, but somehow it never came up. Suddenly the cult had gone from clowns in costumes to everyone's new best friend, someone who might be called upon for an urgent favour sometime soon.

Two Colonial warships had turned up at Berlenhof, ostensibly to defend against any Architect incursion. Idris knew full well they'd have set off before the news broke, and had come to lean on the Partheni.

"They want the regalia, of course," Trine announced mournfully, having lost his chance to work on the things. "Which are here, on this very ship, a mere hundred metres away. And suddenly they are of a far more than academic interest to the authorities on Berlenhof."

"They could, what, just take them down there and make the whole planet Architect-proof?" Olli asked him.

"I'd be willing to wager my ambassadorial status that Hugh

is digging up absolutely everything it knows about the process, my old comrade-in-adversity," Trine agreed. "And maybe it isn't anything more significant than just having the things there. We're all aware that the Hegemony loves ritual for ritual's sake."

"But Hugh don't have the regalia," Kris pointed out.

"No, they don't," Trine agreed. "But—what coincidence!—suddenly they have warships here. How fortuitous."

"They can't just start *shooting*. How will that end?" demanded Kris.

"They think they'll be able to threaten, and we'll cave," Solace said hollowly. "But we won't. It's not what we do. Also, top-of-the-line Colonial does not beat top-of-the-line us. They can't stop us just leaving if we want to go."

"Then why haven't you?" Olli needled. "Just leg it. Everything's simpler for *you* if Berlenhof gets hit, right?"

Solace stared at her. "Hope," she said.

"Which one of you was Hope?" the specialist asked blankly.

"No, I mean the...the idea of hope." Solace frowned. "My people will be *hoping* we don't have to just walk away. They'll be hoping there's a diplomatic solution. And..."

"And what? They're going to be our warrior angels all over again, throw themselves in the way if the Architects come?"

"*Yes.*" Solace was blinking rapidly. "Yes, Olli. Exactly that."

Idris wondered how much of this vaunted hope was her own, that her people were still the heroes she remembered. She'd been in suspension for a long time and the universe had turned.

"*The Angels of Punching You in the Face,*" he pronounced sadly, but ending with a smile. God knew he needed something to lighten the mood. Solace rounded on him, looking for mockery, finding none.

"Enquiry—crew logistical arrangements on sudden failure of diplomacy?" Kittering piped up. He'd been crouching in one corner, puzzling over his backscreen, currently spread on the floor in several pieces.

"Good point. I'm guessing your people won't have time to just drop us off, if you do decide to leg it home," Kris agreed.

"Well," Solace shifted awkwardly. "They did ask...would you agree to come with us? I mean, war or peace, diplomacy or not, I'm supposed to ask."

"And if we say no, that means they let us go, *right*?" Olli asked, with heavy sarcasm. "Maybe give us a little hamper of rations for the journey, complimentary mint candy, that kind of thing?"

"We—they—*we* would contract with you, on good terms. For the services of the *Vulture God* and all crew."

"So long as crew includes Idris," Kris finished for her.

"Why not just take him?" Olli said suddenly. "I mean, you can. The *Vulture*'s in your ship's hold. Even *we* were able to storm this damn bucket when we needed to. You have all the supermarines in the universe, right outside the hatch. Why this goddamn pussyfooting around?"

"We don't *want* to...That's a step we can't un-take, and what use are any of you under duress? You ever think about trying to *force* an Int to do something, really? Hugh might have all the leash contracts in the world, but you can't tell me the Liaison Board doesn't invest massively in psych-conditioning too. Maybe they have slaver cut-outs or some killer implant to keep their hooks in, even. Because it's like those birds they keep on Magda, the expensive hunting ones. The whole point of them is to let them fly, and if they fly then maybe they never come back. But more than that, we don't *want* to. And *I* don't want to. At least *consider* a contract...Largesse or Halma or goods in kind, however you want it. Most spacer crews would be scrabbling over each other for this sort of deal. Is it so bad that it's *us*?"

Olli opened her mouth for the quick retort, then shut it, looking around at her fellows. "Fuck," she said at last. "Actually, hate to admit it, that's not a bad pitch."

"Well it comes down to Idris," Kris noted. "I mean...I'd be for it. I, er, always wanted to see the Parthenon. But Idris?"

He was silent. Their voices had become very far away. He was gripping the edge of the pilot's board, to stop himself falling into the vast well he could feel forming. The jabber of the news mediotype had become no more than static.

His name again, from Kris, then Solace. Then Olli lifted a leg of her walker frame to prod him with its tip. There might have been the tinkle and clatter of Kit reassembling his screen, taping over the cracks. Trine's phantom face with its vacant beatitude. All so far away.

Just outside the ship, the curve of space fell into a void, pulled down by the leaden weight of nothingness. Gravity without mass, because its cause was on the other side of the membrane. In unspace. He knew that Saint Xavienne would be feeling just this, wherever she was. And over where the Liaison Board plied its trade, its conscript Intermediaries would be clutching at their heads, wailing, waking from nightmares—because none of the poor bastards would know what they were sensing. It hadn't happened before in their lifetimes. They weren't veterans, like him and Xavienne.

"It's coming," he told the crew. "It's here."

28.

Solace

Her sisters let Solace stand with the *Vulture*'s crew, in the hastily convened meeting that followed. It was a fiction, obviously. Solace was a Myrmidon Executor of the Parthenon, not some free spacer. Except there was a fierce loyalty to the crew inside her, and it didn't have to clash with her lifelong devotion to her sisters just yet.

The conference chamber was decidedly more crowded than before. The Hegemonic cult had a seat at the table, which made nobody very happy. Sathiel, in his full finery, was the only person in the room with a smile. And Solace wanted to live up to her sorority's name and punch his teeth in.

"Obviously," the hierograve was saying, "the Divine Essiel are far above me." His self-effacement was so shallow as to be two-dimensional. "Their will filters through to humble agents such as myself but dimly. However, their mercy and grace is without bounds. They would, I am sure, extend their protective benevolence over your Colony worlds...if the Council pledged unconditional fealty to the Hegemony. Perhaps a diplomatic barge could even emerge in time to consecrate Berlenhof? The Architect, though it has manifested in-system, appears to be considering the ephemeral grave of its kin before beginning its approach. We may yet have time."

Neither Borodin nor Tact liked any of that. But the mere fact that Sathiel was *here* was telling. *If all else fails . . .*

"So—what if they take the anti-Architect goods and then say, 'Ho, ho, just kidding,' when the Essiel want their back taxes?" Olli murmured.

"If they bow the knee," Trine confided to her, "then the Essiel would consider them part of the Hegemony, O newfound ambassadorial ward of mine. The Hegemony is of course notoriously loath to use its prodigious technological might against foreign powers. A matter of internal truculence is another matter."

"With all due respect," Borodin replied heavily, "we turned aside the Architects before. An Intermediary team are on their way even now."

Solace caught Idris staring at her. His expression was unreadable but she thought she understood it, one haunted veteran to another.

"However, the Council doesn't wish to rely entirely on their efforts," Borodin continued. "Hugh therefore requests that the Parthenon surrenders the Originator regalia, so these can be transported planetside and installed."

"If you believe these precious items can be simply—" Sathiel started, but Borodin cut him off with a sharp gesture.

"We'll take that chance, Hierograve. We've studied. We know we can't duplicate your masters' ability to transport the things. Yet now they're in our hands, we believe we can use them."

And Monitor Superior Tact said, simply, "But they are not in your hands."

Borodin's face closed up. "I won't lie, I did wonder if it would come to this," he said tiredly. Solace had taken the man for a professional weasel but his regret seemed genuine right then. "However, let me at least make my government's request. I am asking, *pleading*, that you hand over the regalia, so we can protect Berlenhof against the Architect. The Architect that is out there right *now*."

Tact's face was impassive, her expression revealing nothing. "No," she said, and Solace's heart froze. *This is it, then. This is how we become what they fear.* She could feel the others' eyes on her: Olli, Kris, even Kittering. It was as though she was their scapegoat, the Parthenon in miniature. She wanted to say something. She wanted to challenge her superior officer, right there. But she was a good soldier, so she stood and said nothing.

Borodin nodded, almost as blank-faced himself. "Monitor Tact, you know our warships the *Blake* and the *Perihelion* have arrived in-system. But we can't afford a shooting war between Hugh and the Parthenon over Berlenhof. Certainly not now the Architect's here; we couldn't risk destroying the regalia. And, let's face it, if we tried to disable your ships before you could leave, we'd take more licks than we gave. We both know that. Wouldn't that make a fine spectacle for the Architect, when it came to make an end of us? Humans fighting humans, like gladiators, for its amusement.

"But...there are over a *hundred million* people on Berlenhof, Monitor. Please consider that number, let it sink in. As it stands, we could only save about nought point nine of a per cent of the population. And you know what? It's not your fault, it's not your doing, and they're not your people. But if you leave now, taking with you the means to save us, then you *are* responsible, and history will remember. The Colonies will remember, and so will every other state and power for whom such things have any meaning at all. You will be writing a terrible chapter in Sang Sian Parsefer's legacy if you simply abandon us."

Tact nodded. "And yet, we will not relinquish the regalia."

Borodin let out a long breath to absorb that and was about to speak when Tact's raised hand stopped him.

"Our possession of mobile but functional regalia has provided an opportunity, Menheer Borodin. The Parthenon is shipbound, with no worlds to protect. But now we have a ship warded against the Architects. This situation may not occur again."

"Menheer Borodin," Sathiel broke in. "Please listen to me. There are other regalia that can be brought here—"

"Shut up," Borodin told him, almost without venom. His eyes never left Tact. "Monitor, there is an Architect *here*, *now*. Are you telling me that, for the chance of some future encounter, you will abandon our millions?"

"No," Tact said. "However, I *will* take from you your Intermediary team, all of them. I'll take them aboard this ship and we'll go out and meet the Architect, armed thus with both sword and shield." And now the faintest ghost of emotion limned the severe lines of her face. "We will *fight*, Menheer Borodin. We will carry the Intermediaries to battle, as we did before. We will not abandon our sis—our siblings. Hugh may have forgotten what it is to be Partheni, but we have not."

Solace heard a hiss of pain, and realized she'd been gripping Idris's shoulder so hard that he was twisting to escape her clasp. She wanted to whoop, to jump in the air and cheer.

She wanted to run over to Tact and embrace the woman. She was a good soldier, and she did none of those things, but a great tide of joy swept through her nonetheless.

Borodin's face remained blank, because he was a diplomat. "I do not have authority to place our Intermediary team on your ship. I'm still supposed to be repatriating Telemmier," he said hoarsely. "However, I can anticipate my orders, when I convey your offer. I don't think we have a lot of choice, after all."

Tact nodded. "Correct, Menheer." Then Idris stepped forward and said, "I'll go." He had to say it twice, because the mics were off the first time. Then everyone was staring at him. He backed up, squinting into their scrutiny as though it was too bright a light.

"I'll go. I did it before. You don't have time to get anyone else. Just me."

Tact regarded him as though trying to work out if his ageless decades had matured him or made him vinegar in the bottle. "That would be appreciated, Menheer Telemmier," she said at last. "Myrmidon Executor Solace, he's in your care."

Just like old times.

*

"I thought we'd go to Borutheda," Olli said, as Idris hovered nearby. She was out on the deck by the *Vulture*'s open hatch, rebuilding the Scorpion's arm.

"You know," the specialist said, not looking at Idris, "when you don't come back, and all. I reckon the shipyards at Borutheda will be busy as fuck from now on, and the *Vulture*'s a good hauler. We won't be doing deep void work after this, what with not having a navigator."

Idris just stood there, letting her talk, shoulders slumped.

"I mean I'll be glad," Olli went on. "Frankly, ship was getting crowded. And you're a weird little sod, Idris. Hard to get on with, you know. Isn't that right?"

"Always having to bail you out," Kris chipped in. "More trouble than you're worth. I could have had a thriving practice, big desk, clients begging."

"Individual of incomprehensible motivation," Kittering added. "Not even safe hands."

"You said it, Kit," Olli agreed. "I mean, you were a decent one-trick pony. But more trouble than you were worth. Look at the mess you got us in. Go run off with your Partheni girlfriend, why don't you?"

Solace opened her mouth to object to that, but the slightest look from Olli silenced her. This was between *them*. And while Solace knew that their jibes weren't serious, she was slow in understanding the real context. This was the crew's funeral for Idris, the same dressing down they'd given Barney and Medvig and then Rollo. The Colonial way to process grief.

"I'll be back," Idris told them all, his voice very soft.

"Like we'd have you," Olli tried, but Solace heard the tremor in her voice. "We'd have to discuss it, me and the crew. Have to decide if we even wanted you back."

"I know," Idris agreed solemnly.

"I mean...running off with a *Partheni*."

"A transaction lacking all consideration!" Kit threw in.

"I'll be fine. I'll be back. I *have* to—"

"We know," Kris interrupted him. "Idris, we know." She put

a hand on his arm, anchoring him. She looked into his eyes, creating that intimacy that Colonials could always manage between them, no matter how many people were about. "You are one seriously stupid man. You were *out*. You always told me how glad you were, that you were really *out*."

"Stupid, I know," Idris agreed. He hugged her and stepped back, leaving Solace next in the line of fire.

But Olli was already puppeteering the Scorpion back into the ship, the mech drone gathering up her tools. "You let anything happen to him, I'll be back for you," she warned, glowering back at the Partheni.

"I'll do everything I can," Solace started, then changed her mind. "You know I'll look out for him. So stuff it up your ass, Refugenik. He'll be safer in my shadow than anywhere."

Olli crooked an eyebrow. "*Now* you're talking like one of the crew."

Idris

When Idris and Solace reached the *Heaven's Sword*'s bridge, Trine was there already. The Hiver had welded a makeshift framework to the deck, which patently offended all sorts of Partheni sensibilities but looked absolutely like home to a Colonial spacer. Between its bars, the Originator regalia floated, revolving gently in their invisible field.

"You *cracked* it?" Solace exclaimed, then Idris saw her glance guiltily at Exemplar Hope and the other officers. The sort of free speech she'd grown used to aboard a spacer ship clearly didn't mix well with Parthenon military discipline.

"Ah well, as to *that*..." Trine started with their usual

self-importance, before setting their face to crestfallen. "Can I duplicate the peculiar standing wave that is enveloping those relics, my comrade-in-arms? That I cannot. Can I maintain the field, once present? Apparently the answer is a resounding yes. So rejoice, therefore."

"Intermediary Telemmier," Hope addressed him, her Colvul strongly accented and awkward. "It is an honour having you on board."

Idris goggled at her. Not least because he'd been on board for some time, and nobody had felt moved to say anything of the sort. Apparently his return to active military service, even if just this once, had changed his status in Partheni eyes.

"I am knowing you served aboard our name ship in this system," Hope continued. "I'd say, let us hope of similar victory, but I shall settle for fewer casualties."

"Likewise, ah, Mother." This seemed to be the appropriate form of address for a Partheni officer, from her curt nod.

A trio of other civilians were marched in at that point, and at their head was Saint Xavienne. Idris blinked at her. "Seriously? They've risking you on this? And I said I'd do this alone."

Xavienne's lips quirked slightly. "It's amazing what they'll agree to, with Berlenhof under the hammer. Idris...How strong are you feeling?"

"How strong are *you*?" spoken with concern, not as a taunt. Close to being of an age, but she seemed so frail, and she'd not been on the front lines during the war. Whereas he had fought but hadn't aged, as though some part of him was still trapped in those years. "Who are these?"

Behind her were a man and a woman, both with close-cropped hair. He was short, lopsided, his cheeks and scalp marked with jagged rayed tattoos. Gang markings, Idris guessed. The woman was taller, gaunt-faced as any famine-bred spacer. Ugly crooked lines of surgical scars stood out about her skull. He answered his own question, seeing that. "Ints, from the Liaison Board."

"The most promising of the current class," Xavienne confirmed, and her tone warned him to keep his opinions on the Board to himself. After all, it wasn't these Ints' fault that they'd ended up in the Program, and they'd be standing by his side when the fight came.

"Davisson Morlay," the man said, without offering his hand and keeping a definite space around himself. He had a trace of an on-planet accent.

"Andecka Tal Mar," said the woman, introducing herself in turn. "I've read a lot about you, Menheer Telemmier."

"That so?" He didn't know what to make of that. "I didn't realize I was...on the curriculum."

"Before the Board," she said. "I studied history."

I'm history. He didn't know whether to laugh or cry. "What the hell did *you* do to end up on the Program, Andecka?"

"I volunteered," she told him. In the resulting staggered silence she added, "I knew this would happen—that they'd come back. And we'd need more Ints."

"I..." In the face of her fierce certainty he didn't know where to put himself. Despite feeling just the same, when he'd signed up with the Program.

"Myrmidon Executor Solace is tasked as your liaison here," Exemplar Hope informed them. "We now proceed out-system towards the Architect. It currently proceeds in-system towards us. Meet her halfways, understand?"

They nodded: Davisson suspicious, Andecka radiating a

wire-tense need for action. They made Idris feel old and tired.

"Exemplar, if our attack is going to work..." Idris paused. He glanced at Xavienne in case she'd rather take the lead, then at the Partheni. He was concerned Exemplar Hope wouldn't understand him, with her shaky Colvul. But Solace was translating smoothly and Xavienne just waved him on.

"If this is going to work," he repeated, "we will need to make contact with it. But I don't know if we can break through if there's a battle underway. I was on a far smaller ship before, at Far Lux. There wasn't any chance of going toe-to-toe with conventional weapons so we didn't try, just led with us Ints." He shrank a little beneath Hope's stern stare. She was a Partheni commander, after all. Fighting was what they *did* and no skinny little Colonial civilian was going to tell her otherwise.

Except when she gave her reply to Solace it translated as, "She understands and will take her lead from you."

"Right then." Idris felt something must be wrong, because people were doing what he wanted and that hadn't happened to him for a long time. *Really? Was it war I was missing all this time? Not helpful.* He faced his fellow Intermediaries. For a moment the thought of him giving them some sort of briefing, like an actual soldier, was ridiculous. But if not him, then who?

"I'll need a room," he told Hope. "We need to talk up a game plan." He shrugged. "Or at least, I'll tell them how it worked out last time."

After that, the others managed a meagre ration of sleep while the *Heaven's Sword* cruised. The Partheni had put out from Berlenhof orbit in good time and the Architect was still getting underway. Perhaps it had delayed to lay a mental wreath by the scar of its sibling's demise. Idris was left to sit alone in the dormitory Hope had given over to the Ints. Solace slept with them, curled on her side on a bunk by the door. She'd been first to slip away with a soldier's enviable ease. Of the others, Xavienne seemed to have the same gift— lying on her back, arms folded across her chest like an ancient queen. Davisson Morlay took a while to drop off, tossing and turning and grumbling to himself. And as for Andecka Tal Mar, the *volunteer*...for a while Idris thought she truly was a kindred spirit, because her eyes never closed. But when he waved a hand before them, he realized that was just how she slept. He wondered if it had always been that way, or whether it was Tal Mar's own personal souvenir of her transformation.

He padded over on bare feet to look down at Solace, wondering at her. She'd left some kind of hook in him, an old rusty one from long ago. If their paths hadn't crossed he'd never have felt the metal of it, buried in his flesh. But now...They'd killed an Architect together. Once. And they'd been together for a little while, in that camp, amongst the mass of war-wounded.

It had been a nightmare place, really, despite Berlenhof's wartime authorities doing everything they could. People there had suffered wounds of the body and wounds of the mind, and Idris had the latter, stricken by his experiences. It was as though the Architect's consciousness had been radioactive in some way, and he'd received a dose just short of terminal. Then there had been Solace with her own traumas. They'd healed each other. It wasn't his first time, not hers either— though her first with a man. Awkward and fumbling and apologetic and, in the long decades after, he got the memory out from time to time and warmed himself by it. Thinking, *At least I had that going for me. Oh, there was saving a planet, killing a god and ending the war. But most of all, I lay within those arms.* As if he was a poet. As if he was anything but a terrified spacer-rat, who just happened to be an Intermediary.

Kicking his heels in the dormitory, he had no idea what she thought about him, but then that was his problem with most people. Having gone where he had, or else having become what he was, reading other human beings was difficult.

He was so glad she was with him, though. Now they were doing it all again. He even encountered the unexpected revelation that, yes, he might actually go with her, if she asked him again. Forsake the Colonies, screw Hugh, sign up with the Parthenon. Be the lone Jack amongst all their Jills, just for her. A terrible reason for committing treason, really. Good thing he'd been ducking the big questions for the last fifty years.

Eventually the alarms sounded, giving the "all-wake." The *Heaven's Sword* segued into an ordered tumult of booted feet and women's voices. Solace was sitting on the edge of her bunk, instantly at full alert. She had a smile for him, a small one, just enough to keep him brave.

"Do we eat yet?" Andecka was asking, and Xavienne was stretching in careful stages. Davisson sat and stared at his hands with hollow eyes.

"We fight," Idris said, his voice sounding small and ridiculous to his ears.

"To the bridge, all speed," Solace confirmed. "Menheers and Mesdams, if you will?"

Trine met them as they entered, practically buzzing with excitement.

"I am detecting a new modulation from within the regalia!" they announced loudly, to the considerable annoyance of Hope and her crew. "And the ship's instrumentalists are reading kindred frequencies from within the Architect. They are *reacting* to one another!"

"That's good, is it?" Idris asked dubiously.

"It is *unprecedented*, my dear old colleague!" Trine exclaimed, their battery of arms waving excitedly. "This has *never* been observed before. This strongly suggests these mobile relics retain their properties in transit. That was by no means guaranteed. Also, these readings will be of incalculable scientific value! I am already planning a symposium."

"That's...great, well done." Idris had no idea what that even meant. "I'm sure that'll go well for you if we survive."

Trine's face beamed at him benevolently. "Oh, I rather feel our survival is in the bag, my old crew-fellow. We bear with us the one known defence against the Architects—mounted within a fighting ship for the first time. What is our enemy going to *do*, precisely?"

"Take it down a notch, Delegate," Solace told them. They rolled their projected eyes but the flow of words stopped and they returned to the regalia. The relics still looked like corroded old junk to Idris, but apparently they were doing their thing. That was all that mattered.

"Ready now?" Hope addressed them then fired off a dense patter of Parsef to Solace.

"We're close now. Under other circumstances, at this distance, we'd be risking the Architect's attention," Solace translated. "We have gravitic shields up anyway, in case Trine's wrong. But so far, it's just continuing to advance on Berlenhof. We're matching its trajectory. And we're ready for you."

Idris nodded convulsively, and Xavienne squeezed his arm. Then she went over to the Liaison Ints and murmured some words of encouragement. Both of them looked ashen and frightened, and Idris suspected he looked the same. Not inside, though. Inside him something had woken that had slept since the war. It sent fire though his veins, and he both loathed and loved the sensation. This was what made him a monster and a war-ender.

He met Solace's eyes and she saw it there too, the wolf within the lamb. *Old Times*. She smiled at him and that was *Old Times* too, and it felt good.

"Medical crew will stand by," Hope told them, because at Far Lux he'd almost killed himself, just as a side-effect of doing his job. Right now he felt invulnerable. His mind was streaming with memories: Berlenhof and Lux; the pain of the Intermediary Program; all the hungry, terrified years of growing up with a war on.

He let his mind out, the wolf loping through the door of its cage after long captivity. Out there, beyond the eggshell walls of the *Heaven's Sword*, was the vast, serrated face of the Architect. And again he made himself small, a dagger, a dart, a needle. He folded his mind until he could hurl his consciousness out along the gravity curve, down towards its immensity. He remembered doing this in hate at Berlenhof, as their armada was torn apart around him. He remembered Far Lux, where he had done this in hope—and had been met by the enemy in its own halls.

You said you'd go away forever. Untrue and he was anthropomorphizing, but still. *Why are you here, now?* In his baffled frustration he bounced off it, falling away from the crystalline complexity of its internal architecture. Then he was back on the *Heaven's Sword* bridge, head already splitting and blood roaring in his ears.

He risked a glance at his fellows. Davisson had blood running from his nose. Andecka's fists were balled up in front of her face, cheeks wet with tears. Xavienne stood ramrod straight, head tilted back and lined face without expression.

Again...

He fell back into that space—the deformation between unspace and the real, where the Architect's consciousness resided. He entered its vast complexity immediately, this time, this mind as big as a moon... He was blundering like a moth, battering the mirrored surfaces within its substance. And somewhere in there was a window onto the thinking part of the Architect, which knew why it did what it did... The thing that made planets and ships into art, and murdered billions. And its species hadn't even known or cared, until it met Idris Telemmier over Far Lux.

Why now? Why come back? Had they been busy exterminating some other species, while two fleeting human generations had come and gone? Had they only granted a stay of execution, and Idris had simply misunderstood? He didn't think so.

What's changed? He rushed headlong through the maze of its mind. He was looking for the monster at the heart of it— so he could demand answers, demand recognition and a future for his people. He sensed the others, as though he was stumbling over the tangled string they left behind. As though he saw their faces briefly in the shimmering confusion of the place. Xavienne's calm determination; Davisson breaking up, mind fracturing; the deadly earnestness of Andecka Tal Mar. She was terrified beyond all reason but was still fighting.

He thought he saw himself in that maze, the Idris that had been. The Idris from Far Lux who had found that one sublime thread to the very heart of the labyrinth, tea with the minotaur, diplomatic relations with the unthinkable. Then as he headed down that way, in search of the warren's heart, he found the Idris from Berlenhof-that-was...he'd been panicked, maddened, failing even as the *Heaven's Sword* had failed. And yet he had achieved just enough back then, slowed the enemy just enough...

For a moment he was back on that bridge again, hearing shouted orders in Parsef, the cries of pain, the accelerators singing, and he didn't know which *Heaven's Sword* he was on. Then he forced his mind out again, following the trail he'd blazed. Davisson was shrieking in his ears like an animal being butchered. Solace was shouting, a hand gripping his shoulder. But he was losing himself again inside the mind of the monster, hunting it, aware that it was hunting too. It was concentrating on something. Something new, different. He was the expert, after all. He knew when an Architect's mind felt *wrong*.

What are you doing? But it couldn't hear him. It was concentrating, that unthinkably vast edifice focusing on something infinitesimally small—something on the human level, like a giant trying to thread a needle. His ears were flooded with screaming now, too many voices, weapons discharging, a sound like stone tearing, a choir of hornets in a rage...He had no frame of reference for these sounds, and couldn't guess if they were real or not.

Then he was out again, the fresh contortions of the Architect's mind excluding him without ever acknowledging him. He stared at the torn-up bridge of the *Heaven's Sword* and reeled. Solace was shaking him by the arm, had been for some time. Abruptly his legs gave out and he fell into her. He was trying to form words but was forgetting how they were made. There were great rents in the metal walls of the bridge and, everywhere, medics were crouching by bodies. He saw Exemplar Hope lying crooked nearby, too much of her insides ripped out for her to have survived. A dozen other officers and crew had been served likewise and there were myrmidons amongst them. Their beautiful armour was rent and buckled, accelerators lying where they'd been dropped from dead hands.

"What—?" Idris said. Because none of this was battle damage. This wasn't what happened to a ship when an Architect took it and mauled it. This was...trivial, small-scale stuff. This was more like the damage people did to one another, for all it left the victims just as dead. This wasn't what happened when they were struck by an entity that could reshape planets.

Mind still whirling, he looked to his fellow Ints.

Andecka was kneeling, clutching at her head. He thought she must still be locked in combat with the Architect, still vainly trying to reach it. Davisson was...dead, he had to be dead. Something had ruptured inside his skull, hard enough to push the whole left side of his head out of shape. Xavienne...

He ran over to her, already stuttering denials. This was not Architect damage. *Something* had struck her, something physical, something sharp. It had carved into her thin body and smashed her to the ground. There were medics here, the Partheni prioritizing her over their own fallen—desperately stitching her and her life together as best as they could. The sight of her injured, perhaps dying, was like a spike into Idris's own heart.

"Idris, stay still," Solace was imploring him. "You're hurt. Let the medics get to you."

"I'm fine, I'm fine," he mumbled, tasting blood in his mouth. He spat it out past his chewed-up tongue. Then he saw Trine. The Hiver's bad leg had been removed completely, severed at the hip, and a handful of their arms were just stumps. Their false face flickered and stuttered as it tried to speak. But its expressions and the movement of its lips didn't match the words that thrummed from their torso.

"Gone!" they buzzed. "Gone!"

Idris's eyes went to the framework the Hiver had set up for the regalia. They were gone, as Trine said.

"What happened?" he managed, meeting Solace's wide gaze. There was blood on her face, he saw.

"They came for the regalia," she told him.

"*They* who?"

"Things, soldiers from the Architect. Crystal things. They punched into the ship. We couldn't fight them, couldn't stop them. Took the relics and left. Idris, we—"

One of the surviving officers yelled something in Parsef, then the whole ship shuddered as bulkheads ground against one another. Sparks flashed from buckled panels and half the screens went dark. It was almost reassuring in its familiarity. *Now* that's *an Architect attack.*

There was more rapid back and forth between the bridge crew, and Solace said tightly, "We can't survive another strike like that. The shields barely held us together." And it was, Idris thought, a remarkable thing that they were still in one piece. That this work of human hands had endured the wrath of an angry god.

But not twice, and so he was breaking from Solace,

bounding over to the pilot's station. "Give me unspace, someone. I am plotting a course," as clearly as possible. He heard Solace translate for him, trusting him. Someone was objecting that they were right in the Architect's gravity shadow and couldn't leave the real. Solace was telling them that they *could*, with Idris as navigator. Didn't they know what he was? Her hand was bruisingly tight on his shoulder, the tension giving the lie to her words.

They gave him everything he wanted and, for that moment, he had the power of a top-of-the-range Parthenon warship at his fingertips. Except before an Architect, that didn't mean very much.

The appalling mass of the thing gave them no clearance at all to get into unspace. It narrowed their options to a single equation, a needle to thread. They were caught between the hungry weight of the world-destroyer and the world it was set upon destroying. But Idris was on fire, half out of his mind, half in unspace already. It was as though the universe simply drew him a new Throughway, for one use only, just for him. He took the battered *Sword* and whipped it out from under the Architect's descending hammer. He yanked them through unspace for a handful of traumatizing, unprotected moments. It would feature in the nightmares of everyone aboard for the rest of their lives. And he had saved the ship, and everyone still living on it. At least until the Architect caught up.

29.

Idris

They shot Idris full of drugs to bring down the inflammation in his brain, and to stem the internal bleeding. Then there were more drugs to combat the sluggishness brought on by the first batch. At least they quietened the hallucinations he'd been getting, of motion at the corners of his vision plus a sense of impending doom. Although as doom was in fact impending maybe that hadn't been a symptom of anything other than actual current events.

He was in a Hugh infirmary, on an orbital over Berlenhof. And if he listened carefully, he could hear staff arguing about which patients could be got out on what ships. He reckoned that same conversation would be dominating the planet below, too. Oh, the powerful and wealthy who owned estates across the beautiful sun-kissed archipelagos of Berlenhof would have their own transport, but right now a fair proportion of Hugh's entire bureaucratic staff would be performing the hard maths with every vessel they had left, working out who could be saved. Luckily, he had a ride. Solace had told him the *Vulture God* had docked at the same orbital. She'd gone to call the crew and tell them their errant son was still alive.

"I don't understand," he said. "It's never attacked like that before. Was it because we had the regalia?"

Beside his bunk, Delegate Trine was perched in a basic walker frame. Both legs had been removed, so he could be given a matching pair. Trine was sick of limping.

"If you're asking me to make an educated guess, old confederate, I don't know." The Hiver's face was disconcertingly absent, their projectors having literally given up the ghost. The remaining silvery bowl showed nothing but a smear of Idris's reflection. "Perhaps this is what Architects *do*, if they encounter Originator gear on a ship? But really, if it can deal with regalia on a ship, why not on a planet? If I were the Hegemony I'd start getting very nervous indeed."

The Architect had launched a couple of its smallest spines into the *Heaven's Sword*, inflicting significant but incidental hull damage. Then the spines had begun fragmenting out into...soldiers, Trine had said. Individual mobile units. They had been made of the same crystal as the spines and took on many shapes. Some were humanoid, most were not: many legs, no legs, serpentine, arachnoid, flying ray-forms and other less recognizable things. Hearing the unfamiliar descriptions, Idris had a creeping fear these were species the Architects had met, and there was only one way that meeting ever went. They were drawn from a great funerary list of extinct civilizations—one with a space on it reserved for humanity.

The stuff the soldiers were made from was simultaneously stone-hard and malleable. Accelerator shot that would pierce a starship's hull had just ploughed into and through them without damage. Energy weapons had refracted from them in rainbows of blinding light. One intruder had been cut in half when Partheni techs explosively triggered a blast door. Overall, though, they had rampaged through the ship to the bridge without serious opposition. There they had taken the regalia. And, when the deck crew and Trine had tried to stop them, they'd responded with lethal force.

"Quite remarkable, really," the Hiver reflected. "They used their limbs to cut and bludgeon close in. But they could also just shoot shards of themselves like living accelerator guns, just chewing up their mass as ammunition. I count myself lucky that I merely lost a few limbs."

Idris closed his eyes but found he couldn't imagine it. "How did they do it?"

"Ah, well." The loss of much of their body hadn't damaged Trine's pedantic tone. "As it happens, old chum, I was able to take some readings."

"While they were *attacking*?"

"Indeed yes."

"While they were killing everyone?"

"For science. I judged that, when my time came to stand between these soldiers and their prize, I would prove a short-lived barrier. Judged correctly, as it happened. But before then, I was able to perform a little impromptu research—and the data raises some fascinating possibilities. I believe the soldiers were just puppets, manipulated by the Architect through incredibly precise application of gravitic force."

Idris's eyes shot open and he sat up in the bunk. "Yes."

"I am glad you concur."

"That makes *sense*. It was doing something, when I was trying to contact it. It was…absorbed, had to bend all its concentration to it. It was making its puppets dance."

"Ah, the power," said Trine wistfully. "The precision. If it weren't so horrible it would be rather wonderful, don't you think?"

Idris grunted. "I guess Borodin and the others are mad at the Parthenon for taking the relics out there. Now we've lost them."

"Most likely, although the loss of the chance to study them is patently the greater woe," Trine said airily. "Honestly, though? I suspect the councillors have bigger things on their minds right about now. Such as saving their families."

Solace came back then, with a chair. It didn't look as smooth as the Partheni model he'd had, and he'd been terrible at driving that.

"I can walk," he told her, hoping it was true. "What's going on?"

"The crew is waiting for you," she said.

In the end he could walk, just. But only after Solace found him a cane. Leaning on it and on Solace, he finally made his way down to the docking ring and into what was surely the smartest, cleanest berth the *Vulture God* had ever enjoyed. Behind him came the merry clatter of Trine's surrogate frame on its six legs.

Olli was working on the ship in her Scorpion, and Idris saw a fair amount of clutter littering the pristine junk; parts that had been inside and were now outside. *Making room for refugees*, he realized. Even the *Vulture God* was needed. Kris had been sitting with Kit and another Hannilambra over a holographic Landstep board, but she jumped up when Idris came in. From her face, she'd expected to see him wheeled in on a gurney. Her relief was palpable.

She hugged him, too hard so that he winced and she

flinched away. Then Olli tapped him on the top of the head with one of her manipulator arms, and Kit fiddled a greeting from his game.

"I notice nobody is particularly concerned about *my* well-being," Trine pointed out.

"We don't know you, Buzzboy," Olli told them.

"Entirely your loss." Trine waved their remaining arms dismissively.

"They said you were hurt." Kris looked Idris up and down.

"I *am* hurt."

"They said you failed?" Olli added.

Idris met her gaze, finding only the usual frankness, not an accusation.

"The Architect is still coming," he confirmed. "We lost the relics, and the ship got crippled."

"He brought us home," Solace said defensively. Olli bristled, then just nodded.

"We're shipping out," Olli said. "They're finding us twenty colonists we can take. Twenty through unspace with no beds, Idris. But *everyone's* carrying. They're jamming three, four, into packet runners, even." Her face was set against tragedy, the way Colonials had lived during the war and in the lean times after. It was habit that came back easily. "I mean, could be worse, right? Matey over there with Kit, name something like Hullaway or some damn thing, came in with a fleet of freighters. Now they've dumped their entire cargo into space, that's maybe another thirty thousand people, if they can cram them in. If they can get them up from planetside in time."

"The Architect...?"

"Still coming," Kris confirmed.

"The *Thunderchild* put out to meet it," Solace said tonelessly. "Also the *Blake* and the *Perihelion*, those two Hugh warships that turned up. 'Buying time with steel.'"

Idris felt his legs start to go, and Solace slid a crate behind him so he could collapse in safety.

"The *Heaven's Sword* barely survived the first direct hit," he said hollowly. "The ships out there, they won't buy Berlenhof more than a cupful of time. It won't help."

"I'll book you another big diplomatic meeting, you can discuss it with them," Olli said. "In the meantime, you coming with us or not? Because if you're out, we can fit in another couple people when we go." But she was watching Idris with a sharpness that belied her air of unconcern.

I failed. But it *wasn't* too late. He pictured the Architect riding the skies of doomed Berlenhof, visible even during the daytime, crystals catching the sunlight. They'd have every trainee Int at the Liaison Board working to stop it...maybe that would be enough. But he didn't believe it. He could stay behind on the orbital and try one last time. But by the time the Architect was that close, its mass dragging at the planet below, it would be too late.

"I need a ship," he said.

The others were all staring at him. "Ships are kind of busy," Olli pointed out.

"Any ship with a gravitic drive—a packet runner, a shuttle, some rich kid's speedster, anything," Idris said desperately. "I *need* a second chance. I have to get out there and do it again. I can save everyone. I *know* I can..."

"Idris, you were on the way to dying when you broke off," Solace told him.

"Then it's my *right* to die trying!" he shouted at her, then put his hands over his mouth, horrified at the great gout of anger and frustration that had come out of him.

Solace nodded, then nodded again, convulsively. "Come on. We'll go see Tact."

The orbital's corridors were cluttered with people and it was hard to push through. Some were plainly evacuating— clutching bags, cases and treasured possessions that were mostly going to end up on the dock floor. *We forgot*, Idris thought numbly. *We forgot what it was like to be hunted. And I've lived to see it again.* He wondered if it had been his destiny to see events travel full circle, the reason for his unnatural longevity. So he should now wither to bones and dust, curse suddenly lifted.

Then they found themselves facing a wall of purple, red and gold, a hurrying band of men and women in high-collared robes. They were led by a man who had finally lost his geniality somewhere along the way.

"Hierograve Sathiel," Solace addressed him coldly. "Get out of the way."

He gave her a wide-eyed stare, but there was neither fight nor authority in him at that moment. He shrank aside and his people flowed past, giving Solace plenty of clearance.

"You wanted people to worry about the Architects? Happy now?" she shouted after him, with venom worthy of Olli. Sathiel made no reply as he fled.

Monitor Superior Tact was closeted with Lucef Borodin when they arrived, but Solace made sufficient noise that they were allowed in. Idris suspected that the two diplomats didn't have much to discuss anyway, at this stage. Borodin hadn't shaved that morning and there were bags under Tact's eyes.

"I *need* a ship," Idris insisted, because he was all out of pleasantries.

"Menheer Telemmier." He couldn't tell if Tact's cold manner was just her, or if she was judging his failure. And why shouldn't she? He certainly did.

"A ship," he repeated. "Get me out there again, on a ship."

"The military force going to face the Architect has already left," she said.

"Bring one back."

"Menheer Telemmier, there's no time. They will be engaging shortly."

"They…" He had a sudden sense of disjointed time. The drugs had upset all his internal clocks. "I need another chance."

Tact regarded him, her expression ambiguous. "That's it, is it?"

"*Please.* Get me out there."

She glanced at Borodin. "I'll see what I can—"

"No," the other diplomat said. He didn't seem very happy about it, but the word was out there.

Tact raised an eyebrow. Idris felt time cascading like sand falling from a broken hourglass into the void. There would be no chance to turn it over again, no more when it was spent.

"The *Colonial citizen* Idris Telemmier will be leaving aboard the liner *Sepulchrave*, which is currently standing by," Borodin said flatly. "Good ship, actually. My own family are on it, as are all non-essential Hugh staff. I'll be heading there soon."

"No," Idris told him. "I'll leave on the *Vulture God* then. With my crew."

"You won't."

He felt a keen need for Kris. But who'd have thought this old argument would raise its head now. "You can't—"

"Menheer Telemmier," Borodin addressed him, "Saint Xavienne died. They couldn't save her."

Idris made a sound like grieving. "No."

"She died," Borodin said heavily. "And that makes you almost the last of the first wave. The hope our new Intermediaries need. Which means we can't let you rush off and get killed facing this particular Architect. I'm sorry."

"I need a *ship*. I can save your fucking planet!" Idris shouted at him, at them both, at all the universe. "Just get me *out there*. I have a right to screw with my own head, if that's what I want." His eyes narrowed, words coming too fast for thought. "You're Magdan, right? Is that what this is about? Lose Berlenhof—then Magda's centre of the Colonies? That what you want?"

"Idris." Solace's hand was on his arm, trying to rein in his temper.

Borodin just looked sad. "I'm going to have my people take you to the *Sepulchrave* now."

Idris looked to Tact. "*Do* something."

She didn't meet his gaze. "This is very much out of my hands, I'm afraid." And a warning look passed from her to Solace. "Right now, Partheni writ is running very thin. This is a Hugh matter."

Colonial soldiers were coming in, four of them. Solace tensed, but under Tact's stern gaze she was not going to make a diplomatic incident of it.

"I could save everyone," Idris said, not shouting now, barely audible. "You just have to let me."

"Get him away, keep him safe," Borodin told his soldiers. "I'll be along in time for the launch."

*

Borodin's people took Idris's stick and put him in a chair, which they drove for him. He kept trying to get out but, each time, one of the soldiers pushed him back down. Not forcefully; respectfully, even.

In that part of his head that made him an Intermediary, Idris felt the Architect out there, getting closer. He didn't feel the world full of people about to be obliterated, but they weighed on him anyway. Bleakly, he knew that Borodin and Hugh were going to be disappointed in him. He wouldn't be able to live with himself and this failure. He'd put himself outside their control, even if release came via the edge of a razor.

After his first attempts at Berlenhof, and Far Lux, it seemed profoundly unjust that he'd be remembered as the man who let a planet die. It was as though the Architects were personally invested in erasing every good thing he'd ever done.

Then they wheeled Idris into what would have been the wealthy passenger lounge, in better times. It was currently crammed full of people shouting, crying, arguing and holding each other. Through the clear far wall, he could see the sleek flank of the *Sepulchrave*, painted with a hotch-potch of colours— a rich man's attempt to replicate the old mismatch of Colonial scarcity. There were ten hatches with umbilicals connected to the ship, and Hugh staff were diligently trying to hurry people aboard as efficiently as possible. The transparent window also revealed some of the planet below. Idris could see the lights of shuttles and lifters rising up from the gravity well, each one surely filled to the brim with the desperate and the lucky.

I could just shout, "Hey, someone else want my place?" and start a riot, he thought. But he said nothing, just sat in the chair while his escort jockeyed, threatened and pulled rank to get closer and closer to the nearest hatch.

I could...I could... But he couldn't. There was nothing he could do.

They reached the hatch, with a trail of angry people resenting their every step. He wondered, with new horror, whether someone at the back of the queue had lost their place for his sake.

"I'm not going," he said and made a game effort to get out of the chair.

"Remain seated for your own safety, Menheer," one of the soldiers said. Idris grabbed at the hand that came for him, but he was too weak. And even if he'd been strong, the man would have been stronger.

"*Help,*" he said, ridiculously. "I'm being kidnapped. I don't want to go. I can save the world..." In the general hubbub, almost nobody heard him. And those who did plainly thought he was deranged. "I'm an *Int,*" he squeaked as the soldier shoved him back again. "I can stop it. Get me on a ship!" Which was even more stupid because they *were* getting him on a ship. Just not in the way he wanted.

"I'll take it from here, Sergeant," a new voice broke in. Idris stopped shouting, because it sounded familiar.

"Who the hell are you?" the lead soldier demanded.

The newcomer was standing behind his chair, and Idris caught a flash of a holographic ID. "Intervention Board," the man said. "We're intervening."

The soldiers were all suddenly quite still. "Sir, we have orders..."

"Mordant House has orders too. We're requisitioning him."

"Sir—"

"Let's get out of the way and let these people board, shall we?"

When the soldier obeyed, Idris knew he wasn't going to end up on the *Sepulchrave* after all. Mordant House was the bogeyman of the Colonies. Mordant House knew all your secrets. It protected the Human Sphere against all threats, and good luck if that threat was *you*.

"You need that chair, or can you walk?" and at last Idris shifted around enough to recognize the narrow, suspicious face of Havaer Mundy.

"If you take my arm, I can walk."

"Fine." Mundy helped him up. The soldiers looked daggers but none of them would challenge Mordant House.

"So," Idris said, as Mundy helped him out of the lounge, against a tide of panicked refugees. "You have some Mordant House ship or something? That can get me out there?" *Please don't tell me I'm just trading one kidnapping for another.*

His heart sank when Mundy said, "Not exactly," but at least they were leaving the *Sepulchrave* far behind, as they moved around the orbital ring towards the shabbier docks. They had to jostle and fight through every corridor, but Mundy seemed to have a way of finding every gap in the current to get ahead. Idris just let himself be tugged along. The man's way with crowds was like navigating unspace to the uninitiated—something magical and mysterious. They were well into the docking band that dealt with freight now, though the only freight shipping here was more people. And all the while the Architect was getting closer.

"Agent Mundy," he said at last. "Where are we going?"

"Where'd you think?"

"I'm not going to be some spook asset." Idris pulled back

trying to resist. He might as well fight gravity; Mundy's long-boned frame bought him a lot of leverage. "I refuse to be some black ops sneak-pilot for your assassins."

Mundy stopped. "'Black ops sneak-pilot'?" he queried. "That's a job description where you come from, is it?"

"I'm not—"

"Telemmier. I am risking a great deal on my assessment of you—not least my job. So just shut your yap and come with me, would you? Because right now I am attracting all the bad kind of paperwork. And I am just desperate to get started on the last report of my career, after I drop you off." He gave Idris's arm a final yank, hit a door release with his elbow and they were standing in a familiar dock. And there was the *Vulture God*.

Idris looked from the ship to Mundy and back. Solace was heading towards them, her eyes on the Mordant House man.

"I didn't think you'd do it," she said.

"Well, I reckon you and I are both exceeding our orders today," Mundy replied. "You're shipping out with them, right?"

"You want a berth?"

He laughed harshly. "That would just about put the nail in the coffin, wouldn't it? No, I'll stay here and clean up the mess I made. Telemmier."

Idris jumped. "What?"

"I met you."

"What?"

"I sat down with you, remember? We had a chat, back before the Harvest turned up and we had to part ways. Right now, I am really hoping I'm as good a judge of character as I want to be. You want a ship, here's your ship. If you can talk them into it. I've also got you departure clearance, at least until someone clocks on and overrules me. Go use it."

Then the man was retreating, seeming to shift crabwise out of the hangar before vanishing. Because Mordant House never did anything in a straightforward way.

Idris turned to the ship, the unlovely, oft-repaired scavenger-hauler that was the *Vulture God*. The drone bay hatch was open, but he couldn't see any of the crew.

"I know you all heard that," he called. *"Well?"*

"Okay, are we going or not?" Olli's voice boomed from the speakers. "Because I just spent ten minutes getting us all ready to leave. Just get your ass on board. Her too."

When he reached Command, they were all there: Olli in her walker, Kris in Rollo's chair, Kittering in his own. And Trine too, to his surprise. Their arms were still mangled, but they had new legs and their face had been restored to its phantom glory. Solace stepped in behind him and leant on the back of the pilot's chair, as he took his place at the board.

"Look…" he started awkwardly.

"You're going to say we don't need to come, that it's dangerous," Kris told him. "Idris, in the general ranking of 'people important enough to get a berth off-planet,' just where do you think we fit? If we're not getting out on the *Vulture*, we're not getting out at all. So we're sticking on board, thank you very much."

"Speak for yourself," Trine declared. *"Some* of us are an ambassador."

"Taking her out," Olli announced, and the ship's bones creaked around them as they lifted off from the dock and passed out of the station's gravitic field into open vacuum. "Idris, she's yours when you're ready. Take her away."

*

He'd wanted the crew in suspension beds, even for the stutter-jump in-system. But there wasn't time. They'd been through it before anyway, were practically unspace veterans. He argued the case as he slung the *Vulture God* away from the orbital, ignoring the angry comms chatter they left in their wake. A couple of Hugh military skiffs hailed them, but they were too little, too late. *Enough politics.*

He sketched out the maths of the stutter-jump always with the sense of Berlenhof as a crushing weight poised at his back. His target destination was unexpectedly complicated, a nightmare maze of gravitic distortions—even without the Architect itself with its disproportionate mass-shadow. Seeing the mess he was dropping into, he couldn't quite believe he'd lifted the *Heaven's Sword* out of it. But then it wasn't just the enemy out there anymore.

The fighting's started. Even at this remove, he could sense the slight shudder as the *Thunderchild* and its impromptu allies deployed their gravitic weapons. They were trying to crack the substance of the Architect, as its ponderous will sought to pin them down.

And the *God* was *In*, falling away from the real into the dream that was unspace and—

Out, exploding back into existence and into the thick of it. For a moment he could still see the ragged shawl of space-time, bent a thousand ways by the fighting. The Partheni warship was deploying its mass loom, four times the power of the batteries they'd used at the first Battle of Berlenhof. Idris saw a spray of cracks flower across those crystal mountains as the strike hit home. But they blurred into wholeness just a moment later, as the Architect reshaped its own substance to heal. Further off, Idris's instruments reported on the *Blake*, a Colonial-built monster shaped like a lump hammer. It had launched a withering storm of super-accelerated shot from its cannon, most of which whirled off to oblivion as the Architect leant on the universe to shift the gradient.

Solace took her place at Idris's back, medkit ready in her hands. Kris and Kittering were just staring at the monstrosity dominating space outside.

"We're too late," the Partheni whispered.

"Not too late," Idris insisted. Although even as he spoke, he *felt* the Architect wrench space around the *Thunderchild*, breaching its overstressed hull in three places. "I need a pilot."

Silence from the drone bay.

"Olli? You there?"

"I . . . Holy fuck, look at that thing."

"It's just like before," Idris told her. "No different to last time."

"She wasn't *at* Berlenhof the first time," Solace said quietly.

"Idris, you famie bastard, I was born in Ninety-fucking-Four," Olli threw in over comms. "Believe it or not, this is my first Architect, see right?" But she sounded more together now.

"Olli, I—"

"You need a pilot," Olli's voice came over the comms. "I got it. Show me where to go."

The others were waking from the spell, too. "Survival opportunities few and falling," Kit announced, skittering over to his own board. He was throwing up unwelcome statistics, specifically the efficacy of the *Vulture God*'s gravitic drive once the Architect caught hold of them. They punched a long way above their weight, but they weren't a warship. Shielding wasn't what they were optimized for.

"I know, Kit, I...Take us in, Olli, I'll...find a way. I promise." *I don't have a way. Maybe it won't look at us. Maybe we're too small for it to see.* But he knew that wasn't true. To the Architect, a single atom and an entire planet were equally worthy of adjustment.

The *Thunderchild* had launched a flight of Zero Points now, little single-woman fighters. Their size wouldn't help, but *many* could make a difference. The Architect had a limit to how much it could divide its goliath-like attention. And yet they would die, all of them. They knew it. They were buying time for Berlenhof, just the same as before.

The *Vulture God* streaked on, a battered old junk-hauler that had no place in the war zone. The other Hugh cruiser out there, the *Perihelion*, was hailing them. It was warning them off, as though they might somehow have missed the crystal half-moon out there murdering everyone. Kris proclaimed they were the cavalry, the Intermediary Program here to save the day.

"Kit," Idris said through clenched teeth. "I know we're basically screwed, but do what you can with the drive to get us some shielding. Just enough to fend off the worst."

The Hanni's reply went untranslated, which was probably just as well. But Kittering bent to the task anyway, slender mandibles rattling away at his board, sabotaging the clean running of the gravitic drive to twist space around them. Meanwhile, Olli had the brachator system hauling them forward from point to point, clipping them in a zigzag course into the heart of the fight. Idris would rather be doing that himself—it was his skill set, after all—but he had a different job right now, and one nobody else could help him with.

Solace's hand closed on his shoulder and he felt a moment

of perfect stillness. It was as though all the duelling gravities and energies out there had cancelled each other out, just for a fraction of a second, leaving only calm and peace.

Idris felt the Architect then, its vast and incurious mind that was focused on turning all these vessels into junk art and filigree. Remaking the universe one clutch of matter at a time. He made himself small and sharp and stabbed like a rapier. And everything receded from him: Kris's voice over the comm, Olli's swearing...his own body, with all its frailties and injuries, all someone else's problem.

We are here. Stop killing us. We are here.

He could feel the Architect's ponderous attention shifting from place to place across the battlefield. Here a Zero Pointer was snuffed out—pilot and vessel turned into lace and sent spinning into the endless void. There, clawing for the *Perihelion*, the Hugh ship's shielding failing, the ring of its gravitic drive rupturing into space. Idris felt the shift and shunt of the Architect's thoughts as it caught the ship's broken pieces and remade them. Each one became a work of art, worthy of a master. Some of the pieces had been crew but the Architect made no distinction. In his far, far distant ears, over Kris's comms connection, Idris could hear screaming.

He felt that he was standing by the feet of a great, slow giant as it tore down a city, block by block. The buildings fell, the people in them screamed and then they were crushed. But the giant only cared about urban clearance. It didn't understand that there were living things in the stone edifices it ripped down.

Except it must. They learned it at Far Lux. That's why they stopped.

He was a tiny little man beating at the giant's heel, hammering at its smallest toe, shrieking himself hoarse. He was the mote in the mind of God, lost in that labyrinth of mirrors and moving parts.

Why have you come back?

And one of his tiny ant punches registered, because the faintest feather edge of the Architect's consciousness acknowledged his existence.

Then he was slammed back into his body because the *Vulture God* was spinning out of control. Trine slammed complaining into the wall and Idris was half out of his chair. He was only saved from breaking his head by Solace grabbing him and hauling him back. Olli was incandescent over the comms. She turned a cubic mile of void blue with oaths Idris had never even heard before, as her Scorpion frame slid across the drone bay to crash into its closed hatch. For a moment she lost all connection to ship systems and they were helpless, adrift. Then she had *The Vulture* underway again, limping and shuddering.

"No more thank you no," Kit rattled off, sending damage reports to all boards. *The Vulture* was just about in one piece, but they'd accrued ten years of wear and tear in as many seconds.

"We've lost the *Perihelion*," Kris choked out. "Gone, dead."

"No more no further impact all tolerances exceeded no," Kittering insisted.

We're not going to make it. The moment the Architect turned back to find them—that would be it. They couldn't move fast enough, shield hard enough. They just weren't *strong* enough to wrestle the monster for control of local space for even a moment. And if tiny Zero Pointers could be pinched into oblivion, detected by the all-seeing Architect—how could they escape its notice?

Idris felt his throat go dry.

Unless...

"Olli," he yelled into comms.

"Busy!"

"You're linked to the ship?"

"I'm *flying* the fucking ship, what do you think?"

"Linked, really linked, right?"

Space shuddered about them, the gravitic shockwave of someone else being wrung out of existence. Yet even with its focus elsewhere, he could still feel the *thereness* of the Architect. This close, it felt as though its crystal needles were being driven into his brain.

"I'm going to stutter-jump us again." And Olli would think he was quitting, getting them out, but he went on, "Only for a fraction of a second. You'll feel it like a big old shock to the system, but no more."

"Idris, I—"

"I need you to just *keep flying her*, Olli. I'm feeding you coordinates for where you'll be flying from when we exit unspace. And I'll keep doing it, again, then again—and you have to keep up with me, okay? So are you linked to the ship? Nav systems, sensor suite, all that stuff. Your eyes, your limbs?"

Olli made a croaking sound over the comms. He chose to interpret that as a yes and jumped them...

...into unspace. Except the moment they crossed out of the real, he was slamming them back in again. He could hear Kris's yelp, the skreeling complaints of Kittering. They were demanding to know what he was doing, and the ship was just tumbling now—falling towards the jagged horizon of the Architect, utterly without control.

"*Olli!*"

"I got it, I got it, damn you, Idris, give me a..." And the brachator drive kicked in. Hauling them away, hand over hand—further from that hungry crystal landscape. Idris felt the Architect register them once more, reach for them, and he jumped them again. Once more, he fed Olli his calculations a split second before they went. Again they were gone, becoming unreal. Then they were back, a hundred kilometres from where they'd been. Now his head was splitting. The pain of those abrupt seat-of-the-pants jumps, the pain of trying to contact the Architect. All getting together and raising a family inside his skull.

But Olli was *on it* now. She was managing the ship from the moment it burst out of unspace—barrelling them through a formation of Zero Pointers, winking like stars on every side, flying the *Vulture God* as though she'd been born with wings. Olian Timo, born a stranger to her human body, had decided, why limit her efforts to that? Any frame, any surrogate shell could be hers. Now she was riding the *Vulture God*'s sensor data, eating the nav information Idris fed her. She saw each new emergence point and assimilated it before they popped into existence there. Always desperately fleeing ahead of the Architect's angry strikes.

And even as his hands jumped and jumped them, Idris let his mind out again. Once more, he fell into the fractured maze of the Architect's body—that was simultaneously its brain. Again, he was seeking that point of consciousness within. Seeking an audience, so he could plead for the survival of his people.

He was plunging through ablating crystalline layers of thought and desire. His mind shouted *We are here*. But the Architect knew this already. It didn't care. And this time around, it really did want to kill them. To unmake their worlds—despite knowing that myriad little minds lived upon them. *Why? Why hate us now?*

I don't hate you.

Those weren't the words; it wasn't quite like that. But his mind took the stimuli it encountered and translated them, awkward as Kittering's artificial voice trying to give words to Hannilambra concepts. Stunned, he was back in his body—just as a great fist slammed against the *Vulture God*'s hull and made it ring like a gong. Abruptly alarms and red warning signs were all over his board and Kit was reeling off the damage.

"Drone bay!" Kris got out. "Breach in the drone bay. *Olli!*"

"Still here," came her grim voice. "Air's gone but I got my own, haven't I. Fucking clinging on, aren't I? Only..." There was a pause. Idris blinked, finding the world red-washed. He had blood in his eyes and his head jumped and stuttered as randomly as their course through unspace. Solace tore open his tunic, the cheap printed fabric parting like paper. She clamped something to his chest, part of the grab-bag of medkit junk the *Vulture* had accumulated over the years. Was it interacting with his heart in some way? He felt only a distant curiosity, as he waited for Olli to keep speaking. He *hoped* Olli would keep speaking.

"Trine," the drone specialist said at last.

"Here and present."

"Get in here. Need your help. I...I've got a lot of failing systems. Took a bit of a knock here."

"I am not a technician," the Hiver said uncertainly.

"You are proof against vacuum, you roach bastard. I need you to *get in here* and do what you can to the Scorpion, before my life support gives. Okay? I would do it myself, but I'm too busy saving all your asses."

"Well, in that case, I shall lower myself," Trine said with dignity. "Myrmidon Solace, as requested," and they passed something to the Partheni. "If I should not return from this—"

"Just go!" Kris shouted at them. The phantom face looked mortally offended, but they went.

I'm going in again. We're jumping, Idris tried to say. But he couldn't get the words out, probably because he didn't seem to be breathing. Solace was on it, though. Whatever she had plugged into his heart had oxygenated his blood, until his autonomic systems stopped sleeping on the job. His brain was still fed, and that was all he needed. He rolled his eyes in thanks but she had no time for that, absorbed in the job of keeping him alive.

So he just continued, passing another set of sums to Olli, keeping them always one jump ahead of the Architect's next sally. And he forced his mind back into it, trying to pick up where he'd left off. *If you don't hate us, why kill us?* He met a vast wall of alien thought and scaled it, driving his hands into the gaps between nameless concepts. He navigated impossible logical contradictions, finding a mind so old that human concepts of time did not apply. A focus so powerful that it could rework a planet at the molecular level—not as an act of brute force but one of loving, careful artistry. Placing every atom perfectly in place. Fit for purpose.

What purpose, though? Why did the Architects rebuild the

universe, one inhabited world at a time? Surely not merely because they could?

Another near miss, distant cursing from Olli, Kris trying to liaise with the *Blake* and the *Thunderchild*. Idris fell out of the Architect again, clawing at it, plummeting forever. The space around them was a constellation of ships—hundreds of Zero Pointers bringing their gravitic drives together to fracture those crystal spines. All while the *Thunderchild*'s mass looms boomed and hammered soundlessly and the *Blake* unleashed hell. It was pumping out such blistering salvos of accelerator shot that even the Architect could not catch every falling sparrow of it. And it was still not enough. It was not even a hundredth of enough. They were flies in the face of God. They were just powerful enough to be worth obliterating.

And still Idris tried to get to the centre of the Architect. He was beating on the doors of its brain, but he couldn't get in.

"New challenger. Unexpected potential trouble!" Kit reported. He harvested more data from the boards, while trying to shore up their shielding. Idris came back to himself, realizing that another ship had stutter-jumped into the midst of the fight. The Hugh military launch that had hailed them as they fled the orbital.

You can't be serious. They've come to arrest us? Don't they know there's a war on? The Hugh ship was just tumbling, the shock of the in-system jump throwing its crew. *But if they stutter-jumped that means—*

He sensed the other mind then, scrabbling at the Architect's consciousness. Andecka Tal Mar, the volunteer. She'd come out here like he had, still volunteering, trying to make a difference.

He fed another set of coordinates to Olli. And presumably Trine was doing some good down there, because she was still alive and guiding the ship. There was the shock of another jump and now he couldn't see, couldn't open his eyes. There was Kris's voice, Solace's voice, all very distant now. The whooping of alarms too, thoroughly someone else's problem.

Perhaps we've just hit the limit of the Vulture's *medical kit. Ah well…*

He could *feel* Andecka out there, fighting and failing—but she'd caught the Architect's attention, just for a moment. He couldn't coordinate with her but he could adapt to what she did. He slid in past her, using the gaps she'd opened in the Architect's concentration. Its mind was elsewhere as it tried to discover the cause of this latest pinprick irritation.

And he was *in*.

It happened as easily as that, the perfect insertion of mind into mind. *Thread the goddamn needle one last time.* And he was in a place of eerie stillness, of pure Zen calm. A single step away in every direction he could see it all: the battle, the ships, the planet, the wider universe…All as remote as if painted in some abstract, expressionist style onto canvas and hung on a wall. A way of looking at the universe that made it seem like no more than bad art—something that could be reimagined, perfected.

He sensed a presence then, though not the looming, brooding Presence that attended unspace. This was something transcendent and beautiful, wise yet infinitely destructive. It was the thing he had howled *We are here!* to, back at Far Lux, so long ago, which had ended the war. It was the mote of *I am* within the vast structure of each Architect.

It became aware of him. Not as it was aware of the ships, as burrs and abrasive parts of the universe outside, that must be sanded down for it to pass smoothly by and achieve its purpose. But as *him*, Idris Telemmier: the thinking individual; the Intermediary.

Why? Stop, please. He tried to picture all the people on Berlenhof, failed almost immediately, but *something* got through. He perceived something in response—but not thoughts, not feelings. These were vast shunting blocks of intent and desire that had to be crammed into a funnel, crushed down meaninglessly small in order to be apprehended by a human consciousness.

We do not hate you.

We do not want to kill you.

And then Idris saw a barrage of images as it picked apart his memories, fragment by fragment. It dissected him, laid out the complete contents of his mind upon a table. Filed him, catalogued, tried to understand this odd evidence of a primitive civilization on the very point of extinction.

He found himself thinking—without consent or volition— about the Liaison Board. And about the Boyarin Piter Uskaro, trying to lay claim to him under Magdan law. He thought about the Hivers fighting to gain independence from their human creators. About the darkest parts of old-Earth history, back when they still taught it. About shackles and chains, duress, mastery and ownership. The Architect found all these things as it taxonomized the contents of his mind, and judged them relevant to the topic under discussion.

He kept expecting it to manifest as a kindly old grandfather, a white-bearded god, even as a monstrous demon. But it was never able to reduce itself to anything so banal or human.

All it could do was pick over his thoughts like a beachcomber, holding those which caught its attention up to the sunlight... until he understood.

You stopped before.

Whips, thumbscrews, chains, orders, punishment, servitude.

Please, not here. Not now. Please.

He had the Architect's whole attention now. Out there, the *Thunderchild* and the others were battering away ineffectually at its substance. But it had ceased to retaliate. The whole awful majesty of its concentration was on one Idris Telemmier, Intermediary, first class.

Please...

The moments cascaded about him, stolen from his memories and thrown in his face. Grief, loss of family, trauma, love, curling up beside Solace in the infirmary camp. Saying harsh words about Rollo, because he'd loved the man like family and that was how you did it. Shouting at Havaer Mundy on Lung-Crow station, because he was terrified of ending up with the Liaison Board and all their evils.

Please... Asking for himself, now. Because he didn't want to be the man who'd failed to save Berlenhof. Because, even though he was definitely dying, he'd never be able to live with himself.

A moment of perfect clarity.

The acceptance of pain, the willingness to go back to punishment. Because, of the two of them there, one of them must face failure. The choices were between Idris punishing himself, or the Architect meeting the wrath of... *who? What possible power could compel them?* But there was *something* there— that was what he had learned. There was an intent behind

513

the Architects. A purpose that was not native to them. A hand that brandished the whip.

Please...

And it left, the whole immensity of it falling away into unspace from the real. It abandoned the Berlenhof system, leaving a scattering of ships and filigreed debris spinning in its wake.

30.

Kris

When Idris regained consciousness, it was Kris's turn on watch. She'd been spending the time recording responses to the Liaison Board's demands, all of which mentioned Idris's name. Some of the demands talked of patriotism. Some spoke of Idris's recuperation and his need for their specialized care. Still more dealt with tenuous legal rights. Her real concerns centred on what wasn't being said. She was worried that some cabal of Hugh representatives was being hastily convened to make an executive order allowing them to march in and take Idris for the good of the Colonies. That would leave her with no legal power to stop them.

They were on one of the Berlenhof orbitals, despite invitations to more lavish facilities planetside. And Kris had made sure they'd docked at the same yard as the damaged *Heaven's Sword*—anything to keep Hugh at bay. The Parthenon's *Thunderchild* was also maintaining a battered, watchful orbit nearby. The *Vulture* crew were still taking advantage of Trine's tissue-thin ambassadorial credentials, which the Hiver Assembly, or at least its Berlenhof representatives, had somehow failed to revoke. Kris had no idea whether the Assembly was playing some complex game, or just completely failed to understand the nuances of the situation. Hivers were an odd bunch, more human than human one moment, utterly alien the next.

Then Idris croaked something, and she watched as he finally opened his eyes. Across the room, Trine abruptly stirred themselves, face flickering into being with their usual slightly superior smile. Trine had to stay in the room, apparently, or it wasn't a proper embassy. Or that was *their* understanding of their responsibility.

Kris's eyes flicked to the medical readouts, which all seemed within tolerance. The Liaison Board's doctor had been in again, although, when he found out the list of things that had happened to Idris's poor body, he had just about given up in disgust. There was, he announced in high dudgeon, nothing more he could do. Apparently, the crew had already broken every rule of his profession and trampled all over the Hippocratic Oath in the bargain. Not that, Kris suspected, he had much truck with any such oath himself, given his employers.

"Right then," Idris said quietly, even as Kris was sending an alert to Kit, Olli and Solace. "I feel dreadful."

"I'm beginning to think," she told him, "that you pick fights with Architects because it's the only way you can get a night's sleep." It was a terribly witty, brave little line. She'd spent ages handcrafting it as she waited by his bedside. Now it came out ruined because her voice was shaking. "How much do you remember? Do you... even remember?"

"Too much," he said hoarsely. "I remember the Architect left. And that was when... Actually, I remember a whole lot of me hurting. Though that might be just the reminder I'm getting now, from all the parts that are still hurting. Damn, Kris, I feel like I died."

"You maybe did," she choked out.

"Again, huh?"

"You... Solace said you lost all brain function."

"That right?"

"For ten minutes, nothing. Then you were back like you'd never been away. That's what she said. I mean, *I* was busy shouting at the Liaison Board ship."

"They were helping too," he told her. "Or one of them was."

"Well I know that *now*."

"I think..." And his eyes weren't seeing her anymore, or the room, or anything so quotidian. "I think it took my mind into it."

"*What?*"

"Just... reproduced the pattern of my mind. All the electricity of it, the precise organization that was *me*, and constructed it inside itself. And then it put me back, when it was done. Exactly as I had been. Every neuron picking up where it had left off."

"That's patently impossible. Probably Solace got it wrong. I mean, she's not a doctor. I mean probably your brain just died."

"Or that, yes." Idris blinked philosophically and one hand reached up to scratch at his chest. Kris stopped him.

"What?" His eyes widened. "I... seem to have a scar there."

"You do, yes." Kris glanced at Trine, who was trying to look disinterested.

"The sort of scar you mostly see after someone's tried to investigate cause of death. Big Y-shaped fellow, you know," Idris couldn't help noting.

"That's right. Solace opened you up," Kris confirmed.

"In the *Vulture's* command capsule?"

"Right there, yes." Kris suddenly began to feel the strain of the last few days, all at once. She clasped her hands to stop them trembling. "She did it because your heart had stopped and she couldn't restart it. You weren't reacting to the drugs, or to the shocks she was giving it, and we didn't have any nanotech. But she'd thought ahead. She had a contingency plan."

"I guess she kept me going, somehow?" Idris looked like he wanted to probe the sealant that had closed up the incision, "Did she put something in there?"

"Indeed," Trine observed. " 'Something.' "

"What was that, then?"

"Me."

Idris opened his mouth, closed it. Raised his eyebrows.

"At the good myrmidon's request, I donated three of my units to act as a pacemaker. She used them to restart and manage your cardiac functions. They remain inside you, so I suppose this makes us family or something? Personally, I feel a grand swell of sibling feeling somewhere within me. I'm sure you do too."

Idris tentatively fingered the ridge of sealant, still staring at Trine.

"They are on autonomous secondment to your cardiovascular system, severed from my swarm. I won't be, ahaha, manually tugging on your heartstrings, my old confederate-turned-proxy-relation, worry you not." Trine's face looked insufferably pleased with itself.

Then the others were piling in, Kit first, then Olli in her walker, and at last Solace, in her uniform coat. She sent Kris a glance that pleaded *Is he really all right, then?* and Kris sent her a nod.

"Oh wow," Olli observed. "You look really, really ill."

"Thanks," Idris said sourly, then blinked. "You look ropey yourself."

The specialist's exposed skin was blotchy with broken blood vessels and the whites of her eyes had gone a solid red. "That's because Trine's a shitty mechanic," she accused.

"You're still alive, are you not, my dear ingrate?" Trine retorted. "And, I would add, I've been performing a mechanic's work on your ship—"

"Poorly!"

"...Work on your ship. And yet, I am the only one not drawing some manner of recompense," the Hiver finished haughtily.

"All contracts to be negotiated ahead of performance," Kit chimed in merrily. The Hanni seemed to have come through the whole ordeal better than any of them.

"Perhaps I should start charging you for the use of my embassy," Trine suggested darkly.

"Open to negotiation!" Kittering announced.

"So..." Idris looked from one to the other. "Fill me in. The Architect went away. As we are where we are, I assume it hasn't come back yet. What happened next?"

"It's been two days since then," Kris told him. "Mostly what's happened is we've been dancing around your bed—because everyone is very deeply interested in you."

"Kris has been running interference," Olli noted approvingly. "What's that you said, Trine?"

"Telling people to go to hell in such a way that they enjoy

the trip," the Hiver supplied. "It's been a privilege having you on the diplomatic staff."

"But...tell me they've been making preparations beyond that?" Idris said weakly.

"I think the consensus is that we've all had a nasty scare, but the Second Architect War has been headed off before it began. Thanks to you."

Something buzzed in Idris's chest, just at the edge of hearing, as Trine's severed components did something to modulate his heartbeat.

"But it really *hasn't* ended. It hasn't been headed off *at all*," he told them, and at their collective blank looks, he explained, "They're coming *back*. They have to. They don't even want to, but they will...Do people seriously think this is over? And they're back to the politicking—already?" A louder buzz then, as he tried to prop himself up in bed.

"Idris, you can't just—" Kris started, but he was shaking his head, wild-eyed.

"I need to speak to people. I need to *tell* them. Borodin, Tact, anyone. Get them, call them—Trine, do ambassador stuff, do *something*."

Havaer

Chief Laery was not much of a proponent of the "walk and talk" meeting, for obvious reasons, but this time, she'd decided to take the scenic route with Havaer Mundy. They were walking along a viewing gallery set into the satellite that was the Intervention Board, hence the de facto new Mordant House. She'd donned a humanoid frame, just a subtle one beneath her robe. If you didn't listen out for the whine of servos or note the odd shifting of struts about her hips, you'd almost miss it. Havaer shortened his own long stride to match her pace.

"You've allowed yourself quite a lot of leeway on this one," she told him, staring out at the starry immensity beyond. Berlenhof's blue horizon was just starting to show itself beneath their feet.

"I'm aware that there's a disciplinary with my name on it, Chief, waiting in the wings," he confirmed, stoically. He had crossed several lines to extract Telemmier from Hugh custody and it had paid off. But that didn't mean those lines magically moved to just beyond the toes of his sandals.

"Ah, drama..." she said dismissively. "Not right now, Havaer. It's on your record. It's circling above you, ready to drop its payload, but we need every good agent we can get. Even those with a distressing tendency to think outside the box. Perhaps especially those. Why did you do it, in the end?"

"Because I'd spoken to him, he'd been right about the Architects returning and he had more information than any of us."

"Those are usually the sorts of people we detain, rather than letting them go," she observed drily. "But in this instance, the results certainly speak for themselves."

"You'll tell me to go get him now though, I take it?"

"Not outside the realms of possibility," she confirmed. "Though if Borodin and his clowns do *their* job, *we* may not have to act. And I fear the matter may be taken out of our hands. But to move to our next problem: ever been to the Hegemony, Havaer? The *real* Hegemony, not just some turn-coat human colony."

"Couple of times. That's our next problem, is it?"

"This business with the hierograve, Sathiel, and his fake Architect evidence. I don't like it. I think the Essiel might have bitten off more than they can chew when they started taking on human converts. Human cults tend to proselytize, and it's changing the passive Hegemonic dynamic. Mark my words, we'll have some flashpoints there in the next few years."

"The Hegemony's issued a formal statement on the *Oumaru*?"

"I don't think the Essiel even understand the problem. All rather beneath them. Although I'd like to think we've caused some consternation when we showed their damn relics aren't actually all *that*. I would like that very much. Bring them down to the mud like the rest of us." She chuckled, a singular event. "And here are our visitors, just ahead of schedule. The legendary efficiency of the warrior angels."

"I don't..." Havaer squinted into the void. Were there three points of light out there, which had been absent a moment before? They were moving, cruising at an angle to Berlenhof, making an oblique approach.

"The *Lady of the Night*, the *Sister of Mercy*, the *Witch Queen*," Laery reeled off, staring past her own reflection. "Yes...the Parthenon had three warships within striking distance, just a few days away. Until they were underway, we didn't even know they existed. Very hard to get intel from that quarter. Can't infiltrate spies into *that* sisterhood."

"I know our own reinforcements have turned up too," Havaer advanced cautiously. A grab-bag of Colonial military vessels had pitched in over the last few days. They'd been summoned by packet runners and the first wave of Far Lux refugees, expecting to go toe-to-doomed-toe with an Architect. Not that they'd have been in time anyway.

"It had looked as though we could keep Tact and her mob in their place, before their ships arrived. Allies we could put back in their box once we didn't need them anymore. Yet with the *Thunderchild*, the *Heaven's Sword and* these new arrivals, they can punch harder than we can, if it comes to it."

"It won't come to it."

"It won't, now they *can* punch harder," Laery replied with bleak humour. She sagged and her exoskeletal frame didn't, doing odd things to the contours of her shoulders. "Yes, I'm sure you'll be disappointed, but your disciplinary will have to wait. It's going to be all hands to the pumps, Agent Mundy. Now and for the foreseeable future."

Kris

"We're within our rights to consider this an act of war!" was the first thing Kris heard as the crew entered. Because this time, the diplomats had started without them. The talks weren't taking place on a Partheni ship either, but in a well-appointed conference room on the Hugh orbital. Although it seemed to Kris that the parties preferred to stand and shout at one another, rather than sit in comfort.

"If you choose to view it as an act of war, that's up to you. But see where it gets you, Menheer Borodin," came Monitor Superior Tact's acid reply. "However, wearing my diplomat's mantle, I'd say our 'relief force' shows our commitment to humanity in general, not just our own people. And our determination to defend them against any threat."

Approaching the square central table, Olli tapped forward in her walker. She loudly yanked two chairs away with a metal leg, making room at the table for herself and Idris, whose walker she was also piloting. He hadn't much liked that, but he was almost endearingly hopeless at moving the thing about himself.

"Ah, Menheer Telemmier." Borodin turned smoothly to smile at them as though he hadn't been shouting at the Partheni a moment before. "I'm delighted to see you with us again. I've been asked to formally extend the Council of Human Interests' sincere thanks. Your actions headed off a humanitarian disaster on a scale we've not seen since the war. And I add my own personal thanks to that. We owe you a great debt."

"Does that mean you'll *listen* to me this time?" Idris rasped. He still looked nine-eighths dead to Kris's critical eye, slumped in the walker with his bare feet dangling.

Borodin directed a sideways look at Tact, who just stood watching. Seeing no help there, he sat so he was on a level with Idris. "Of course, Menheer. And I imagine you and your crew would like that recognition made into something... more concrete?"

"It's *not over*," Idris said. "They'll come back. Maybe here, maybe elsewhere... and soon too. Not in years, not in decades. Soon."

Borodin's face closed up. "With all respect, Menheer, how can you know such a thing?"

"I was in its mind," Idris explained tiredly. "It did its level best to show me exactly that. To make me understand what was going on. The Architects aren't doing this for fun. Something is *making* them come. They're under duress, just something else's servants. Something that wants us gone, all of us."

"All humans?"

"All thinking life. Look at Ash's people. Look at the Naeromathi. And it'll be the Hanni and the Castigar in time. We're just the current project. They want us gone, or at least not concentrated on planets. And don't ask me why. I don't know why. I don't think the Architects know either. If 'why' is a concept they even have. But it's like this: the Architects recognize humanity as life, as thinking life. They recognize themselves as thinking life too. That's a kinship. The Architects went away when we made them face up to that. And now their masters have caught up with them and set them on us again. Because their masters don't give a damn."

"Masters. Or creators?" Tact asked, with admirable sang-froid.

Idris shrugged painfully. "No idea."

"Well..." Borodin swallowed. And doubtless panicky communications were already radiating out from the orbital, sent by the clerks listening in on this conference. "Menheer Telemmier, I do hope that you're wrong..."

"Menheer Borodin, I have been inside the Architect's head. If you have someone who is in a better position to know than me, wheel them out. Have *them* state their case. What has Andecka Tal Mar told you?"

"That you went further than she could," Borodin admitted.

"Well then. The war's *on*, Menheer, Monitor. Maybe I've bought Berlenhof a period of grace, but that's all. Now, I've said my piece—" Kris saw him looking around to check on the crew—"let's go."

"You must have more to say," Borodin said quickly.

"Whatever you learned, what you experienced...We need to know *everything*."

"I'll send you a report."

"Menheer Telemmier, we really do need you. I thought we needed you before. But now...if the Architects *are* still coming for us, we need you more than ever." Borodin had stood again, pushing his chair back. "The Liaison Board wants—"

"Over my dead body."

"Menheer—"

"My client," Kris broke in, as the diplomat glowered at her, "is exercising his rights of free travel and association as a Colonial citizen. There is currently *no* special order restricting his movement. He is also travelling within the aegis of Ambassador Delegate Trine—here at my left hand right now. My client will regard any attempt to prevent him from leaving this room, or this orbital, as an attack on his liberties. It could also be an act of aggression against the Hiver Assembly In Aggregate. In addition, we are in the presence of Parthenon representatives. Should any hostile acts be committed by Hugh, they may take diplomatic action of their own." It was all just word salad, really. It hardly gave Idris any ironclad protection against Hugh. However, if Borodin felt that the Parthenon—or even the Hivers—might take her words seriously, that could be enough. That uncertainty left a gap that they might just be able to squirrel through.

Borodin looked sick, almost desperate, that smooth veneer of etiquette peeling away. "Menheer Telemmier," he said softly, "do not turn your back on your people, *please*. We are in dire need of Intermediaries, a new class to protect our worlds against the Architects or their masters. Saint Xavienne is dead.

We've lost the Intermediaries' chief teacher and inspiration, the one rock they had. We need *you* to take Xavienne's place. You wouldn't ever have to face an Architect again, even. Just help us with the Intermediary Program. And believe me, you won't want for anything. The Colonies would make you their hero."

"Stop." A barely audible plea. "I can't. I'm not strong like Xavienne. I can't do it."

"You've proved you are—" Borodin started, but Idris held up a shaky hand.

"Xavienne had to watch us die," he said. "Us volunteers, the first class. I remember all the faces who were there at the start, who didn't survive the conditioning, the surgery, the chemical diet. Who didn't survive you trying to make *us* into *her*. And I saw how it hurt her, how she felt every death. But she kept on, because she had to, and we kept on because we had to as well. Because there was a war on. Thirty, Menheer. Thirty of us walked out of the Program as Ints. And now you have the Liaison Board, and you take criminals and put them through the factory. If you're lucky, then one Int walks out alive out of every *hundred* who go into the grinder. And those Ints of yours, you want to know something about them? They're useless, Menheer Borodin. They'll never fend off an Architect. None of them, or almost none."

If Idris looked nine-eighths dead, Borodin was pushing for ten-eighths himself. "Why ...?" he managed.

"Because they don't want to be there. They're *slaves*."

"A leash contract is—"

"Slaves. Enforced labour without right or choice. And you know what the Architects are, for all their power? Slaves, Menheer. And if you're a slave sent to chastise someone, and that someone sends their own slave out to plead for their master's life, how well disposed do you think you'd be? Volunteers, Menheer. You cherish and take care of Andecka Tal Mar and anyone else like that, who give themselves willingly to the process. More of them will survive, for one thing, and what you get out of it will be worth having...not just a tame commercial pilot, but someone who can defend your worlds."

Kris watched Borodin's face, saw his quick mind changing tack. "There *will* be volunteers," he promised. "Once people understand that the threat is back, and it's real, they'll put themselves forward. Just like you did in the war."

Idris nodded, looking defeated. "You're probably right," he whispered. "But I still couldn't watch them die. Because our brains aren't the same, not any of us. Everyone gets cut up differently, trying to shape our brains to match Xavienne's. It's stupid, wasteful. And mostly it fails. I couldn't live with it. I'm sorry, Menheer."

"Menheer Telemmier," Borodin said, at his most reasonable despite his pallor, "your crew would be compensated. *You* would be compensated. We would do everything we could to insulate you from the...negative aspects of the role." He blinked. "Menheer Telemmier?"

A stab of worry went through Kris, because Idris was very still. It wasn't inconceivable that he'd actually died on them, right then and there. Then he said, "No," although there was a thoughtful tone to it. "No, Menheer. I'm not your man. And I'll go against the Architects again, no doubt. I'll likely die doing it, next time or the time after. Because even success kills, in this game." He shook his head, and suddenly everything seemed to be funny to him. "Oh, Menheer, I won't abandon anyone. I just won't take on this responsibility. I volunteered, back in the day, because I was needed. I'll do my bit now for the same reason. However, I won't go near you or your Liaison Board. Not now. Not ever."

Solace

Monitor Superior Tact had left for the *Thunderchild* by the time various conversations amongst the *Vulture* crew had been concluded. So Solace had to commandeer another packet runner to get her over from the orbital to her superior's ship. And every moment she was gone, she worried in case the *Vulture God* might not be there when she returned. Perhaps the crew would reconsider what they'd said, and just take off without her. No matter what she or anyone tried to pretend, she wasn't quite one of them—and maybe never would be.

Tact's room had holographic representations of every Partheni ship in the system projected around the walls, the display dominated by the five warships currently at her disposal. More Hugh forces were doubtless on their way, and that kind of pissing match was likely to end with someone doing something rash unless the Parthenon backed down. After all, Hugh *couldn't* back down because they were above their own administrative capital. Situations like these made Solace glad she wasn't a career diplomat.

"You've requested a face-to-face meeting, so I take it you're here to make a final report on your mission," Tact observed. She was watching those warship images: each one with the face of its Exemplar projected over it, all those sister-close likenesses.

"Mother, I am," Solace confirmed.

Tact nodded. "When I sent you to turn Telemmier, nobody could have known just what was about to erupt. I don't doubt you did absolutely everything in your power to recruit him peaceably." She brought up a virtual board and dispatched a brief communiqué. The display showed it as arrowing off to the *Lady of the Night*. "Of course, recent events show us as even more in need of an Intermediary Program. We are looking at the other two first-class Ints who yet live, though neither of them appears as disaffected as Telemmier. I understand he's not a joiner, though. Not them, not us, not anyone."

Solace took a deep breath. "Mother, he *will* join us."

Tact went very still. "Clarify, daughter. Are you stating a fact or merely your belief in some future change of heart?"

"He has agreed to come with us and help us with our Intermediary Program. With conditions."

"Well of course with *conditions*. He's a Colonial spacer, and they never did anything for free if they could avoid it," but there was a jag of excitement in Tact's crisp voice. "How did you possibly manage it, Solace?" Tact had turned away from the display entirely, now, the Partheni fleet circling unregarded behind her head. Her face crinkled abruptly into an oddly fond smile, which looked utterly alien on her face. "Don't tell me the mediotypes are true and the Colonials are hopeless romantics after all?"

Solace felt herself colouring. "No, Mother. Idris... Menheer *Telemmier* knows that we will need Intermediaries— that is, all humanity, all intelligent life will need them. And he doesn't trust the Liaison Board to help. What's more... the Colonial method of developing Intermediaries is flawed, wasteful. Telemmier said only a rare few have the right sorts of brains, and they can't know before the procedures whether a brain's right or not. But..."

"Yes?"

Solace looked at the ships, at their captains, seeing in them Tact's own features and knowing her own were just like them. A genetic legacy of Doctor Parsefer's genius and hubris. "We vary less than Colonials, Mother. If we can train *one* Partheni Intermediary, we should be able to train many, with far less failure, far less loss. *If.* That's what Idris is betting upon. That our more limited genetic range has that potential. That we can raise a class of Ints *without* killing most of them—because we're alike. More alike than any two Colonials who aren't close family."

Tact digested that for a moment, then glanced up with a sly expression. Perhaps she was wondering if Idris and Solace's shared history hadn't played *some* part, after all. Solace wondered that too, she really did...And these were odd thoughts to have about someone who was the wrong gender and whose chest she'd been wrist-deep in not so long ago. In those *Sách vê faim* mediotypes, the Colonials were always fighting for people's hearts. But that probably wasn't what they meant.

"They had conditions, you said," Tact reminded her.

"Idris wants to bring along the *Vulture God* and its crew."

"I'm sure we can throw sufficient Largesse their way."

"They don't just want credits, they want a contract with the Parthenon," Solace clarified. "They want to work for us, legally. They think that will at least give them some protection against Hugh interference. Of course they'll do their best to outwit us on contract terms and so on. The usual. But they're good people and good at what they do. And who knows when we might need a..."

"Shabbily maintained salvage vessel," Tact finished for her. "Yet strange times, strange tools, yes. Do we get the Hiver academic in the bargain? I couldn't work out whether they were crew or not."

"Delegate Trine will go wherever they can learn most about the Architects. Which means not yoking themselves to us or anyone else. But if we have an appropriate research opportunity they'll come running. If we want them."

"We do," Tact agreed. "Which brings us to you, Myrmidon Executor Solace. Where do *you* see yourself, in all of this?"

Solace straightened, feeling her future fall out of her own hands after this brief. "I'm at your disposal, Mother. As always. Although...I did wonder if the newly contracted *Vulture God* would need a formal Parthenon liaison? To smooth over our new working relationship."

"And you're volunteering yourself, I take it."

"Yes, Mother."

For a difficult moment she thought Tact was about to pass judgement on her. Something about unsoldierly sentiment. The danger of attachments outside your sorority. The general perfidy of Colonials as a class and male Colonials in particular.

But Tact simply said: "Very well. You have yourself a new mission," and she regarded Solace with a faint smile. Perhaps in her youth, she had even watched the same kind of mediotypes.

"Call the *Vulture God* and say we're on," Tact continued. "And tell them to get that little Hannilambra factor over here to talk terms. Don't let them think they can simply name a price, either. If it's a contract they want, it's a contract they'll get."

"Yes, Mother!" And Solace turned smartly on her heel and marched out. There was a future out there, and it was a terrible one. It included war and whole planets dying in the shadow of Architects. They were living in a fractured galaxy and it must come together, or it would fall into darkness one star at a time. Yet just then, her own personal star seemed bright. And she was smiling to herself as she went to hail the *Vulture*.

THE UNIVERSE OF THE ARCHITECTS: REFERENCE

Glossary

Architects—moon-sized entities that can reshape populated planets and ships

Aspirat—Partheni intelligence services

The Betrayed—the violent extremist wing of the Nativists

Broken Harvest Society—a Hegemonic criminal cartel

Colonies—The surviving human worlds following the fall of Earth

Council of Human Interests ("Hugh")—the governing body of the Colonies

Hegemony—a coalition of species ruled by the alien Essiel

Hegemonic cult—humans who serve and worship the Essiel

Intermediaries—surgically modified navigators who can pilot ships off the Throughways, developed as weapons against the Architects during the war

Intermediary Program—Colonial wartime body responsible for creating the Intermediaries

Intervention Board ("Mordant House")—Colonial policing and intelligence service

Kybernet—an AI system responsible for overseeing a planet or orbital

Liaison Board—current Colonial body responsible for creating Intermediaries en masse for commercial purposes

Nativists—a political movement that believes in "pure-born" humans and "humanity first"

Orbital—an orbiting habitat

Parthenon—a breakaway human faction composed of parthenogenetically grown women

Throughways—paths constructed within unspace by unknown hands, joining habitable planets. Without a special navigator, ships can only travel along existing Throughways

Unspace—a tenuous layer beneath real space, which can be used for fast travel across the universe

Characters
Crew of the *Vulture God*

Rollo Rostand—captain

Idris Telemmier—Intermediary navigator

Keristina "Kris" Soolin Almier—lawyer

Olian "Olli" Timo—drone specialist

Kittering "Kit"—Hannilambra factor

Musoku "Barney" Barnier—engineer

Medvig—Hiver search and catalogue specialist

Myrmidon Executor Solace—Partheni soldier and agent

Other key characters

The Unspeakable Aklu, the Razor and the Hook—Essiel gangster

Harbinger Ash—singular alien prophet

Heremon—Tothiat

Chief Laery—Havaer's superior in the Intervention Board
Luciel Leng—administrator on the Lung-Crow Orbital at
    Huei-Cavor
Mesmon—Tothiat
Havaer Mundy—Intervention Board agent
Doctor Sang Sian Parsefer—founder of the Parthenon
Yon Robellin—biologist on Jericho
His Wisdom the Bearer Sathiel—Hegemonic cult hierograve
Albas Solier—Mordant House operative on Tarekuma
Monitor Superior Tact—Solace's superior in the Aspirat
Livvo Thrennikos—crooked lawyer on Tarekuma
Xavienne "Saint Xavienne" Torino—the first Intermediary
Delegate Trine—Hiver archaeologist
Boyarin Piter Tchever Uskaro—nobleman from Magda

Worlds

Amraji—world destroyed by the Architects
Berlenhof—administrative and cultural heart of the Colonies
Earth—world destroyed by the Architects
Far Lux—where Intermediaries ended the war
Forthbridge Port—where Saint Xavienne first managed to
    contact an Architect
Huei-Cavor—prosperous world passing from the Colonies to
    the Hegemony. Site of the Lung-Crow Orbital
Jericho—wild planet rich in Originator ruins
Roshu—a mining world and Throughway hub
Scintilla—planet noted for its legal schools and duelling code
Tarekuma—a lawless, hostile planet

Species

Castigar—alien species with several castes and shapes, naturally wormlike

Essiel—the "divine" masters of the Hegemony

Hannilambra ("Hanni")—crab-shaped aliens, enthusiastic merchants

Hivers—composite cyborg insect intelligences, originally created by humans but now independent

Naeromathi ("Locusts")—nomadic aliens that deconstruct worlds to create more of their "Locust Arks"

Ogdru—a species from the Hegemony that produces void-capable navigators

Originators—a hypothetical elder race responsible for the Throughways and certain enigmatic ruins

Tothiat—a hybrid of the symbiotic Tothir and another species, often human. Phenomenally resilient

Ships

Ascending Mother—Partheni warship

Broken Harvest—flagship belonging to the criminal cartel of the same name

Cataphracta—Partheni warship lost at Berlenhof

Dark Joan—Partheni packet runner

Gamin—freighter lost in transit during the war

Heaven's Sword—Partheni warship, both the original that was destroyed at Berlenhof and its replacement currently in service

Oumaru—Hegemonic freighter lost in transit

Pythoness—Partheni launch

Raptorid—private yacht of Boyarin Piter Uskaro
Samphire—Colonial warship at Jericho
Sark—Broken Harvest ship
Thunderchild—Partheni warship
Vulture God—salvage vessel captained by Rollo Rostand

TIMELINE

107 Before: Probes sent by Earth to neighbouring star systems
attract the attention of an alien ship. Humanity's
first alien contact follows shortly afterwards. Once
the initial revulsion over the wormlike Castigar
fades, humans begin to learn about unspace,
Throughways and the wider universe. The Castigar
themselves have only been travelling between stars
for under a century and have a practice of making
small colonies on many planets, but not engaging in
large-scale colonization. Castigar ships reach deals
to ferry Earth colonists to habitable worlds they had
discovered. They also give humans some details
about the Naeromathi and the Hegemony.

91 Before: Humans establish their first interstellar colony on
Second Dawn, a planet with a dense ecosystem of
plant/fungal-like life. Second Dawn is pleasantly
balmy for the Castigar but proves difficult for humans.

90 Before: Humans establish a colony on Berlenhof, a warm
world with 90% ocean coverage. This thrives and is
patronized by a number of powerful companies and
rich families.

88 Before: A colony is established on Lief, an ice world in a
system with valuable minerals in several asteroid

belts. A colony is also established on Amber, a hot world with a crystalline ecosystem where humans live in cooled domes.

75 Before: Several minor colonies are established in other systems with Castigar help, mostly for industrial purposes. Reliance on the Castigar for all shipping is becoming problematic to expanding humanity, and to the Castigar. Castigar scientists work with humans to help them build their own gravitic drives.

72 Before: The first human gravitic drive spaceship, the *Newton's Bullet*, opens the doors to a greater era of human colonization.

61 Before: On the forested world of Lycos, humans discover their first Originator ruins.

45 Before: A Naeromathi Ark arrives in the colonized Cordonier system and begins dismantling some of the inhabited world's moons. Contact goes poorly and degenerates into fighting. There is never a formal Naeromathi–human war, as there is no Naeromathi state to declare war on. However, other Ark ships are seen across the Throughway network, and there are several clashes with losses on both sides.

25 Before: Contact is made with the Essiel Hegemony as a result of human travel and expansion. Initial contact is not hostile but humans find it baffling as they and the Essiel fail to understand one another. Human diplomats recognize that the Essiel appear to be offering humans some kind of master–subject relationship. However, they are confused that it does not appear to be accompanied by threats. In retrospect, warnings about the Architects were present, but not grasped. Over the next decades human emissaries understand that the Hegemony appears to value Originator ruins, though not displaced Originator relics. Several worlds with Originator sites are effectively sold to the Hegemony as a result.

22 Before: As a response to conditions on Earth, and what she sees as deep flaws in human nature, Doctor Sang Sian Parsefer and her allies found the Parthenon. They genetically engineer what they consider to be an ideal version of humanity. The Parthenon is founded as a military force and uses parthenogenetic vat birth as a means of creating human beings artificially. This happens more swiftly than natural means would allow. The Parthenon pushes the limits of human science and is viewed as a threat by the rest of humanity.

5 Before: A Castigar ship brings the alien Ash to Earth, warning of the arrival of the Architects. Few take him seriously; the Castigar themselves have not encountered the Architects. But some nations and groups do make limited preparations.

0: An Architect larger than Earth's moon exits unspace close to Earth. It reworks the planet into the bizarre, coiling structure now familiar to all, causing appalling loss of life and tearing the heart out of the human race. Every spaceworthy ship evacuates as many people as it can carry, but billions are left behind to die. The ships flee to various colony worlds. Some reach them, others founder, insufficiently prepared for the voyage. The Polyaspora begins, as does the Architect War.

15 After: The largest solar system colony on Titan is deconstructed by the Architects around 7AE. Over the next few years, several extrasolar colonies are also reworked. Every human colony is on high alert, with evacuation measures in place as standard. Many colonies become short on food and supplies. Attempts to fight the Architects fail to even attract their notice.

21 After: The small religious colony on Charm Prime establishes communication with Hegemony envoys and becomes the first human Hegemonic cult cell. In return, the Hegemony establishes a shrine, and their human cult declares that the Hegemony can ward off Architects. The majority of other colonies do not believe this, and some claim the Hegemony controls or can even summon Architects to scare humanity into accepting alien overlords. There is little human take-up of Hegemonic rule for the next few decades.

28 After: Experiments in autonomous distributed intelligence, originally intended as a resource-stripping tool, are turned to the war effort. The first Hive entity is developed and added to humanity's arsenal.

43 After: In the midst of war, the first Hannilambra–human contact occurs—with Hanni venture-ships narrowly escaping a hostile response when they turn up at Clerk's World. The Hanni will subsequently create a sporadic lifeline of goods, at cost, to beleaguered human colonies. They will also transport humans from colonies under threat.

48 After: Architects at Lycos leave without touching the colony. From this and other clues it becomes clear that the Architects do indeed have some relationship with Originator sites and their relics. The shrine at Charm Prime is found to contain Originator relics and there is a doomed attempt to use these to repel Architects from other colonies by simply transporting them off-world. After the destruction of Karis Commune, whose inhabitants relied on relics taken from Charm Prime, the Hegemony manages to communicate dire news: only they can transport relics in a manner that retains their anti-Architect properties. Between now and the end of the war, a number of human colonies will accept Hegemonic rule in return for such protection.

51 After: The Architects come to Amraji, a large human–Castigar colony swollen with refugees. There is a considerable human military force in place already, owing to the arrival and depredations of a Naeromathi Ark. Parthenon, Hive and regular human forces attack the Architect to buy the evacuation more time and the Naeromathi join the battle on humanity's side. Combined efforts allow over half the colony's population to escape off-planet. However, this initiative also results in the majority of the defenders being destroyed, including the Ark. The "Amraji Peace" is no more a formal human–Naeromathi détente, any more than the hostilities were a war. But from here onwards, fighting between humans and Naeromathi will be minimal.

During these years, at the height of the Architect War, humanity is living hand to mouth under the constant shadow of annihilation. Everyone lives with an emergency bag and a knowledge of where to go if the worst happens. The entire species suffers from a multigenerational traumatic shock.

68 After: A refugee transport, the *Samark,* arrives at Forthbridge Port at the same time as an Architect. Aboard is Xavienne Torino, aged 15, who claims that she can hear the Architect's thoughts. Through a process that is entirely mysterious at the time, Xavienne is able to demand that the Architect leaves the system. To everyone's astonishment, it does.

76 After: Human scientists work with Xavienne Torino to isolate the precise genetic and neurological fluke that allowed her to interact with the Architects by way of unspace. By 76AE, the first generation of artificial intermediaries has been developed. Of the suitable volunteers, less than ten per cent survive the process and come out sane. Idris, one of the first generation, is 20 years old when he completes the Program.

78 After: Battle of Berlenhof. The wealthiest and most populous human world detects the approach of an Architect—and military forces race to intervene. The full force of the Parthenon navy, several Hive lattices, human regular forces and alien allies fight to preserve the world. The defenders pay a colossal cost but top-of-the-line Parthenon weapons are able to damage the Architect. Early use of Intermediaries also appears to be effective. However, of the eight Ints deployed, three are killed and another two go insane trying to contact the Architects. Yet Berlenhof is saved.

In the next six years, the Architects destroy two more human colonies. In each case, a spirited defence only buys time for a more thorough evacuation.

80 After: The Intermediary Program reaches its greatest strength with thirty combat Intermediaries. Their training builds on the lessons learned at Berlenhof. They begin meeting the Architects when they manifest, making contact, trying to get the creatures to notice them. Their attempts prove more and more successful.

84 After: Intermediary successes culminate with Idris and two other Ints contacting an Architect at Far Lux. They report that the enemy was momentarily aware of them this time. After this event, there are no further Architect sightings.

As people realize that the war has finally finished, three generations after it started, human society and economy are in a poor way. People are desperate, colonies are under-resourced and overpopulated. There is no real political unity and friction develops between needy colonies and alien neighbours. Growing discontent seems likely to fragment the Polyasporic human presence into dozens of feuding states.

88 After: The Council of Human Interests or "Hugh" is formed. This happens when the various human colonies come together to prevent internecine war and to regulate their affairs. The initial line-up does not include many smaller colonies. It also excludes expatriate communities within alien colonies, who will be given a voice at a later stage. However, it does include both the Parthenon and human colonies that have sworn fealty to the Hegemony.

96 After: The Hivers, the cyborg intelligence developed during the war, remain under human control but elements of this distributed intelligence find ways to demand independence and self-determination. There are several brutal human crackdowns on Hive cells that refuse to perform their functions. The Hive cites its service during the war as a reason to grant it independence.

103 After: Human worlds sworn to the Hegemony make vocal attempts at proselytizing, including some terrorist activity. Following this, Hugh votes to exclude human colonies that have sworn allegiance to the Hegemony from its ranks. There are fears that a war with the Essiel will result, but this never manifests. The Hegemony's stated policy, as translated by its human mouthpieces, remains that the Hegemony is ready to accept the fealty of any who wish to join it.

105 After: The political struggle over the future of the Hivers comes to a head, as the Parthenon faction demands it be released from human control. The decision to allow this, forced through by Parthenon military superiority, is contentious. The Hivers are released from service and promptly evacuate to worlds outside human control and unsuitable for human colonization. The Hive's initial contacts with its former masters are almost entirely though the Parthenon. Over time Hive elements will re-enter human space and commerce to offer their services and skills.

107 After: More than twenty years after the war, the first stirrings of the Nativist movement are felt. This manifests as increased hostility towards alien powers, especially the Hegemony. It also shows in antagonistic behaviour towards human elements seen as deviating from a "traditional" human lifestyle, especially the Parthenon. Hugh has only been in existence for nineteen years at this point, and many human colonies are still in a very bad shape. Many traditionally born humans believe that the Parthenon intends to impose its "unnatural" way of life on all of humanity at gunpoint. Others fear that the Hive will take revenge for their previous servitude. Another popular Nativist belief is that Hegemonic cultists—both overt and hidden—are a fifth column on many worlds, aiming to manipulate governments into submitting to alien overlords. There are riots, demonstrations, coups and popular movements.

109 After: The Betrayed movement starts to gain traction. They spread the story that the Architects could have been fully defeated save that certain parties struck a deal to limit human expansion and power for their own benefit. They include amongst these "betrayers" the Intermediaries, Parthenon agents and aliens.

The Betrayed fan the flames of anti-Parthenon and anti-Hegemony feeling and enact several terrorist attacks against Parthenon citizens.

110 After: The Parthenon officially secedes from Hugh, declaring its fleet and colonies a state outside traditional human control. War is feared but does not materialize, and diplomatic relations are maintained. As a result, relations become perhaps less fraught than in the last few years of the Parthenon's Hugh membership.

Over the next decade, human colonial life slowly improves, but political differences become ever more divisive. Hugh's ability to influence the recovering colonies decreases, as more extreme and populist factions take over. The larger and more powerful colonies form a relatively self-interested core. On the fringes of human space, there is a rich melting pot of humans and aliens prospecting, salvaging, colonizing and exploring.

123 After: Present day.

ACKNOWLEDGEMENTS

My thanks to my agent and editors for all the work they've put in to this book. In addition, given the strain of the last few years, my heartfelt thanks to the community of fellow authors and creatives who've been my mental health safety net when I've needed them.